Praise for *The Last Passenger*

'Astonishing'
Ian Rankin

'The premise is excellent . . . [a] mile-a-minute,
bite-your-nails-to-the-quick ride of a novel, but I
will tell you to trust this writer because I guarantee
you'll enjoy where he takes you. Extra kudos for the
final twist, which brought me great pleasure'
Observer

'A rollercoaster ride. I barely had any nails left by the end!'
Good Housekeeping

'This heart-stopping premise is one of the
best openings to a book I've read'
Sunday Express

'The apex of suspense writing'
Steve Cavanagh

'Thrilling and terrifying in equal measure with a
brilliantly heart-stopping ending. So good!'
B.A. Paris

'Expect not just the unexpected but strokes of genius'
Imran Mahmood

'Brilliant, twisted and oh so clever. *The Last
Passenger* is Will Dean at the top of his game.
And just wait for that killer last line'
Chris Whitaker

'A fast-paced, snakily plotted treat for fans
of the modern psychological thriller'
Vaseem Khan

'Will Dean is a master storyteller - this book is real edge
of the seat stuff! I loved it. And what an ending!'
Catherine Cooper

Also by Will Dean

The Last Thing to Burn
First Born

The Tuva Moodyson Thrillers

Dark Pines
Red Snow
Black River
Bad Apples
Wolf Pack

WILL DEAN

The Last Passenger

HODDER

First published in Great Britain in 2023 by Hodder & Stoughton Limited
An Hachette UK company

This paperback edition published in 2024

4

A CIP catalogue record for this title is available from the British Library

Paperback ISBN 978 1 529 38287 7
Hardback ISBN 978 1 529 38282 2
Trade Paperback ISBN 978 1 529 38283 9
ebook ISBN 978 1 529 38284 6

Typeset in Plantin Light by Hewer Text UK Ltd, Edinburgh
Printed and bound in Great Britain by Clays Ltd, Elcograf S.p.A.

Hodder & Stoughton policy is to use papers that are natural, renewable
and recyclable products and made from wood grown in sustainable
forests. The logging and manufacturing processes are expected to
conform to the environmental regulations of the country of origin.

Hodder & Stoughton Limited
Carmelite House
50 Victoria Embankment
London EC4Y 0DZ

www.hodder.co.uk

'. . . one knows not what sweet mystery about this sea, whose gently awful stirrings seem to speak of some hidden soul beneath . . .'

Herman Melville, *Moby-Dick*

'Nothing is so painful to the human mind as a great and sudden change.'

Mary Shelley, *Frankenstein*

To librarians. I've visited libraries my whole life. To escape, to warm up, to learn. Librarians are the protectors of those spaces. They help us find what we are looking for, even when we're not even sure what that is.

1

Stepping aboard a ship is an act of faith. You place your life in the hands of the captain and crew. You decide, actively or passively, to offer up your autonomy, and oftentimes that decision is not one that is easily reversed.

'Welcome aboard, ma'am.'

I take a tentative step and hand over my voyage card. Below me, through a gap between metal plates, I see a sliver of darkness: a structural crack allowing me a glimpse of the water below.

'Ms Ripley. Have a lovely voyage.'

'Thank you.'

Pete follows.

'Mr Davenport, welcome aboard the *Atlantica*.'

He compliments her hat and then we walk into the ship proper and although we're not the first to board we're among the first hundred or so. We head deeper into the grand Ocean Lobby, me dragging my carry-on suitcase, Pete unencumbered.

I am not a natural traveller. My instinct is to stay close to home and to surround myself with the familiar. I look on with awe as people like Pete catch flights and trains without a care in the world.

'Seven storeys tall,' he says, pointing to the mural that dominates the lobby. It's an Art Deco depiction of the Atlantic Ocean in bronze relief created by a lauded Senegalese artist. Our destination is there on the left. The Atlantic coast of America.

We arrive at our cabin and my pulse is racing. Pete opens the door.

I scan our room – *rooms*, plural – my mouth slightly ajar. 'You promised this was a last-minute bargain. I'm paying for the next trip, remember.'

'It *was* a bargain,' says Pete. 'When I booked, all the Diamond cabins were taken. This is only Platinum. And it was a bargain thanks to you never making your mind up.'

I kiss him. 'I'm here, aren't I? With you? We're actually doing this.' Then the realisation hits me. 'Oh, no, we forgot.'

He frowns.

'The sea-sickness pills.' I retrieve the blister pack from my carry-on case. 'We were supposed to take these half an hour before boarding.' Just the thought of monstrous Atlantic waves makes me nauseous. The way they undulate. Their inherent, unbridled force.

'We're still in Southampton and we're still docked.' Pete opens the curtains and points to the harbour buildings and city beyond. 'Relax. We can take them now.'

I hand him one and take one for myself.

I start to say *Could you pour us some water* when I hear the sound of a cork being eased gently from a champagne bottle.

'Careful,' I say. 'That sounds expensive.'

2

'It's included,' says Pete. 'You can relax now, Caroline. Forget the café work and the lunch deliveries. Don't worry about the family. Just take some time out for you.'

I like it when he calls me Caroline in his bass-baritone voice. I take a deep breath and he hands me a glass. We swallow the scopolamine tablets.

Our luggage is already here. I do all the things I'd usually do in a regular hotel room on dry land. I check the bed linen's clean and I unpack and then I familiarise myself with the bathroom. Check there's a working hair-dryer. Two of the miniature bottles of L'Occitane shower gel and shampoo make their way into my suitcase. They're for Gemma. I promised her. She's looking after the café for me, managing the rota, and checking in on Mum, so really it's the least I can do.

Pete's sitting with his feet up on the balcony. Navy cotton shirt, jeans. 'This is the last sight of Britain we'll see for a while,' he says.

'Not quite Doncaster, is it?'

He stands up, glass in hand, and walks over to me, maintaining eye contact. 'All we will see for the next seven days straight is indigo blue, and each other.' He takes a deep breath. 'True ocean and uncharted depths. This dock view might not be much, but I'm making the most of my last glimpse of home.'

The ship's horn blows ominously.

Please stand by for the emergency signal.

The announcer explains how we all need to take part in a muster drill. He says it's mandatory under international law. We set off, carrying our life vests, and the atmosphere in the corridors is a mixture of excitement and trepidation. It reminds me a little of school immediately before exams. As I walk hand-in-hand with Pete I peek inside some of the other cabins. Larger than ours. Folded clothes arranged on the beds. I know I shouldn't snoop but I can't help it.

The crew wear their life vests but we're told not to put ours on yet. A man pushes his wife in a wheelchair as she eats a red apple. I eavesdrop. People comparing the ship, and the drill, to others they've experienced. A mixture of British, French, Spanish and American accents.

We make our way to the A3 Muster Station, located in the central section of the *Atlantica*, beneath the main funnel that doubles as a rock-climbing wall, and close to the main Grill restaurants. Our voyage passes are scanned and we're shown how to put on our life vests, and told how the crew will escort us to the correct lifeboat. I am straining to hear, to take in this important information, but Pete's carefree, chatting with other guests, checking his watch.

I have an idea of the layout of this gargantuan vessel now. The bridge is located at the front of the ship above the Captain's Lounge, and below that is the ship's theatre. Set back a little is the vast Ocean Lobby we entered through. Behind that are the Grill restaurants. Behind all that, towards the stern of the ship, are the ballroom, observation rooms, library and engines.

We're told there's strictly no smoking in cabins or on balconies. No irons may be used. No candles may be lit. I start to feel uneasy. We're told we must not throw anything overboard. In the event of an emergency we must leave our luggage and proceed to the relevant muster station carrying our life vests, important medication, and warm clothes. In the event of fire we're told to crawl if necessary.

I glance over at Pete for reassurance but he's reading a news story on his phone. In the distance I glimpse a teenager with curly red hair travelling with her parents. She looks as though she doesn't want to be here. We're told not to take lifts as we may become trapped between floors in an emergency. At the end of the drill we put on our life vests, following clear instructions from the crew.

After the drill we dress for dinner, except Pete is more focused on trying to *un*dress me. This is officially our thirteenth proper date and he's acting like a teenager. Maybe it's because we've left land. We're out at sea now. The motion of the ship. The corridor outside our Deck Nine cabin is remarkably long. Dark red carpeting, soft underfoot. He slows and pulls me in close and bends his head down to kiss my neck. I close my eyes for a moment and then when I start to feel dizzy I pull away and look into his eyes and tell him I'm so hungry I could eat a buffalo.

Hundreds of doors and a gleaming chrome rail along the wall for use in rough seas. There are couples dressed more formally than us. Perfume and expensive cologne with notes of citrus. Excited expressions.

We walk through the Ocean Lobby, past an ice sculpture scale model of the ship, past the Nantucket Spa and the Cape Cod Cigar Lounge, and on to the main restaurant.

'This is the Gold Grill,' says Pete. 'Eight out of ten passengers will eat here. We're dining in the Platinum Grill on Deck Ten.'

We ride up in the glass lift and enter our Grill room. Towering flower centrepieces: calla lilies and frothy white hydrangeas. Carved ceilings and elaborate crystal chandeliers. Pete tells me they are Venetian and I tell him I know they are. It's the most ornate room I have ever seen.

The foghorn blows and I feel it.

A man wearing a bow tie approaches. 'Let me show you to your table.'

'Thank you . . . Tom,' I say, glancing at his name badge. Tom smiles and I can sense Pete roll his eyes. But if you've ever waited tables, your legs aching, your back hurting, you never forget what it's like to be treated as a human.

'This is Gloria,' says Tom. 'We'll be your servers for the entirety of your stay here on the RMS *Atlantica*. This table will be reserved for you for the duration of your voyage.'

They leave us and I say, 'This is lovely, isn't it? I feel guilty about Gemma and Mum.'

'This is *your* holiday,' says Pete. 'Well-earned. You need to learn how to wind down.'

Canapés arrive. Crostini with salmon mousse. Tiny spoons filled with asparagus *velouté*. We order. I choose the wines.

There's no ring box in Pete's jacket pocket. There can't be; it'd be far too early, unlike him, too rash. Gemma thinks he has plans but I'm convinced this is a straightforward week-long romantic getaway. I try to put the notion out of my mind.

By the main course I start to relax, and sense that the couple on the table next to ours are becoming increasingly uptight so I make an effort to reduce my volume.

Then Pete cracks a joke about his younger brother and I burst out laughing.

'This your first crossing, is it?'

The lady asks the question with all the poise and focus of a matador stabbing a bull.

'Sorry?'

'I asked if this is your first ocean crossing?'

Her husband keeps eating his smoked salmon.

'Seventeenth,' I say.

She looks livid. Emerald-green dress and crimson nails.

'And Peter here was conceived on board the *QE2*, weren't you, Peter?'

'Terrible storm,' says Pete with a glint in his eye. 'Dreadful winds off the coast of South Africa. Almost sank her.'

'How . . . unusual,' says the lady with the tight bun and shoulder pads. Her bun's tightening with each passing minute. She leans in closer to me. 'In all seriousness, tonight is casual, dear, but when at sea we tend *not* to wear sneakers after six in the evening. I'm only telling you to spare your blushes.'

I look at my shoes. 'Oh, these? I have a special dispensation.'

Her husband starts to mumble something but I interrupt. 'Bunions.'

The lady mouths the word back to me and I nod.

We actually manage to have a nice chat after all that. She apologises for being highly strung and I apologise for being giddy and juvenile. We talk about New York and their plans to travel to Boston to walk the Freedom Trail, and then up to Maine. They explain how the *Atlantica* is an ocean liner, roughly double the size of the *Titanic* and half the size of modern cruise ships. He describes those disparagingly as *floating condominiums*. She's very eager to reinforce how we're not currently dining on a cruise ship. It's an ocean liner. For her there is significant difference.

'This is the finest cruise ship I've seen,' says Pete.

I nudge him under the table, urging him to stop.

'We're on an ocean liner,' remarks the lady, not letting this go. 'The shape of her hull, you see. Built for rough seas and all weathers. She's for *crossing*, not cruising. Think of her as an alternative to a scheduled aeroplane. She's transporting us, not steaming around in ridiculous circles.'

We finish our coffee and wish the couple a pleasant evening. I apologise to them again for being raucous earlier. Pete and I take a walk out on deck. Cold, salty air and hushed voices; seabirds perched on railings and couples flirting, excited at the thought of what's to come. There are lights on the horizon: coastal towns and ships entering the English Channel. We are leaving that world and entering open seas.

'Come on,' says Pete, smiling. 'I have a surprise for you.'

Was Gemma right? I've always assumed it'd be me who asked.

He leads me, walking quickly, excitedly, back down to the Ocean Lobby.

I can't think about it. I'm too old to get excited about something only for it not to materialise. I've experienced enough disappointment in my life. I'm past all that.

We walk by the concierge, a tall, bald man with a kind face and a birthmark under his eye, and he says *good evening* to us and then I overhear his colleague say something about *fair winds and calm seas* to another couple.

We walk on and, despite my better judgement, I am excited about Pete's surprise.

'Come over here,' he says.

Hand-in-hand, he cajoles me to the threshold of the casino.

'Oh, no,' I say, pulling away. 'Sorry.'

'Roulette.' His eyes light up. 'Come on, it's my favourite. It'll be fun.'

I stand firm, my body rigid. 'No, Pete, I mean it. I can't go in there.'

'Three games, that's all.'

The excitement in my tummy has turned to acid. 'Let's go back to our cabin, please.'

'It's so early. Blackjack, then, if that's more your thing.'

I pull my hand away and the air cools between us. 'Please, Pete.'

We're both sober again.

'OK, of course. I'm sorry.' He looks confused. 'What about a drink at the bar instead?'

I point to the casino. 'Not in there.'

'The Captain's Lounge? They have a notorious cocktail list.'

I take a deep breath and make an effort to smile, to narrow the gap between us, to walk this back, and then I slide my hand into his. 'Sounds good.'

We sit by the window and watch the blackness outside. The seas are calm and the ship's hardly swaying at all.

I drink a gin fizz, slowly, silently, and Pete sips a single malt.

'You want to tell me?' he says.

No, I don't want you to know yet. It's too early. Too complicated to explain.

'Not really. I don't want to ruin the mood.'

'Don't worry about that.'

I drain my glass and he does the same. I take a breath.

'My father had a . . . problem, you see. It made things quite difficult for Mum, Gem and me when I was growing up. Dad was good at covering things up but bad at pretty much everything else, gambling included. I can't help blaming him, in part at least, for Mum's decline. A therapist would probably tell me I blame him for a lot of things.'

'I'm sorry,' says Pete. 'Dangerous habit.'

'Sometimes – and he was a good man in other ways, don't get me wrong, he never hit us or even shouted – but he'd take Mum's shopping money, her housekeeping. He'd even help himself to our birthday money some years. Gemma said it was like living with a magpie. He was gentle and kind most of the time, but he was supposed to be keeping us all safe and he never really did.'

'When did you lose him?'

More drinks arrive. I take a sip of my second gin fizz.

'Twelve years ago. Almost thirteen. For the last decade of his life things seemed better. He and Mum stopped arguing so much and we all thought he was in recovery. He wasn't taking from us any more so there was a sense of relief. He had a sponsor and followed the twelve-step programme to the letter. But then, years later, he was caught.' I shake my head at the memory of it all, the shame. 'Our world fell apart. He'd taken a significant sum from the charity he worked for. A charity he loved, helping local veterans with housing and job interviews, retraining, setting up their own small businesses. He took their money through false accounts and creative book-keeping. It went on for years. Later he said he'd thought he'd be caught long before it got so out of hand.'

'I had no idea.'

The group next to us order a magnum of Krug champagne.

'The worst of it was the way neighbours and friends looked at us after the news broke. Front page of the Doncaster *Evening News*. *Local man rips off our heroes*. Mum even considered moving. It was starting to make her ill. Sorry, I didn't mean to ruin the mood on the first night.'

'Not at all.'

He places his hand on mine for a moment, and I am tired.

'The afternoon before he was due to appear at the police station Dad said he needed a walk to clear his head.' I glance out at the window, at the dark sea. 'He took his own life that evening.'

'I'm so sorry, Caz. I knew there was some sadness in your past but I had no idea. I promise you I will not set foot in that casino the whole time we're on board. I give you my word. I didn't know. I feel awful for stirring all this up.'

'We don't really talk about it any more. Gem can't handle it. It's not your fault.'

Piano music. Soft jazz from the 1940s. Raindrops tapping against the angled windows.

'Did you know about your father's habit when you were little?'

I look around at the well-heeled passengers casually sipping their sidecars and martinis without a care in the world. Talking about this, here, seems unreal.

'I had an inkling. Mum was always there for us but we'd go for days with no heat. Electricity cut off because he'd lost on the horses or at the dog track. Mum would go without meals, bless her, so we could have dinner, saying she'd already eaten; she'd even put a dirty plate in the sink to prove it. And then I started skipping dinner, pretending I'd had something in town after school, so she and Gemma could eat.'

'That must have been tough.'

I take the chance to lighten the mood. 'Slightly different from your childhood.'

Pete smiles. 'Ampleforth was far worse.'

I kick him.

'I'm being facetious, of course,' he says. 'But it was pretty awful in its own Dickensian way. School dinners, cold rooms, church before rugby and not seeing my parents for weeks on end. We suffered too, you know.'

We head back to our cabin. The atmosphere has changed since our conversation. It's subdued. He needs some time to digest it all. Or maybe now he realises why I haven't had a serious long-term relationship in over twenty years and he's having second thoughts. I wouldn't blame him.

I move the curtains and look out at the black, ever-moving sea.

Raindrops streak down the glass.

Pete tells me he has a headache coming on so we climb into the comfortable yet unfamiliar bed and switch out the lights.

I wake the next morning, stretch, and instinctively reach out for him.

His side of the bed is empty and the sheets are cool.

He's not there.

2

A dull ache behind my eyes.

'Pete?' My voice is more of a croak. 'Pete, are you there?'

No response.

The ship is moving at full speed, I can tell. Twenty-nine knots from the Rolls-Royce engines. I remember reading about the details on the journey down to Southampton.

I open the balcony door.

Empty.

The fresh November air is chill and I retreat back to the cabin, my arms wrapped around myself. He'll be in the bathroom. We haven't been together for long but I've already noticed he likes to read *The Economist* and the *New Yorker* in the bathroom.

I knock gently on the door and start to ask if he'd like a cup of tea but the door gives way to my knuckles and creaks open. The light's on but the room is unoccupied.

He went to breakfast without waking me? Of course he did. He knows I'm tired from work, from one family crisis after another. He let me sleep in.

I fill the kettle and switch it on.

My phone has no reception, something we've been told to expect from time to time out here, and my stomach is uneasy. Maybe it's the motion of the waves or maybe it's the fact that Pete didn't think to leave a note or a text. He usually leaves a scribbled note with a misshapen heart.

I pull on jeans and a jumper and scrunch my hair on top of my head and take my key card and step out into the corridor.

Thirty seconds later it hits me.

All the other cabin doors are wedged open.

Every single one is unoccupied and unlocked.

I walk along, frowning, confused, my mouth dry.

They're all empty.

Beds made and luggage gone.

My heart starts beating harder against my ribs. I break out into a run. At the end of the long corridor I take a lift down to the Ocean Lobby.

There's nobody here.

I run through the Captain's Lounge and the Gold Grill and the library. No crew. Not a single passenger. A ship as large as a small town with no people around.

They'll be gathered somewhere for a safety briefing, queued up next to lifeboats holding their lifejackets.

I take a lift up to the main deck. Same feeling in my gut as when Dad walked away that fateful day.

Not a single human being on any of the windswept decks or promenades. Nobody waiting by the lifeboats.

The breeze blows my hair over my face and I start to panic.

It's as if I'm trapped on a runaway train.

No, this is worse.

The RMS *Atlantica* is steaming out into the ocean and I am the only person on board.

3

I missed something, I always do. Some kind of emergency evacuation. I was so taken aback by Pete's casino suggestion that I missed some key piece of news, some scheduled drill.

I sprint up a flight of stairs and burst out on to the deck, my heart pounding.

The lifeboats are all here. Still tethered and untouched.

No sea birds in the sky.

A blank canvas.

So, they re-docked at Southampton and disembarked without me. But why would we still be steaming into the north Atlantic with no passengers on board?

It's important to stay calm. There is a perfectly rational explanation for all of this. There's something obvious I've missed.

Why didn't Pete wake me in the night?

I walk around the deck, my legs unsteady, and follow the running track. There is no sign anything's wrong, but there's no sign anything's right either. Not a crew member or a noise apart from the gentle hum of the engines in the background. That must mean the engine rooms and the bridge are manned, surely? A skeleton crew of professionals who can explain to me in simple terms what happened last night.

A pain in my abdomen.

I do not feel well.

It takes me almost two hours to explore, with increasing desperation, all the public areas of the *Atlantica*. In the belly of the ship I head to the main restaurant for Gold-class passengers. The Gold Grill: two storeys high, hundreds of tables, not a single one of them occupied.

'Hello,' I call out, and then louder. 'Hello?'

My voice echoes inside the cavernous room but the swirling carpets dampen the echo to a sinister whisper.

I step out to the rear decks.

A small pool and two Jacuzzi hot tubs.

Empty.

The sprawling wake of the ship presents itself in front of me. I look out at what I've left behind even though the land of home is now too distant to spot. That's the thing with horizons – Pete and I discussed it on the drive down to Southampton – you can only see a dozen or so miles. You think the horizon is far away but it never is. Especially not at sea level.

I try my phone again but it's no use. I send three messages but they just sit there on my screen refusing to budge. I send two emails and they linger in my outbox.

'Hello?' I holler, but my voice is carried out to sea on the breeze.

No seagulls.

No life at all.

I run now, panicking. What am I missing?

I have never felt so small, so impotent.

Up to the Platinum Grill, past the very table we dined at last night. Empty. Through to the sumptuous Diamond Grill. Mahogany and mirrors. Gleaming ice buckets by tables. No crew arranging silverware or polishing parquet floors. One table in the far corner already set. I run back to the Ocean Lobby with its piano and sweeping staircase, my guts twisting from the strangeness and from lack of breakfast or coffee.

The lobby is vast and silent and I resent it. Unmoving lifts and the blinking lights of slot machines in the casino with nobody to press their plastic buttons or feed them money. I walk to the purser's desk and check the desktop computers. They're operational but they're not online. The screensaver shows the RMS *Atlantica* but when I move the mouse the screen is blank.

It must be some kind of malfunction. A gas leak or a hull breach below the water line. They took everyone off the ship as a safety precaution. I wish Gemma was here, she'd know what to do. I'd say we're heading to a shipyard somewhere in France or Spain for urgent repairs before the next crossing. But we *are* crossing. I stop to take a deep breath, to calm myself. If we'd needed repairs they surely would have taken place in Southampton?

'Is there anyone here?' I ask, shakily.

It feels wrong to yell *help*. Pathetic, somehow. Fraudulent, even. I'm not in peril. This is the most luxurious mid-size ocean liner in the world. I am not in any physical danger.

I walk through the Nantucket Spa massage rooms. Not a soul. Only rolled towels, massage tables, unlit scented candles and expensive-looking oils.

The Cape Cod Cigar Lounge is quiet. A well-stocked humidor and zinc-topped bar with no human behind it to mix me a drink.

I need a drink.

Outside is the Diamond Lounge. I take a coffee from the machine and eat two ginger biscuits from a packet. I might get caught. We only have Platinum tickets. This is an area we're not entitled to use and I'd like a uniformed officer to walk over to me; discreetly inform me I'm in the wrong lounge and offer to help me find a way back to Platinum.

But no such officer arrives.

I walk up two flights of stairs on this maze of a ship, my head pounding, drawn to the bridge, to the well-trained women and men who are steering. I don't want to bother them if I can help it. They'll probably feel guilty, me left here all alone as the only passenger. Will they turn the ship around or send out a tender?

And then I remember the ship's theatre. The space is enormous, capable of swallowing almost every single passenger for a performance of *Guys and Dolls* or Bizet's *Carmen*. I run down the stairs, smiling, ready to be reunited with Pete. He'll embrace me and then we'll laugh about it.

He'll probably tease me for the remainder of our voyage.

I want to be teased.

The doors to the theatre are closed. The carpet has stars and planets, and the TV screens outside display our current location. We're west of Ireland now, in true ocean. There is no land mass visible on the map. We are surrounded by hundreds of miles of deep, inhospitable sea water and we're steaming further and further from home.

I approach the doors of the theatre and push them open.

The auditorium is empty and the stage is velvet black.

'Hello,' I call out. 'Can anybody hear me?'

I wait, my pulse throbbing in my ears. I can sense my heart rate and I can almost hear it, like holding a conch shell close to my temple.

No one replies.

The run back to my cabin takes twelve minutes, sweat pouring down my back.

Pete's nowhere to be found.

His watch sits on the bedside table, the only sign he was ever here. I pick it up and strap it to my wrist. It looks large and clumsy. I smell the leather strap and hold it against my upper lip.

Out on our balcony I see that the waters are choppy and the wind is picking up. He could have fallen overboard? No, anything but that. It wouldn't explain everyone else going missing.

What *could* explain that?

I do what Mum used to do when life became too much for her. If he'd spent the Christmas food budget or sold the family television she'd scream into a pillow and then splash cold water on her face. I don't scream, but I do wash my face and wet my hair. I need to think straight. I need to get a message back to the police, back to the coastguard, back to Gemma.

Phone off. Hard reset. Phone back on again.

No signal.

The messages have failed to send. The emails still linger in my outbox.

I jog back to the bow of the ship. I run down unfamiliar flights of stairs and turn through corridors of Gold-class cabins, the doors closer together, the carpeting less extravagant, and then I discover a side exit where the carpet ends and the floor is rubberised. I cross the threshold and knock on crew doors. They swing open. Unlocked. Tiny, cramped rooms with bunk beds and no windows, not even portholes. Photos of relatives taped to the walls. Make-up and deodorant cans. I am intruding. Are we below the water level here? Just the thought of that makes me shudder.

'Hello?' I ask, out in the corridor.

The echo is louder here. Not as many soft furnishings to absorb my anxious tones.

I run up to the highest point of this section of the ship.

The bridge.

Strictly crew only. No passengers allowed.

I try the door.

It's unlocked.

I pass through and walk out on to the central section of the bridge.

'Hello?' I say, apologetic. 'I know I'm not . . .'

But then I stop talking because the bridge is completely deserted. The view in front of me is empty chairs and screens and endless ocean.

There is nobody in control of the ship.

4

There must be an officer here. A skilled engineer or chief mate. A skeleton crew of highly trained professionals responsible for this mammoth vessel. I remember reading how the *Atlantica* cost over six hundred million dollars to build.

'Hello?' I say again, but my voice ricochets off the instruments and radar screens. I can see the whole of the front part of the deck from here. A clear view out of the windows. Deep waters past the continental shelf to the abyssal plain; a sea that may as well be bottomless.

I've never had an issue with surface swimming. Sometimes I even enjoy it. But I cannot tolerate being underwater. If I go under then I panic.

There are two leather chairs, one each side of the main control console, and seeing them unoccupied is unnerving.

'Where . . . is everyone?'

No reply.

I try to make sense of the panels: the gauges and lights and joysticks. The only thing I can ascertain is that there's nothing ahead of us on the radar screen. Nothing behind us either.

We are alone.

I am alone.

There is a GPS route map showing our current location and the route we've taken so far from Southampton. West, between the mainland and the Isle of Wight, and then west through the English Channel past the tip of Cornwall, and onward. No stops. No pauses to disembark almost a thousand passengers and six hundred crew. No slowing to anchor next to another passenger ship so the people on the *Atlantica* could get off due to an emergency: a breach of a bulkhead or a noxious chemical leak. According to the route screens there have been no stops. We've averaged twenty-seven knots and we're now steaming at twenty-nine.

I perch on the edge of one of the chairs, built for a captain or a first officer.

Firm leather.

Eerie silence.

My instinct is to reach for the handbrake, which is a preposterous idea. There is no brake, not that I can see, and why would I want to stop in the eastern north Atlantic? What good would that do? I check my phone again but it's not connecting. And then I see the radio on the side of the central console.

Thank goodness.

I pick up the handset and inspect it, trying to work out how it functions. I press a button but then I pause and look around and yell, 'I'm going to call the coastguard now. If there's someone on this ship you should come and stop me.'

No noise save for the gentle hum of the screens.

'Hello?' I say into the radio, the button depressed, my voice unsteady, trembling. 'This is Caroline Ripley on the RMS *Atlantica*. This is a mayday call. I repeat, this is a mayday call. We have no crew. I don't know how to steer the ship. We need urgent assistance from the coastguard. Mayday. Mayday.'

I release the trigger and look at the radio receiver.

I stare at it.

Waiting.

There is no reply. No one informing me a helicopter is already on its way with experienced operatives who'll remove me from the ship and take back control and explain to me calmly, with authority, exactly what happened to everyone.

Nothing.

This vessel is sailing by autopilot, of course it is. My nephew, Martin, Gemma's youngest, explained it all to me. Martin's technical for his age. Aspirations to one day become a civil engineer and design bridges. He said the *Atlantica* is similar to a jumbo jet, only a hundred times heavier. The ship will navigate its own way to New York, and then, as we approach the city, an experienced pilot from the harbour authority will board and safely guide the ship to its mooring. The thought of that helps loosen my chest. A *pilot*. Someone with knowledge, qualifications, and an unflappable demeanour. All I need to do is wait this out.

But as I walk away from the abandoned bridge there's still a voice lingering in my head, a monotone whisper, telling me Pete's gone and he's gone forever. The first man I've been able to trust since Dad betrayed us all. The only person to ever feel like a soulmate, even though I've never told him so. That ghoulish voice is saying that hundreds of people don't just disappear from an ocean

24

liner at sea. It's telling me that this is merely the opening scene of a nightmare.

I jog to the main decks and check the lifeboats. Some of them are used as tenders to ferry passengers to and from the ship in smaller ports. But most are state-of-the-art lifeboats, completely enclosed, unsinkable, self-righting, capable of holding more than a hundred passengers each. They have independent engines and emergency supplies. Worst comes to worst I climb in and set off slowly back towards England. For some reason the thought of being alone in a much smaller boat is almost more comforting than the thought of being alone on this Goliath-sized liner. Almost a dozen decks, hundreds of passenger cabins, and me completely and utterly on my own. I am more vulnerable than I've been since the day my father took a walk to clear his head.

I scream, 'Where are you, Pete?' at the sea, and suddenly I'm tired, weak at the knees, and I stagger to a deckchair and slump into it. I want to be in his house close to Hatfield Moors sitting on his scruffy leather sofa with the fire lit, ash all over the hearth, and him placing a vinyl record on the complicated turntable he's so protective of. It was a gift from his brother and he won't even let me put a drink down near it. I'd give anything to be curled up with him right now with a glass of wine and his ancient cat purring on the next chair. I could not be further from that world. The momentum of this giant steel structure is relentless. Powering forward, away from home, towards the mid-Atlantic trench, the deepest part of this ocean, thundering on, stoical, perhaps set to collide with the Statue of Liberty at thirty knots in five days' time.

I sprint back to the bridge and linger with my hand over the main controls. I won't stop the ship but I could slow it down? Allow a rescue vessel to catch up?

I don't touch it. Knowing me, I'll make the wrong decision.

After calling out another frantic mayday on the radio I say, 'I'm stopping the ship. I'm going to do it. If you want to prevent me then now is your chance.'

Nobody answers.

I rest my shaking hand on the thrust lever and pull it gently towards me.

The speed displayed on screen stays at twenty-nine knots.

I pull it harder.

Twenty-nine knots.

I pull it back to the five knots zone.

The *Atlantica* stays at precisely twenty-nine knots.

I swallow hard and drag my hands up and down my face, clearing my eyes, rubbing my forehead.

There's a rational explanation, there always is. Mum taught me that. She was always fascinated by science, especially physics, even though she never had the chance to study further at school. She borrowed popular science books from the local library and she always said, *You need to look at the potential logical reasons. Look at them one by one.*

Everyone's gone, even Pete. He left me here alone. The ship won't slow down. So, there must have been an emergency of some kind. An evacuation. I'm no expert in how these things are carried out. Maybe another ship came alongside and everyone walked off. I don't see why Pete would have left me here all alone but there will be a good explanation. Mum would also have asked, *Have you checked absolutely everywhere, Caroline? Are you sure? There's always somewhere we miss.*

I spend two hours working my way systematically through each deck. I don't obey rules or safety messages any more; I stray from passenger lounges and elevators to the galley kitchens and crew-only zones. I even locate the captain's quarters, with direct access to the bridge. 'Captain?' I call out. 'I'm sorry but I need to come in.'

An empty suite with its own immaculate kitchenette with espresso machine. No signs of panic or past emergencies. A perfectly made bed and a stack of unread international newspapers on his coffee table.

There's a detailed plan of the ship framed on the wall. Blueprints. I can see the engine room at the rear and the gas turbine electrical unit below the main funnel. Food stores are marked out near the base of the ship on Deck Two. Deck One is recycling, desalination, water processing, food waste, carpentry, laundry. A large ballroom at the rear and a dog kennel on the highest deck.

There could be crew here. There could still be help.

As I walk back along Deck Five, my legs weary from all the running, exhausted by the sense of fever-dream unreality, I can feel the power of the ship, its bulbous bow slicing through the waves. It's as though I've regressed to a child left behind at a holiday camp when the season ends and the weather starts to turn.

There is no noise apart from my noise, no voice apart from my own.

'Anybody here, please?' I say, but my voice cracks.

There is a noise.

A soft tapping in the distance.

I focus on it and squint with concentration. The noise is faint. I walk down three flights of steps and the tapping is regular and it is growing louder.

Crew only.

I enter a workshop area, and then follow a long corridor with a squeaky floor.

There are ducts and cables threaded along the ceiling area.

I step to a bulkhead threshold.

Sliding power-operated watertight door.

Compliant with SOLAS regulations.

Do not open at sea without reason.

I've read about these. They're to keep each segment of the ship watertight in case we hit an object or run aground.

Close immediately after opening.

Do not block.

I take a deep breath and press the button.

The door opens slowly. It's heavy-duty reinforced steel and it's moving at about quarter the speed of a lift door. This deck is below the water level. An alarm beeps as the door slides into the recess in the wall.

I peer ahead into another identical crew-only corridor.

I take a step.

The tapping is louder now. Much louder.

The far end of the corridor is dark, a faint light flickering from down by the floor.

I walk twenty metres, the alarm from the open watertight door still bleeping ominously behind me.

I adjust my gait in a vain attempt to stop my shoes squeaking on the floor.

The tapping stops.

There is a figure in the shadows at the far end of the corridor.

He's standing quite still, uplit, facing the wall. His nose must be touching it. He's wearing overalls and his right leg is kinked at an unnatural angle.

'Oh, thank God.' I say.

The tapping stops.

5

The man turns to face me.

'I'm so happy to see you,' I say, smiling, frowning, holding out my hand.

He looks at it and, after a long pause, says, without much emotion, 'I thought I was the only person here.'

'Me too.'

He stares at me. 'I thought you had left.'

I frown and swallow hard.

'I'm Daniel Cho.'

I let out a sigh of relief. 'What happened, Daniel? Sorry, I'm being rude. I'm Caz. Caroline Ripley.'

'Scottish?'

'English.'

He shakes my hand and we walk back towards the watertight door I came in through. His gait is unusual somehow.

'I woke up and meditated like I usually do,' he says. 'Went down for a workout and the ship was completely empty.'

'Does your phone work? Please tell me you've been able to contact someone.'

'Nothing,' he says. 'I was inspecting the wiring back there, trying to reboot a router.'

'Did it work?'

'Not so far.'

We arrive at some kind of control room and I know I should be wary of Daniel, wary of any man I don't know, but I don't have many options right now.

'Do you work on the ship? Electrician?'

'No, I'm just a normal passenger like you.'

I point at his overalls. They say *Atlantica* on the back.

'Oh, this? New gym gear. Borrowed the boiler suit to cover up while I worked. This was hanging in the crew area so I put it on.'

That seems strange to me but I let it go.

He starts stepping out of the suit. Daniel's younger than me. Ten years younger, maybe. He looks like a professional athlete.

'Did you notice anything last night?' I say. 'This morning? Noises? Anything strange?'

'I sleep well. Felt like a normal night.'

'For me too.'

'Most likely we headed back to Southampton and everyone disembarked. Perhaps some kind of union dispute or safety issue.'

'No, not according to the bridge,' I say. 'The maps and monitors.'

'You've been on the bridge? It's open to us?'

'I just walked in there.'

Daniel looks at the control room screens. 'I'm pretty sure this readout is the total amount of electricity we're generating. And this is the amount of power we're currently using. That's exhaust analysis.'

I wonder what Pete might be doing right now. Where he might be. It's so alien in the modern world not to be able to contact your loved ones or know where they are.

'What do we do now?'

'I honestly don't know,' he says. 'Search the ship, I guess. Find some way of communicating. A sat phone or long-wave radio.'

'I want to leave the ship now.'

He frowns.

'I don't feel safe on here.'

'I don't feel safe either,' he says. 'But we *are* safe, and that's what's important. If you think about it, this is one of the most reliable ocean liners in the world. It's due a refit but it's still built like a tank. Have you seen the YouTube videos of her going through hurricane-force storms in the Caribbean?'

'No. I don't think I could watch.'

'We're safe on here. Sorry, what did you say your name is again?'

'Caroline Ripley. Call me Caz.'

'There'll be some mundane technical reason why everyone left the ship, you know. We either docked some-place or else smaller boats came to collect everyone off the *Atlantica*.'

'Oh, I know that.'

'Why don't you search the rear of the ship for sat phones, radios, anything like that? Try any gadget you see, any computer. I'll do the same in the front half. Let's meet in the Ocean Lobby at two o'clock. You OK with that?'

'Sure,' I say, tentatively. 'I can do that.'

Part of me doesn't want to let him out of my sight.

Being together seems so much better than being alone on this vast liner.

By half-past one I've found nothing of use. Most of the crew cabins are perfect, as if nobody ever slept in the beds. There's hardly any luggage left. Few signs that performers and chefs and bartenders were woken up in their sleep by some pulsing alarm or siren. How would you remove a thousand people off a ship in the middle of the night in the middle of the ocean? *Why* would you do such a thing?

In the Ocean Lobby, close to the casino and in the shadow of the sweeping staircases, Daniel is sitting in an armchair holding an iPad.

'You have connection?'

He shakes his head. 'We need to send some kind of emergency distress call.'

Distress is the right term for this. Pete and I needed a break together, a chance, a week away from the café deliveries and staff shift calendar, to really connect. And all we have is distress.

'I tried the radio on the bridge but nobody answered. It's like we're floating around in our own bubble. Did you see any satellite phones?'

'Nothing's working,' he says, not looking up. 'This is starting to really freak me out.'

'Don't say that. We're missing something, missing the obvious.'

'My mom used to tell me I'd always look for complex solutions to simple problems. Not like my brother.'

I look at him and he meets my gaze.

'Brother's an orthodontist,' he says, scowling. 'Former·
college football line-backer and soup kitchen volunteer at
our local church. Two inches taller than me, three down-
town dental surgeries, working on a fourth. Two polite,
overachieving kids and a nice six-bed in the 'burbs.
Whereas I live in a van.'

'You . . . live in a van?'

'Let's get to the upper decks and see if we can figure
out how to launch a tender.'

The carpets are plush underfoot and the ship is steady
and smooth. From time to time I think I can sense the
faint leftover aroma of someone's perfume from last
night – notes of grapefruit or sandalwood – and it brings
home how quickly everything turned upside-down.

We reach outdoors and I ask, 'You know much about
ships, Daniel?'

'Not really, not on this scale. I teach water sports in the
summer, downhill skiing in the winter. I know the basics
but the *Atlantica* is built more like a city than a boat.'

Out on the running track deck, Daniel pulls off a white
steel panel to access the lifeboat release mechanism.

'How much range do these have?' My words are
muffled by the wind so I repeat them.

'These? No idea. But they'll have survival food and
water. We'd manage. If things go south we'll jump in one
and float away. You think we're in shipping lanes here?'

'I have no idea.'

In the distance I watch a piece of plastic wrapped in
netting float by. It looks microscopic down there in the
water. Martin, Gemma's boy, has been regaling me with
stats about the ocean ever since he heard I was taking this

last-minute trip. How a hundred per cent of the moon has been mapped but only five per cent of the ocean floor. He told me the Australian box jellyfish contains enough toxin to kill thirty humans. I bought him a '1001 facts' book for his twelfth birthday and I find most of the oceanic references deeply unnerving.

'If we're in the main lanes we'll stand a chance of sending up flares, catching someone's attention. Hell of a horn and a whistle on this ship.'

'The library?' I say. 'There might be maps or information on commercial shipping lanes?'

We walk there and split up. Daniel checks the reference section and I look for books on the *Atlantica* itself. Shelves and shelves of illuminated hardback books, and study tables with green leather armchairs and elegant lamps. This is nothing like my local library, the place I sought comfort and safety most weekends as a girl. That was tatty and underfunded but the books were read and reread and they were loved. The librarians were knowledgeable and kind. This library looks fake in comparison.

I turn to the history section and notice the desk in the corner.

All on its own, pushed up against the window.

Bedsheets hanging down on all sides.

I gesture to Daniel and, together, we step closer.

The bedsheet curtain twitches.

I crouch and pull it to one side and there's a young girl hiding underneath and she's wrapped in blankets.

6

'There's a kid under there?' whispers Daniel.

I bend down and lift the bedsheet curtain again.

Her eyes are huge. Curly reddish hair falling around her shoulders. Fourteen, maybe fifteen years old. She's gripping a book so hard her thumbnails are white.

'It's OK,' I say. 'You can come out. You're not alone.'

She mutters something under her breath.

'What are you doing under there, sweetie?'

'I'm doing research.' Her voice is confident. Assured.

'Research?'

'I am *trying* to do research.' Her tone is acidic now.

'My name is Caroline. Caz.'

She starts to extricate herself from the den under the library desk. 'Does either of you have the slightest idea what happened on the ship earlier today?'

'What's your name?'

'What on earth happened to everyone?'

'We don't know yet,' says Daniel.

'It took my mother and my father,' she says.

'What do you mean?' I say.

'They're gone. They were in the next cabin and I went to sleep with them there and when I woke up this morning they were both gone. No message or note. No clothes in the wardrobe. No suitcases. Vanished into thin air.'

'I'm sure they're OK,' I say.

'You are not sure,' she says. 'You have no idea.'

The girl has a Welsh accent and I underestimated her age by a few years. She smells faintly of roses. She reminds me of someone. Perhaps a girl I went to school with.

I hold out my hand.

'Caz Ripley,' I introduce myself again. 'We'll find out what happened.'

'Will we? And how will we do that, exactly? I've been trying to communicate with the coastguard, with anyone, all morning, and to no avail.' She's panting now. Working herself into a frenzy. 'My phone won't connect. What do you suppose is *wrong* with this ship?'

'What's your name?' asks Daniel.

'My name's Francine,' she says. 'Frannie.'

Daniel takes a deep breath and says, 'Frannie, I'm Daniel Cho. I'm kind of a water guy. I work around boats, always have done. I'll make sure we find your parents.'

She seems to take some reassurance from that. Maybe it's because he's been around ships before or maybe because he looks like a cliché stock image of a lifeguard.

'What are you reading under there?' I ask. 'Navigation books? Maps?'

She says, 'I was reading an exploratory analysis of the events surrounding the *Mary Celeste*.'

Daniel and I glance at each other.

'You studying it in high school, Frannie?' asks Daniel.

She narrows her eyes. 'I'm twenty-one years old.'

'You're twenty-one? You said you were travelling with your parents . . .'

'Yes, so? Trip of a lifetime, supposedly. We're celebrating their silver wedding anniversary and now they've both gone. Dad's not well. Have you noticed how all the small boats and lifeboats are still attached to the main ship?'

'We noticed,' I say.

'So what happened here?'

'I don't know,' I say. 'There must have been an evacuation of some sort.'

'The sort where everyone takes their luggage and makes their beds before they leave? What kind of evacuation is that, Caroline?'

I'm taken aback for a moment. 'Caz. Call me Caz.'

She shakes her head and looks up to the ceiling then back at us and she says, 'I'm sorry. You didn't deserve that, I'm just a little jittery over here. Your phones aren't working, are they?'

'Not uncommon this far out at sea,' says Daniel. 'We're nowhere near a tower, so we're dependent on the ship.'

'*Dependent on the ship,*' says Frannie, sweat beading on her upper lip. 'That about sums it all up. The three of us are totally dependent on this ship.'

I want Pete to walk in. I want this to end.

'People survive weeks or months on small fishing trawlers,' Daniel says. 'I think we'll be just fine on board the *Atlantica* for a few days until we reach New York.'

'Oh, OK. You think we're still headed for New York?'

'Sorry?'

'Look at the sun, Daniel. You too, Caroline. Right now this ship's headed due south. If we stay on this course, the first land mass we'll hit will be the Antarctic ice shelf.'

7

Daniel stares out of the window, scratching the stubble on his neck.

'She's right,' he says.

'Of course I'm right,' says Frannie.

My breathing is shallow. I need to focus on deep breaths the way Mum used to.

'There's nobody steering the ship,' I say, more calmly than I feel. 'We went up to the bridge and there's nobody at the controls. It's locked on autopilot.'

'I understand what this is,' says Daniel.

My heart lifts. We both look at him.

'The navigation system detected bad weather so we're skirting a storm, is all. We'll be heading back to due west just as soon as we're in safe waters.'

'*Safe waters*,' says Frannie, dismissively.

'That makes sense,' I say, trying to convince myself. 'A modern ocean liner like this would automatically deviate around a storm system. Of course it would. That's logical.'

'There's nothing logical about this ship, Caroline.'

'Call me Caz, Frannie, please.' Only Dad used to call me Caroline. He never once shortened my name. Mum called me Sweet Caroline before she stopped recognising

my face. Gem calls me sis. Pete only calls me Caroline
when he's flirting.

'My best friend back in Swansea is Caz. We've been
friends since primary school and we went through
Brownies and Guides together. So I'll call you Caroline if
you don't mind.'

'We need to find some perspective on this problem and
carve out an actionable plan,' says Daniel. 'Stay calm and
get organised.'

'I am calm,' mutters Frannie.

I start biting my nails, something I haven't done since
my teenage years. We should not be here. The three of us
are going round in circles and my chest is tight.

'We need to eat something,' I say. 'Let's start there.
Basics. Sandwiches. We'll think more clearly with food in
our stomachs.'

'We're not your kids, you know,' she says.

I pause and look at her. What a hurtful comment. But
then, I suppose, she doesn't know. Only a handful of
people in the world do.

'I work with food, Francine. I run a small, busy café.
I'm a business owner, responsible for the livelihoods of a
dozen people. Now do you want some food or don't you.'

'OK, you're right,' she says. 'I'm sorry.'

We walk uncomfortably to the main Gold Grill restaurant. This place seats five hundred passengers at any one
time. An ice sculpture of the Statue of Liberty sits at the
centre of the room and it has melted down to the point
where it's barely recognisable.

'Let's use that table,' I say, pointing. 'Collect plates,
paper, pens. I'll prepare some food.'

'I'm gluten-intolerant,' says Frannie.

'No problem.'

The galley kitchen is ten times the size of my entire café. Stainless steel electric ovens and chef stations and gleaming worktops. The floors are tiled and the knives are resting on magnetic strips. The fridges are pretty much empty but I make up two plates of sandwiches and a cheese omelette for Frannie. We eat in silence and we all share the same wide-eyed expressions on our faces. I think it's because we feel perversely safe on this solid vessel, and at the same time utterly vulnerable.

'Best omelette I've had in years,' says Frannie. 'Really. I owe you.'

I wasn't as confident as her when I was twenty-one. Twenty-eight years ago I could barely speak to strangers or take a train by myself. Any notion of self-belief I have now has been accumulated over decades, a little at a time.

'Let's share plans,' says Daniel, wiping his mouth. 'Strategies and theories. We can go around the table. Spill whatever thoughts are in your head, no matter how unhinged they seem. Caz, you go first.'

I shake my head. '*You* go first.'

'Fine,' he says, and then he drains his glass of mineral water. 'Modern-day piracy. I know, but hear me out. The well-armed teams you hear about in the Gulf of Oman, off Somalia, Gulf of Guinea, Strait of Malacca. It's a genuine issue. Can you imagine how much a small group of pirates would be paid in ransom for a thousand *Atlantica* passengers? Factor in precious wedding rings, cash, other saleable jewellery. When I think about it I'm surprised this hasn't happened before.'

'Oh, it's happened before,' says Frannie. 'Cruise ships are attacked because they don't have private security in the same way cargo ships and oil tankers do. No mercenaries on board to shoot back. There was this one case—'

'So why did they leave us three?' I ask.

'Because there were never any pirates here, Caroline,' says Frannie, pushing her plate away, sitting up straighter. 'They'd have woken us all up. Also, pirates would, at the very least, have stolen the lifeboats and tenders. They're valuable. Realistically, they wouldn't have wanted a thousand ordinary people either. Raid the ship, firing into the sky, and quickly take phones, cash, earrings, items they can liquidate quickly – that I can see happening. Maybe a couple of wealthy-looking Diamond-class duplex cabin passengers. *Maybe*. But not everyone. Civilians are a liability. Unpredictable. This wasn't modern-day pirates.'

Daniel adjusts his posture. 'So, what's your theory?'

The sun disappears behind a cloud and the cavernous dining room darkens.

'This has happened before, believe it or not,' she says. 'In fact it's happened numerous times throughout history, just not recently. The *Lady Lovibond*, the *Flying Dutchman*, the *Princess Augusta*, the SS *Valencia* – I could go on. The legends vary but I can assure you that numerous well-maintained ships have been found in open ocean with no crew or passengers on board. Utterly deserted. They're sometimes referred to as ghost ships.'

Daniel shakes his head and mutters, 'Please.'

She half-smiles and then bites her lip. 'It happened, though. I'm not sure you get to be dismissive if it happened over and over again, Daniel. At least two dozen well-documented events. Insurance companies don't pay out until thorough professional investigations have been completed. In every single case the cause was declared unknown. Why would a well-paid crew desert a perfectly seaworthy ship?'

A long silence.

'Well?' I say.

'As I said, they've never been fully explained. There are theories of madness brought about by the doldrums phenomenon, or by the specific mathematical resonance of certain wave patterns. One Lithuanian professor theorised that rare algae phosphorescence caused some kind of hysteria, a form of mass mania.'

I frown. 'You think people jumped overboard?'

'I don't personally think that, no. I'm just saying these historical events are still, to this day, even with radar and satellite images and so on, unexplained. And it's human nature to feel unsettled with anything left unexplained. We developed the Big Bang theory to explain how our universe came to exist in the first place even though it can never conclusively be proven correct or incorrect. Ditto with every major monotheistic religion. Where there are gaps in our knowledge, we fill those gaps with best-guess theories and philosophies of convenience.'

'So your theory is that this is some kind of modern-day *Mary Celeste*?'

'My mother and father are gone, Caroline, that's all I know. We're a very close-knit family on account of me being their only child. We speak every day on the phone and . . . I'm sorry . . .' She fans her eyes with her hands.

'I'm freaking out that I can't reach either of them. My therapist says I have a tendency to spin out of control.' Her breathing quickens. 'Where are they? I never even had a chance to say goodbye. Or to explain what I did.'

8

The chandeliers flicker for a moment.

'What happened, Frannie? You can tell us.'

She shakes her head. 'No, I can't.'

'We need a plan of action,' Daniel says. 'Something concrete.'

Frannie nods. 'What do you propose?'

He goes quiet so I take over. 'We have ample food down in the stores on Deck Two. We have the desalination plants. We have heat and light. We have shelter. All the elements we need to live comfortably. The autopilot seems to be sailing the ship safely as per usual.'

'I say we try to get word out to other ships but we don't panic,' says Daniel. 'Panic can be lethal. I remember one time hearing about my high school history teacher's brother. He was an experienced kayaker, one of a group who travelled to Alaska. They made all their scheduled stops but then lost their bearings when the fog came down out of nowhere and caught them off-guard. Eventually they managed to find the shore. Half the group followed a wise old outdoorsman and stayed put. They built a shelter and melted snow for water. The other half panicked and decided to ignore the older man. They walked away to find help. The group who stayed were discovered months later: hungry, emaciated, but alive.'

Frannie raises her eyebrows.

He looks down at the floor. 'The other group were never found.'

'Your teacher's brother?' I ask.

Daniel doesn't reply.

Frannie and I glance at each other but say nothing. A vast painting of a Venetian canal scene looks down on us in this windowless room. Some tables are set but most are bare.

'Let's stay calm, and, if possible,' he says, 'we should try to enjoy the voyage.'

'*Enjoy the voyage*?' says Frannie, standing up. 'Sorry, but what are you talking about? My parents are missing. Caroline's boyfriend vanished from her cabin earlier this morning. Just because you're here alone, you must realise we will not be enjoying anything until we're sure everyone's OK.'

'I didn't mean it like that,' says Daniel. 'Listen: when I'm teaching someone to ski off-piste for the first time, or surf a big wave, I tell them to lean into the experience and let it happen. To stay loose and relaxed is to survive. That way you don't crack and make a dangerous mistake.'

I already know I have made a dangerous mistake. I'm usually the person in control of the situation, the responsible adult, the spider in the web. That's who I am. Checking maps before setting off, making sure each tyre has the correct amount of pressure, filling up with petrol in advance. I am the grown-up so others can relax. It's been that way ever since Dad died. The only way I can hold everything together, and resist the same urges that caused so much misery, is to stay in control.

'I think what Daniel means is we should have focus,' I say.

Daniel nods.

'Let's split up so we can cover more of the ship.' I clear the corners of my eyes. 'Do you both have watches?'

Daniel nods again. Frannie shakes her head.

'You have your phone, though?'

She nods.

'Let's regroup at four p.m. on the bridge. Search every space on the ship for flares and emergency smoke beacons. Anything we can use to signal to a passing sailboat or bulk carrier.'

'And phones, radios, anything like that,' says Daniel. 'I have some experience with electronics, circuit boards. I'll try to rig something up to broadcast a basic SOS.'

At five to four I arrive on the bridge carrying two phones and other scavenged items. Daniel and I crossed paths a few times during the searches but I didn't meet Frannie once. Running through carpeted corridors, sometimes the same corridor over and over, you start to lose your sanity. It's like being locked inside a steel maze.

Red hair.

She's sitting slumped, cross-legged in the captain's chair staring out at sea.

'You find anything useful? Radios? Flares?' I ask.

'Nothing.'

'*Nothing*?' I can't help scowling as I make a show of placing down all the smartphones and chargers and iPads and plastic bottles I've collected.

'Are they water supplies?' she asks, gesturing to the bottles.

'For messages. There are hundreds more in the recycling area on Deck One. We write a simple SOS note, or better still we print something off on a printer, then release all the bottles and hope someone will read one.'

'Worth a try,' says Daniel, joining us. 'I picked up three flares. There should be more on the lifeboats.'

'I did find something,' says Frannie.

'What?'

She smiles. 'A dozen beautiful dogs.'

'They're still here?'

'Fully occupied kennel. Twelve in all. Well, I should have said eleven beauties and one beast.'

'What are you saying?' asks Daniel.

'Remember, this is an ocean liner not a cruise ship,' she says. 'It's normal to have dogs on board. Kennel accommodation so people crossing from one side of the ocean to the other can bring their beloved pets. Less traumatic than a long flight. Only they're not all pets, I don't think. I think one of them is a Caucasian Shepherd dog.'

It feels alien to have dogs on board. Out-of-kilter, somehow.

'My parents have dogs,' says Daniel, and then worry lines deepen across his forehead. He takes a moment and mumbles, 'You would never leave your pet on a ship. I mean, if people evacuated, they'd have taken their dogs with them, surely. No way a dog-lover would leave their precious pet here all alone.'

'My parents left *me* here all alone,' says Frannie.

I clear my throat because I don't like their pessimistic tone. 'Most of the suitcases are gone, mine included. But I did find some luggage. Do you think it's worth us opening up all the cases, rifling through people's personal belongings for phones and things?'

I would hate for strangers to look through my bags. When the newspapers investigated our family, digging up old photos and paying cash for quotes from school friends and colleagues, it was as if our house had been cracked open for the whole world to look inside and judge.

'It's justifiable,' says Daniel, still clearly spooked at the thought of dogs being left behind. 'But it's unlikely we'll find anything with sufficient range. The phones are not working because there's no signal. That's a ship-wide issue.'

Frannie says, despair in her voice, 'How did this *happen*?'

We don't answer.

The world is carrying on as normal in every direction from here. People cycling to work, stepping on buses, beginning their school days, and we are lost.

Frannie takes a deep breath. 'My dad's an engineer. He told me the whistles and foghorns on this ship are so powerful they can be heard ten miles away. We should give them a blast.'

'Or a Morse code SOS signal?' I say.

'Yes,' says Daniel. 'Dash, dash, dash, dot, dot, dot, dash, dash, dash.'

'I have absolutely no idea what you're talking about,' says Frannie. 'Sorry.'

He lets his finger hover over the horn button. And then he braces himself and presses it.

There is no noise.

Nothing.

9

Colour is draining from the sky: blues morphing into slate greys and whites. Not a bird or insect to look at. The sea smells rancid all the way out here. The largest wilderness of them all, and we are stranded in the centre of it.

'I don't like this ship,' says Frannie. 'It's as if it's taken against us.'

Daniel knocks the metal structure. 'Steel, rivets and aluminium. Worst case scenario, if there's a computer system malfunction and we don't feel safe on board, we'll launch a rigid lifeboat or an inflatable survival raft and we'll muddle through. It won't be comfortable but we'll survive. A cargo ship or gas carrier will pick us up.'

I stare out at the waves. They look petrol-green now. The palette is unreliable. Everything here, it appears, is unreliable.

'Do you think there are distress beacons on the lifeboats, Daniel?' I ask.

'Of course!' A smile spreads over his face. 'See, we just needed to think this through. Well done.'

We walk down flights of stairs lined with photos of old liners from the steam era – ships with masts as well as funnels – through an atrium leading off the Gold Grill, and arrive on deck. We locate the lifeboat stations.

'How do we get access?' Frannie asks, peering over the side of the safety rail. 'And how do we drop them down to the water level? We must be ten storeys up.'

'We're not launching,' says Daniel. 'Just hunting for gear. I'll go in.'

He tries and fails to open the main access hatch from the deck so he clambers up a white-painted steel structure. I can hardly bear to look because he's now directly over the water, away from the safety of the deck and the rails. He steps precariously on to the orange-covered lifeboat and it starts to sway.

He opens the roof access hatch.

Except, he doesn't.

'What is it?' I ask, shouting, the wind blowing my words away.

'What?' yells Daniel.

'What's wrong?'

'It's locked,' he calls.

Locked? Are lifeboats ever locked? Again, I miss having people with expertise close at hand. Trained and experienced. I miss not being able to look things up with the click of a button. I am not accustomed to being this out of my depth, guessing, scrambling around in the dark.

'Maybe you need a crew pass or a key?' asks Frannie.

'What?' he screams again.

He climbs back to the main ship, and then he slips and loses his footing. His arm slams into the metal beam and he winces.

'Are you OK?' I shout.

He winces harder and nods.

'Take it slow,' yells Frannie.

He proceeds more cautiously. When he's safely back we read the instruction panel for how to launch a lifeboat. It explains how passengers should board the vessel in an orderly fashion, wearing their life vests, and how the person in charge needs to oversee this, and how, once the hydraulic system has lowered the boat to the water, two people need to release the tethers so the lifeboat can power away from the ship. It says nothing whatsoever about locks.

'This must be the VIP tender,' says Daniel, rubbing the underside of his arm. 'Sometimes Diamond-class guests have their own craft for visiting port stops. They pay extra to be the first people off the ship. This must be it.'

Frannie squints into the distance.

She raises her arm and extends her index finger.

A plane is approaching.

10

'Help us!' screams Frannie, waving her arms frantically in the air.

'Stop,' says Daniel, angrily. 'It's pointless. That's a commercial four-engine plane flying at nine thousand metres. It cannot see you.'

Frannie barges past him and heads for the stairs. We follow her up to the main sun deck. Frannie starts dragging recliner chairs on to the centre of the teak boards.

'This ship looks like a pine needle floating on Lake Superior from way up there,' he says, almost yelling at her, the vein in his forehead protruding. 'They can't see us, Francine.'

I realise what she's doing and start helping her.

'Over there,' she says. 'Get started on the "O". Daniel, make yourself useful.'

He shakes his head, but then he understands. He starts to drag chairs.

By the time the plane is directly overhead, Frannie has almost finished her 'S' and I've made the top curve of my 'O'.

'It's too late,' says Frannie. 'We were too slow.'

I keep working. 'There will be other planes. Let's extend these letters. We must have eight hundred chairs on the ship. SOS as tall as the whole deck. Someone will spot it eventually, call in our position. Some low flying aircraft. A helicopter, maybe.'

Daniel wipes sweat from his brow and drags more chairs to form the centre section of our desperate message.

Three letters from three confused stranded shipmates. A young Welsh woman with freckles and attitude forming *Save*. A hungry forty-nine-year-old café proprietor finishing *Our*. An Asian-American water-ski instructor setting out wooden seating to complete *Souls*.

'Not to put another dampener on your spirits, but there won't *be* a low-flying plane or helicopter.'

We both turn to him.

'My uncle was a plane transporter before I was born. The way small planes are delivered across continents, from Europe to North America, for example, the planes that fly at three thousand metres, is via Iceland and Greenland. No way you can fly a single engine across open ocean. Same goes for rotary aircraft. They have limited range. The only things we'll see in the skies all the way out here are stars and high-altitude jets.'

'I disagree,' says Frannie. 'Because, well, you're wrong. The astronauts above us living inside the Space Station might zoom in and spot us. A Delta flight might have to drop altitude to avoid a storm cloud. The pilot might see the ship. We need to do anything we possibly can to not appear like a normal ocean liner. Now, double up the chairs like I have. We need to make this bold.'

The plane has left us behind. It glided noiselessly over us, through darkening wisps of cirrus cloud, and it ignored us completely.

For the first time in a long time, I miss my mother. Not superficially, but with my whole self. She doesn't often know my name any more, thinks I'm one of her carers, but occasionally there's a lightning-quick flash of recognition. She had such a lot to put up with in her life. She deserved joy in her old age, not this.

'What we really need is fire,' says Daniel. 'Our only hope of signalling is a fire to show another ship we're at risk. Smoke rising miles into the sky. A trail to mark our location. Otherwise we may as well give up.'

'I don't think you can light a fire on board a ship,' I say, rubbing my arms to stay warm. 'Pete and I were discussing it on the drive down to Southampton. I asked if the Diamond-class cabins have real fires, like they did on the *Titanic*. Not real fires – I know that's not possible on a modern ocean liner – but alcohol fires or gas fireplaces. He said, *Fire is the biggest risk to a modern cruise ship or liner, more so than icebergs or running aground.* Apparently modern radar systems can prevent collision, but fire, caused by electrical malfunction or a drunken passenger smoking on her balcony – that can place an entire ship at risk in minutes.'

Driving down in his old Audi, his hand on mine, I could never have predicted any of this. *I hope you're safe, Pete Davenport.*

'She's right,' says Frannie. 'It's too risky. We need to find the smoke-signal flares you were talking about. That, and messages in bottles. We need thousands and thousands of messages in bottles. Attach them to anything eye-catching that floats. At some point someone will pick one up out of the water.'

I swallow, picturing how large the Atlantic is, realising it could take months for someone to pick up a bottle and read the message inside. I remember Martin, my nephew, saying the Atlantic Ocean was over six times the size of Russia's landmass.

'Could have been my fiancée on that plane,' Daniel says, staring into the sky at the fading contrails. 'My little girl, too.'

I turn to him. 'They didn't travel on the ship with you?'

He shakes his head. 'This is kind of a business trip for me, so just one ticket. It's complicated. And, well, we're not officially together at the moment. I mean, we're together, but we don't live together. She and I need to sort things out. I live out of my van mostly, send money back to her. We're not a conventional family, I guess. We don't really believe in that.'

'Free spirit?' I say.

'You think I'm a jerk, and that's fine, I know it sounds that way, but, honestly, I struggle with modern life. I'm not good indoors or working routine jobs. Ocean, lake, beach, mountain I can manage, and I can work hard, but I can't live cooped up like other respectable people. I've tried being like my brother with a mortgage and a 401K but it doesn't work out. My head can't take it. Jess understands that, I'm pretty sure she does. I mean, it's not as if I'm with other women. I'd never do that. I'm just not good at being penned in.'

'But you're engaged to each other?' I say, pulling the last few deckchairs into place.

'It's our compromise. She'd like to be married but I'm not ready so right now we're fiancée and fiancé. We're committed, in our own way, but we still get to be individuals, you know?'

'I've known guys like you,' I say, my tone a little more harsh than I intended.

He frowns.

'Some of them grew into family men, and some grew lonely. Be careful you make the right decision.'

He walks away.

I'm opening up much earlier than I usually would. It's not that I'm close friends with Daniel and Frannie, far from it, but we are connected by our shared circumstance. *In extremis*, you skip the small talk, I've noticed, and focus on what matters. An hour on board the *Atlantica* is like a month on dry land.

'I think you can do things your own way, your own style,' he says, somewhat defensively, coming back. 'Most of the guys I went to high school and college with are married but they're either having affairs or they're medicated or they're watching sports in their basements and giving up on life. Jess prefers me at peace and she likes to see me fulfilled.'

'She manages, though? With your daughter? That's a lot of daily work, a lot of responsibility.'

'She's a great mom,' he says. 'The best.'

'Sounds like it.'

Frannie runs to the edge of the deck and leans over the railing.

'Careful,' I yell.

'Hey!' she screams down towards the water. 'Hey, you!'

'What is it?'

I peer over the edge and the height makes my legs unsteady. It's like looking over a cliff or a roof terrace guard rail. There are papers and cardboard boxes fluttering in the air, scattering along the surface of the water.

Another box is flung overboard.

There is someone else on board this ship.

11

I want it to be Pete but I know in my heart this isn't him. I can't explain how I know but I do.

We run down the central staircase. Daniel takes two or three steps at a time so he opens up a lead in front.

'Be careful,' says Frannie. 'We don't know who it is. And we don't need you with a broken ankle.'

Daniel's out of sight now but I can hear his footfall on the carpet. Dull thuds.

We arrive at the Ocean Lobby, the central hub of the RMS *Atlantica*.

Daniel isn't here.

'Hello?' I say.

Again, everything looks normal but nothing looks normal.

The sound of glass shattering at the far end of the lobby. Frannie and I run past the ice sculpture, now a nub, unrecognisable as the *Atlantica*, and head past the Nantucket Spa towards the arcade of shops.

Daniel's standing there, panting, bent double, his hands on his knees.

Watching.

We join him and there's another crash and jagged glass fragments scatter around our feet.

I see the man for the first time. Ten years older than me. Around sixty or so. Bald. Manic-looking.

'Are you OK, man?' asks Daniel. 'What are you doing?'

'Join me,' says the older man, his voice low and gravelly. 'But be careful. Don't cut yourselves.'

We step over broken shards of glass and enter the jewellery store.

'Are you all right?' I ask.

He holds up his arms and I see his watches. He's wearing six or more on each wrist, the hang tags and stickers still attached.

'Do you need a quality timepiece? Fine young people like yourselves, well, come in and take a look.' And then he smiles and announces, 'Black Friday, flash sale.'

The atmosphere on the ship changes in an instant. We were afraid before, confused, but there was no lawlessness, no sense of anarchy. I look around, some form of muscle memory kicking in, waiting for a security guard.

The man doesn't look well.

'You can't just take all these, you know,' says Frannie, her face full of scorn. 'You'll get into trouble.'

'I'll get in *trouble*?' says the man, indignant. 'Sweetheart, they don't know what trouble is till they've met me. Do you have any idea how much I paid for my Diamond deluxe cabin? Butler pantry, premium wines, massages, baby grand piano, the works. And this is what I receive? I expect just and fair compensation and nothing more. I picked through the earrings and necklaces but there's still some quality branded jewellery left. Go on, treat yourself to something nice.'

'You can't just take these,' says Daniel.

'Are you going to stop me?'

'No, it's just . . . there will be consequences, you know?'

'At my age, in my condition, consequences aren't what they used to be. You see this?' He points to a gold watch. 'My uncle Theo used to tell me all about this piece. Speedmaster, it's called. Landed on the moon with the Apollo 11 astronauts back in '69. I was sat in a trailer park in North Carolina hearing all about this model of wristwatch, and Uncle Theo never got to own so much as a Timex his whole life. Taken from us at the age of forty-nine. Asbestos will do that to a man. So, now, maybe you understand. This here is my watch now. Gold version of the very one that travelled to space.'

My father never had a nice watch. He was like any other working-class dad back then: cheap shoes and a small second-hand car, basic home, no luxuries. But the amount of money passing through his hands was unfathomable. All that cash and he never spent a penny on himself, or us.

Frannie starts to walk towards a handbag stand.

'Help yourself, young lady. Tomorrow you might go missing like my friend John did earlier this morning.' He clenches his fists and then opens them. 'Gone. Full-grown man vanished into thin air. Whole place is cursed. Live your life like today is your last and one day you'll be right.'

'What were you throwing into the sea?' I say. 'Messages? Help messages?'

He snorts dismissively and picks up another watch from the floor.

'Warranty cards, boxes, inner boxes, anything linking back to the specific watches and serial numbers. There can be no official trace, you see. Why would I be sending out messages in the middle of the ocean?' He snorts again. 'I don't need rescuing. I'm fine right where I am. The most luxurious liner on the planet, with all the finest foods at my disposal and no Gestapo ship police telling me where I can smoke my cigar and when I can eat. I think I'll give this crossing a five-star rating once I'm home.'

'You were travelling with your friend?' I say. 'Same cabin?'

'Met John years ago at a convention. I'm in the vending machine business, East Coast, primarily. John's done well for himself up in Indiana. We travel together, now and again.' He looks at Frannie and then at me. 'We're both single.'

'You have any idea what happened last night? Or early this morning?'

'It was this morning when it all happened,' he says.

I step towards him. 'What did you see?'

'I went to bed just before midnight, watching news on the TV. Some kind of problem with the faucet in my cabin so I had to use bottled water to brush my teeth. Another inconvenience. Woke up at nine this morning and John was gone. We usually sit on our respective balconies on liners like this one: strong coffee and not too much small talk before breakfast. Realised the whole ship was empty apart from you three.'

Frannie puts back a tan ostrich-skin handbag. 'You knew we were here?'

'You make enough noise. You'd think we were sinking the way you three run around.'

I'm stunned. 'You mean to say you didn't think to come and say hello? Let us know you were OK?'

'We're not friends . . .' He gestures with his hands for me to tell him my name.

'Caz.'

'Caz?'

'Short for Caroline.'

'With a zee?'

I nod.

'It's not like we're travelling together now is it, Caz? We're not friends. I wanted to think before I acted.'

'And your first act,' says Daniel, 'was to come down here and loot a jewellery store.'

'I'm a long way from looting. I'm securing early compensation for my loss of enjoyment. I'll clear it all with my lawyer before we hit American waters.'

'Your mobile working?' asks Frannie.

'My what?'

'She means your cell,' says Daniel.

'No, it's not, and I don't mind that too much. I came on this vacation to get away from my clients, from my staff. Cell's dead for three more days, I'll be quite satisfied.'

I don't have the measure of this man yet. Daniel and Frannie seem relatable, familiar almost, but I will keep a close eye on this unpredictable passenger.

'Well, then, if you'll excuse me, I'm overdue breakfast. Well overdue. What do you think – the best food on the ship: Diamond Grill or the Captain's Club?'

'The food's all down in the stores on Deck Two, not in the restaurant galleys,' I say. 'The restaurants are almost completely empty from what we've seen. You'll need to bring it up and cook it for yourself.'

He sticks out his lower lip. 'Would you mind showing me those stores, Caroline? I'm awful peckish.'

'Call me Caz.'

We head out from the lobby down the stairs to the stores at the bottom of the centre of the ship. There's a refrigerated room for cut flowers, the colours dazzling, another for fruit and vegetables. I notice wooden crates of grapefruit from South Africa and pineapples from Costa Rica. One room for fish, stacked in ice, and one for meats and poultry. Boxes of pheasant and partridge, and a chest labelled *Wagyu*. There's a dry storage room the size of a tennis court. Vats of flour, sugar, salted nuts and Italian pasta. I take eggs and cheese and bread. Frannie brings up fruit and salad. Daniel collects milk and yoghurt and smoked German sausage. The looter, however, decides to collect lobster tails and beef fillet.

'What's your name?' Frannie asks him.

'Smith,' he says, sucking the tail meat from a cooked lobster as he walks, juice dribbling down his unshaven chin. 'You can call me Smith.'

12

Some people are good at forming cliques and investing in new friendships. I am not one of those people. Gemma can make friends with strangers on trains and in the supermarket queue but for some reason, for many reasons, it takes me a long time to trust a person.

Daniel and I prepare food in the industrial galley kitchen of the Gold Grill restaurant.

'You believe that guy?' he says.

'I've met worse.'

He slices bread and starts to mix eggs for the French toast. There's something about the way his face stiffens with concentration. Daniel sets his jaw the exact same way as someone I had a vague crush on years ago, but I can't recall who: some actor from a sitcom or a model from an advert in a magazine. Perfect skin and bright, alert eyes.

As I cook on the induction stovetop, my mind wanders to Gemma. She'll be panicking now at not having heard from me. Her nerves are always on edge. Are we on the mainstream news yet? How does this story look? Are there people out searching the ocean for us? She'll be frantically calling my dead phone, reaching out to relatives, trying Pete, sending messages, confusing Mum with it all. My sister is my rock in so many ways but she is a fragile, weathered rock, complete with deep stress fractures. We only really work well when we're together. She still has regular meetings with her sponsor, just as Dad did, and she needs predictable routines in order to thrive. I dread to think what this will do to her, and, consequently, to the café. It's not the business I'm worried about *per se*, although it took years of work and failures to make it work; it's the lives that rely on it. The kitchen and delivery staff, many of whom are lifelong friends now, and their extended families. They each have rent to pay and mouths to feed. My sister's kids, my mum's nursing home fees, the repayments to the charity – it all relies on the café.

'I said do you want syrup on your French toast?'

'No,' I say. 'No, thank you. Just sugar and cinnamon.'

Smith and Frannie have set the table but by the look on her face she's been left to do most of the work. Four places set in a room this cavernous looks absurd. Like forgetful children who turned up at their school on a Saturday and have to fend for themselves in the dining hall.

I want Pete by my side. He's at the age where he's worked through most of his neuroses, given up on vanity projects, survived his midlife crisis, sold the sports car. He says he's found a good level since meeting me. The thing that made me fall in love with him, in addition to his face and his intellect and his humour, is how he makes me feel safe. Ever since Dad's truth broke I've felt the need to protect myself within a bubble. Not so with Pete.

I'm not alone any more on this ship, but I am excruciatingly lonely.

'Something smells good,' says Smith.

'I can't go on calling you Smith,' I say. 'What's your first name? You know ours.'

'People call me Smith. If that isn't polite enough for you, then feel free to call me Mr Smith.'

He tucks an RMS *Atlantica* motif napkin in his shirt collar and eats a mouthful of French toast followed by a mouthful of lobster tail.

'Where are my manners?' he says. 'Would anyone like champagne?'

Frannie shakes her head.

'Are you allergic to champagne, young lady?'

'I'm allergic to you,' she mutters under her breath, and I can't help but smile.

'That's not an allergy,' he says, standing up. 'Sounds like an intolerance. All the more for me. Caz? Daniel? Are you going to help me drink the bottle?'

So this is how we come to be sipping vintage champagne on board an empty ocean liner. Four strangers at a round table large enough to seat twelve in a room designed for hundreds.

'Best lobsters I've had outside Georgetown, Maine,' says Smith. 'Sweet as candy.'

Daniel finishes his food. 'We might be stranded on this ship for days. I suggest we take a few minutes to introduce ourselves properly.'

Smith looks at him, his head at an angle. 'Don't I know you from someplace?'

'No, I don't think so.'

'Have we met before? I recognise your face. I never forget a face. Let me think . . .'

Frannie and I look over at Daniel.

'OK, there are a few posters,' he says, dismissively. 'Could be that, I guess.'

'You're on posters?' asks Smith. 'Tell me, what goods are you advertising?'

'Nothing, really. I received a free crossing, that's all. I'm due to give four lectures, each one lasting an hour with Q&A sessions, and I get a free Gold-class ticket in return.'

'Gold class?' says Smith, shaking his head. 'Might as well stay in a Ramada. Better off in a Motel Six, my man. You should have negotiated harder. Never accept the opening offer, Danny. Never do it.'

'I'll bear that in mind.'

'You a scientist, then? A physicist? Or are you espousing some of that personal wellbeing *be kind to yourself and light a smelly candle* nonsense?'

Daniel smiles. 'Tiny homes.'

'Tiny what?'

'I live in a van most of the time.'

'And that's supposed to be a good thing?' Smith says. 'No offence, but people want to learn how to live in a van like you? State of the world these days.' He sips his champagne, holding the flute carefully by the stem. 'Makes my head spin.'

I feel the urge to defuse the hostile atmosphere. When Mum and Dad argued I was always the one to create a distraction or be naughty myself to deflect attention. I cannot abide a brewing conflict.

'Ecological responsibility and living with a small footprint,' says Daniel. 'Recycling, sustainability, saving water, insulation. That kind of thing.'

'I think that's really interesting,' says Frannie.

'Of course you do,' says Smith. 'Asian Adonis over here gives a lecture on how to open a can of tuna fish and you'd queue up for a ticket.' He glances over at me. 'I suspect you both would.'

'What kind of van do you live in?' she asks.

'I converted a—'

'What *kind* of van does he live in?' says Smith, more animated now. 'Who cares what kind? What, you camp in a Walmart parking lot and shave in the patron restrooms? What'll be the next thing? Maybe I can give lectures on my friend John's psoriasis. You live in a van and lecture us all on it. Stop the world, please; I'd like to get off.'

'America's a free country,' says Daniel. 'I can surf and ski most days. I'd call that a win.'

'Are you American?'

'I thought we were going to introduce ourselves,' says Daniel, his voice turning severe. 'Like adults.'

'You're introducing just fine,' says Smith. 'Are you American, Daniel?'

'I am.'

'You are.'

Daniel swallows hard. 'Korean-American.'

Smith smiles.

'What's that supposed to mean?'

Smith shrugs and eats another lobster tail, juice spraying his napkin.

'My parents came to Chicago in the fifties,' Daniel says. 'I was born in a small town by Lake Michigan and I've had a love for the water ever since.'

'Well, you came to the right place, man,' says Smith. 'What about you?' He turns to Francine. 'Are you here on a school trip?'

'Are you here on day release?'

Smith coughs. 'Backbone. I like spirit in a woman. Tell us about yourself, Frannie.'

She turns away from him to address me and Daniel.

'Francine Jane Pepperdine. I'm twenty-one. From Swansea. Dad was a miner years ago, small town; now he runs a machining outfit and Mum runs the office. I live in Birmingham at the moment, in the Midlands. Studying there.'

'What are you studying, Frannie?' I ask.

She looks pensive and wipes her mouth on a napkin. 'Studying . . . philosophy, I suppose.'

'Oh, watch out,' says Smith. 'We've got a genius at the table.' He narrows his eyes. 'Say, Francine, what am I thinking about right in this instant? What's going through my head?'

'Might be my chair if you keep on like this.'

Smith whistles and shakes his finger at her.

'Anyway,' she goes on. 'My parents were here on the ship with me. It was their silver wedding anniversary. Well, it's today, I guess.' She pauses for a few seconds. 'Twenty-five-years together. We're very close, closer than my friends are to their parents. I don't know why I'm telling you all this, but, you see, they both think I'm studying nursing.' She smiles but she looks sad. 'It's a white lie that got totally out of hand. They never stayed in school past fifteen or sixteen. We shouldn't even be on this ship, not with how their business is going; Mum tried to talk him out of it. They both thought I should study something practical, something that'll lead straight to a secure job, an NHS job, and they were probably right. The idea of me reading philosophy might give Dad a stroke so I never got around to telling him I switched. He acts tough but he has heart problems.' She stands up suddenly from the table and her speech quickens. 'Oh, God, he needs to swallow two tablets every day to keep his heart working. If he doesn't have . . .'

'Have you checked his bags?' I ask.

But Frannie's already running away.

13

The air smells sour. Leftovers and unwashed bodies. With every passing minute the ship feels more isolated and less solid.

'Just the grown-ups left,' says Smith.

'She's an adult,' I say through gritted teeth. 'Cut her some slack, please.'

'Slack, please? Nobody ever cut me any slack, Caz Ripley with a *zee*. Slack creates weakness.'

His voice echoes in this empty Grill room.

'You introduce yourself, then,' I say. 'Go on. How come you turned out so perfect?'

He smiles and pushes the empty lobster shells away from himself. 'First question is, how did we end up on this grand old ship all by ourselves with no supervision?'

'We don't know,' says Daniel, tersely. 'Did you hear anything? See anything?'

He shakes his head. 'I took my medication and went to sleep and then, bang, whole place was deserted.'

'Medication?' I say, sitting up straighter. 'Did you happen to take sea-sickness tablets? Motion-sickness medication? Scopolamine? Did we all swallow the same pills?'

'No, I just took my usual meds. Prescribed by my personal doctor.'

'But could we have been drugged?' I ask. 'I've read about psychedelics. Drugs that alter your consciousness, your sense of self, your grip on reality. My sister had some awful experiences, but that was years ago. Mind-altering substances. Is it possible we're not quite, you know, *here* right now? Some kind of waking dream?'

Smith almost falls of his chair laughing.

I am not warming to this man.

'That's it,' he says. 'This dining room is packed full of passengers; it's the free drugs that make them invisible.' He staggers over to the next table and theatrically says, 'Well, how do you do? So lovely to meet you all. What an eventful crossing we're having.'

'Don't,' I say.

'Are you crazy?' he asks, turning to us, his hands on his hips.

I snap back, 'How do you explain it, then?'

His tone softens. 'I have no idea, but I didn't even take motion-sickness pills. Mine were sleeping tablets, the same I've taken for years. This is not some hallucination. I should know: I lived through the seventies. This is real. We're on a ship and we're completely on our own.'

Frannie arrives back in the Gold Grill clutching something tight in her hand.

'Dad's meds were still in his bathroom,' she says, weakly, a strand of red hair across her forehead. She's holding a plastic box with separate compartments for each day of the week. 'He wouldn't leave without them, not even in an emergency. Mum would never let him. He needs them to stay alive.' Her hands are shaking.

'Maybe he hopped off at Southampton if the ship returned in the middle of the night,' says Daniel. 'We don't know anything yet. He might have new medication from some other doctor or pharmacist. For all you know he's back home in . . .'

'Swansea,' she says, unconvinced.

'Nope,' says Smith. 'This ship never turned back.'

'You don't know what you're talking about,' I say, rubbing Frannie's shoulder to reassure her.

'I've been on two dozen crossings and cruises,' he says. 'I usually book myself a VIP bridge tour – comes with my Diamond cabin at no extra charge. I like to see the view from way up there, the screens. Feel the power of the vessel and talk to the men in charge. I went up earlier today and it's clear from the maps and the nav route monitors that we powered out past the southwest tip of England, past the coast of Ireland, and into the Atlantic Ocean, and we never looked back, never even slowed down.'

'So, then, where is everyone?'

I try to steady my breathing.

'Search me,' he says. 'Could be there was some kind of mass event. There have been strange occurrences in the past, you know: hundreds died at Jonestown, nine hundred and eighteen of them if I remember correctly, all on the same day. What would prompt that kind of self-destructive action? Almost a thousand souls, gone. Similar numbers to our ship. Makes you think, doesn't it? Who knows if this was caused by something in the food or the water supply on board. A kind of trance, something from the audio system, a vapour emitted through the air vents. The only rational explanation to me is that a thousand passengers woke up in the middle of the night and quietly, solemnly, threw themselves overboard.'

14

The mood is sombre. Back home if we're downbeat for too long Gemma or one of her children will break the tension. Here, there is no one to perform that role. The tension persists and, building slowly like a storm cloud, it intensifies.

When we drove down to catch the ship the verges of the country roads were coated with fine snow, so ephemeral it vanished seconds after settling. My world was turning the page from autumn to winter and that seasonal shift was reassuring. Out here there are no seasons and there is no constant. We are in flux.

'So, what do we do now?' asks Frannie, breaking the silence. 'How do we find help?'

'What do you want help for?' says Smith, leaning back in his chair. 'Think about it. Two English girls, two American guys. A five-star luxury liner with all the food, cigars, periodicals and old-world wines we could wish for. I suggest we enjoy this while it lasts and then worry when we see the shore of Long Island.'

'I'm not English,' says Frannie.

'Sorry?'

'I said I'm not English, I'm Welsh.'

'What do you want, a certificate?'

'It's pitch dark outside,' I say, changing the subject. 'Should we switch on the deck lights? Lights we can control from the bridge so other ships can see us?'

'Smart plan,' says Daniel.

'You two go play sailors and I'll enjoy a Cohiba in my hot tub and watch the sun go down. Of course, if my cabin happens to be on the wrong side of the ship for a sunset I'll just move to another one. A man could become accustomed to this level of freedom.'

'What are the risks?' asks Frannie.

'I suppose I could drop my cigar.'

She turns her back on him. 'What are *our* risks? Things we should be conscious of.'

'A collision,' says Daniel. 'With a ship or an island or a floating shipping container or a large piece of debris.'

'Or an iceberg,' I say.

Smith shakes his head.

'There have been large ice fragments spotted this far south,' says Frannie. 'One of us should keep lookout.'

'A ship like this sails itself,' says Smith. 'The ship's computer senses a problem on radar, it'll automatically divert; I've seen the radar tech in action. Six hundred million dollars this thing cost to build, so rest assured all the latest safety systems are in place. Now, if you need me I'll be in my tub.'

Frannie glances at me, relief in her eyes. Smith has confirmed what Daniel said earlier: the ship may have been heading south instead of west this afternoon. There'll be a good reason.

Smith walks away, flat-footed, and we fall quiet.

It strikes me that I haven't heard a bird sing or seen a car or motorbike for a long time now. Life, as I'm used to it, church bells and buses and the sound of people talking in the café, laughter and gossip, background traffic, the sight of my neighbour's cat crossing the street – I miss it all.

'Should we take shifts?' I say. 'Lookout shifts?'

'I don't see there's much point if we can't actually steer the ship,' says Frannie. 'What's the point in spotting something if we're powerless to move?'

I'd rather know, personally. I'd want to brace myself.

Five minutes later Smith comes rushing back. He looks pale. Smaller, somehow.

'I changed my mind,' he says, not looking at our faces. 'I'll stay with you.'

We watch him pad closer to us. His posture is that of defeat.

'Eerie out there all on my own. I know what I said but the ship is so empty.'

'The other risks,' continues Daniel, coldly, 'are fire or rough seas.'

'She's built for rough seas,' I say. 'Pete told me how the *Atlantica* is built with a sharp, deep hull. Extendable stabilisers. It's designed for rough ocean crossings. Otherwise I'd never have boarded.'

'He was in your cabin this morning?' asks Daniel.

I point to my wrist. 'I just have this left.'

When I first saw his watch on its well-worn calf-leather strap, I thought it looked like something an old man might wear. It seemed too small and delicate. I thought he was similar, if I'm honest. My first impression of Pete was that he looked a generation older than I feel. His clothes, his shoes, his home, his orderliness. But it didn't take long for me to warm to him. It's not just that I can trust him, although that is extremely attractive. It's that he makes me genuinely happy. I laugh when I'm with him. He took me to a regional opera house and the main tenor was ill so he was replaced by an understudy. As soon as the young man took to the stage and started to sing, terribly, Pete muttered, 'Oh, piss off,' and I had to leave so as not to disturb the other audience members. Not my finest hour, and not his either, in fact it sounds cruel now I remember, but we laughed all night and had the most wonderful time. Sometimes it's wise not to trust a first impression.

Daniel tries his phone again.

'Nothing?' I say.

He shakes his head.

'My old man walked away when I was seven years old,' says Smith, dragging another chair closer to rest his feet on. 'Two days before my birthday, it was. We owned a trailer park in Arkansas. Seventy trailers or so, modest enterprise. Mom ran it as well as she could, gave people chances, second chances, third chances. View of the Ouachita Mountains in the background, small convenience store on the lot – it wasn't a bad place. People had to keep their dogs on leashes and there was no loud music permitted after nine. Anyway, one morning I woke up for breakfast and there was a note in his cereal bowl. It was weighed down with the spoon. Said how he was leaving town. Had things to do. How I should take care of my mom and not be too much bother.'

'Did you ever see him again?' asks Frannie.

He looks up. Smiles. 'I was hoping for a bike for my eighth birthday but he never showed up. I did see him one time, years later.'

'I'm sorry,' I say.

'Imagine not being man enough to tell Mom to her face.'

'What other risk factors are we—'

'No,' says Smith, sharply, cutting off Daniel, raising his hand in the air. His face has turned a shade of purple. 'There are no risk factors. That kind of talk breeds anxiety and madness. We're on a secure ship that's under its own steam, navigating by GPS autopilot. We're warm and we have plenty of food. Quell your panic, stay calm, and rest easy. In four days we'll be in New York with a unique story to tell.'

He pours himself another glass of champagne.

And then all the lights turn off.

15

There are no windows in this Grill room. It's as dark as midnight on the Yorkshire moors after an overcast day. So black I can't make out my own hand in front of my face.

Daniel says, 'The back-up generators will kick in soon.'

I can hear fresh anxiety in Frannie's breathing. She is repeating something but I can't make out the words.

The restaurant seems larger now, much larger, as if the walls are moving away from us, and Frannie's incoherent words are ricocheting off the ceiling. The ship feels unsteady, pitching back and forth.

Smith switches on his phone's torch function and says, 'It's just a power outage.'

Back-up lights flicker down by the floors, marking routes to emergency exits.

'Generator,' says Daniel, sounding relieved. 'Ships have secondary systems. It's OK.'

But Frannie's eyes are fixed open and she's chewing her lower lip. The room has transformed, in an instant, from bright lights, elaborate chandeliers, table lamps and spotlights to complete darkness, and now to a dim, stuttering glow down by the floor.

'Are we . . . going to sink?' she asks. 'If we sink slowly

we may not notice until it's too late. I need my lifejacket.'

'We're not sinking,' I say, moving closer to comfort her. 'It's just the power. Smith, turn off your phone torch, you may need the battery life.'

'I don't appreciate you telling me what to do.'

Daniel walks over to a serving area close to the galley and then returns with a handful of flickering candles. They're battery-operated. Ideal for a ship where naked flames are too hazardous, and yet passengers expect a sophisticated ambience at their evening meal.

'How many are there?' asks Frannie.

'Dozens,' says Daniel. 'But they're weak.'

Frannie takes a handful.

'We need to check on the electrical controls,' I say. 'Daniel, you seem to be the most technical among us?'

'Not really. Built out the van, and my van before that. Solar, diesel heater, LED lighting strips. Basic things I learnt from a book. I'm not a—'

'You're the best we've got,' says Smith. 'I never even changed a lightbulb the right way.'

I have an urge to run upstairs to the decks, to seek out fresh air, but I resist that urge.

'You go down to the engines or up to the turbine and electrical plant,' I say. 'There might be a screen explaining the cause of the power cut? Maybe it's something we can reset.'

'I'll try,' he says.

'Smith, I'm not telling you what to do, honest, but can you go back to the bridge? See if there are any alerts. See if the navigation equipment is still working from the back-up power.'

He nods.

'Frannie. Collect more battery candles together and maybe try to find us proper torches.'

'No naked flames on the ship,' says Smith.

'Flashlights, I mean. Battery-operated flashlights. Collect four lifejackets as well, and whatever gear you find that might be helpful.'

She switches on the torch of her phone and goes to leave and then she says, 'I'm sorry, I only have four per cent battery. I can't do this. I drained my phone searching through photos of Mum and Dad all day, their dogs, my college friends. The battery's almost dead.'

'Take this,' I say, giving her mine. 'It's OK, we'll swap back later. Conserve the lights as much as you can, though. The emergency strips should be enough for you to find your way.'

'And what are *you* going to do?' asks Smith.

I don't like his tone. Take away basic comforts and authority figures and it's not long before people reveal their true personalities.

'I'm going down to the food stores. If the power's out, the refrigeration units are probably off, which means everything's going to spoil. The way the air is out at sea, the humidity, food will turn rancid fast. God knows how long we'll be on this ship. I need to make sure we don't run out of food.'

16

The stair rails are cool to the touch.

I walk down four flights into the central crew-only area of the ship. Emergency lights flicker off for a moment and then brighten again.

The drone of machinery.

Deck Two.

The ankle-height lighting is more subdued in the crew-only sections. My shoes squeak on rubber floors and they clang on stainless steel steps. All I have to help me are two imitation candles in the cold, sweaty palm of my right hand. I can see my own blood: fine capillaries feeding my fingers with oxygen. The candles flicker to their unnatural pre-programmed rhythm and light the corridors in weak yellow light, and the shadows cast on bare walls sway this way and that.

I shouldn't be permitted in this part of the ship.

This is not my domain.

The ship's Rolls-Royce engines purr in the background. One deep breath and then I pass through into a new stretch of corridor with large framed noticeboards on the walls and perhaps a hundred wheelchairs strapped tight together by staircase C7. It is normal to have this many wheelchairs here? Couples celebrating their diamond wedding anniversaries, office-workers taking a well-earned transatlantic voyage to mark their retirement, families voyaging across this vast body of water for the first time in their lives. So many stories in one finite space. So many unanswered questions.

I can't see more than two metres in front of me.

One of the dinner table candles dims and then switches off.

It's fine. I have one left and I have Frannie's phone. I hope she's managing up there on her own. She seems so vulnerable at times, like my sister twenty years ago. Except Francine has beautiful freckles and, as far as I can tell, no opioid dependency.

Eventually I reach the meat stores. If the chillers and freezers are off, there's going to be tonnes of food that goes to waste. Sides of Aberdeen Angus beef and organic pork tenderloins. Plump corn-fed chickens, wild ducks and legs of New Zealand lamb.

I use the candle to locate a button for the watertight fireproof door that divides one section of the ship from the next.

I press but nothing happens.

I try it again, pressing harder.

Nothing.

I use Frannie's phone to illuminate the area, to find any instructions I might have missed. But I'm doing everything right. It says *Stand clear of the door at all times. Do not linger. Do not place any object in the way of the door. This door will not sense an obstacle. Keep closed at all times when not in port.*

I press it one more time.

Nothing.

I switch off the phone and head back the way I came. The lifts are all out of action so it takes time to walk up above water level and then along and then back down to Deck Two. I approach from the other side, towards the fruit and veg stores and the dry stores. At least these won't be affected too severely by refrigeration failures.

Only, the door is the same as the other one.

It's locked tight.

We need electrical power to open it. There is no manual override I can see.

I switch the phone torch back on and run to the fish stores, cold sweat running down the small of my back, my arms held out in front of me so I don't crash headfirst into a metal pole or door.

An identical watertight door.

I cross myself for the first time since Dad's funeral and then I press the button.

It does not move.

And then it dawns on me like a weight being placed gently on my back, around my shoulders, over my neck.

We're completely alone in the mid-Atlantic.

And we have no food.

17

There's a clang somewhere close by, the sound of metal hitting metal, and I drop my imitation candle. It breaks into two pieces. I bend down to mend it and the lights come back on, the real lights, full lights, blinding me.

And then they turn off again.

I wait for the emergency lighting but this time it doesn't come.

Weariness mixed with dread.

I use the torch function of Frannie's phone and make my way through the corridor, skirting baggage carts and precarious stacks of navy blue dining chairs.

The phone dies and I stand motionless.

Pitch black.

I don't remember ever being anywhere quite as dark as this. Below the water line, several decks away from any natural starlight or moonlight. It feels as if I can sense the water pressure on the other side of the steel hull. Pushing. Squeezing the worryingly thin plate metal and testing each and every rivet. My heart pounds and I start to jog, sweat on my brow despite the falling temperatures. It only takes one rivet to fail. Perhaps the machining was off, or human error led to a mistake when forging the alloy, a structural weakness introduced accidentally due to a last-minute shift change or a supervisor being hungover one morning two decades ago.

I make it to the staircase and now at least I have something to cling on to. Gripping the handrail, I run higher and higher as if rising through some deep Æolian cave system, some condemned mine. I need to be as far above the water line as possible. Deck Three, Deck Four, Deck Eight. I burst out into fresh air and dash to the rail and breathe.

It was like being underground down there. But worse. That was *underwater*.

My breathing steadies and I stare out at the nothingness of the north Atlantic Ocean. Not a twinkle anywhere on the horizon. Not a boat or a seabird or a buoy. It is us and it is only us.

With Pete by my side this might be manageable. We'd lean on one another and keep each other's spirits up. His black humour would help; it always does. Stupidly, I thought he might propose on this voyage, and instead I have to deal with this unfurling nightmare all on my own.

I imagine Gemma in the café cleaning up after a busy day, wiping down, removing the milk from the steamer and the salad from the sandwich bar. She'll be taking out the rubbish or balancing the till. Or else she could be spiralling out of control again, texting her narcissistic ex-husband, injecting in his flat, leaving her kids, *their* kids, my precious niece and nephew, to fend for themselves like last time. To bathe themselves and feed themselves and put themselves to bed. Is she checking on Mum in the care home, or is she lying on the grimy linoleum floor of his kitchen with a rough leather belt tight around her arm?

'Caz,' says Frannie, behind me. 'Are you upset?'

I wipe my face. 'No, I'm fine. It's just being out here. The power going off. I'm cold and exhausted all of a sudden, but I'm OK.' I force a smile. 'Some bloody holiday this turned out to be. At least we have the stars.'

She puts her arm around me and says, 'Each one of them an independent self-sustaining source of light and heat.'

'Exactly what we need right now. Light and heat.'

She ignores me and says, 'Billions of kilometres away. Hundreds of billions of kilometres. And we can still see them clearly with the naked eye. We're not witnessing our own sun shining on them and detecting that light energy. They're creating their own. And it is so unimaginably powerful that we each have the privilege to notice it for ourselves. But it's not new light. We're looking into the past right now, a unique lens, a glimpse of history. Looking up at these stars, we are experiencing the purest form of time travel. We're standing here together looking back through millennia and we are experiencing old light.'

Neither of us says anything for a long time.

'Did you find much?' I ask.

She holds up a fabric tote bag that I haven't seen before. 'This. Four torches. Lots of lifejackets and lifesaver flotation rings; I didn't collect those because I've checked all the life rafts and there are plenty. Found three lighters and I've taken out food from people's cases. Not much, unfortunately.'

'You've been going through people's cases?'

She pauses.

Swallows.

'Do you think that's wrong?'

Do I? I suppose I do. But I also think we must do it. Sometimes you have to pocket your moral compass and find a novel way to navigate.

'Like feeling through a dead man's pockets, to be honest,' she says, shuddering. 'It's so personal, isn't it? The items people pack. Medicine and old tatty underwear and condoms. Latex gloves and chestnut hair dye. Such intimate, personal things.'

'You found medicine? That could be useful.'

'I didn't think.'

'Let's set up a makeshift pharmacy. So we can treat any injuries.'

'I'm supposed to be a nurse one day, at least in the eyes of Mum and Dad. They've always dreamed of me being a senior ward nurse, just like my aunt. But you seem to be better than me at all that.'

'You'd be surprised the cuts and burns you see in a café kitchen over the years. And I worked in a kindergarten before that. I'm used to getting my hands dirty. Plus, out here, with no phones or television or . . . people, I'd like to keep busy. It'll stop me from thinking about how we got into this mess. I don't know where Pete is, and the longer this goes on, the more I worry I might never see him again.'

We set off walking, guided by starlight.

'Have you been together long?' she asks. 'What's he like?'

'Not really,' I say, pulling up my collar. 'I'll be fifty next year and I've stopped wasting time with all the exhausting game-playing. He's a good man. Makes me giggle like I used to years ago. If you like someone, you have to get on with it and give it a chance. That's what I think, anyway.'

'I have something to look forward to, then.'

The truth is, my dating history is bleak. I'd almost given up when I bumped into Pete and the thing that made him stand out from all the others was how he listened. That's how low the bar was. I've had relationships with decent men who *pretended* to listen. Conversations that might have looked fine from the outside but I knew in my heart those men wanted to be somewhere else. When I met Pete it felt as if I already knew him. Had known him for years. He never tried to push me in any particular direction. My last boyfriend, years ago, was uncomfortable around my family; he was always itching to leave. Pete's not perfect – he snores horrendously, he's very particular about his music and antiques, he can be secretive, and he's not the most spontaneous person in the world – but he is secure in his own skin.

'What do you think of these two?' she asks. 'Smith and Daniel.'

'Part of me thinks Smith's the kind of man who drinks too much on an aeroplane and insults the staff and has to be strapped into his seat by the passengers and stewards.'

She points at my face and says, 'Exactly. He is the type.'

'And Daniel is the type to voluntarily restrain him and then go quietly back to his seat to watch a movie. But it could be worse. My sister was married to a parasite for

eight years. I'd trade Smith for Gemma's ex any day of
the week.'

'I thought you and Daniel were a couple when I first
saw you both in the library.'

'Honestly?'

'I just assumed, I don't know why. You'd made a good
couple. I'm just saying.'

I blush and turn my face away. 'I'm not sure Daniel
would agree.'

'He likes you.'

'Oh, please.'

'What was the fridge situation like? Do they have a
separate generator or are they starting to warm up?'

I look at her. Unsteady after that abrupt segue.

'What is it?'

'They're all locked down, Frannie. Whatever the watertight doors are called below deck, the heavy doors
designed to contain catastrophic flooding, they're locked
shut now. Unless Daniel fixes the electrics, I can't see
how we'll reach any of that food.'

'*Any* of it?'

'Each compartment down there is sealed. Fire safety,
or in case we hit rocks.'

'Could we hit rocks?' she says, alarmed.

I read a non-fiction book once that Mum bought me,
which means Gem bought me, last Christmas. It tried to
put into perspective the magnitude of various natural
phenomena. Mountains, lakes, deserts, planets, caves.
Some of the descriptions were unnerving, but there's one
fact I find strangely terrifying and soothing at the same
time: the depth of the sea. It's so extraordinarily deep,

when compared to the Eiffel Tower or the Chrysler building, that the human mind struggles to visualise or comprehend it. And so, because of that, you can't really worry too much.

'The Atlantic is three and a half thousand metres deep on average,' I tell her, with mock authority. 'More than double that out here in the middle. We're not going to hit any rocks. That's one worry we can eliminate.'

'But we have some food in the galley kitchens, right?'

'They're pretty much empty. The system works the same way as in my café, only on a grander scale. You bring supplies from the stores to the prep areas, which are also down on Deck Two, and then send them by service elevator to the kitchen, where dishes are finished off and plates are assembled and checked at the pass. Frannie, I don't think we have enough food for one more meal.'

18

When you've experienced someone you trust rifling through your possessions, taking what belongs to you, violating your private space, lying to your face, you find it difficult to trust anyone ever again. I would have given Dad my money if he'd asked. From that day on I was on guard, watching my back, hiding things, double-locking every door.

'You said you found food in passenger cases,' I say. 'How many cases have you looked through?'

'Maybe a hundred,' she says. 'A third of them, I guess. And then there are the crew things in their cabins, I haven't searched those yet. Some of them are empty. I also spotted a drinks vending machine in the crew mess.'

'We need to take stock of everything we have. We'll need to establish a food room and a meds room.'

'But, Caz. I'm talking mini bags of pretzels taken from planes. Sticks of chewing gum and half-eaten chocolate bars. You can hardly call it food.'

In my head I see the stores we have in the café. I can picture them in exact detail. The fridges and freezers, the dry goods shelves, the condiments, the sacks of coffee beans. Everything labelled and organised. We have fresh deliveries most days from suppliers. If there's one thing I understand it's that people eat significantly more food in a week than they think they do. If they were confronted by it all, stacked in a pile, they'd be shocked.

'We can't waste a single morsel of food.'

'I'm cold,' she says, cupping her hands in front of her face. 'It must be close to freezing out here.'

The gravity of our situation hits me in waves. I think our wellbeing is precarious and then I realise, just a few moments later, that it is much worse than I feared.

'We need blankets.' I start coughing and Frannie looks concerned. I try to reassure her I'm OK, and the coughing subsides. 'There are blankets in each cabin, right? Or duvets. We'll use them for tonight until the power's fixed.'

'Look how dark the ship looks with no lights,' says Frannie. 'It's an absence. Other ships won't see us. What if we're out of power for the whole of the crossing?'

We walk cautiously towards the bridge and then, from deep down in the belly of the *Atlantica*, we hear the muffled tone of a man calling out for help.

'Smith? Where are you?'

We grab two of the four torches out of her bag and run down the stairs towards the noise but now it's more like sobbing. Desperate, breathless cries for assistance.

'Where are you?' I yell.

We pass through the Diamond Grill Room, our torch beams flying around the veneered walls of the grand restaurant, struggling to pick out deranged swirls in the carpets, showing glimpses of our blurry anxious faces in each Art Deco mirror. Past the entrance to the Nantucket Spa, past the casino, now lifeless and impotent with no electricity coursing through its crooked machines. I've always been troubled by fruit machines and one-armed-bandits. Slot machines. They look innocuous enough to most people. The thing I find sinister is that they, more so than card tables or roulette wheels, hold the power to draw me closer.

He's bent double at the entrance of the Ocean Lobby, the triple-height atrium I arrived in when I boarded the ship yesterday with Pete. Feels like a week ago.

'I can't . . .' he says.

We run to his side and shine our lights directly on to his face.

'Are you OK?' says Frannie. 'I used to volunteer for St John's Ambulance. Where are you hurt?'

He shakes his head.

'I'm not hurt,' he says, panting. 'I was trapped in the long corridor, down there.' He points towards the front section of the ship, towards the suites and large Diamond-class cabins. 'When the emergency lights went out I was left in complete darkness. I've never been anyplace so black. I couldn't see my hand in front of my own face and the passageway was endless. Hundreds of locked doors, one after the other, on and on. Like being in an unravelled maze, blindfolded, dizzy, no end to it. Felt like I ran for miles, like the ship was growing in length, extending. I could hardly breathe. The electric failure must have locked all the doors down there. I couldn't get access to a single balcony, couldn't breathe fresh air. I couldn't find my way out of the blackness.'

I pat his shoulder. 'It's confusing down here in the dark. Here, have my flashlight.'

He takes it and his hand is shaking. His face looks older in the harsh beam from Frannie's torch. Jowls and dark circles under his eyes.

'I need air,' he says.

We walk slowly past the grand piano and on towards the casino. I direct us away from its entrance. I will not cross that line. Even with no electricity those machines and felt-topped gaming tables still possess some malevolent force, some dark magnetism that I refuse to test.

'Did the bridge have electricity?' Frannie asks. 'Some kind of back-up generator for the equipment?'

'The screens are all out,' he says, defeated. 'Only the analogue instruments are working. The compass says we're headed due north now. There's a speedometer-type dial that says we're still cruising at twenty-eight knots. Cruising to where is what I want to know.'

I rub my temples and slow my breathing. 'We can launch a lifeboat in the morning. Everything will be better with daylight.'

Smith holds up his hand. 'Listen.'

He shines his torch – my torch – out into the vast room and it picks out the bronze mural the ship is famous for, the steps from the ornate, twisting staircase, and the glass-walled lifts.

'Footsteps,' whispers Frannie.

'Daniel?' I whisper back. And then I say, 'Daniel, is that you?'

The footsteps grow louder.

'Engines are still working,' says a familiar voice. 'Eighty-eight per cent capacity. Screens are off but they seem to be working fine regardless. Plenty of fuel in the tanks. What's wrong with him?'

I turn to Smith and he's still visibly shaking.

'I need to leave this fucking ship is what's wrong with me. I want dry land, cars and drive-thru restaurants. This is not what I paid for.'

'Frannie,' says Daniel, 'would you take him up to the decks? I need to show Caz something.'

'You need to show me as well,' Frannie says, her eyes suddenly angrier than I've ever seen them. 'I need to—'

'I'll show you straight after,' he says. 'I'll show you both. Can you take him to get some air first, please? He doesn't look well.'

She thrusts the bag with the rest of what she found at me and storms off with Smith, their silhouettes shrinking into the distance, discs of light from their torches bouncing off the walls. I open it and take out another torch, and hand Daniel the other.

'What is it?' I say quietly. 'You can't get the electrics back up?'

'I can't, no. I don't understand how the systems work; they're a long way from the basic wiring I've worked on before. But it's not that.'

I frown.

'Look.'

He flicks on his torch and shines it at his feet.

It takes me a moment to register what I'm seeing, and when it hits me I gasp and cover my mouth with my hand. Daniel's boots are soaked. His trousers are wet to the ankle and there are dark footprints leading back from him towards the bridge.

My body stiffens. 'No.'

'Two feet or so in the garbage-sorting and recycling area. It's Deck One. The base of the ship.'

I have to wait a few seconds in order to get the words out.

'We have a leak now?'

'I don't know. It's just one room and the walls looked intact. The water level isn't rising.'

'What can we do about it?' I start to feel hot, feverish. 'Pump it out? Buckets? Oh God, we need to leave this ship.'

'I managed to close the bulkhead watertight door and seal the room. Tried that in reverse for the other locked doors but they still won't open. I think they're designed to be easy to close but there's some kind of mechanism to overcome in order to open back up. Officer keys, maybe. The ship designers knew what they were doing. We'll be fine.'

'That,' I say pointing to his boots, 'is not fine, Daniel. It is far from fine.'

'We have propulsion but we have no electricity,' he says, placing his hand on my shoulder. 'That means no light, no heat, no comms, no navigation equipment. We're back sailing in the eighteenth century.'

'It's worse than that,' I say. 'We have no food, either. You and I need to go back down there and find a manual override.'

He holds up a finger, looks around.

We both go quiet.

'Dripping water?' he says. 'Up here as well?'

'We must warn the—'

'Wait,' he says, guiding me towards the centre of the lobby. 'I think it's this.'

I shine my light on the ice centrepiece of the Ocean Lobby, or what's left of it. When I boarded with our carry-on bags it was a two-metre-long ice sculpture of the RMS *Atlantica* and now all that's left is a receptacle stand collecting the meltwater, a misshapen funnel waiting to melt away, and a plastic box in the approximate-to-scale position we're now standing in. The box is opaque Perspex and it is half the size of a shoebox.

He holds his light to the lid of the box.

Words etched into the plastic, as if by hand.

Cursive script.

Frantic.

Looping letters, but childlike.

It says *Do Not Open The Box*.

19

I stare at the box and then at Daniel's soaked boots.

My day-to-day life seems suddenly distant and fragile. Time reversing. I am losing whatever confidence and strength I have built up over the years.

As a teenager I felt constantly out of my depth. I never had a best friend at school like the other girls in my class. I had friends and we ate chips together in the market-place and we laughed, shared secrets, but they were always someone else's best friend. That continued into my twenties. It wasn't until recently that I made peace with the fact that I am who I am, and that my family, Pete included, is my world.

'Was this box here the whole time?'

'I have no idea,' says Daniel. 'I never looked closely at the ice sculpture. The box is translucent plastic. Frosted. Maybe it was *inside* the ice *Atlantica* the whole time?'

'*Do not open the box*,' I say out loud. 'Why would we even want to open the box?'

'I don't understand.'

'You think there's one inside every sculpture on the ship? A form of chemical coolant to prevent the ice from melting too quickly?'

'If that's the case, it didn't work. Most of the model ship has drained into the drip tray.'

'But it could have extended its life?' I say. 'Usually, with power, there are bright lights in the lobby. And when the *Atlantica* is passing through the tropics it must be warm in here.'

He looks sceptical. '*Do not open the box*. What could be inside that warrants that form of warning? Something acidic or flammable? A hazardous material?'

'Can we touch it?' I say. 'Not open it. Keep it closed, but just lift it up?'

He thinks about that.

'I don't think we should.'

Goosebumps rise up on my arms. The whole ship is losing any residual heat it once had. Gemma and I became pretty good at sealing windows with clingfilm each winter. We learned the importance of hot water bottles and sharing bathwater. When the electricity was cut off we managed with candles and the fire, sleeping in hats sometimes, but that was there and this is here. I am not equipped for this.

'I think we should leave it exactly where it is,' he says. 'We don't have any back-up, any first responders. If the contents were to set off a chain reaction or a fire we would be powerless to save ourselves.'

'You're right.' I take a deep breath. 'Of course you're right. We leave the box alone. Come on, let's tell Frannie and Smith not to go near it.'

I think back to school. To reading *Lord of the Flies* in English literature class with Mrs Hutchinson. Those boys all alone to rule themselves. Group dynamics and power struggles. Voting on key decisions. Dividing into teams. Ralph and Jack and . . . Piggy. The shock of what happened.

'You think Smith will listen to us?'

'I think he might. He was pretty shaken from the power outage. I think he'll be reasonable.'

We take the steel stairs the crew use to access the running deck. Safety notices all over the walls. Dining trays stacked and stowed in a corner. We emerge into the passenger area and step outside.

The wind is whistling and the chilled air is laced with salt and the iodine tang of old seaweed.

'Frannie?' I say. 'Smith?'

The only thing I can hear is the distant howl of a dog from the kennels on the deck above. The dog howls again: a singular animal far away from its natural environment, sitting with its neck bent up to the sky.

We walk quickly towards the front of the ship, past the covered saltwater pool, and I recall the brochure boasting how the pool cover doubles as a dance floor. We head past the rock-climbing wall that forms part of the funnel, past the shuffle ball court, past the bulbous radar equipment.

Something different in the air.

As we reach the front third of the ship the wind changes direction.

The bow of the ship is burning, flames leaping up into the sparkling night sky.

20

Daniel breaks out into a run.

The flames grow in ferocity, crackling, climbing into the sky. I sprint as fast as I can along the dark deck. Is this the cause of the power outage? How do you extinguish a fire at sea?

'If we need to break into a lifeboat, we will,' says Daniel, as much to himself as to me. 'There will be time.'

The scene is otherworldly. A fire on a ship is what you observe before it disappears beneath the waves to be replaced by steam. And yet there is no panic here. If the ship were full of paying passengers there would be screaming and people filming on their phones but today there is none of that, no one to bear witness to this peril.

Black smoke.

We emerge at the bow.

Frannie and Smith stand warming their hands against the flames. They've built a makeshift bonfire at the front portion of the ship, the section that's white steel rather than wooden deck. They're down below the breakwater, the angular metal wall built to deflect high waves from the main structure.

'Come down and warm yourselves,' says Smith.

'What the hell are you doing?' asks Daniel.

They frown and peer back at us. 'We built us some heating. Thought you might be grateful.'

'It's just a stack of deckchairs,' says Francine, apologetically, moving to evade the smoke. 'He had a lighter and I took newspapers from the Cape Cod Lounge. We didn't think it would grow this big but the varnish on the chairs is fuelling the flames.'

'You didn't think to have a chat with us before setting the ship on fire?' asks Daniel, shaking with rage. 'You didn't think we should talk about this?'

'It's warmth and it's light,' says Smith. 'The fire can't spread. We're on solid steel plate. Relax, warm yourselves up.'

The glow *is* comforting in a way, and I find myself drawn to the heat as our forefathers have been drawn to it for millennia. My hands have been growing steadily colder these past hours. Another stack of newspaper catches, the glare intensifying. The fire is making my shoulders loosen and the intensity of it on my nose and forehead reminds me of a bonfire just last week in Pete's back garden. He positioned several buckets of water around the burning branches and grass clippings, careful not to let the flames grow out of control. No such caution here.

'I thought it might work as a beacon of sorts, too,' says Frannie. 'Something other ships might see. Planes, maybe. You don't normally see a bonfire on the front of a ship.'

'With good reason,' says Daniel, moving chairs and cushions away from the flames.

'Give her a break,' says Smith. 'It was my idea.'

Daniel's hands are balled into fists. I can see the rage in his eyes and I understand in this instant that if we descend into violence there may be no way back.

'Let's stay civil,' I say.

'Civil?' says Daniel, shaking his head. 'We need to act like a cohesive team. That's what we need to do. Listen, if I'm out surfing reef breaks, if I'm skiing off-piste some-place new, there's no way I'm making a big call without consulting everyone else in the group. We depend on each other from now on. Like the buddy system for divers; it's built on mutual trust. We live or die together, you both understand that?'

Smith doesn't answer.

'You two find anything else in the lobby?' asks Francine.

I squirm.

Daniel shakes his head and then he spits into the fire.

I look at him and then Smith. 'Well, we did find a box down there. It was inside the ice sculpture of the ship. It says not to open it.'

'OK,' says Smith, poking the fire with a charred broom handle. 'So, what's inside the new box?'

'We don't know. We didn't open it.'

'Probably a safety alarm,' says Smith. 'Maybe it'll alert the coastguard.'

'Why the hell would they have that hidden inside an ice sculpture?' says Daniel. 'It's not connected to anything. No wires.'

'I'll need to check this box for myself,' says Smith.

Daniel holds out his arm and Smith stiffens at the gesture. 'See it tomorrow. It's pitch black down there. Like a nightmare.'

'We have flashlights.'

'They're needed up here,' says Daniel, holding his ground. 'What do you three think about strapping a flashlight to the bow of the ship, one port and one starboard, one on the stern? We're a floating city out here, and as soon as that fire goes out we'll be invisible to other vessels.'

'Makes sense,' says Frannie.

'So, now you think our fire is sensible,' says Smith, stepping away. 'A beacon, as young Francine points out, but also a safety light to avoid collisions. Well, look at how that turned around. From disaster to saviour in five minutes.'

'The fire will have to be enough,' I say. 'Let's save our batteries.'

We collect more chairs and stack them close, but not too close, to the bonfire. Daniel brings up eight powder extinguishers and four fire blankets and positions them around the blaze. We sit and we do not speak. There's a lot of coughing. Recliner cushions are passed around. I place three on top of each other and lie down under a pile of blankets and then, with the heat of the fire at my back, thinking about her beautiful face as I do each and every night, trying to remember her features, wondering if she looks like me, is she's well, if she forgives me, I stare out into the dark north Atlantic Ocean, close my eyes, and fall into a deep sleep.

21

When I wake there's acrid smoke in the air and my cheeks are so cold I can hardly feel them.

Slowly, the scene comes into focus. Glowing embers. One armrest of a teak recliner smouldering away in the ashes. Piles of recliner cushions and blankets like a make-shift campsite at the end of the world. The white-painted steel floor blistered and blackened from the heat. And then, beyond, the sea. Our constant companion: neutral, yet complicit. Flat as a mirror. These are what they call the doldrums. Metallic blue reaching out to meet the sky like a solid membrane.

I stretch.

The thing about being stranded on a ship this size is that somewhere inside yourself you ache for a living thing: a tree or a blackbird or a floribunda rose bush. Something green, chaotic, sprawling, with its own life to live. Last night we burnt chairs because there is no true firewood to be found. There's no natural untreated timber of any kind. The floors are flat and hard and uniform, and the walls are made from dead oak and mahogany, each panel of lacquered veneer about as far from a living breathing tree as it is possible to be.

'Good morning,' says Francine.

'You all right? You sleep OK?'

She nods and smiles. Her cheeks are red and her freckles look darker in the day's harsh light. 'I like this place better after sunrise. Even below deck, you can see where you're going. See what you're dealing with.'

I take a deep breath of sea air.

'The others?'

'Daniel's on the bridge looking for files on how to repair the electrical system. Smith's hunting down breakfast. Says he's hungover and needs bacon.'

I smile. 'He won't find any of that.'

'That's what we told him.'

'He's down there with the plastic box on his own?'

She shrugs and puts on her yellow-rimmed sunglasses. 'He acts the fool but he won't open it. He wouldn't do that. There's a lot of front with him, a lot of ego, but I think most of it's show. Underneath, he's just as unsettled as the rest of us. Got talking to him last night when you were both down in the lobby, when we built up the fire, and he seems decent deep down. I think it's important that we trust each other.'

Trust each other.

I'm starting to trust them, but I'm not entirely sure I trust myself.

I stand and rub the sleep from my eyes. The air is damp. The ship is still moving at full speed. My hair feels dirty and my scalp itches.

'He was here with his best friend,' she says. 'Might be more than a best friend from what I gleaned. Poor guy has angina and type two diabetes. I think Smith's genuinely worried about him.'

'Of course he is. Last night I had a vivid nightmare about Pete down on the sea bed, underneath us all, staring up, his eyes locked open. And I know you're worried sick about your parents.'

'You think they're all safe on an island or another ship?'

I pause a little too long, and then sigh. 'I hope so. I'm starting to have my doubts about the whole world.'

She sits up and frowns. 'What do you mean?'

'Look out there.'

'Caz, you're scaring me.'

'I'm sorry. Ignore me. No coffee in my system yet.'

She starts turning around on the spot, looking out at the unreal flatness in every direction, the lack of waves. It looks as if you could take a casual walk on the surface of the sea this morning. As if some unnamed deity laid out indigo silk in every direction.

'What could have happened? What were you talking about just then? Like an accident or something?'

'No, no,' I say. 'I was just talking nonsense out loud. Probably high on all the fumes from the fire.'

'But you do think something might have happened?'

I rub my eyes again. 'Some kind of accident? Maybe, yes. Why haven't we been rescued yet? A ship this size – why haven't we been visited by some other boat, some plane? You'd have thought we'd have received a message on the radio, at least before the power went out.'

'What kind of accident?'

I shake my head. 'I'm really not the woman to ask.'

'Well, who is?'

'My niece might know. Alice is almost your age and she's obsessed with CERN, the scientific underground laboratory in France. Or is it Switzerland?'

'I think it's both.'

Alice is a vibrant green sapling, who somehow pushed her way up through poor-quality soil, and now that she's grown roots and fronds she is becoming unstoppable. I'm so proud of her I can't put it into words. She's a survivor.

'My niece told me the work they're doing there – the Higgs-Boson particle and so on – is so next-level that the lead scientists admit they don't fully know the potential consequences of their own experiments. Something to do with quantum theory. I don't understand it, but Alice said it was so advanced that, at some point, those physicists have to make their best guesses and then press the button.'

She looks agitated again. 'What's that got to do with us on this ship?'

'Who knows, Frannie?' I snap, hungry, tired. 'How do a thousand passengers disappear into thin air? How does an ocean liner fall off the edge of the world?'

'I need coffee,' she says.

'You and me both.'

She smiles. 'Did you ever read Jung?'

I look at her.

'The concept of shadow aspect, or shadow id?'

I shake my head.

'It's similar to the Freudian unconscious, kind of, only more elegant. It can be positive or negative, but Jung told us how everyone carries a shadow around with them.

Animal instincts, anxieties, repressed childhood memories. The irrational side.'

'I think I understand.'

'We'll see each other's shadows in the coming days.' Her voice is unsteady. 'See our own shadows even, true shadows, perhaps for the first time. We can hide them for a while but eventually, under these conditions, they'll rise to the surface.'

I walk over to the deckchairs and place another on the remnants of the fire. 'Let's start with that coffee. There will be instant sachets in the cabins. And potentially ground coffee in the lounges and restaurants and bars. We have fire and water.'

Daniel arrives back from the bridge. He's wearing a fleece blanket around his shoulders and he's carrying six lever-arch files.

'Are you OK?' I ask.

'I'm not hopeful I can fix anything but I have to try.'

'Want coffee?'

'Very large one, please. Strong. Four sugars.'

'*Four*?'

'I need it, Caz.'

'If we don't find food . . .' says Frannie, and then she trails off.

Daniel places down the folders on his stack of recliner cushions and stretches and says, 'We'll find food.'

'But if we don't.'

He and I look at each other and then he says, 'Humans can survive three weeks with no food, three days with no water, three hours with no shelter, three minutes with no hope.'

'I'm hungry,' she says.

'Hunger and starvation are two different things,' he says. 'We can make do with no food, or what scraps we can salvage from lounges and bar fridges. Lemons and bags of nuts will keep us going if we can't find better. Nobody's going to starve.'

Smith walks through the glass doors on to the deck and he's carrying a dinner tray covered in miniature bags of pretzels and sachets of ketchup and mustard. 'Any of you fine people in need of breakfast?'

'We're going to make coffee,' I say.

'Ah, then I am the harbinger of bad news, friend,' he says. 'I just discovered that, on this ship, at least, no power means no running water. None of the faucets are working any more. None of the toilets, either. So we'd better pray it rains.'

22

I head downstairs to the closest bar and Smith's right. The taps have run dry.

Three weeks with no food.

Three *days* with no water.

Suddenly my throat is parched. Underneath the gleaming bar is a row of stainless steel fridges. I open the first one. Empty. I open the second one. Also empty. There are no soft drinks or bottled mixers here. There's liquor, every kind of liquor you could ever wish for, but there's no water or soda.

'Dry,' says Daniel, to himself, running into the bar, his eyes darting around for answers. 'No running water. The toilets aren't working, the shower by the pool isn't working.'

'The pool,' I say. 'We still have the swimming pool.'

'Chlorine. A dozen other chemicals. I used to be a lifeguard in high school: trust me, the water in a public pool is treated. You can't drink it. More than a few mouthfuls and you'll be seriously ill.'

My head starts to ache. He was a lifeguard in high school? I cannot imagine that life. I feel so far from home hearing that. *Further* from home.

'And the other, covered pool by the funnel's climbing wall is salt water. Undrinkable.'

I adjust my ponytail. I have the urge to take a shower because I know I can't. 'Then we need to take stock. Scavenge what we can and make a list of provisions. Worst case scenario we'll need to ration whatever water we can find.'

He looks at me. 'What about the box?'

'What about it?'

'Seems irresponsible just ignoring it.'

'What else should we do?' I bend down to check the final fridge. Empty. 'It clearly says *do not open the box*. Let's not make this even worse than it already is. Find the others and let's meet at the theatre in fifteen minutes. We haven't explored all the dressing rooms and make-up rooms yet. Maybe there's something back there. A small crew kitchen or bar.'

He leaves to locate Francine and Smith.

I walk towards the theatre but take a detour down a long, dim corridor with passenger cabins on the left side and a blank wall on the right. The corridor isn't completely dark at this time of day; there's weak daylight from the doors at each end.

Seeing my shadow reminds me of Frannie's words. Am I too trusting? If I were shut in an underground car park with two male strangers I wouldn't be at ease for one minute, so why is this any different?

I try each door. Locked, possibly due to the electrical failure, possibly due to some kind of security protocol being tripped. I need to gain access to a room. I need to gain access to *my* room, but that can wait. We must collect the contents of each minibar: small bottles of mineral water and orange juice, snacks and chocolate bars and bags of roasted salted nuts. My mouth starts watering at the thought of it. I take a run-up and kick the door but it does not open. I turn my back on it and kick like a mule but nothing. And then I remember that these doors open outwards into the corridor. We'll need tools to break in.

No passengers, crew, power, heat, lights. Nothing. No radio or phone signal. No internet. No food, and, perhaps most importantly, no water.

I head to the front of the ship, towards the Captain's Lounge, and this place appears less pristine than it did yesterday. In the dull light I notice imperfections and scratched paintwork; damaged veneers and paintings hung at slightly incorrect angles. Yesterday this was a world-class ocean liner but today, after our fire on deck, it's as though I'm exploring an abandoned psychiatric hospital or mothballed boarding school.

Muddled voices from the stairwell. The three of them heading to the theatre for our next pathetic action plan.

I'm cranky now. Hungry and dirty and I'm sweating into the fabric of my clothes. Where is the *real* help? Where are the emergency services with their sirens and expertise? They don't exist this far out at sea. Each maritime country has its own coastguard, its own air-sea rescue services. But all the way out here, in no man's land, international waters, where the ocean is as deep as Mount Everest is tall, deeper even, there is no on-call assistance.

I reach the theatre and together with the others we explore the auditorium and the backstage rooms. We find one quarter of a Hershey's bar. Walking out on stage makes me queasy. I'm not someone who craves attention. I am not a spotlight-seeker. If you look for me in a group photograph you'll inevitably find me at the back. I take in the plush red curtains, the hundreds of empty padded seats, the reversal of what I consider to be normal and safe. I shouldn't be here, facing the impotent lighting rigs.

We walk back to the grey ash of our new impromptu hearth.

'Seems wrong burning this part of the ship,' I say. 'Look at all the damage we've already done. The ship isn't ours to burn.'

'We didn't die in the night,' says Smith. 'You can repaint steel; you cannot bring back a life.'

I think about that for a long time.

The wind picks up, cushions gliding over teak, mirroring the clouds above.

After three hours of scavenging in the public and crew areas of the ship, I make my way back to the sun deck. I rearrange our SOS sign laid out in recliners and wait for the others to join me. They arrive one by one, their clothes dusty and smoky, their faces filthy. Frannie's carrying her fabric tote bag. Daniel has two buckets and Smith's carrying another dining tray. They deposit what they've found on to the decking.

Five mini bags of salted pretzels in total: three plain, two cheese and chive flavour. One half-eaten bag of Cheetos rescued from a bin. Three bottles of water, all opened, all with a few drops in the bottom. Sixteen limes and twenty-one lemons, all fresh. A small airline-size can of Coca-Cola. Two snack bags of mixed nuts and one kid-size bag of gummy bears. An airport bagel still wrapped in its airtight pack. Qantas airlines. Drops of moisture clinging to the inside of the plastic.

'Is this everything?' I ask.

'There's also a vending machine down in the crew area,' says Smith. 'It's next to an ATM and a ping-pong table. I spotted it yesterday, but now it's locked behind heavy watertight doors.'

I take stock of the food. 'We'll live, but we need drinkable water. We must have plenty of water.'

'You don't have to tell me,' says Smith. 'Vintage champagne yesterday and now I can hardly swallow, my throat's so dry. I came aboard this ship to relax and unwind. Paid good money. When I get back to the States, the first thing I'll do is call my lawyer.'

'Caz is right,' says Daniel. 'We need much more water than this.'

We all look out at sea. The cruel, basic irony is not lost on us.

My mind is beginning to play tricks on me. There are moments where I remind myself that I am, in reality, lucky. Assuming Pete is alive and well – and that is an assumption I have to make – I'm fortunate to have family and friends and a life of routines. I still have that life in Yorkshire, waiting for me, and it's much more than Mum ever had. And yet there are other moments where I do feel sorry for myself. Confined here on a ship with no answers and no access to information. There are times I know I must pull myself together, be practical, and then there are other moments where I'm tempted to withdraw from the others and hide in bed the way I used to as a teenager, duvet over my head, pretending, dreaming, insulating myself.

'The minibars in the rooms,' I say, my voice flat. 'We'll need to break the doors down.'

'Right,' says Smith.

'Same with the locked fridges in the bars. No way we can break through watertight doors but we can smash our way into fridges. We can use extinguishers or stools.'

Daniel leaves to look for a crowbar.

'I saw the box,' says Smith, his eyes down. 'I didn't touch, I promise, but you have to admit, it is a temptation. What do you think it's for?'

I shake my head. 'I don't know.'

'I know you don't know. But what do you think?'

'Maybe it's a key?' asks Frannie.

'I thought that,' said Smith. 'Could be some kind of key inside.'

'Or an emergency beacon?' asks Frannie.

'In an ice sculpture?' he says. 'No. It might be a surprise for a guest?' He perks up. 'Could be an engagement ring? The ice melts and some twice-divorced guy takes a knee in front of everyone. Maybe that was all planned out in advance with the concierge. Might be a two-carat princess-cut diamond in that—'

'It's just some unpronounceable chemical used to keep the ice from melting,' I say. 'As Daniel said.'

'You two seem close,' says Smith, smiling for a brief moment, scratching the back of his hand. 'Working together, helping each other, going off for private chats. The *de facto* mom and dad of the ship. Nice that you get on so well. Don't you think so, Francine?'

23

There's a clump of birch trees growing in the square outside my café and I'd give anything to see them again. White, papery bark that catches the morning light. Local schoolchildren have planted daffodils and grape hyacinths in their shade. I took them for granted all these years, watching their fine upper branches sway with the breeze in the early hours before staff and customers arrive, before the till is open, before the noise ramps up. Sitting at a window table with the door locked, hot cup of tea, anticipating the day.

Frannie informs us she has two dogs at home. She says if there's wet dog food in the ship's kennels, that should help keep them alive until we can find water. She volunteers to take responsibility for them.

'I'm going to retrieve whatever tools I can find from the bridge,' says Daniel. 'What are you two going to do?'

I detect an edge to his voice. A sternness.

'Are you feeling OK?' I ask.

'I'm just hungry,' he says. 'Sick and tired of this ship. We all need to pull our weight around here. I can't be the only one trying to fix everything.'

'*Trying* to fix everything,' says Smith, his hands deep in his pockets.

'What did you just say?'

Smith and I set off through the interior of the ship to let Daniel cool off. We walk through dim, unlit, unheated corridors and crew rooms. From comfort and luxury to something altogether more unnerving. Deeper and deeper. Eventually, after double-checking the framed deck plans that flank each bank of lifts, we reach the turbine control room and the workshop.

He picks up a small hacksaw and then discards it. I open a cabinet and find screwdrivers and vices and a soldering iron still in its box.

'No hammers,' he says.

'There's that, though,' I say, gesturing to the fire axe affixed to the wall. 'That'd break through a door.'

He takes it from its emergency casing and we make our way towards the more expensive cabins.

'Doesn't part of you want to take a peek inside the box?' asks Smith. 'Just a glimpse? I'm asking in confidence.'

'I think we should keep it shut.'

He clears his throat. 'Let's try these rooms. Platinum, not Diamond, but they'll still have decent minibars. Small bottles of wine, even.'

I am weary. My legs ache and I can sense a migraine stirring deep inside my skull. 'Let's find Daniel and then we'll try.'

'Why do we need him? I don't report to anybody, never have.'

'Fine, go ahead. Smash through. Just be aware the repair cost may be added to your final tab.'

Smith raises the axe above his head and it scrapes unceremoniously across the ceiling, dislodging a tile.

Then he repositions himself for a side swing and pulls the axe back for a couple of practice attempts. It looks as though he's swinging a seven iron rather than a fire axe.

'Stand clear,' he says.

He pulls back the axe and brings it quickly around and deposits the sharp edge in the wall next to the door frame.

'Damn lights are off. I can't see clearly.'

'Have another go.'

He tries to extract the axe from the wall but it is embedded. He levers it and arches his body but even when I try to help, heaving at the far end of the hickory axe handle, it is stuck firm.

'We don't need to talk about this,' he says, wiping sweat from his brow. 'With the others, I mean.'

I smile. 'I guess we don't.'

We head back to the harsh white sunlight of the top deck. Then, as soon as Smith leaves to visit a non-functioning guest toilet, I betray his confidence and tell Daniel about the fire axe failure. He jogs off immediately to locate it.

I stare at the lifeboats, my hand shielding my eyes from the glare. Four of them are tenders and the other eight are solid orange vessels. The longer this goes on, the more inviting they look. Boats we'd be in control of. The thought of having the ability to switch on an engine is comforting. But then so is the enormous bulk of the ship we're living on. If we swapped the *Atlantica* for Lifeboat No.7, would we regret it after a day on the open ocean? It would be a one-way ticket, a decision we'd likely be unable to reverse. The sea won't remain this calm for long. If we're stuck in a tropical storm on board the *Atlantica* I'm sure we'll manage fine, but on a small lifeboat? And then there's the reduced likelihood of being spotted. On balance I think I'll take my chances on the ship.

Francine tells me the dogs are healthy but restless. She tells me how the large dog growled so fiercely when she approached the cage that she wasn't able to take him out for a proper walk or a toilet break.

'I'm used to working dogs,' she says. 'We had Rottweilers and Alsatians when I was a girl. But this one's different. Maybe the breed was developed to protect livestock from predators. He's scared or he's angry. I can't get close.'

'Then don't get close,' I say. 'Keep your distance. This will all be over soon.'

Smith walks soberly to the railings and throws a deck-chair cushion into the sea. Normally I'd admonish this behaviour but today it seems pointless to do so.

We take our torches and go below deck.

Daniel has managed to remove the axe from the wall and he uses it to smash a hole through the door of the cabin Smith failed to access. Part of the wall comes away from the ceiling and there's dust and debris all over the carpet.

Chaos out of order. The status quo crumbling into something altogether more menacing.

He walks inside, panting, and checks the minibar. Then he sits down on the king-size bed, defeated.

'What?' I ask.

He doesn't respond.

'Daniel?' asks Frannie.

'I'll try the next cabin. I'll keep trying all of them. This one's completely empty. No bottles in the minibar, no food.' He stands up and checks the kettle. 'Even this is dry.'

Frannie looks at me, wide-eyed.

'I'll keep at it,' he says, sensing her fear. 'It's just that I've been fasting and it took a lot of energy to smash through the door, energy I don't have to waste. I was weak already from the lack of calories. I know, it's pathetic.' He looks up at us and smiles a sad smile. 'Thought I'd at least get a cold Pepsi for my labour, you know?'

'We're going to the library,' says Frannie. 'To research options to filter water. Some kind of trap for rain or fog. We're going to need a lot of water so I need to figure out how to capture it.'

'I'm going to the medical centre down on, what, Deck Three? Deck Two?' I say.

'Two, I think,' he says. 'Do you feel sick?'

'Preventative.' I need to take stock; it's something I always do at the café and it never fails to calm my nerves. 'I don't want Smith dying on us because we didn't have medicine on hand.'

Daniel braces himself and then he smashes his axe into the next door. It takes eight solid hits to break through.

'Damn it,' he says, holding his head in his hands.

'You hit yourself?'

'My eye,' he says, cursing under his breath. 'I got dust in my eye. Damn, it hurts. Take a look for me.'

One leg inside the cabin, one leg still in the corridor, Daniel holds his head up to face me. I shine my torch. The beam of light picks out a splinter the length of a matchstick embedded deep in his pupil.

'It's going to be OK,' I say, unsteady on my feet at the sight of it. 'Hold steady.'

24

'Oh,' says Francine, taking a step back after seeing the splinter for the first time. 'Oh, my God.'

I look at her with an expression that says, *You were right to choose philosophy over nursing*.

'Can you pull it out?' he says. His eye is watering now and it is reddening. 'Take it out of my eye.' He's opened his palms, fanning his fingers.

I hold my fingertips over the splinter but he withdraws.

'I'm sorry.'

'Hold still if you can. I'll be gentle.'

I try to steady my arm and then, slowly, carefully, I pinch the end of the splinter and extract it.

He crouches down, still half in the room and half out, and covers his injured eye with his palm.

'Are you OK, Daniel?' asks Frannie. 'Can you see?'

He stands up and blinks and tries to show us. He has tears streaming down his cheeks. He can't keep either eye open.

'It looks OK now,' she says, although there's no way she can tell. 'There might be a mark, a red dot, but it'll heal.'

'Caz?' he says.

I touch his elbow. 'I'm here. You'll be OK. I remember my dad stabbed himself in the eye with the tip of a knife one time when trying to extract a cork from a bottle of red wine. He was already a little drunk. It healed fine. Had a small blemish on the surface afterwards but it was hardly noticeable.'

I don't mention that he required two operations: one immediately after the accident and one a month or so later in the Manchester Royal Eye Hospital.

I help Daniel to the bed and Frannie checks the minibar. There's a momentary pause before she pulls the door.

'Well?' I ask.

She turns to face us. 'Nothing,' she says.

'I should have flown home with my ex,' says Daniel, defeated. 'This ship should be condemned.'

'I thought you said she was your fiancée?' asks Frannie.

He grunts that away, one hand shielding the injured eye. 'The main bars have large locked fridges. There will be drinks in there. Ice, maybe. What I wouldn't give to suck on an ice cube right now. You and Frannie go, and I'll get back to work with the axe after I've caught my breath. Go on now, both of you.'

Frannie looks at me and whispers, 'What if his eye gets infected?'

I turn away from Daniel and say, in hushed tones, 'That's why I'm going to the medical centre. I'll bring back the supplies we need. Frannie, talk to Smith. Maybe offer Daniel the small can of Coke from upstairs. The sugar might help if he's in shock.'

It takes me almost an hour to discover that the medical centre drugs are all locked away in secure rooms and the only areas I can access are the waiting room and the children's play area. A wooden game with coloured beads to be pushed along wires. A stack of well-read Pippi Longstocking stories. A doll in a saffron-yellow dress. I can't help but stare at the doll. Every time I see a lifelike one it takes the air from my lungs. They make me consider what may have been. I look away. There's a defibrillator on the wall but with no power I'm not sure how that will help us. What I need is gauze and bandages and seasickness tablets and antibiotics and anti-diarrhoeal medication.

There's banging from a stairwell above me so I jog up to find Daniel swinging his axe again, attempting to break into the bar fridges. He looks like a crazed escapee in Frannie's yellow-rimmed sunglasses. Swinging the axe to sheer off the stainless steel doors.

The fridges are empty.

Every last one of them.

'This doesn't make any sense,' he says, panting from the exertion. 'These bars should be fully stocked. Drinks and olives and lemons. Ice chips. The ship was full of people.'

'If everyone left at, say, three a.m., maybe that's when they were due to get restocked from the stores on Deck Two?'

He sits down heavily on a leather bar stool.

'I'm so thirsty,' he says. 'Frannie, pour me a drink, please.'

She frowns and looks over at the bottles on the wall. Vodka and gin and bourbon.

'Liquor?'

'I need something wet.'

'It'll dehydrate you.'

'I don't care.'

Frannie pours him Grey Goose vodka. Daniel drinks it down and then coughs.

'Another?' she asks.

He shakes his head. He looks pale and sweaty, either from the shock of his eye injury or from lack of hydration.

'I think we should go to the top deck. Find you some fresh air.' I touch Daniel's arm. 'Get you some food in your stomach.'

We reach the Jacuzzi and the wind is starting to gust.

'No fire for us tonight if this weather keeps up,' says Frannie. 'We'll burn down the whole ship.'

'Best thing that could happen to it,' grunts Daniel.

'Where's my Dr Pepper?' shouts Smith from the pool. He's standing in the shallow end with his shirt off.

'Everything's been empty so far,' yells back Frannie, her curly red hair plastered across her face. 'Every single minibar. No drinks. What are you doing in the pool? You'll catch hypothermia.'

'You can't *catch* hypothermia,' mutters Daniel.

'Taking a bath,' says Smith. 'Found me some lavender soap. I'll be done soon.'

'I might do the same,' I say.

And then Smith climbs the steps from the water and we all turn in unison because he doesn't have a stitch of clothing on.

'I'm in a towel now.'

Daniel squints, opening and closing his injured eye.

'There's a hospital room someplace,' says Smith, tightening his robe belt. 'Fully equipped. They can even do minor surgery, I checked it before I let John book our tickets.'

'But all the meds are locked away.'

'Let me dress and then I'll look at your wound,' says Smith.

He dries off and dresses on deck and then wraps himself in a blanket complete with *Atlantica* motif.

'Hold your face to the light, Danny.'

Daniel walks away instead. 'Lifeboats,' he says. 'It's the only thing for us.'

I hold out my palm. 'Wait, this needs to be a joint decision, I think, and personally, well, I feel we'll be safer to stay together on board the main ship. Look at those clouds.' They've morphed from heavy white to gunmetal grey. Towering storm clouds casting shadows all over the surface of the sea. 'We could be heading into that weather system and I for one don't want to be strapped into a tiny lifeboat.'

Daniel turns to me. He looks completely exhausted. His lips are starting to crack.

'They have emergency supplies on each one,' he says, his voice low. 'Fishing gear, water rations, dry biscuits. They might have radios, or at least distress beacons. More flares. We need to break into a lifeboat somehow and take out what we need.'

'Fine,' I say. 'We can try.'

He staggers to the nearest boat on the starboard side and within minutes it's clear the lifeboat is locked securely, just like the one we tried before.

'What kind of negligent company locks up their lifeboats?' says Smith, his face twitching with anger. 'Another point for my lawyer. This group will have to sell three cruise ships to afford my settlement the way this is unfolding.'

'I read somewhere that lifeboats and rafts activate from water pressure,' says Frannie. 'Think they mentioned it in the muster drill. There's a sensor or switch and they become usable once the ship starts to sink or get into trouble.'

Daniel shakes his head. 'There must be some kind of mechanism that's stuck. Because of the power outage.'

He sits down on a deckchair and, once again, covers his eye with his hand.

'I say we release a lifeboat into the water and let it open up for us,' says Smith. 'It'll trigger some kind of hydrostatic pressure switch and unlock.'

'We shouldn't waste a lifeboat,' I say.

'We have plenty,' says Daniel through gritted teeth. 'And besides, if it opens we'll climb in and take what we need. It won't be a waste.'

'Access it from all the way down there?' I say, leaning over the rail. 'We must be ten or eleven storeys up.'

He coughs and shakes his head again.

'You're hungry,' I say. 'Injured. We need clear heads.'

'The boats lower into the water slowly from their own cranes and winches,' says Daniel, as if to himself. 'Like a pulley system. It's gradual. The cables are supposed to be released by the officer in charge of the lifeboat. So ours won't be released, right? It'll sit in the water, door unlocking, assuming Frannie is right, and then one of us can shimmy down the cable, climb into the lifeboat, and, I don't know, send up the emergency rations in a basket or something. Then the other three help pull that person up.'

'*Relaxing cruise*, they said,' says Smith, picking at his thumbnail. '*Trip of a lifetime*, they said. Diamond class with butler service. *Only the best in the world*, they said.'

'I'll do it,' says Frannie, pushing her shoulders back. 'I'm strong and light. As long as I don't look down I think I'll be OK, but I'll need a secure harness.'

'This job's for me,' says Daniel. 'My idea, should be my neck on the line.'

I shake my head. 'Frannie's right. You really don't look yourself, Daniel. And we need you up here to haul her back in.'

He walks over to the mechanism holding up the lifeboat and examines signs and judges the pulleys and safety notices.

The sky looks irate: the colour of an old bruise.

'If we can take harnesses from the climbing wall and rig them up securely then we'll be able to lift her back to safety. Smith, are you prepared to help?'

'I'll do what I can.'

Twenty minutes later Frannie's strapped into a rock-climbing harness and her ropes are tied off on the steel superstructure of the ship. Daniel tests its load-bearing capacity and declares it to be good enough.

'You lower yourself down the cable. Take it steady but know that we've got you, OK? If you grow tired or freak out we will not let you fall, do you understand? I've rigged it that way. We won't let you get hurt.'

She looks terrified but she says, 'I know you won't. Just hold on to that rope, all of you.'

'Are you sure you're willing to do this, Frannie?' I say. 'You don't have to. We can try again tomorrow when it might be calmer?'

'I'm scared to climb up things but I've abseiled down a cliff in Snowdonia before. Needed hypnotherapy for months before, but I managed it. My therapist told me if I face my fears I can overcome them.'

I don't know what to say to that.

'We'll send down a basket on another rope,' says Daniel. 'Fill it with water and—'

'Food and fishing gear and any portable radio equipment and flares and star maps. I remember,' she says. 'Don't worry.'

'And if you see a radio.'

'Mayday, mayday, mayday. This is the RMS *Atlantica*. We need urgent assistance. Mayday, mayday, mayday.'

I smile. 'You can do this, you know.'

'Everyone ready?' asks Daniel.

We nod.

Daniel releases some kind of metal pin painted red and the crane arm swings over us into position and the cables stiffen. Then the lifeboat starts its descent towards the sea. It's calm, steady, as an emergency protocol should be. Two decks down, five decks down.

The wind whistles.

'Almost there,' says Daniel peering over the guard rail. 'Let's do this quick. In and out.'

He looks at Frannie and she bites her bottom lip and then nods. Daniel tightens her harness one last time.

'Almost there,' he says again, looking down at the boat. 'Splashdown. OK, Frannie, you've got your gloves on, start making your way down the cable. We'll take your weight from up here. We will not let you fall.'

'Guys . . .' says Smith.

'What?' I say.

'Look.'

The four of us peer down at the boat far below us.

We watch as the lifeboat cables detach and the vessel pitches to one side, and then, silently, it sinks beneath the waves.

25

I stare down at the blank water, my mouth agape. It's happening again. A downward spiral. A slippery descent we are not in control of. When we were told of the true extent of Dad's lies it was as though the ground gave way beneath our feet. He fought it at first, claimed it was a loan, told Mum calmly it was a short-term problem, that there was paperwork to support what he'd done, that the board trustees of the charity had verbally approved his actions. By that point I was desperate for him to stop.

'I must have done something wrong,' says Daniel. 'Or in the wrong order. I screwed it up.'

Smith's rubbing his eyes as if he can't believe what he just witnessed.

'It's an accident,' I suggest. 'A practice run. There are lots more lifeboats on the ship.'

'You three don't get it yet, do you?' says Smith, a crazed grin spreading across his face. 'That was a lifeboat built for, I don't know, a hundred people. More? And it just sank in calm waters. Lifeboats don't sink, guys. They cannot sink.'

'We still have some water,' I say, slowing my breathing, trying to stay on the level. 'I say we make up a small fire and brew coffee. Help us all to think clearly again. Take a time out.'

They don't reply; they just stare down at the flat, grey water far below us.

'I'll build the fire,' says Daniel.

'I'll help,' says Frannie.

'I need a real drink,' says Smith, walking away, dejected, back into the shadows of the ship's interior.

It takes us a while to get the embers hot enough to boil water in the saucepan I borrowed from the Platinum Grill galley kitchen. I make instant coffee from plastic sachets we scavenged from a lounge, and we all take more sugar than normal. My mug scalds my hands and I let it.

Pain I'm in control of.

A blessed distraction.

I think back to when Dad was sick years ago, before the truth came out. Moving from a general ward to a room with one other patient, a kind, long-haired man, and then into intensive care for almost a week. Optimism slipping away with each move. We'd hold up faded photos for him to look at, photos of family holidays in Scarborough and Blackpool. The machines around him were multiplying, a new cannula or sensor added each day. Higher levels of care. He was desperate for sleep and I'd explain to him as best I could that the constant nurse visits and IVs and catheter checks were important for his improvement. He'd complain of people screaming or crying in pain at night. How the room never became dark enough for him to be able to sleep properly. We understood the medics were helping him. I knew he was lucky to be there. But he grew so desperate for home, for peace and quiet, for his own bedroom with a view out over his neighbour's back yard and the hills in the distance. We didn't know at that point how much he'd stolen over the years. Gambled it all away with seemingly no joy to show for it. But even if we had known, I'd still have visited him in intensive care. I'd have hated him for those days but I'd still have been there, brushing his teeth and reading to him.

He recovered after a long convalescence, and then, later, we came to understand the true extent of his deceit. Perhaps his secrets contributed to his sickness. The toxicity of maintaining such a complex web of lies. Much later, on the day he stepped off the bridge, it was like a sudden release from a pressure valve. I'd put so much effort and strength into willing him better, and then willing the news away, willing Mum some peace, that the finality of his death, the visit from the police – it caused all that pent-up energy to burst out all at once. I cried and wailed, and, looking back now, I am guilty of not holding back in front of Mum and Gemma. I'm the strong one who pulls it together and I failed them both. The police officers made us strong tea with plenty of sugar. It's a basic thing but it helped us through those terrible hours.

'This is the best coffee I've ever had,' says Daniel.

Frannie and I both smile.

'It feels like rain,' she says. 'Does it feel like rain to you?' She starts to arrange buckets and plastic sheets in anticipation.

'I hope it rains for days,' says Daniel, his eye twitching.

I miss the weather of home. Light drizzle one minute, dappled sun the next. Gentle, undulating fields and blackthorn hedgerows adorned with raindrops. Wild rabbits dashing across misty public footpaths. The sunsets this time of year.

'It'll get cold, though,' I say, recalling the sleet we left behind just a few days ago. 'If it rains we can drink but we will freeze quicker. A hundred years ago there would have been real fireplaces down below in the state rooms, and coal furnaces powering the propellers. If it rains, we're reliant on blankets and body heat.'

'We'll manage,' Daniel says. 'That lifeboat, though. I thought they were built to withstand hurricanes. Self-righting. It sank like a rock.'

There are moments each year when I start to lose my mind a little. I recognise them, and I can always bring myself back from the brink, I've done it many times before.

I hope I can do the same on board this ship.

'It's all the way down there on the sea bed,' I say, staring out at the horizon, at our alien aquatic world. 'Thousands of metres down below us. Tens of thousands of metres. Resting on the sea bed in complete silence. No other ships down there. Resting, seemingly pristine, with bleached humpback whale bones at the bottom of the sea.'

'The midnight zone,' says Daniel.

'Sorry?'

'That part of the ocean. Marine biologists and ocean-ographers call it the midnight or bathyal zone. It's constantly very cold, just above zero, and the life down there is unearthly. Needle-teethed viperfish, giant squid and anglerfish. Translucent amphipods. There are eel-like frill sharks down there that people call *living fossils* on account of their brown skin and blank eyes. They are the depths where no sunlight can ever reach.'

26

Silence can cause the mind to wander, to venture into dark places. It's taken me this long to become accustomed to hours on end without screens, phones, constant news flow. I have more time. Too much of it. Now I find my thoughts meandering between longing for home, for the dales and moors, the market stall hustle on a Saturday, the background music we play in the café; to worrying about Mum and what she has endured, still endures; to Pete and his cancer scare earlier this year, and his stubborn reluctance for me to meet his family. He says they haven't been close for decades but I still yearn to meet them. I want to see photos of him as a boy.

I join the others.

'I think it might be wise to try another mayday broadcast from the bridge,' says Daniel. 'Depending on our course we could be closing in on Bermuda, or Greenland, or St Helena.'

'I'm heading to the library,' says Smith, staring out at sea. 'My first visit since grade school. Middle-class kids from the 'burbs used to make fun of me back then. Kevin Parkinson especially, nasty little bastard. I got my alphabet mixed up, spelling things the wrong way, numbers too. I'll go look for basic electronics manuals; you never know your luck.' He glances at me. 'You both go with Daniel, go on.'

'No, I'm going to check the food stores again while we have some light left. Try all the approaches one more time.'

'The watertight doors will be sealed shut. No room for negotiation there.'

'I'll go anyway.'

It turns out Smith was right. I still can't gain access and just knowing how many tons of potatoes and egg pasta and fresh beefsteak tomatoes and string beans and smoked bacon reside beyond the steel doors makes my stomach growl. If I were back home Gem would make me a Caesar salad with charred chicken, generous with the croutons, easy on the anchovies. She serves it to me when she senses I'm low. Somehow she always knows.

My torch is dimming. I only use it when I have no other option, but it's losing its power. I manage to venture most of the way to the bridge with it switched off because I'm growing familiar with the layout. The shadows and the migraine-pattern carpets are still disconcerting, though. I have a sense inside myself that the ship has taken against us.

Two newspapers are neatly folded on a table outside the captain's private quarters. They're dated the day Pete and I left Doncaster in his Audi.

The bridge is quiet. It's another area you naturally expect to find manned, lit up, beeps and radio chatter, women in uniform at the helm. Layers of professionalism and experience. Well-rehearsed protocols enshrined in company policy and maritime law. But there is nothing here except for a tired waterski instructor nursing his untreated eye.

'Any luck?'

'Nothing is working.' He bangs his palm on the desk. 'I'm tempted to never leave the continental United States again as long as I live.'

'This'll be over soon. A few more days and some veteran pilot from New York harbour will board the ship by boat or helicopter and he'll calmly take control and dock the ship safely and then he'll explain exactly what happened.'

Daniel looks up at the ceiling. 'I need to see my daughter. It's already been too long. I know now that I haven't seen enough of her growing up, I even missed her fourth birthday.' He grits his teeth and swallows hard. 'I need to make it up to her.'

'You will.'

'Will I?' He shakes his head and blows air from his mouth. 'Fatherhood didn't come naturally. I don't know why it didn't, I have no excuses. My dad was always at home in the evenings, playing chess with us, always at Little League games. He was good at all that, although I've never told him as much. I'm an absentee parent. The useless guy who sends toys in the mail and then misses every fucking party, scared I won't be able to communicate with my own daughter's friends. I have never once looked after her on my own for more than a couple of hours, can you believe that?' He shakes his head. 'It's pathetic.'

'You'll do just fine,' I say. 'The great thing about little kids – she's four years old, right? – she'll forgive and forget, I promise. She'll love you unconditionally as long as you start being Dad from now on. No harm done. Can't say the same for your fiancée – I'm just being honest with you – but you can still have a beautiful relationship with your daughter. That isn't ruined, far from it.'

He sits up straight, focuses. 'I wish we still had GPS co-ordinates on screen. I hate not knowing exactly where I am. How far away we are from land. It's like we're going around in circles, drifting. I want us to move towards somewhere.'

I place my hand on his shoulder. His breathing slows and he puts his own hand on top of mine and we stay like that for a moment, locked together.

'None of this makes sense.'

'Even so,' he says. 'There's usually a straightforward explanation. It could be that we're overlooking it. Some kind of ship systems failure meant everyone disembarked at Southampton. Wiring trouble. We didn't get the memo for some reason. Now we're lost in the mid-Atlantic.'

'They wouldn't have let the ship sail off with no crew.'

Daniel scratches his head and Frannie and Smith both arrive on the bridge.

'I've built another SOS from deckchairs,' says Frannie. 'Opposite end of the ship. The stern, right? And I've been reading up on the inflatable life rafts on board.'

'We need to prioritise—' says Smith, but Daniel cuts him off.

'Wait,' he says.

We turn to face the open doors behind us.

I hear it. Very faint, in the distance.

'I don't hear anything,' says Smith. 'Quit playing games.'

'I do,' says Frannie, moving to the doors.

A tune I remember learning in music class at school.

Rachmaninov's 'Rhapsody on a Theme of Paganini'.

27

'A piano,' says Daniel. 'There's someone on board . . . playing a piano?'

We turn together and start running down the stairs.

'Wait, I can't move as fast as you,' says Smith.

Frannie slows to help him but Daniel and I keep going.

The piano is being played live. Not recorded. I can sense the difference. It's being played beautifully.

'Who is it?' I ask. I'm excited but I'm also weary. Too many things have happened.

'Whoever it is, they must have been here the whole time. Watching us. Why didn't they show themselves?'

There is movement in the air. Rolling waves of vapour. We are deep inside the ship, running lower and lower, and there is a damp breeze inside this stairwell.

'You feel that?' I say.

But Daniel's out of earshot now, outrunning me.

A fine mist. Like a hill fog, or tropical humidity.

The tempo of the music intensifies to the point where it's almost too fast to be recognisable as Rachmaninov. Heavy, thunderous keystrokes.

'Wait for us,' says Frannie behind me, her voice fading.

I pause to catch my breath and wipe the moisture from my face. The music is close. I think it's coming from the Ocean Lobby . . . or the casino.

I will not go in there.

'There's a voice too. What are they saying?' asks Frannie, touching my hand as she catches up with me. 'What is that? I can't make it out.'

I stop for a moment and listen intently, my face damp, the scent of unwashed bodies in the air.

'I can't hear,' says Smith between heavy breaths.

The music quickens to the point where it's just noise.

'Box?' says Frannie. 'They're saying something about a box.'

I focus and cup my hands behind my ears.

The stairwell is dark, almost impossible to see each other, just outlines.

'Open . . . the box,' says Daniel, running back to us looking hopeful. 'Listen closely. They're speaking slowly over the piano but I think they're telling us to open the box.'

'That's it,' says Frannie.

'I think it's *do not* open the box,' I say. 'There's a noise before *open*.'

'I'm going to the piano,' says Smith. 'You're all hearing the noise of the ventilation system. Hunger-induced hysteria. There aren't any words I can make out; your minds are playing tricks.'

We make our way to the Ocean Lobby.

The mist is thicker down here. Like a trapped cloud.

'There,' says Daniel, pointing at the black grand piano positioned between the two sweeping staircases.

'It's a self-playing piano,' says Frannie, as the tempo slows down. 'That's good news, right? There's power, at least. We have *some* electricity.' The tempo is normal again. 'The ceiling light. The music. We can unplug it and use that socket. Charge our phones. Plug in a heater, maybe.'

Rachmaninov's symphony ends abruptly and the cover of the piano's keyboard slams shut.

The solitary ceiling spotlight brightens.

It buzzes.

The box on the ice sculpture drip tray is illuminated.

'Power's coming back,' says Daniel. 'That's good.'

A wall-mounted TV switches on and the whispering stops. A blurry image on screen sharpens gradually into focus. The bottom half of a woman's face. Black skin, crimson lips, perfect white teeth.

The lips break out into a shallow smile.

28

'Good evening, passengers,' says the voice.

Her accent is American and her intonation is that of a self-assured newsreader.

We stand perfectly still. Spellbound.

'Who . . . who are you?' asks Daniel.

There's a long pause and then she says, 'You can call me Admiral.'

I try to swallow but my mouth is too dry.

'This means we have electricity now,' says Smith, looking furtively at each of us in turn, and then to the screen. 'The TV's working so we can eat proper food again. Water.' He sighs. 'We're going to be OK.'

'Francine, Caroline, Daniel, Mr Smith. Passengers of the RMS *Atlantica*, you are being broadcast live around the world. Please do not curse.'

'What is this?' asks Frannie.

'We need to leave the ship now,' I say, to the face on the TV. To the *Admiral*. 'We must leave this ship tonight. You cannot—'

Daniel speaks over me and says, in a deep voice, 'Who are you and what do you want?'

The lips on screen don't move.

'My parents, though,' says Frannie, her tone desperate, pleading. 'Are my parents safe? Do you have them? I want to know what happened, Admiral, please.' She starts to break down. 'Show me them, if you can. I need to know they're OK. I want to talk to them. Dad's not well. Please, Admiral.'

The lips on screen don't say anything for a full minute.

'What do you mean, *broadcast*?' I ask.

The other lights in the lobby come on gradually but they stay dim. Then spotlights shine into our faces and the lips on screen say, 'Please, all of you, take a seat and allow me to put your minds at ease.'

We drag chairs closer to the screen. Daniel's face is pure desperation. Same for Frannie. Smith looks exhausted.

'Two days ago you boarded the RMS *Atlantica* destined for New York City. What you didn't know was that you were in fact destined to become media pioneers.' She smiles, shows us a little teeth. '*Atlantica* started to air the moment you boarded. The pilot episode was screened for free on various platforms. All subsequent episodes have been offered on a pay-per-view basis.'

'I never agreed to any of this,' says Smith, crossing his arms. 'Screened? I'd like to speak to my attorney. His name is—'

'The episode with the sinking lifeboat,' she says, cutting him off, 'was watched by an audience in excess of the last Super Bowl. You each have multitudes of loyal admirers and exuberant fans. Newspaper headlines and magazine articles are written each day in your honour. Congratulations, passengers.'

'Bullshit,' says Smith.

The screen turns off.

29

'Admiral?' says Frannie. 'Admiral? Please come back.'

The screen stays blank.

'You're pleading with a television,' says Smith.

'He'll apologise,' says Frannie, urgently, pointing back at Smith. 'Please come back. He'll talk nicely this time, won't you?'

Smith mutters something to himself and then he says, 'If I wasn't half starving, I'd . . . I'm sorry,' he says. 'Fine, I apologise.'

We wait, standing under a three-storey-high ceiling with a small opaque plastic box behind us and a dark TV screen in front. My heart is beating hard in my chest. I need this to be over. I need to eat and to see my family, see Pete. I'm not interested in why we're here. I want to leave.

Please come back.

The TV screen switches on and the lips return. But her smile is gone.

'I'll urge you again to moderate your language. Now, take a seat again. I'm going to talk through what will happen on board the RMS *Atlantica* from this point forward. Think of this experience as the chance of a lifetime. I understand you may be puzzled, so I'll ensure you each have the opportunity to ask me one question per day.'

Her skin is flawless. Moisturised and professionally made-up. The camera zooms in and her lips are perfect. I can only imagine what my dry, cracked lips would look like on a screen that size.

'Strictly one question from each of you per day at six p.m. Is that understood?'

We all nod.

'Excellent.'

'She can see us,' whispers Daniel.

'Of course she can see us, we're on TV right now,' whispers Smith. 'They're broadcasting us being starved.'

'How can you see us?' Frannie asks her.

'Thank you for your daily question, Francine. It may help to think of this ship as your own live, interactive studio. The vessel contains thousands of active cameras, like the weatherproof CCTV systems you've already spotted out on deck. They're all operated remotely. The same goes for microphones. If you look around closely enough you'll find some of them.'

'But are my parents OK?' asks Frannie.

'Strictly one question per passenger per day, I'm afraid.'

Frannie looks distraught.

I glance at Daniel and he looks back.

Part of me yearns to ask her about Pete, to find out exactly where he is and what happened to him. If he's healthy, because his blood pressure is still too high, his cholesterol, and I'm curious whether his brother's knee operation went well, whether someone's feeding his old ginger cat. But I take a moment to reflect and then I ask, in the clearest voice I can manage, 'Are all the other passengers safe, Admiral?' because that should give both Frannie and Smith some reassurance.

'They are safe.'

Daniel and Frannie and I stand up and hug each other. We squeeze tight and gesture for Smith to join but he stays seated, shaking his head.

'This is all BS,' he says. 'BS, the lot of it. I've never been tricked like this in my entire effing life.'

Daniel detaches. He stands up straighter and says, 'Is my daughter OK, Admiral?'

The lips say, 'Yes, Eva is fine.'

He looks skyward and mutters something to himself. 'And my fiancée?' he asks.

'One question per passenger per day.'

'I'm keeping all the watches,' says Smith, defiantly, pulling up his sleeve to reveal at least three on each arm. 'Call it advance partial compensation. A deposit. A levelling of the weighing-scales of justice. Now, connect me through to my lawyer immediately.'

'That wasn't a question,' say the lips.

'Alright,' he says. 'His name is Jack Norton, he's a partner at Blathe, Ware and McCann out of Charlotte, North Carolina. Can you put me through to my attorney?'

'No, I'm afraid I can't,' say the lips.

And then the screen goes blank again.

30

When we emerge back on deck the rain is coming down in sheets and the foaming waves force the ship to rock to and fro. We are a tragic, unkempt quartet, and we each digest the news in our own way. Smith is mumbling to himself and Daniel is checking the walls for cameras and microphones. Frannie looks haunted.

'No fire tonight, not in this storm.' Her eyes widen. 'Oh, shit, we left the blankets outside.'

'No swearing,' says Daniel.

'That was just for the live broadcast, wasn't it?' she says. 'They can't control our speech the whole time.'

Control. We have some limited answers but it's as though we have unknowingly, incrementally, sacrificed our individual liberty in the bargain. Four starved puppets operated via invisible strings from far away.

'I never consented to be on any kind of show,' says Smith, behind us. 'As far as I'm concerned this is false imprisonment. Kidnap. You can't inform people that they're on TV. You cannot just inform them of it after the fact. That's not how real life works . . .'

He trails off.

'She told us everyone else is safe,' I say. 'She said *every-one*. That's the main thing. They must have disembarked at Southampton. I guess our drinks were spiked or something. For some reason we were chosen.'

'They can't just *choose* people,' says Smith, shouting to be heard over the wind. 'I am a sovereign citizen of the United States. They don't get to choose. *I* get to choose. I have constitutional rights, granted to me by God, and I'm here for a Diamond-class ocean crossing back to America.'

I can still hear the piano music inside my head. The memory of it.

'My sister, Gemma, used to be obsessed with a particular reality show. She'd watch the main programme but she'd also watch the audition tapes to see how the producers selected housemates. I remember her explaining how they didn't just want a dozen of the most outlandish people. They didn't want quiet, passive people either. The producers were always looking for the perfect mix of confidence, relatability, and a hint of inner darkness.'

'Darkness?' says Frannie.

'The unexpected. You know, something spontaneous or unusual.'

'The Admiral seemed nice, though,' says Frannie.

'Are you out of your fucking mind?' says Smith, spitting as he speaks. 'She seemed *nice* to you? We're in the middle of the Atlantic with no food or power being overseen by a maniac talking through a television screen. She seemed *nice*?'

My stomach aches, it's so empty. I am unsteady on my feet so I lean against the steel wall of the ship.

'We don't even know what this is about yet,' says Daniel. 'My guess is they'll bring in a pair of presenters. This will be the pilot episode, isn't that what she said? They want our reaction and they're getting it. But all these TV shows follow essentially the same format. Entertaining viewers in their living rooms. They want us to entertain them.'

'I'm not entertaining anyone.' I shake my head, almost shuddering at the thought of it. 'I'm trying to get us through this with our lives intact. I'm not an entertainer. Not even close. I can't tell jokes or sing in tune. That's not who I am.'

Frannie looks around, squinting. 'Cameras everywhere. Are we being watched right now? Or is there a delay so they can edit the footage if we make a mistake?'

'You can ask the nice lady tomorrow at six p.m.,' says Smith.

Daniel dashes off to collect any blankets that aren't already soaking wet and then when he's done we reconvene in the stairwell.

In any other circumstances we would never have met each other, never mind talked to one another. Our paths would not have crossed.

'We need to stay dry and we need to find heat,' says Daniel, back with armfuls of damp blankets. 'Let's think straight. Help each other.'

Smith's face folds in on itself to form a twisted scowl and he says, 'Could you try to be a *little* less obvious? Playing up for the cameras. That's what this is, right, Danny? I saw you look at that CCTV camera just now and say your line. You're trying to impress all the young women watching on their iPads, but you could be more subtle about it. Will you be working with your shirt off next? Is that your strategy?'

Daniel throws a blanket at him with such force it almost knocks Smith over.

'Stop it,' says Frannie.

'We need to stay warm,' I say. 'It's close to freezing out there and not much warmer inside. The ship is losing any heat it once had. I think we should find four rooms next to each other and set ourselves up with as many blankets as we can find. Focus on the basics. You think we can fashion a safe fireplace with a chimney leading out of a window somehow? Using metal ducting? Maybe we can take foil survival blankets from a life raft on deck. Lay out extra buckets to catch water.' Smith starts to interject but I cut him off. 'Let's discuss what the Admiral told us once we're sure we'll live through the night.'

31

The ocean is raging: white-tipped waves and rolling swells so powerful they lift the ship and move it around like a bath toy, tilting it, pushing its structural integrity to the limit.

Something is creaking.

Chairs slide across the floor in groups.

Eventually we decide two of us will try to feed and walk the dogs, while the other two stay indoors to gain access to rooms.

'I'm not going out there again tonight,' says Smith. 'It's freezing and slippery, and I can't stand the blackness. When the skies are cloudy like this I can't see a damn thing. I think the youngest two should go out and tend to the dogs. Better eyesight.'

Frannie and I head up to the kennels while Daniel and Smith try to smash down doors.

As we're walking up the stairs, clinging to the rails, all the lights flicker on. Not the emergency lights, the real lights.

'Oh, thank God,' says Frannie. 'This means heat and water, right? They must have fixed the problem.'

'Food,' I say. 'Let's go down and check the food stores.'

We head back down, delighted with the new brightness. It makes such a dramatic difference to our mood, to how terrifying this place can become after sunset. Deck Five. Deck Three. We're too scared to try the lifts. I can't imagine being stuck in a broken lift between floors on this ship. We arrive on Deck Two and the watertight doors are still locked shut.

'I thought they'd fixed the problem,' says Frannie.

My stomach growls. 'I don't think there ever was a problem. The TV worked, didn't it? The piano that played itself – that must have had electrical power. The engines ran the whole time. If the Admiral were here in person I'd insist we leave right away. I think they're keeping food from us on purpose.'

'But . . . why? Why would anyone want to do that?'

'Ratings? Who knows. It's not moral.'

I notice something in the mirror. The etching is Art Deco and the glass looked as if it moved. A glitch. I stare at it, avoiding the two increasingly gaunt reflections. I keep moving my head, focusing, cupping my hands to the surface of the mirror, adjusting my posture to stay upright as the ship crests another wave.

'Is there somebody behind there?' I ask.

'What?'

I pick up a chair and hold it out at arm's length and take a run at the mirror.

It shatters.

A multi-lens camera stares back at us, swivelling, adjusting its apertures, refocusing on our faces.

32

Jagged shards of mirror all around us. I look down and see myself; broken and multiple at the same time. A deconstructed kaleidoscope.

'Hidden cameras?' asks Frannie, peering into the recess. 'She said CCTV; she didn't mention this. How many cameras could there be?' She spins on her own axis. 'What about the showers yesterday morning? What about the toilets? Oh, my God, I think I'm going to be sick.'

Fragments of glass skid across the floor as the ship pitches, and then they skid back to us.

I stare into the camera lens and grit my teeth and say slowly, 'You need to open the food stores now. I don't care if you give us rations, you can let us eat bread and water, but we need access and we need it tonight. The storm is intensifying and Smith is increasingly weak.'

I wait, breathing heavily, even though I know this camera can't reply to my hollow demand. It cannot grant me my wish.

The lens looks back at me, resolute.

'Open the doors!' I scream.

Frannie picks the chair up off the floor. 'I'll smash the whole thing.'

'No point. There are probably a hundred more on each deck. Leave it.'

We climb up the stairs dejected. My mouth had been watering all the way down. The lights were bright and we'd made contact with another human, no matter how odd that contact was, and I could almost taste the meal I would have prepared. First, a pint of water to quench my thirst. Two pints. And then something hearty but immediate. Mature cheese, salty French butter, digestive biscuits, grapes, quince jelly, savoury cold cuts and cured hams. Crisp green apples. Thick chunks of bread with a proper crust. Nothing fancy, just a pub ploughman's and then maybe a fat slice of chocolate fudge cake, like the one we serve in the café, our third bestseller after vanilla sponge and lemon with poppy seeds. But instead we have nothing. Instead of that feast, we have electric light and no food at all.

'You're going to think I'm crazy . . .' says Frannie.

'No more crazy than me for stepping on board this ship.'

'The dogs are keeping me on the level.'

We pass through the centre of the ship. Through the double-storey Gold Grill and up through the smaller Platinum Grill. I think about what Frannie said. We weave through tables set with linen cloths, wine coolers at the ready, one attached securely to each table. It's a miracle they're not sliding across the room. Perhaps it's the carpet or that they're so heavy. Could they be bolted down? There are hundreds of empty chairs. A chandelier the size of a family car twinkling above us, shifting, the crystals clinking gently as they move in sync with the ship.

'Just walking up there and feeding them,' she goes on. 'Letting them out to run around. Stroking them and reassuring them that everything will be all right even though I have no such reassurance myself. Making eye contact with a living thing that has learned to trust me and take comfort from me. Having them to look after. Maybe my parents were right all along; maybe I should be a nurse. I don't know. But I'm happy the dogs are on board.'

'Me too.'

'All except one,' she says, her tone turning serious. 'I wish the shepherd dog was back home with his owner. He scares the other dogs and he scares me.'

We reach the stern and the air is colder tonight, as though we've crossed into a different realm, into an uncharted northern sea. The ship's exterior lights are on. That means less risk we'll be accidentally rammed and sunk by a container ship in the middle of the night. It's some consolation.

When I climb the interior stairs to the highest point of the ship, my breath clouds in front of my face.

'Right now people might be watching me, judging me, discussing my past,' Frannie says. 'Mum and Dad could be tuned in watching us talk right now. I never signed up for it. Even in Aristotle's day there was a clear distinction between private life and public life. I'm not one for public life. That isn't me. At school I never volunteered for anything that would mean I'd be in the limelight. No musicals or school plays. I'm a background person. A wallflower. I don't want to be talked about or analysed. I find the idea of a shoulder massage completely unbearable: the vulnerability, the exposure, the self-indulgence of it all. I can't help thinking this crosses a line. What'll be next? Disclosing medical data and bank account statements on television? We need privacy in order to thrive and feel secure. We require the concept of contractual consent in order to trust others. They're bedrocks of modern society. But, honestly, hearing the Admiral reveal our reality, I felt disbelief and relief all at the same time. Like, it doesn't make any sense but at least it makes more sense than it did before.' She shakes her head. 'I'm rambling. Lack of food making me talk nonsense.'

'I think I understand what you're saying. I thought this was some kind of administrative error at first, heads miscounted, checklists ignored, shortcuts taken, me – us – left behind. Then I didn't know what to think. At least seeing Lips – that's what I call her; I'm not sure she deserves the title of "Admiral" – means I haven't completely lost my mind. Almost, but not completely.'

The dogs' area is comparatively normal and untainted. Elsewhere on the ship there are toilet cubicles cordoned off with duct tape, smouldering fires on deck, collections of saucepans to catch rainfall, smashed jewellery shop displays, stacks of open suitcases.

We pass through a gate and enter the dog-walking zone. The safety barriers here run all the way down to the decking so small dogs can't accidentally fall eleven storeys to their certain deaths. We pass the twee ornamental lamp post complete with wraparound pee drain, and head into the kennel building. A large windowless room with chairs and tables for grooming.

Frannie approaches the door to the room where twelve dogs are kept in large crates.

Barking and yapping. The sound of claws scratching against metal.

She pushes the door open.

The largest dog bares its teeth, its hackles raised on its back, its tail in the air.

With a low voice Frannie commands the dog to sit but is keeps on snarling at us, drool falling from its teeth.

'It's all right,' she says to me. 'They're all in steel crates. We can let the others out and leave him inside his own cage. We can still feed him. Now it's raining we can refill his water jug.'

This pocket of wildness. I wonder if viewers see any parallels between the dogs and our pitiful quartet. The quiet one, the conniving one, the aggressive one, the leader.

'You open the other cages,' she says. 'Let out the smaller dogs but make sure you don't step too close to his door. The longer he stays locked up, the angrier he's getting. Dogs need to feel like they're part of a pack. They need affection and exercise. He's had none of that.'

The locked-up dog's eyes are blank. I can see his incisors as his lips retract and his growl is as deep in pitch as the ship's engines.

We take the other eleven dogs outside. A Labrador, a bulldog with a red collar, two boxers. There's a Border collie with a shiny coat. Two poodles and the rest are terriers, spaniels and mixes. They all wear collars. Frannie fetches two hair-covered tartan blankets that used to rest on the upholstered chairs and passes me one. I wrap myself in it and go outside. The wind almost pushes me back in and two of the dogs are shaking, either from fear or cold. We make sure they relieve themselves by the lamp post or imitation tree. And then we take them all back inside, away from the storm-force winds, and we fill up their bowls. Each dog has its own food stored in its own stainless steel locker. The water bowls track the roll of the ship, and I am mesmerised by the fluid motion. Their food is a mixture of kibble and meat from cans. In a perverse way it reminds me of the café. I'm usually most content mixing egg salad or coronation chicken behind the counter, watching as dozens of regular customers find comfort in our menu items. Reading or chatting, watching their phones, wearing headphones or working their way through a weekend newspaper. There's something safe about a well-organised café with patrons and content customers and steamy windows. Something beautiful about it.

'It's starting to stink in here,' says Frannie. 'The Caucasian Shepherd. I don't like him but I pity him, you know, sleeping in his own filth. I wish I could take him out for half an hour. A brisk walk around the running track and a game of catch.'

'You can't,' I say, firmly. 'I had a dog when I was little. Buster, his name was, nothing like that beast, just a spaniel cross, but he was an important part of the family. When I was eleven or so we found out he'd dug his way out of the back yard. Our neighbour screamed, we all heard it. But she hadn't been hurt; it was worse than that. She had an infant daughter. Our neighbour told Dad Buster had bitten her daughter on the leg. Nothing too deep, thank goodness, but teeth marks. One puncture wound. Little Emily needed a tetanus jab. What I'm saying is, we cannot risk that dog getting loose. It's aggressive, and none of us can stop an animal of that size. If someone's bitten, and the bite becomes infected, we can't access any of the ship's medicines.'

'Oh, but they'll help us out, though,' she says. 'The TV people, I mean. They have a duty of care, Caz, a strict code to abide by. We're on their ship so they'd give us emergency treatment if that happened. Wouldn't they?'

33

We say goodnight to the dogs. One terrier stares at me with deep brown eyes and he looks shaken. Pete and I have talked about adopting a similar dog one day. The thought of it weighs heavy in my chest. I try to comfort this little dog but it's clear he doesn't want me to leave. I don't know if it's the wind outside that's spooked him. Frannie and I take two black liners from a roll next to the dog waste bags and flea powder, and we wrap our heads against the rain and head out on to the stern deck.

Tremendous gusts now. A weather vane device attached to one of the funnels is spinning manically, and the ship rises and falls with each swell like a ride at a run-down amusement park.

We step inside and use monogrammed towels to wipe rain from our faces. Although the corridors and atria are dry and protected from wind, they are as cold as walk-in fridges.

'If we didn't have these dog rugs . . .' says Frannie.

In truth, my dog, Buster, never did bite the leg of our neighbour's daughter. I said that to warn Frannie from straying too close to the Caucasian Shepherd dog. I don't want her to pity him. In some circumstances a blatant lie can be justifiable. Buster never bit anyone. I found out the truth that night and I only told Mum what happened decades later, in the quiet, numb days after Dad's funeral. She wasn't as appalled as I'd thought she'd be. She and Gemma lived through it as I did, only they understood Dad better than I ever could. Mum because she grew up with him, together since they were sixteen, and Gem because she inherited more of his self-destructive impulses. Dad was visiting the fixed-odds betting machines on the high street back then. He'd visit them every day, superstitious about which machines to play in which order, about what he ate for breakfast, about the socks he wore that time he won a jackpot. He was obsessed with horses and greyhounds; I can still recall the names of distant racecourses and winners. I used to think they sounded so exotic. Aintree, Newmarket and Chepstow. Ascot and Kempton Park. Horses with names like Galileo, Kauto Star and American Pharoah. He didn't frequent casinos much at that point, but he did bet on illegal fights at the local boxing gym. Dad would insist on placing a wager on the gender of a newborn baby. He'd go from pub to pub and bet how many peanuts were in a bag. It was like eating for him. An autonomic action he had to perform each and every day. When I was eleven he sold our beloved family pet, a dog Gemma and I received as a joint birthday gift. Buster was always gentle around the neighbours' kids. Dad took him to the back door of our local pub, the Red Lion, and he sold him for twenty pounds cash to settle a football bet.

My sister still doesn't know to this day.

34

Frannie decides she wants to walk through the Ocean Lobby again. She wants to check the screen in case the Admiral came back, in case she has softened her stance, become more humane and granted us extra questions. I accompany her on this hopeless mission and there is a mixture of longing and dread in her eyes.

We pass through the Platinum Grill. Ornate. Lots of space between tables. I find the place Pete and I dined two nights ago and I can't catch my breath. The actual chair he sat in. I stroke the wood and run my hand over the cushioned seat. My chest swells. The time before. Back then the room was full and I took my safety and privacy for granted. I'd give anything for Pete to walk into this Grill room right now with his dimpled smile to tell me it's all over. I'd even welcome the small-minded couple back. I'd welcome them with open arms.

The Gold Grill restaurant below it is vast. Empty. Like a film set after hours. Corridors that should be teeming with passengers in tuxedos walking from their first sitting dinner to the theatre for a gala performance of *The Mikado*. Hundreds of people, new friendships forming and fracturing, affairs brewing, flirtation, the unpredictable effects of dry martinis, gimlets, manhattans and whisky sours, the thrill of a walk on deck during this tempest, or a nightcap in someone else's cabin. None of that.

Empty vestibules and faint echoes.

We pass beautiful mirrors framed by oak panels and I assume every one is a pair of eyes. Following us everywhere we go.

'If we went berserk, started attacking each other with steak knives, how quickly would they be able to intervene?' I ask. 'I mean, running a speedboat out to us would take too long, wouldn't it?'

She looks at me open-mouthed.

'It won't happen, Frannie. Just a hypothetical.'

'It's television,' she snaps. 'Lips said *broadcast*. So there are strict standards. I covered it in media studies A-level. Duty of care. Codified regulations and codes of best practice. I was thinking before, while I was feeding the little spaniel, the one with the limp: the media company who manages all this must offer us food at some point.' She smiles sweetly, nodding. 'They'll have to feed us, Caz.'

We reach the door of the Grill room.

'How can they control what we ask?' Frannie says.

'What do you mean?'

'It feels like school all over again. Putting up your hand to ask a question. Being selected, deemed worthy to speak. I loathe that Lips controls what we can ask her. That the screen turns off when she's done. It's one thing to limit what we're told, but quite another to curb our ability to ask questions. Makes my skin crawl, that kind of Orwellian oversight. Like we're meant to be seen and not heard.'

'Maybe we should call her Admiral when we chat. We don't want her to take against us.'

Frannie looks anxious.

We arrive in the Ocean Lobby and it appears almost normal except for the stack of unusable iPads and phones littering the floor, and the four chairs facing the TV screen. The piano is quiet and the Perspex box still sits where the ice sculpture once was.

'People adore their dogs,' she says, frowning. 'They grow attached to them. Like family members.'

I think back to Buster. To Dad's betrayal.

'What I can't quite comprehend,' says Frannie, 'is, if everyone else left this ship voluntarily, then how come they were happy to leave their pets behind? Daniel was right all along. My parents are dog people. It breaks their hearts if the dogs are left in a local kennel for a week when they travel. Mum fusses about them having the right food and she calls the kennel owner for updates. Something here doesn't add up. There's no way dog people would just abandon their pets.'

35

It's unsettling to look out hour after hour and not see anything.

I'll glance out of a window or stare at the horizon from the observation deck, the area housing spare propeller blades, and there is nothing to observe. Back home I can always see the Minster, the main church of the town, designed by George Gilbert Scott in the reign of Queen Victoria. It's grounding in a way: a kind of totem or anchor point. Here everything is blank and featureless and in constant motion.

It's not difficult to locate Daniel and Smith. Frannie and I follow the banging noises up to Deck Ten and then walk to the far end of the corridor. I check the deck map framed on the wall because I'm not familiar with this section of the ship, and I notice that the rooms are much larger here.

Smith's using the fire axe to hack away the last remnants of the door to Diamond-class Suite Seventeen. Next door, in Suite Sixteen, Daniel sits cross-legged on the threshold.

'We wanted to wait until you guys arrived before we went inside properly.'

'Two rooms?' I say. 'I thought we were going to have four, one each? It's not like there's a lack of empty cabins on the ship.'

Smith wipes his brow and says, 'You want to try breaking through a door with this axe, you be my guest. Anyway, I took the liberty of upgrading us. Daniel was Gold; Frannie and her parents were Gold Plus. You, Caz, were in Platinum with your boyfriend. John and I both had Diamond, but even we didn't have access to one of these. Now we've all been officially upgraded.'

I shake my head. 'The only thing I care about is—'

He raises his hand and says, 'Ladies and gentleman, please allow me to introduce you to Diamond-class Suite Seventeen.'

We follow him inside.

'According to *Cruise Ship Monthly*,' says Smith, enunciating his words, 'these duplex suites are considered to be *among the most luxurious floating accommodation ever conceived of*. Direct quote.'

The suite is impressive, if a little imposing for my tastes. A living room with plenty of polished wood trim, a downstairs cloakroom and shower room, a butler's pantry, a kitchen, a small dining room. There's a double-height section with sweeping staircase.

'There's actually an upstairs part?' Frannie asks.

Smith nods. 'That's what duplex means. I believe the word's derived from the Latin for *you can't afford it*.'

She ignores him and checks the sofa. She half-converts it to a bed and then lets it re-form into a sofa again. I walk upstairs and the others follow me. Small gym area, king-size bedroom, two bathrooms, two dressing rooms. With the double-height windows I have the sense that I'm not on a ship any more.

If only.

'I didn't even have a porthole,' says Daniel, smiling. 'Just a blank wall with a print of a seascape. Look at this place.'

'You gentlemen take this one,' I say. 'Frannie and I can have the other one.'

An hour later we've collected together our monogrammed blankets and whatever warm clothing we can find, and we've congregated in the guys' duplex.

'I don't like to sleep in my van when it drops much below zero but occasionally I have to,' says Daniel. 'Heating's challenging in a confined space. Propane and diesel heaters work, but if your ventilation is inadequate you'll die quietly in the night so I rely on passive insulation, trapping as much of my body heat as I can in my sleeping bag.'

'Sounds mighty unhygienic,' says Smith. 'And you give lectures on this?'

'I wish we had sleeping bags,' says Frannie.

'We have the room blankets from housekeeping plus the wool kennel blankets,' says Daniel. 'We have layers, that's the most vital thing. Fur and wool trap air. You guys ever camped out when it's really cold?'

Frannie and Smith shake their heads. I nod.

'I camp up in the Yorkshire moors when I can. Maybe four or five times each winter. I almost catch frostbite every time, but the sunrise views are worth it.'

'Do you camp with your sister?' asks Frannie.

'Not Gemma's cup of tea, camping. No, I do it on my own. That's the way I like it. I carry a heavy stick but I've never had trouble, I don't stray too close to civilisation. Lightweight tent, sleeping bag, couple of eggs, bacon, freshly baked bap from the café, gas stove, tea bags, milk and sugar. Paperback novel. A little whisky before I fall asleep. Best way to clear my head. I use that time to think things through, work out what's troubling me, keep the demons at bay.'

I haven't taken Pete yet; I'm not sure he'll be keen. Actually, that's a lie. He'd love to come but I need to protect this tradition for myself, keep a place and time to be selfish and deal with black thoughts, at least for a while longer.

'Daniel's right,' I say. 'We all need to cocoon ourselves properly tonight. Blankets under and over. Keep a hat on if you can and keep your body heat trapped inside.'

'We're trapped inside, all right,' says Smith. 'I have never felt so trapped in my entire life.'

Daniel interrupts him. 'Don't talk like that, Smith. I'm not good with confined spaces and you're not helping.'

'I'm sorry,' says Smith, his eyebrows high on his forehead. 'Genuinely, I am. I only meant this is some kind of dystopian prison. We're felons now?' He scratches his cheek so hard he leaves red marks. 'Incarcerated without trial or sustenance. What did I do to deserve this? Feels like I'm trapped in a game only nobody's thought to tell me the rules.'

36

When we finally say goodnight to the guys they're flipping a coin to see who'll have the bedroom and who'll take the sofa bed on the lower level. Smith's already raided the duplex bar and lined up Finnish vodka shots for them both. Daniel's been more focused on retrieving buckets of rainwater from the main deck.

'These are the clean, unused mixing bowls and saucepans, the ones we can drink straight from,' he says. 'We must not mix these up; it's very important. Rainwater in garbage cans and buckets needs to be boiled properly, for a few minutes at least, before it's safe to drink.'

Frannie and I visit a fresh suite of restrooms on the deck below, some old reflex causing us to go together. Or else it's apprehension and the desire for back-up. I'm disgusted at myself each time I leave a cubicle without flushing, but with no electrical power on an ocean liner there is no flushing. There's no vacuum suction. Each stall is single-use.

I know I shouldn't use our precious rainwater to clean myself but I need this if I'm to sleep tonight and it's too stormy to go out and visit the pool. The water drains into the basin and it is grey in colour, streaks of fine grit staining the porcelain like minuscule glacial moraine. I use a scavenged airline vanity pack toothbrush and paste, and sigh with pleasure. You take that everyday freshness for granted until it's ripped away from you. I'm still exhausted, but I feel a little more human than I did an hour ago.

I lift my shirt to wash my body and then stop dead. If I'm facing a mirror, that means cameras could be watching. Not in the restrooms, surely. They couldn't do that. They wouldn't be allowed. And then I remember popular reality shows from a decade ago where they installed cameras in bathrooms, in bedrooms, even in shower cubicles. Some of the cameras were night vision or infrared, capable of watching the housemates in darkness.

Slowly, I put my shirt back on properly. Would the others be as reserved? Would anyone on this ship do the opposite to gain attention?

Sleet accumulates on the duplex windows.

We have our room, at once luxurious and sparse, but we have no security. Being in what is essentially a hotel room with no lockable door feels horrendous. Imagine sleeping in a Hilton superior double open to the public corridor outside. You couldn't do it. We push tables and vases and chairs and a desk to cover the gap. That way, if someone tries to enter during the night, at least this should slow them down. We'd be able to hear them coming.

I'm not paranoid or overly safety-conscious; at least I don't think I am. But, like every woman I know, I've been followed down alleys, stared at in car parks, leered at on buses. Men have come over to sit next to me when all the other seats are unoccupied.

I offer Frannie the bed and I take the sofa. But just as my shivering subsides and I start to feel warmth under my blankets she appears like a sleepy child on the bottom step of the staircase and asks if I'll sleep with her upstairs. This hits me in the gut. In my dreamlike state I don't immediately recognise her as Frannie. I see her as what could have been.

'It's an enormous bed, there's enough room,' she says, walking down another step. 'I'm sorry, Caz. I just can't be up there all on my own.'

Wearily, I drag my blankets upstairs and wrap them around myself on the bed.

'I have so many questions for Lips,' she says, her voice soft and unsteady. 'Twenty questions.'

I don't say anything. I'm drifting off, exhausted, warmth spreading through my body.

'If this is a gameshow,' she says, her words vague, filtered through my tiredness, 'then will there be a reward? Lips said this could be the chance of a lifetime. So what do we stand to win?'

And as I close my eyes and slow my breathing, my last conscious thought isn't what we stand to win.

It's what we each stand to lose.

37

I wake up to sunshine streaming through the floor-to-ceiling windows. Dust particles floating in the middle distance, warmth returning. I look to my side and Frannie isn't there.

I sit bolt upright.

It's happening again.

Panic surging through me. I'm panting. Alone on this ship.

I leap out of bed and run downstairs.

Nobody.

'Frannie,' I say. 'Francine!'

The bathroom door opens and she's standing there casually brushing her teeth, her red hair framing her pale, delicate face, a blanket around her shoulders. 'What's wrong?'

'Nothing. I'm so sorry.'

She finishes brushing her teeth. 'You snore like a bison, Caz Ripley.'

'I do?'

'Some kind of primitive yak.'

I clear the corners of my eyes. 'I told you I should have stayed downstairs. Did you manage some sleep despite the snoring?'

She rinses her toothbrush and says, 'Once I stuffed my ears with cotton wool I slept like a baby.'

I stretch, calming down, my pulse settling. 'Me, too. But I'm starving now. I've never been able to feel this many ribs. When do you think will they open up the food stores?'

Frannie doesn't reply because my question is rhetorical and she understands that. We are not privy to information. We are drip-fed truths, and the next four will be granted to us at precisely six p.m.

'Look what I did,' she says, pointing.

I walk into the spacious shower room. 'You're a smart one. This is good. Taking back a little power for ourselves.'

She's covered most of the mirrors with taped newspaper. The fire alarm and sprinkler are taped. There's a headline, on the diagonal, about diesel prices, and another about the election. So many words to read, so much insight, whereas now, here, we have none. Frannie's covered every possible lens or aperture. Our bathroom might be the only private space on the whole ship.

'At least now we can put on our clothes in peace. Not have to watch our backs or change under a robe.'

'Thank you, Frannie.'

'I'm going to check on the other two. You take your time. Still no running water, but at least enjoy the privacy.'

She leaves and I check there are no uncovered sprinklers concealing wide-angle cameras. I prepare for the day as best as I can. I'd love a shower or a hot bath, the kind where your brain stem grows numb from the heat, where you're warmed to the core, but I'll settle for a dip and wash in the top deck pool. It's odd how quickly you miss the everyday routines, the ones that help make us all feel secure. Texting back and forth with Pete, checking the news app on my phone, having a mug of peppermint tea with Gem after we close up for the night. I miss my terraced house. Pete bringing home a takeaway and carefully placing out all the containers and setting the table. He insists on crockery and cutlery, which I think is ridiculous but I'm old enough to know when to pick my battles. I long for the sound of my neighbour's daughters playing video games too loud, too late, and the scent of my foaming supermarket lavender hand soap, the one I keep by the kitchen sink.

None of the switches in the room work. They've permitted us lighting but they turn each one on and off as they see fit. They do not allow us to operate stoves or televisions or computers. None of the sockets charge our useless phones or tablets. We've been thrown back to a different time, and the most alienating aspect is our lack of access to up-to-date information. I can visit the library and read old news, and there's merit to that, but I'm programmed to seek twenty-four-hour scrolling newsfeeds. I'm used to casually wondering about a subject and then searching it in an instant, mindlessly, on my phone. Being able to call my sister to ask her opinion or check a free GPS app if I'm lost. Finding out the time or the longest rail bridge in the world or trawling for an old email from Dad before he stepped out the door 'for a walk', and a drive to Humber Bridge, to 'clear his head'. And now I'm stuck here, with infinite questions and no outside help to answer them.

When I reach the breakwater at the front of the ship, the fire is glowing, a dining table spitting as it burns.

Frannie and Daniel sit together, close, drinking from expensive china cups and saucers. The contrast is jarring. If I squint, this could be a post-apocalyptic cave drawing. Dirty jeans and grease-stained shirts. I'm reminded of how Einstein is said to have remarked how World War Four will be fought with sticks and stones.

I announce my presence. 'Good morning.'

'Would you like coffee?' asks Daniel. 'I'm not ashamed to tell you I'm taking mine with six sugars now. We have no food but the sugar will keep us going.'

'Six sugars it is, then,' I say. 'Thank you.'

'You're welcome.'

'Let's hope our dentists aren't watching.'

'Oh, mine certainly will be,' he says. 'My overachieving brother will be tuned in. He'll be critiquing my every move.' He smiles to himself. 'I always craved a chance to prove myself to my parents, to show them I could do impressive things if they gave me a little more time. And now I'm here, wasting away on a deserted ship.'

He pours coffee from a saucepan that's keeping hot away from the flames, perched on the charred armrest from a recliner. He hands it to me. 'Strong and sweet,' he says. 'Hot, and slightly bitter.'

'Rather like myself,' says Frannie.

I laugh.

Frannie's face turns from mischievous to serious. She places her cup down on the deck.

'I think you should tell her now, Daniel. You have to tell her what you saw.'

38

The wind gusts and the flames flare and crackle, green and turquoise in among the warm tones, thick smoke blowing from port to starboard.

'What did you see?' I ask.

I move closer to the fire and hold out my hands. Goosebumps cover my forearms. The wind calms and the sky is birdless and matt grey.

Daniel takes another sip of coffee and says, 'We're down to the last mini bag of pretzels. I thought we'd finish it today and then beg Lips for rations. Or break into life rafts.'

'What did you see, Daniel?'

'It was earlier this morning. Smith was still fast asleep on the sofa bed. I didn't look through his bags or anything, I swear I didn't, I wouldn't, but I needed toothpaste, so I thought it would be best to check his bag of scavenged things rather than wake him up. He's a lot older than we are and he needs rest. He looked exhausted yesterday . . .'

'Tell her,' says Frannie, poking our fire with the blackened tip of a croupier's stick taken from a roulette table. Just the sight of it makes me uneasy.

He takes a deep breath. 'Family pack of Twinkies in Smith's bag.'

Suddenly my blood sugar plummets. Knowing there are snacks, food, *junk* food, quick calories, energy, delicious ready-to-eat items somewhere on board and one of us is hoarding them – the very thought makes me feel faint. 'How many?'

'Pack of twelve mini bars,' he says. 'He's eaten two.'

'The bastard.'

'I called him worse,' says Frannie. 'We could have had three each.'

'We still can,' says Daniel. 'We'll allow him one more and then we share the rest between us. It's the only way we can manage this fairly.'

'Did you confiscate them?' I ask.

He shakes his head. 'I thought about it. To be honest I even thought of eating my share in the bathroom the instant I spotted them, popping each from its wrapper and devouring them. But then I'd be just as culpable as him. Should we confront him, or retrieve them and leave him with one?'

We don't reply. The flames splutter as the gale intensifies, and heat reaches out to touch my dry cheeks.

'Morning,' says Smith, walking towards us in what looks like two or three white *Atlantica* robes. 'What's cooking for breakfast?'

39

He's wearing white *Atlantica* flip-flops scavenged from the gym.

'Sit down, Smith,' I say. 'We need to talk.'

He tightens the belt of his robe.

'What's your real name?' asks Frannie, hands on hips. 'I'm tired of calling you by your surname. If that even is your surname. We've all been straight with you. Anyone watching will understand your true identity by now. Your life history is probably printed in every major newspaper in the world, warts and all. Seriously, what's your name?'

'Seriously? It's Smith. It's what I choose to go by, and I'd appreciate it if you would respect my wishes.'

Frannie looks down at her boots and scoffs.

'We know about the Twinkies,' I say. 'Daniel saw them.'

'Anyone explained to you Santa Claus isn't real yet? Because that's going to be some let-down, let me tell you.'

'This is life and death, Smith,' I say, a little louder and angrier than I'd intended. 'You know how damn hungry we all are.'

He bites off a sliver of fingernail and throws it into the fire. 'We're on TV, right now, yes? They're not about to let us all starve to death on live television. That's a certainty. They've pushed the limits before: *Fear Factor*,

Big Brother, Survivor. They'll push us, agreed; they already have done. But there will be food, guys. This is more of a prolonged dietary fast, only it isn't managed by us. Sanitised entertainment to hold the attention of folks with nothing better to do, give them a half-hour of escape from the fact that they work two jobs just to pay rent on a damp two-bed condo and put their child, who never speaks to them, through grade school. They've strategised for eyeballs and ad revenue. Attention is their goal. They're not about to let any one of us perish.'

'Look at me,' I say. 'I don't care much for your theories right now. There are three people sitting round this fire with empty bellies and then there's you. Daniel said you have ten Twinkies left in the box. I hope you enjoyed the two you ate last night. I hope you savoured them while the three of us tried to sleep with our stomachs rumbling.'

He turns his back on us slightly. 'There aren't – well, there aren't ten left.'

Daniel stands up. I can see his arms tense.

'I had four for breakfast just now. There are six left and I'm willing to share some of them with you all even though strictly speaking it's my private food. I bought it, so I rightfully own it.'

Daniel steps closer to him and sets his jaw. I recognise this atmosphere from being outside pubs as they close. The electricity.

'Possession is still nine-tenths of the law, even out here.' Smith pivots, looking me in the face before moving his gaze back to Daniel. 'If you're going to hit me, get on with it. Otherwise sit down and let me explain some realities.'

Daniel retreats a few paces and Smith continues in a more soothing tone.

'I paid hard-earned dollars for a nine-hundred-square-foot cabin with multi-jet Jacuzzi tub. Paid for early embarkation and late disembarkation. All tips included. VIP excursions with our own deluxe tender. Paid for the finest food on the open sea. What a sick joke that turned out to be. Paid for butler service and premium liquor. I have a right to more than someone with a Gold-class ticket. I'm sorry, I know that's tough to hear, but it doesn't make it less true.'

'Just because you paid more, that doesn't mean you can expect better treatment now,' I say. 'This is a whole different world from before.'

'Again, with the greatest respect, Caz, I disagree. This is the same world it ever was; it just became a few shades darker. I paid; I have greater resources, so I am entitled to more benefits. That principle has stood since the dawn of mankind.'

'I'm going to collect the Twinkies now,' says Daniel, his voice almost robotic, as he leaves us.

Smith sighs. 'He might be younger than me, more physically capable, but something tells me he's never had a real confrontation in his life. Where I grew up there was no such thing as a clean fight. You get caught up in a Friday night altercation in my old neighbourhood, you finish it as quick and as brutal as you can manage. Escalation of violence. You have to take an eye, or a life, to save your own hide, you do it and then you learn to live with yourself, maybe in a different state. I made my peace with all that a lifetime ago.'

I miss birdsong.

Some days, when Mum doesn't remember who I am, or when my delivery team have their own marital or financial problems at home, or when I stumble upon an old betting slip hidden away in a shoebox or drawer, I'll jump in my Fiat and drive out to Sprotbrough Bridge. I'll park close to the Falls – nothing too spectacular or tourism-worthy, but I'll stop there and open all the windows and sit and listen to rushing water and birds in the surrounding trees. When I'm losing purchase on reality, starting to spin out of control, considering stupid shortcuts to pay back Dad's debt, those birds bring me back.

Despite all the posturing, Smith handed over the six remaining Twinkies without any drama. He didn't even attempt to hold one back for himself.

'Fair's fair,' he says afterwards. 'I could have been difficult, negotiated, but I see you three painfully hungry and I'll always try to help out a neighbour.'

'Don't you fucking dare,' says Daniel.

Smith moves closer to a CCTV camera, the kind shaped like the bottom half of a sphere attached to the underside of an awning, and he says, 'I hope you saw what happened just now: the full story, I mean. Sharing food is an age-old gesture of goodwill. Breaking bread together. These three are good people; I want you to know that. And now they've got the food I brought. I just try to do my best.'

We spend the day scavenging. Daniel and I look for food, breaking down doors to cabins and crew mess areas. We find enough to keep us going for another day or so. Sachets of Sweet'n'Low, tiny cartons of UHT milk, a bag of Tayto potato chips, a half-finished bottle of Mountain Dew.

Smith's been looking for anything we can fish with. He says he learnt how to hunt and forage from an Oklahoman gentleman his mother lived with briefly back on the trailer park. The man showed him how to snare rabbits and squirrels. How to shoot pigeons with an air rifle and white-tails with a .22. Smith says if he can rig up some line, a makeshift hook from the workshop or kitchen, some form of bait, he might be able to catch us a cold-water fish. The thought of it propels me through the day. Me, by the fire, tonight, cast-iron skillet resting over glowing embers, pan-frying four freshly caught sea bass or pollock. Taking the flaking flesh off the bone for the others. Eating them with Taytos. Fish and chips, *Atlantica*-style.

From four p.m. we let the fire die down. Frannie's paranoid that if we leave it unattended it'll rip through the whole ship and leave us bobbing around the middle of the ocean wearing lifejackets, sleek grey shadows beneath the waves, fins, Lips trying to communicate to us in a shipwreck down on the sea bed three thousand metres below.

There's a strange buzz of anticipation in the air tonight. We all know we'll have the chance to ask one question each, unless Lips has changed the rules, which is always a possibility. Strictly *one* question each. I've thought up a dozen and still can't choose between my top three. I must be strategic.

I wash my hair using tepid rainwater from a garbage can, warmed by the fire then taken to our private bathroom by way of a mop bucket. The shampoo smells expensive, and it probably is, coming from this class of cabin. I don't know if it's different from the normal shampoo from the room Pete and I shared or if it's just that everything else has turned rancid. The flower arrangements throughout the ship rot and wilt. They smell like roadkill. Make-up feels ridiculous in these circumstances but I catch Frannie applying lip-gloss. She looks anxious again. A little manic. We will be in public tonight, so perhaps that's it. We already are in the public gaze, I guess: a troupe of non-consenting marionettes. I step out into the main living area of our cabin and look around. Mirrors, plug sockets, light switches, TV sets. Cameras everywhere, monitoring our every move.

The only private spaces we have are inside our own minds. The thoughts we conceal from one another. From ourselves.

We step out into the corridor.

Daniel's washed and combed his hair, and Smith has moisturised the top of his head.

'Shall we?' he asks.

We start walking down towards the stairs and then Frannie turns to face a mirror, and, as if speaking to herself, she says, in very clear English, not much louder than a whisper, 'This is an appeal to any lawyer, human rights advocate or charity organisation. We have not consented to any part of this experience. I urge you to contact law enforcement. Talk to your local politicians. Call the authorities. Before this gets out of hand, you must intervene. Don't just sit and watch us. *Help us*.'

The mood in the Ocean Lobby is subdued after Francine's desperate plea to the cameras. I'm sitting with her by the black Steinway piano, and Daniel and Smith are playing catch with a tennis ball they found in a crew room.

'This will all be over soon, Frannie,' I say, with mock confidence. 'They'll supply us with food and water, and then before you know it we'll dock at the Brooklyn Cruise Terminal. That's the part we need to ready ourselves for. If this show has as many viewers as they're alluding to then we'll need to brace ourselves for the media storm. I don't like being on board the *Atlantica* but I'm almost as scared to set foot back on dry land.'

I haven't been scared since my schooldays, since the Watkins sisters made my life miserable. Their father was a butcher and Dad owed him money. They said they would keep the secret, promised me, and then they went and told everyone in our class. I went from a normal, relatively carefree girl, at least in school hours, to a timid shrew. Everyone was looking, whispering, pointing the finger. They'd leave coppers in my school bag. One time I was hit by a two-pence piece in the school yard. I hardened myself in those later years, in sixth form, and ever since.

You never forget.

'I'm going to check into a hotel at JFK and order room service and take a long, hot bath,' she says. 'No interviews. No press. I'll book a plane ticket home and go and stay with my parents, sleep in my old room, eat Mum's steak and ale pie, help Dad with his newspaper crosswords. Forget any of this ever happened.'

The distance between Daniel and Smith has widened. They're lobbing the ball as hard as they can and half the time they fail to catch it and it bounces off the walls or against a fine oil painting.

It's odd how quickly this kind of petty lawlessness becomes the norm.

By five to six we're all seated facing the TV. We're waiting for our measly, rationed contact with the outside world, discussing what questions we'll ask, making sure there will be no overlaps, to garner as much information from Lips as we possibly can.

But if they made me choose between answers and a dry sandwich I confess I'd take the sandwich. You're strong, until you're not.

'I could see myself doing a regional radio show,' says Smith, tennis ball tight in his fist. 'Always fancied hosting a live show each week, on sports and movie reviews, call-ins and the like.'

'I want to go back to normal,' says Frannie. 'My studies. My friends.'

Daniel says, 'You will. But I'm starting to realise that's not what I want.'

I frown at him.

'I've been dwelling on how, you know, selfish I've been these past years, doing whatever I wanted, not compromising, not showing up when people needed me. Justified it as me being an outdoorsman, a surf, mountain and lake guy, which wasn't difficult as all my buddies are pretty much the same. I'm someone who needs to be in nature, not tied down to mowing the same patch of grass every Saturday.'

'Everyone's different,' says Smith, some sympathy in his voice. 'Don't beat yourself up about it.'

'My daughter wishes she could see me more regularly, that's all I know. She wishes I'd pick her up from kindergarten. Do the everyday things like mail a letter with her or take her for strawberry ice-cream in the mall. I had my ears closed to all that because I wanted to live on my own terms, but in reality I've just been denying my only kid the simple things she wants. I need to make some major changes.'

Smith's expression morphs, as though he's questioning whether Daniel's epiphany is authentic, or performative.

Dad was pretty reliable when it came to showing up, I have to give him that: he was never an absentee parent. It's more that he quietly, cunningly, destroyed things. He was present, he picked me and Gemma up from school in the early years, he never missed a birthday or nativity play, but in many ways he represented a form of slow, insidious rot. Damaging us all gradually, all of the time; wearing away at Mum. She'd always made it clear how our birthday and Christmas presents – from Nan and Grandad, from uncles and aunts – how they were precious and how we had a responsibility to look after them because people had worked hard to earn that money. Grandad was a cab driver and Nan was a cleaner with a wicked sense of humour. Later on she was the most popular dinner lady at school. My uncle William was a scaffolder and could never stay with the same crew for more than a few years because he had a notoriously short temper. Aunt Joan was a factory worker, made components for vacuum cleaners in one of the largest factories around. Gemma and I would receive ten pounds for Christmas, sometimes fifteen. We'd keep it in our matching money boxes in the room we shared. Later on Mum opened accounts for us at the local building society and we each received a bank book. I'll never forget the books: they were blue faux leather and mine made me feel grown-up and responsible. I liked that. Gemma spent her money as it came in but I saved almost all of mine. Hundreds of pounds over the years. I thought maybe I'd use it to buy my first car when I was older. But when I reached the age of fifteen my account was emptied down to the last penny. Apparently, parents or guardians can do that. They can legally withdraw your money in one lump sum. About eight Christmases' worth. Eight birthdays. Odd jobs and babysitting money. All wasted on some miserable horse race in another county.

Daniel walks over to the mirrored wall and holds his palm up to the glass and whispers something. To himself, or to the cameras, I can't tell which.

The screen brightens slowly.

Lips appears.

42

'Good evening, passengers.'

We all say hello except Daniel, who just stares at the TV with his arms crossed tight over his chest.

'A beautiful day on the ocean,' she says, smiling brightly, her teeth perfectly straight. 'I hope you're all having a pleasant voyage. One safety notice before we begin: we ask that you do not start any fires in any other section of the RMS *Atlantica* besides the steel bow deck area you have already designated for the purpose. Fires are the nemesis of any seafaring vessel.'

My instinct is to ask what the penalty will be if we do start another fire. A fire to keep us alive. To cook on. But I hold back in case she counts that as my question.

'In the past twenty-four hours you have been mentioned in numerous parliaments and forums around the globe. You were featured on the front pages of national newspapers and have been the subject of debates in both the Oxford and Cambridge Union.'

We need basic food.

'Now,' says Lips, 'do any of you have any questions?'

Francine clears her throat.

'What is this show, Admiral?' And then, desperately, she adds, 'When can we leave? When can we eat?'

'Only one question per passenger per day, please,' says Lips. 'I'll take your first. What is this show? You are the four remaining passengers on board the RMS *Atlantica* bound for New York City, USA. For most of your time aboard, all you need do is sit back and enjoy your journey. Viewers watch the show. They gain a unique insight into what it's like to be a passenger on one of the world's finest ocean liners. By the time you see a coastline again one of you will be crowned victor. Isn't it just the most exciting thing?'

The room falls quiet.

Smith squeezes the tennis ball in his hand, his forearm tensing.

'I've seen shows like this,' says Daniel. 'What do we stand to win?'

'What do you stand to win? The winner of *Atlantica* will receive five million US dollars.' Her face is replaced for a split-second by an image of a cheque. 'The three runners-up will each receive smaller participation awards of fifty thousand US dollars.'

'*How* do we win?' I ask, and then, immediately, I feel cheap for my choice of question.

'How do you win? You will each be asked to complete one personal challenge. The challenge will test your wits, courage, intellect and stamina. If you fail, you will be eliminated from the competition. Elimination does not mean you leave the ship. You will essentially play on, enjoying life on the open sea, but you'll no longer be entitled to a participation award. If you successfully complete your challenge you will be eligible for the main prize, and as a minimum you'll go home with fifty thousand dollars. As it stands, you each have a one in four chance of leaving with the main prize. You each have a twenty-five per cent chance of taking away that life-changing sum.'

Lips smiles again.

Smith says, 'I don't understand anything. You mean to say . . .'

Lips says, 'Allow me to continue. If you prefer to leave the ship now, by your own volition, this is your unique opportunity to do so. This is your chance; just say the word and preparations will be made. Also, if you stay but feel unqualified to complete your personal challenge you may nominate one of your fellow ship-mates. This will not affect your eligibility for the prize or the participation award but it may adversely affect how viewers vote. Mr Smith, you may ask your question now.'

He needs to ask about food or drinking water. We agreed before that one of us must ask about food and water. If there's no food and water there's little point in talking about prizes or challenges.

Smith clears his throat. 'Are the winnings tax-free?'

Daniel covers his face with his hands and Lips says, 'I'm afraid you'll need to consult your financial advisors on that matter.'

I stand up and she commences talking again, taking me by surprise. I sit back down.

'The four challenges are: Air, Water, Body, and Mind. You each need to commit to a challenge this evening. We judge you've had sufficient time to become acquainted with each other, to understand personalities, strengths and weaknesses. You now have precisely one minute to agree among yourselves who will perform each challenge.'

A clock appears on the screen. Sixty seconds.

'Your time starts . . . now.'

43

'What was it again?' asks Smith. 'Mind, Body. Spirit . . .?'

'Mind, Body, Water, Air,' says Frannie. 'Some kind of mythological connection. Essential pagan symbolism. Elemental—'

'I think I'll leave the ship,' says Daniel, cutting her off. 'I really don't think I can . . .'

We all stare at him.

'Me too,' I say. 'I want to go home.'

'Good decisions, to be honest,' says Smith, grinning. 'Both of you. Bravo, very smart.'

Frannie scowls at him.

'I think you should both take some time to consider this,' she says, looking at us in turn. 'I can't stay here alone with . . . I mean, let's stay together a little longer at least. We're just starting.'

'We're running out of time, people,' says Smith. He looks at Frannie and says, 'Fifty-fifty for the big prize, kid. I really thought . . .'

He doesn't finish his sentence.

Daniel looks torn.

I try to imagine what Pete would do in this situation.

'I guess I don't have much choice,' says Daniel. 'Frannie, I'm not leaving you here. We'll stay on together for a while.'

Smith rolls his eyes.

'Who's strongest?' says Daniel. 'They should do the Body challenge.'

'Perhaps it's not that literal?' I say. 'Maybe it is. I don't know, I can't think straight, I'm so famished.'

Should I stay with them? My head is screaming for me to accept the chance to get away from this ship but my heart isn't so sure. The three of them look strangely vulnerable now when I look at them. Gemma will be able to hold things together a little longer, surely. I need to trust her with that. And then there's the prize money. I could pay back the debt in full. I could wipe the slate clean and buy Mum some peace at last, some respectability, before it's too late.

'I'll stay a while longer and help, of course I will. We'll need to work more like a team from now on. For the challenges, Frannie is the quickest, I'm probably the most stubborn, you're strongest, Daniel.'

'Twenty seconds,' says Lips.

'The very thought of Air makes me uncomfortable,' says Daniel. 'Like I might suffocate in a small space. I think it's best if I do Body. Is that OK with you all?'

'I can't do Water,' says Frannie. 'I'll do Mind or Air. I'm terrified of the water. Can't swim well. I panic.'

'I'll do Water, then,' I say. 'I'm scared of heights and Air might mean heights. But I'm OK at surface swimming.'

'Ten seconds,' says Lips.

Smith looks at Frannie and says, 'You want Air or Mind?'

'I guess I'll do Mind?' she says. 'I used to play chess at county level. I'm studying for my degree right now, and—'

'What does *Air* even mean?' asks Smith. 'Flying?'

'Time's up,' says Lips.

'Daniel will do Body,' says Smith. 'Caz decided she'll do Water. I'll do Mind and Frannie here will do Air.'

'Very well,' says Lips.

'No, I said I'd do Mind,' says Frannie, her finger in the air. 'We agreed. I'll do—'

'Street smarts,' says Smith, tapping his head. 'No offence, Francine, I'm sure you'll ace your book studies, philosophy and all, but this is a game of chance on an abandoned cruise ship. I believe I'm better qualified.'

Have I made a terrible mistake? No, I can still leave at any time. I'm a law-abiding, tax-paying adult. Nobody can force me to stay; it just seems that way.

'The challenges are set,' says Lips. 'When, at any time of day or night, you hear the *Atlantica*'s foghorn sound, you'll be expected to congregate at this location no matter what you might already be doing. You will be given ten minutes. If you are not here ten minutes after the horn blows you will automatically be disqualified and therefore rendered ineligible as winner or participant.' She purses her lips for a moment. 'Good evening, passengers. I wish you all fair winds and calm seas.'

The screen goes blank.

44

I had a boyfriend in my thirties who'd present me with limited choices. For months he'd offer me a choice between two restaurants, or three movies. Mike was a plumber with three men working for him. He was intelligent and he made me laugh. It took me a while to realise he was manoeuvring me, granting me a strange kind of superficial autonomy, always on his terms. He set the parameters and he cunningly controlled everything we did together.

So I left him.

'Air?' says Frannie, as we exit the Ocean Lobby and walk back to our cabins. 'What do you think *Air* means? Holding my breath for a minute? I wouldn't like to hold my breath for too long. What if I'm trapped in a small room with no air, like, buried, or in a sealed cabinet? Caz, I'd like to swap if that's OK. I'm scared of hearing that foghorn now.'

I loop my arm in hers and say, 'It could just be catching tennis balls thrown to you on the deck. Could be birdwatching when we're closer to shore. Don't panic before we know the facts.'

I'm saying this because it's true but also, like Frannie, I'm anxious about not being able to breathe freely. Air is not the challenge for me. But I meant what I said. I'm not being completely disingenuous. Logically the challenges could mean a thousand different things. We just don't know.

When Dad was working through his twelve-step programme, one of the things he reiterated was learning to live a new life with a fresh code of behaviour. He never managed to stick to his, but back then I pledged not to leave anyone alone. It was an unspoken pledge. Dad said he'd felt alone his whole life. Battling with his addiction, and failing, all on his own. I decided I wouldn't leave Gemma alone with her battles, and I never did. I promised not to leave anyone in need alone with their demons. Frannie, Smith, Daniel and I entered this together. We have muddled through each strange day as a team. I can't abandon them at the first easy opportunity. My father broke his pledge and then he shattered it into a thousand tiny pieces.

I will not do the same.

Smith stops walking. 'Do you have any idea how much money they'll be making out of us? Five million sounds good when you hear the number but we'll need to halve that after tax and expenses. A media company streaming to millions of pay-per-view subscribers, if the show blows up and becomes popular – merchandising agreements, ad revenue, product tie-ins – will stand to make a fortune. A genuine fortune. I knew a talent agent once, nephew of a client, and he gave me an insight into that world. The people behind this reality show could be making tens of millions of dollars. More, if they syndicate. And they generate that from the comfort of their beachfront houses in Malibu and hilltop mansions in Hollywood. We're literally starving with no clean water and they're making all the real money.'

'We're in it now,' says Daniel, walking away. 'It's not like we had much choice.'

'We can still leave,' I suggest. 'They gave us that one chance, but they can't keep us here against our will. It just seems that way. Their control is an illusion. It requires us to play along. We could all leave together.'

They don't look convinced.

'Reminds me of the old gladiator battles,' says Smith. 'Ancient Rome. The Colosseum. Augustus, Nero, Caligula, Hadrian. Peasants fighting each other to the death for the titillation and viewing pleasure of the élites.'

'Bread and circuses,' says Frannie.

'Bread?' says Smith. 'I'd swap any one of these watches for a single slice of stale white bread.'

'*Panem et circenses*,' says Frannie. 'Superficial appeasement of the people. Credited to Juvenal, I believe, a Roman poet born after Christ's time. It means the powerful remain powerful by way of distraction and cheap satisfaction of the most base and immediate needs of the masses. No need for meaning or civic involvement. Give them cheap bread and entertaining circuses, or in this case, a sadistic show set on an ocean liner, and said masses will remain distracted, quiet, and docile. The powerful stay powerful and the others stay – well, the others.'

'Look who swallowed a history book,' says Smith.

'We're not fighting each other, though,' I say. 'Not like a gladiator battle in an amphitheatre. This is just a show, remember that. There will be no fighting. They vote, we leave, and life goes on.'

There's no conviction in my voice because I cannot be sure that life will go on as it did before, and I cannot be sure we won't be forced to compete with each other. The format of this experience is so different from anything I've come across. I'm used to being able to recite pasta and dairy re-orders off the top of my head, juggle staff shifts, develop new recipes, and I have our team holiday chart saved to memory. But here I can't even predict what the next hour will look like.

'I'm not sure,' says Daniel. 'A format like this will only work if there is escalation. Sure, Bob in Montana was thrilled when he first watched a bunch of nobodies confused on an empty ocean liner, scavenging in the dark, arguing over Twinkie bars and setting fire to the steel deck. But that won't keep Bob from turning over to ESPN and reruns of *Cheers* for long, now, will it? Bob in Montana needs sex or violence to keep him from switching channels.'

'Well, they won't get either on this show,' says Frannie. 'Bob's going to be mightily disappointed.'

'Whoever pays Lips's wages won't let that happen to Bob,' says Smith, a serious expression on his face. 'Mark my words.'

Frannie and I open the door to our duplex.

Smith and Daniel open the door to theirs.

And then the foghorn blows.

45

Panic in the air.

'What does that mean?' asks Frannie. 'A challenge? Not already, surely?'

'Didn't even let us eat dinner first, did they?' asks Smith. 'Not that there is any.'

Daniel looks dour.

This is like school PE all over again. Picking teams, the domineering master, being thrown out of your comfort zone, not knowing what's coming next. Back then I forged notes from Mum. Here, there's nowhere to hide.

'First challenge,' I say to Frannie, forcing perkiness into my voice. 'Don't worry; it might not be that bad.'

We walk back to the Ocean Lobby in silence. Nobody utters a word but we must all be thinking the same thing. Mind, Body, Air, Water. What order will they come in? How difficult? We retrace our steps. If someone loses a challenge they'll be forced to remain on board even though they won't be eligible for a penny. If anything will stir division and resentment, it will be that.

'Quite the gamble,' says Daniel.

I tense up.

I wait a few seconds and then I ask, in a casual tone, 'What do you mean?'

'Choosing people for challenges before we know what the challenges consist of. Listening to Lips. Trusting what she chooses to tell us. You and I gambled when we decided to stay on board, after she gave us the chance to leave. We're gambling for the unknown.'

'I'm not gambling, though,' I say, trying to keep my voice even. 'This is not a gamble for me. I just want to go back to my family.'

'But if that were really true you'd be on your way home by now. Think about it.'

I bite my tongue and keep on walking.

I won't leave Frannie. And I might be able to pay off Dad's debt if I stay. They're moral reasons to stay here. The ends might just justify the means.

'I suggest we agree that whoever wins the main prize splits it with the other three,' says Frannie. 'I'd like enough for my father to fix his business and stop working. If we split it equally that'll be well over a million each. No friction, no competition. We make a collective pact, a community decision. That way we win and Lips loses.'

'I like that,' I say, nodding. 'Then there's no gamble.'

'First of all,' says Smith, clinging to the handrail of the staircase as we descend back to the lobby, 'you're not taking into account tax, Frannie, because, with all due respect, you probably haven't paid any yet. Less than a million each, it'll be. Significantly less. Then you factor in charges from advisors, admin fees, exchange rates, bank charges, accounting costs. It isn't that much money. Let's say you clear seven hundred thousand. In pounds that's more like half a million. Divide that by years left – for you that's likely to be over fifty – and you'll receive less than ten thousand a year, not counting what you generously gift your father. And that's ignoring the most insidious tax of all: inflation. It's not that much money when you break it down.'

'So, you want to win it all? You don't care about us?'

'I think they've engineered a fair game,' he says. 'We all have an equal chance.'

'I don't know if I'll manage it, but if I make it to the end I'll try to build a place,' says Daniel. 'Read about it in a water sports magazine one time, a park in Norway, I think, a little island camp in an archipelago. They taught blind kids how to sail dinghies. Long summer camps with singing and cookouts and sailing instruction, all the commands by loudhailer. It struck me hard because Mom lost most of her sight when I was in fifth grade. It would be good for those kids to experience the exhilaration of sailing and kayaking. Those activities helped me so much when I was confused, growing up awkward in the shadow of my brother, and I think they could help them. I won't be able to afford an island or anything, but maybe an old gravel pit or rural lake, do some of the landscaping myself with an earth-mover. The place in Norway was peaceful. I'd like to bring something similar to the US.'

'I see what you did there,' says Smith, winking. 'And I admire you for it. No doubt right now you've garnered the admiration of everyone watching. I'm impressed, I really am. But I'm living in the real world, Danny. I'm sorry, but I'm not sure how your worthy waterpark dream fits in with the slightly more suburban plans you outlined to me earlier.'

Daniel looks puzzled.

'To acquire a large family house and a Porsche.'

'Sorry?' says Daniel, his face hardening.

Smith turns to a CCTV camera and looks up and says, 'I'm sorry if this shatters any illusions, but he mentioned a six-bed home, room for his fiancée and daughter, and a Porsche. No shame in that. A 911 Targa, I think he said. I don't know much about these things.'

Daniel walks off.

'We need to hurry up,' says Frannie. 'Lips said we have ten minutes. Caz, you really think we should split it?'

'I'm not sure,' I say, telling the truth in spite of myself. Considering what Smith said about deductions and expenses, I'd need more than a quarter to pay the whole debt. 'This isn't gambling, though, I know that much. No form of gambling I've ever heard of. If I won I'd help you three out as much as I could, you have my word. Main thing is my dad left a shadow that hangs over our family. I've paid off some over the years, and that hasn't been easy. In fact, this is the first foreign holiday I've ever had.'

I laugh out loud at my own words, I can't help it. *Holiday.*

'Some luck,' says Smith.

'If I pay off his debt it'll make a difference to a lot of innocent people. But also, selfishly, I feel like my dad might rest in peace if I fix some of the damage. He can release himself from all the guilt, all the bad feelings, as strange as that sounds. And then my family can move on.'

Daniel walks back to us and says, 'I'm losing balance. I've never been this hungry in my damn life.'

We head into the Ocean Lobby and it's right in front of us. *Do Not Open The Box.*

The TV brightens.

There's one word on the screen.

MIND.

46

Too much adrenaline can weaken you.

It can push you to meet a challenge, but a surge has the potential to cause heart damage and sleep problems. I remember reading about the symptoms after receiving Mum's diagnosis, sitting in a waiting room searching desperately for answers on my phone. Like any relative in that moment, I went down rabbit holes and dead ends, seeking answers. Adrenaline can actually be dangerous.

'I'm up,' says Smith. 'Mind.'

Frannie looks at him. 'It's what you wanted.'

The lips appear on screen. She's not in the exact same position as before because I can see a scar on her upper lip. A mark from an old piercing. Suddenly, in this light, she seems human and flawed. Perhaps we can reason with her.

'Welcome, passengers. Your first challenge is Mind. Mr Smith, this will be your personal challenge. In a moment I'll ask you to make your way to the ship's library. You will then be locked inside for the duration, and you will need to ascertain the rules and goals of the challenge for yourself. You will follow any safety instructions and directions given. This will be a solo challenge but your fellow passengers will be free to view and hear from the adjacent chess and backgammon room. I wish you all fair winds and calm seas.'

'The library,' says Smith. 'The damn library? I guess they want to make a fool of me on national TV, make me a laughing stock so I lose votes. *Look, he doesn't even know the classics; he never read any important books.* Maybe I should give up now.'

We try to reassure him and then we walk in single file to the rear of the ship. Through the Gold and Platinum Grills, and on to the Diamond Grill.

I do not like not knowing what to expect.

We reach the doors of the library. Literary quotes are engraved into plaques on the walls.

'You don't have to do it if you don't want to,' says Daniel.

Smith turns to us. 'Wish me luck. And don't jeer at me if I mess it up. I never had much education.'

He walks inside and we hear a *click* as the frosted glass door locks behind him. We go into the chess and back-gammon room. Green felt tables and chequerboards. The wall dividing us from Smith is clear glass. There's a TV in the corner and it's showing us a close-up of his face.

'Timer, I see a sand timer,' he says, his words piped to us through speakers. We talk back, but it's clear he cannot hear a word we say.

'OK, I have a puzzle here on the table. Some kind of crossword, I think. Bunch of words with no letters. Let's see. Six words. Oh, there's one letter here, there's an X near the end. Last word. What does this mean? Six words. How am I supposed to figure this out?'

He walks around the bookshelves. There are over eight thousand volumes on board ranging from travel books to romance to literary fiction to young adult to crime to biographies. Mahogany cabinets inlaid with marble. All of them tastefully lit.

'Can you guys see the crossword?' asks Daniel.

'I see the table,' says Frannie. 'But it's too far away.'

'*Mark my words*,' says Smith, questioning, inspecting the top chamber of the sand timer. 'It says *mark my words* on this timer. Is that a threat? *Mark my words*. Am I looking for a book written by an author called Mark? Mark Twain?'

The black volcanic sand of the timer drains through into the lower half. I'd estimate he has an hour or less to complete this challenge. I would not want to share this ship with a man like Smith if he loses and no longer cares about the public's view of him. If he's ineligible for the prize, it will make things so much worse for the rest of us.

'Bookmarks,' says Frannie, whispering. Then she turns and says to us, '*Mark my words* means bookmarks.'

Daniel nods.

Frannie bangs her fists on the glass wall and screams, 'Look for bookmarks,' but Smith doesn't hear us. The ship is well-known for its soundproofing. They make a point of mentioning it in the brochures and on the website. Each cabin and each entertainment zone is isolated from the next.

Your peace, quiet and wellbeing are guaranteed aboard the RMS Atlantica.

The crew of the RMS Atlantica *wish you fair winds and calm seas.*

Smith runs around the bookshelves looking increasingly frustrated. He opens a case and the camera zooms into the label. *Business and self-help.* He pulls out books and then, seemingly not finding whatever he's looking for, he drops them and runs over to the computers. They're not operational. He opens the Young Adult cabinet and looks over the novels. He pulls out one copy and then places it back. Then he exclaims, 'Ah,' and picks out another book. The camera zooms in. On the screen I can see it's a paperback copy of *The Hate U Give* by Angie Thomas. Complete with its very own bookmark.

47

The bookmark discovery gives Smith extra energy. He looks hopeful all of a sudden, dashing from case to case, discarding books and pulling out anything with a bookmark. One book lies damaged on the carpeted floor and I see Frannie wince when she notices it. He checks the sand timer and I'd estimate he still has two-thirds of the black grains left in the upper chamber.

We offer encouragement through the glass but not only is it soundproof, it's also one-way. It probably looks like a large mirror to him.

Within ten minutes there are stacks of books piled haphazardly on the table next to the crossword puzzle. Large tomes and slender paperbacks. Non-fiction, epic fantasies and hardback thrillers with sprayed edges.

'What now?' we hear him say. 'I can't work through all these. I'm not much of a reader.' He picks up a book and flicks through it. 'Where's the clue? How do I complete a crossword with no clues?'

I yell, 'What do the bookmarks say?' but my words bounce back off the glass and settle on the floor.

He flicks through the pages of each book, panting. The location of the bookmark in each is seemingly random. Some on blank pages, others on pages of dense text.

From the screen we can ascertain that each bookmark is printed with an image of a brain, but nothing else.

'Shit,' he says, and then he looks up at a camera in the corner of the room and he says, meekly, 'I'm sorry. I apologise.'

The confidence seems to be draining away from him with each passing minute.

He starts to read out the titles of books containing bookmarks. He reads them as if they'll answer the riddle for him. '*The Hate U Give. Eileen* by Ottessa Moshfegh. *Invisible Girl* by Lisa Jewell. *One by One* by Ruth Ware. *Grown Ups* by Marian Keyes.' He's shaking his head in frustration. '*Rattle* by Fiona Cummins. OK, I admit it; I haven't read all these books. I haven't read much since school if I'm honest. I'm not much of a reader.' He carries on. 'I'm more of a TV guy. *Harbour Street* by Ann Cleeves, *The Whisper Man* by Alex North, *Coronado* by Denis Lehane, *Smoke and Ashes* by Abir Mukherjee. What am I looking for here? *Hell's Bells* by John Connolly, *Kitchen Confidential* by Anthony Bourdain. I think I watched that one on cable. I liked that guy. *I Capture the Castle* by Dodie Smith. *Heaven, my Home* by Attica Locke.'

'He has no idea,' I say.

I, also, have no idea.

'The X,' he mutters. 'X marks the spot, right? That's my clue. Six words, sixth word. God, I never finished a crossword in my whole life. Six words. It's not my fault; books and school just aren't my world. Last word has an X in it. Is this what they call a cryptic crossword puzzle? The word is six letters long, X is the fifth letter.' He scratches his head. 'Focus on that. Screen out the rest. Six letters.'

He dashes off to collect a dictionary from the non-fiction section but then he discards it.

I have to stop myself from biting my fingernails.

'There can't be that many words with an X in that position,' says Frannie.

Daniel whispers to himself, 'Laxative, spandex, Felix, exactly, mixture, toxic . . .'

Smith dashes over to the timer and it's half-empty at this point.

'I knew I should have done Air. Crossword puzzles at my age – the nerve.' He looks up at the camera again, sweat glistening on his head. 'You know how much I paid for my ticket? Diamond class. Booked and paid for through Blue Horizons Travel Agency in Wilmington, North Carolina.'

Frannie's counting on her fingers.

'What is it?' I say.

She whispers to herself and then she says, 'Galaxy?' She looks at me, and then at Daniel and says, 'Could be galaxy.'

We scream *galaxy* at the glass, hoping the combined volume will penetrate, but he doesn't notice.

Daniel counts on his fingers. 'It's *The Hitchhiker's Guide to the Galaxy*,' he says, flatly, counting the letters out again. 'It fits.' But he sounds small. Defeated. 'It was written by Douglas Adams. One of my dad's favourite books when I was growing up. I remember him laughing as he read it on a beach in Florida. I borrowed it when I was in high school and it's completely brilliant. Hilarious. And he has no chance of getting it right.'

'Well done,' says Frannie, her voice as flat as Daniel's. 'You did it.'

'For all the good it will do.'

After yelling and cursing for what seems like an hour, Smith works out the word and says, 'Galaxy?' Then he says, 'Some kind of poem or phrase ending with galaxy?'

He looks over at the pile of books on the table.

The camera zooms in on his eyes.

And I see something click.

48

He counts the books. There are twenty-nine in total. He counts the missing letters in the puzzle. There are twenty-nine. Thirty letters in total including the X.

'He's figured something out,' says Daniel.

The room darkens as a cloud moves in front of the sun.

'One clue in each one of these bookmarked books,' says Smith. 'Each book leads me to one letter or number. I have an X. I have Galaxy.'

We observe as he finds books with titles that start with the letters that make up *Galaxy*. This must be how it feels for viewers at home. We know the answer and he doesn't and that anticipation, that sense of being complicit, on the inside, is intoxicating.

Smith's smarter than I gave him credit for. He lays out the books. *Grown Ups*. Then *Americanah* by Chimamanda Ngozi Adichie. So that's a G then an A. *Last Victim of the Monsoon Express* by Vaseem Khan. *An American Marriage* by Tayari Jones. Then the X, and then *Your House Will Pay* by Steph Cha.

'I got it. Galaxy. There, I knew it. Five books plus the X.'

He starts laying out the other books on the patterned carpet.

'So . . . what do I do now? What comes next?'

The camera zooms in on the timer.

'Oh, wait,' says Frannie.

There's a pinhole in the exterior of the upper chamber. Not only is black sand leaking into the lower chamber, it's also pouring down the outside of the glass.

The game is rigged.

He's running out of time.

49

Smith doesn't notice. If he saw the sand timer I think he'd quit on the spot. Instead he diligently rearranges books. After five minutes or so he has the two '*the*' words made up from *The Demands* by Mark Billingham, *Home* by Toni Morrison, *Educated* by Tara Westover, *Transcendent Kingdom* by Yaa Gyasi, *Hearts in Atlantis* by Stephen King and *Exit Music* by Ian Rankin.

He's feeling the pressure, wet patches under his arms, but he's managing.

The camera zooms in on the sweat beading at his hairline and, again, the sensation of knowing about the sand drama when he doesn't is a powerful one. I feel dirty acknowledging it.

He forms '*Guide*' from *Gone Girl* by Gillian Flynn, *Under the Net* by Iris Murdoch, *Insidious Intent* by Val McDermid, *Deception* by Denise Mina, and *Echo Park* by Michael Connelly. And then, before he completes the word '*Hitchhikers*', he yells, '*The Hitchhikers Guide to the Galaxy*. I got it. Let me out. I'm done. Get me out of here.'

But nothing happens.

He checks the timer and frowns and runs to it and lets the black grains of sand run over his hands. He swallows hard and locates the actual book: Douglas Adams's comedic science fiction masterpiece.

I'm anxious for him. I have a bad feeling about this.

He runs back to the table to complete the riddle.

'What more do you need me to do? I solved it.' He grimaces, looks around for answers. 'How much time do I have?'

He flicks through the pages. 'Why did they put me in a goddamn library? Evil swines. How did they know? There's no need to humiliate me. What did I do to deserve this?'

'Something from the story,' says Daniel, rubbing his forehead. 'I can't remember. It's been so long. There was a key question in the book, in the story. It's well-known. A number.'

Smith murmurs to himself, mumbling words from random pages. He reads and he reads, the sand almost completely gone. This is taking too long. He flicks through pages and runs his finger down text, dismissing it, growing more agitated. Only a few grains of sand remain. And then he focuses in one section and follows the line with his fingertip. He looks over at the timer. He reads the passage again and then he stands up and yells, 'Forty-two. The answer is forty-two.'

An audible click as the door to the library unlocks.

Smith closes his eyes and exhales with relief.

Lips appears on TV screens and computer screens throughout the library. A hundred sets of red lips.

She says, 'Congratulations, Mr Smith. You successfully completed the Mind challenge. Follow your answer and the fruits of your labour will be plenty. I wish you fair winds and calm seas.'

The screens turn off.

50

This is the first time I've understood the impact of a show like this. It's not the monetary prize or the scale of the ship or the manipulative games that are addictive for viewers; rather it's the strong psychological impulse, rooted in childhood, to be in on a secret.

Our door opens.

We run out to congratulate Smith.

'You did it,' I say, patting him on the shoulder. 'Well done. You were so clever in there.'

'It wasn't that difficult,' he says, in disbelief, wiping sweat from his forehead. 'I found all the books. I cracked the code.'

'Forty-two,' says Daniel. 'She said to follow the answer. You think that's Cabin Forty-two?'

We pace to the end of the corridor, Frannie and Smith discussing the books and how we'd also come to the answer but couldn't communicate it through the glass wall.

'I don't think there is a Cabin Forty-two,' says Daniel, scanning the deck plans.

After an hour of searching we locate Maintenance Room Forty-two, deep in the belly of the ship.

Smith tries the door.

It creaks open.

Vacuum cleaners and cleaning carts. A wall of tools and containers of various sizes.

In the centre of the room are six cardboard boxes. One of them sits directly beneath a printer on a shelf. Each box has a letter painted on it. S, D, F, C, P, L.

'Can we open the archive boxes?' asks Francine. 'The plastic one in the lobby clearly says *do not open*. Can we open these, you think?'

Daniel approaches a box and says, 'No instructions not to open. There are four here with our initials. These must be the rewards for cracking the code.'

'You're all very welcome,' says Smith, breaking into his box like a child on Christmas morning.

I start to open mine carefully and Smith says, 'Just a bunch of papers in this one. Paperwork from a printer.' He looks up at the smoke alarm sensor on the ceiling and says, 'Do we look like we can live off paper?' The words spit out of his mouth. 'I'm starving down here.'

'Mine has food,' says Frannie. 'Olives, lemons—'

'It's not *yours*,' says Smith, rushing over to her cardboard box. 'It's mine, technically, as I won the challenge.' His face is red again. 'I'll decide which box I take after we open them all.'

'But my name's on it,' she says. 'It says F for Francine.'

'I have a fishing net,' says Daniel, holding up white webbing. 'This is very good news. But can I fish off a ship like this? At this speed?'

'Give a man a fish,' says Frannie. 'But give him a net . . .'

'Can *we* fish, you mean,' says Smith, standing straighter, stretching his stiff back. 'Assuming I let you borrow my net. Forty-two: let's not forget how we won all this. *The Hitchhiker's Guide*. All the bookmarks. Do not forget how this happened. What do you have, Caroline?'

I sort through the bottles.

'Water. Six small bottles. And tonic water. Again, six small bottles. Why don't they allow us to drink properly? Why are they playing these cruel games when we have a massive desalination plant, and the food stores are packed to the rafters on Deck Two?'

'Olives and lemons and tonic, ladies and gentlemen ,' says Smith, gathering the items together into one box. 'I'd say they want us to hit the bar to congratulate me on my victory. Not only am I still in this fine contest but now we can drink like kings. Gin and tonics all round.'

We take stock of the other two boxes, one with six pairs of wool socks and one with six red fire blankets, and forage the room for anything else we can use.

The printer is dead. Unresponsive. No power.

I spot Smith leafing through the papers from his box.

'What are they?' I ask.

He doesn't answer for a moment. He's engrossed. Frowning. 'Photographs,' he says, finally, his eyes scanning the papers, widening. 'Printed pages as well, but look, I think these are photos from the night everyone disappeared.'

51

We begin with four vodka tonics in the Cape Cod Lounge, each one with a slice of fresh lemon.

'Don't touch the photos, just the edges,' says Smith, as he passes the photographs around as though they're his own family portraits, his own precious possessions. 'Be careful.'

Frannie glowers at him.

'They might be used in evidence one day,' he says.

That makes me pause and think.

Evidence.

We take turns to look through them. Fourteen in all. I'm already tipsy from drinking vodka on an empty stomach. The grainy, long-distance telephoto images look like Polaroids. Photos of hundreds of people disembarking the *Atlantica* in the middle of the night. No moon in the sky, just a trail of passengers, some with no luggage, each an ant from a disturbed colony.

'I can't make out that sign,' says Daniel. 'Frannie, your eyes are better than mine. What does that say? Harbour, or something?'

Frannie steps behind the bar and brings back a tumbler. She places the glass over the image and the sign comes into focus.

She takes a moment and then looks up at us. 'Cork International Cruise Ship Terminal.'

Daniel nods. 'They all left at Cork in the early hours and then the ship carried on with only us four on board. This is starting to make sense.'

'Sixteen passengers,' I say. 'If we include the dogs.'

'That reminds me: I need to feed and walk them,' says Frannie. 'Someone else come with me, please. I don't like being close to that one dog on my own. Especially at night.'

Smith goes with her this time. His mood has lifted since winning his challenge, since finishing his drink.

'Do you recognise your partner in the photo?' asks Daniel, when we're alone.

This is the first time anyone on board has referred to Pete as my *partner*. But he was my partner. He still is. The *boyfriend* title seems insufficient and infantile. He's my partner. The first man I have loved in years. There have been dates and short-lived relationships but nothing that worked. I'm too guarded to look far into the future but when I imagine my fifty-fifth birthday, or Gem's fiftieth, he's right there by my side.

'I can't see the faces clearly enough,' I say. 'They're too blurry and too dark.'

'I didn't know any of them so it's not worth me looking. But I'd give anything for a recent photo of my ex and my little girl. Blurry is fine, wouldn't matter, I just want to know they're safe.'

'They'll be OK,' I say. 'Watching you.'

'They tell us they're OK but how do we know?' He sips his drink. 'Out there in the normal world, every time I receive a text message or email with photos of her I drop everything to look at them. Her playing soccer with her mom in the garden, baking together, dressing up.'

A pang in my stomach.

I push the dark thought from my head as I've done a thousand times before and drain my glass. 'The TV company will be looking after them, Daniel. Keeping them updated. Lips said they're safe; she said it out loud on live television. We have to trust her. And to be honest with you I'm relieved after that Mind challenge.'

'Relieved?'

'It was tough for Smith, I know that. The sand timer was rigged and he felt out of his depth in a library full of books. But it wasn't *that* tough, was it? I've seen worse on reality TV shows. I've seen people break bones attempting ski jumps, if you can believe that. Smith wasn't in any physical danger.'

'I'm livid,' Daniel says. 'I'm not relieved at all. I didn't take the lecturing gig to be a performing seal. I worked hard on those talks. And here we are playing word games to entertain viewers all over the world, people who are free to leave their homes, eat what they want, see who they want, all while we're deprived of basic necessities. It's like turning a prison wing into a reality show just by making the camera feeds live. It's not ethical.'

'Don't trivialise prison,' I say. 'This is still a luxury ocean liner. We're not in prison.'

'Have you ever been to prison, Caz?'

'No.'

He stiffens.

'Have you?' I ask.

He looks up at the ceiling.

'You don't need to talk about it.'

'I'd rather you find out from me than Lips or a tabloid newspaper after we get out. Let me tell you . . .' he pours us both another vodka tonic, this time with less tonic as we're already running out '. . . there isn't as much difference between that and here as you think. State penitentiary or a deserted ship lost someplace in the middle of an ocean. There isn't so much difference. Either way, you lose your liberty and your privacy, your agency, your sense of time, your faith in others, and you always have the sensation deep in your gut that things are about to turn a whole lot worse.'

52

Two hours later we're all tired and half-drunk. Except Smith. He's staggering around smoking Cuban cigars he scavenged from a humidor, one in each hand, both lit, drinking dirty martinis as if they're glasses of water.

We're wrapped in blankets. We've moved the chairs around so we have two each: one to sit in and one as a foot-rest. Frannie's drifting in and out of sleep, her feet clad in two layers of wool socks. There's a sense of relief in the air: survival, but backdropped by increasingly extreme hunger. I honestly thought they'd give us food today. Biscuits or emergency rations. Ten minutes' access to the stores, perhaps. The baiting of us with olives and lemons feels extra-manipulative. As though they want us to drink and make fools of ourselves for the public.

'You think we have a fish in my net?' asks Smith, slurring, ash falling from his cigar. 'A shoal of them? Yellowfin tuna, maybe? I don't even like fish but I'd eat a dozen right now if we had them.'

'I checked half an hour ago,' says Daniel. 'The drop from the stern might be too high. The ship's travelling too fast, maybe, or the engines are too noisy, I don't know. I think we might catch something eventually but it's going to take a while.'

Daniel's chair is pushed next to mine. We're close. His thigh is by my calf and I am appreciative of the heat. I feel better with him so near.

'Why did you go to prison?' I ask. 'You don't have to say.'

Daniel turns to me and sighs. Vodka in the air. 'I hit a guy outside a bar. I was much younger. He insulted my ex, hounded her, made a nuisance of himself. I lashed out and hurt him pretty bad. I still regret it.'

The mood in the room cools.

'Honestly, I was disappointed with the prizes,' says Smith, trying and failing to pull up his new socks. He has them inside out with the label still attached but I'm not going to tell him that. 'At least we can light the next fire with my useless paperwork. What kind of reward is papers? Jesus, it's cold in here.'

It's so cold there's ice forming on the insides of the windows. Crystalline mosaics spreading inward from the frames. There's wind and squally rain outside so a fire would be unwise. It'd be unwise if we were sober, but in the state we're in it could be suicidal. We're all accustomed to having security, uniformed officers, people in authority around on a vessel like this. And then when they're all gone you realise how quickly things can spin out of control.

The disembarkation photographs were reassuring for a while. Pete must be one of those distant, grainy faces. He'll have walked off the gangplank on to Irish land. To safety. He'll have been worried sick even though he's outwardly always composed. Reserved, even. I know he can suffer with anxiety. He's told me there have been bleak times in his life; times when he couldn't face getting out of bed for days on end, days where he had to cancel trips and work events. His parents died within a year of each other and that affected him profoundly. Now he'll be watching TV, his glasses perched on his nose, cat by his feet, reading about us in the newspapers he has delivered to his village house. He'll want me home with him. A dinner in the café, after hours, doors locked, with Gemma and the rest of the team. Laughing and eating leftovers straight from the aluminium serving trays, and drinking the sauvignon blanc Gem always buys by the crate.

Frannie says something and I snap back to the present, to my increasingly inebriated fellow passengers.

On closer inspection, the other papers from Smith's archive box are unsettling. One is an Excel spreadsheet. It takes Frannie a few minutes to decipher that it represents audience data. Breakdowns by demographic and region. Average duration of each viewing session, percentage of screen time focused on each passenger. She's figured out there are tens of millions of people watching our every move – and that's old data. Could be more now. They're mostly viewing through phones and tablets, but some on regular televisions. There are spin-off podcasts and reaction videos. She says the average viewing session is well over an hour. She says that's extremely rare these days.

'Where are you going?' Daniel asks Smith.

'What do you care, lifeguard? I passed my challenge already. Gonna punch me in the nose like the poor guy in the bar, are you? No, I didn't think so. You enjoy the fruits of my labour and I'll go where I please.'

'You fall down the stairs and I'll need to come help you.'

'Always the hero.'

Daniel mutters something under his breath.

The final paper is a printout of the comments section on YouTube. It's from the pilot episode of the show; we can see that by the title and the time stamp. There are over six hundred thousand comments. The only three highlighted and liked by the channel, Amp Media, are deeply unsettling.

One says *If Caz and the Asian guy get it together the other two will be toast.*

The next says *With Smith's felony history there's no way I'd be locked on a ship with that dude. I'd rather jump overboard lol.*

The final comment says *They don't have a clue what's coming next, do they? SOS in deckchairs. WTF. They're gonna need more than that.*

53

I wake early, harsh sunlight slicing the zinc-topped bar in half, the blinds not up to the task of keeping this room dark.

Shapes in corners. I can see Frannie's red hair erupting from a pile of blankets and I can see Smith next to the bar sleeping on a chair wearing only one shoe.

I rub my eyes. I'm going to need a wash in the pool today. A good long wash.

'Hey,' I say, croakily, spotting Daniel by the stairwell. 'Are you OK?'

He has his arms crossed. Fully dressed. Wet hair combed neatly. A serious expression on his face.

'You don't know?' he says.

'Know what? What's wrong?'

'Let's wake them up.'

He proceeds to walk to Frannie and Smith, coughing animatedly, and then stamping on the floor.

'Come back later,' says Smith, his words slurring. 'Much later.'

Daniel stamps on the floor again.

'Begone,' says Smith.

'Wake up. Both of you. This is important.'

Smith takes off a blanket and starts coughing and wheezing and rubbing his face. He groans and stretches and then makes an attempt at standing up.

'You're still drunk,' says Daniel.

Smith rubs his temples.

'Frannie, are you OK?' I ask. 'Did you get some sleep?'

She squints through barely open eyelids and nods and then she smiles and slips on her tennis pumps and staggers over to us. 'What time is it?' she asks, wrapping a blanket around her shoulders and jumping up on to a leather barstool. Then, after a pause, rubbing her eyes, 'What *day* is it?'

'Something's happened,' says Daniel. 'And I need whoever did it to step forward and take responsibility. It's that simple.'

A long silence.

'It was me,' says Smith. 'Take me down to the cells.'

I remember the comment about Smith's criminal history. I ask him about it and he explains it was a driving offence from years ago.

'Why did you do it?' asks Daniel.

'My head's broken,' says Frannie. 'Would someone please explain to me what on earth is going on?'

'Tell her,' says Daniel, scowling at Smith.

I don't like the vibe in this room.

Smith checks the glass next to him, sniffing the contents, then drinks what's left. 'I'm sorry, OK. It's not like there aren't other restrooms you can use. I'll clean it up later when my stomach can tolerate it. I apologise. It happens at my age. These things happen.'

'What?' says Daniel.

'I missed the urinal. Went all over the floor. All over one shoe. I apologise. It was a rough night and my balance isn't what it used to be. I won my challenge; I was celebrating.'

'Not that,' says Daniel.

Smith looks at him and frowns.

'The box,' says Daniel. 'The box in the Ocean Lobby. The one from the ice sculpture. Somebody opened it.'

54

I'm reminded of the Stanford prison experiments. Pete and I watched a documentary about it once at his place. The way the students were divided into inmates and guards in a mock-up prison beneath Stamford University. I was shocked at how the so-called guards embraced their roles, taunting the prisoners and quickly abusing their authority.

The planned experiment was halted six days into its fourteen-day run.

Group dynamics are notoriously unpredictable.

People are dangerous.

'I didn't open it,' says Frannie, screwing her face up. 'Don't look at me like that. I went out on deck for ice when Daniel suggested we needed ice for the drinks. You said there might be some in the buckets and pans of rain-water. That's the only place I went, I swear.'

'You were gone an awfully long time, Francine,' says Smith.

'There's a lot of deck,' she says, defensively. 'I wouldn't have opened a box that says *do not open*. Do I strike you as the kind of person who would do such a thing?'

'What's actually in the box?' I ask.

Daniel shakes his head.

'Tell us. You have to tell us.'

'Did you open it, Smith?' asks Daniel. 'When you were drunk? You could hardly walk or talk by the end of your session. And you were gone for far longer than Frannie was. Where were you all that time?'

'I was ruining my shoe, I already explained it. You don't think I would have remembered opening a box in the lobby? I remember every detail of last night. The bookmarks, the *Hitchhiker's Guide* book, the lot.'

'You're still under the influence,' says Daniel.

Smith says. 'Where were you, then, Caz? Strangely quiet this morning. Where did you go?'

I look around at their faces, the light from outside intensifying. Distrust. Us turning against each other. *Lord of the Flies*, reimagined. The beginnings of a headache or migraine behind my eye sockets.

'I went out to clear my head. I hate getting blurry – you know, tipsy. Don't like the lack of control, so I went up on deck in the rain to drink water from a saucepan and breathe some fresh air. I was thinking about my sister, Gemma, if you must know. How the stress of my being away will be weighing on her. And her rotten ex-husband, who's never paid what he owed, still loitering in her neighbourhood, still trying to worm his way back into her life. They share kids. It's complicated. I was thinking about her.'

'You happen to go down to the lounge and open a box?' says Smith.

'No. I wouldn't have done that. Daniel, what was inside the box?'

'Consequences,' says Daniel.

'I'm too old for this,' says Smith. 'What kind of consequences?'

Daniel lowers his voice. 'As you know, the box had words etched on the lid. *Do Not Open The Box*. Inside, etched in the same font, on the base, was one word. *Consequences*.'

55

The fire on deck burns bright and clean. We're using bar stools from one of the many crew areas instead of deck-chairs because the indoor furniture has less varnish. It burns without releasing noxious fumes. That's an important consideration when you're in the middle on an ocean with no medics at hand.

Daniel is out checking the lifeboats and tenders, seeing, once again, if he can gain access. He's taken the axe with him this time. Smith's still ranting about suing the ship owner and the media company. He says – and I think he has a valid point here – that even on a reality show you still need adequate safety measures in place. Sure, the lifeboats are most likely rigged to operate as soon as the ship sinks, or moments after an alarm is set off. Maybe they can be activated remotely. But not knowing if we can use them is tantamount to slow-burn mental abuse.

I throw another stool on the fire and the embers lift and catch the wind and fly high into the grey Atlantic skies.

When we were collecting the stools, I took a minute out for myself. I found a secluded crew cabin and, facing a mirror that likely conceals a camera, I recorded an apology of sorts. A private confession. I explained to Pete and

Mum and Gemma and my niece and nephew how I'm partly responsible for all this. Whatever fresh pain Mum is experiencing, unable to comprehend why I'm not visiting. I'm partly to blame for not leaving when I had the chance. Mainly to blame, even. I talked directly to Gemma and told her how proud of her I am, for managing the café and the family. At that moment I had to bite the inside of my mouth to stop breaking down. Because it's quite possible she's not managing at all. Due to my selfish act – this so-called holiday, a show I didn't quit when I could – it's possible she's at her ex's place rolled up in a ball on his bathroom floor. The café might be closed. Staff unpaid, rent unpaid, instalments to the charity stalled. All because I took a – let's call it what it is – gamble. When Pete asked me if I wanted to go away on an ocean liner to New York I should have listened to my gut and politely declined. Instead I gambled everything I've worked so hard for. I risked my family's security. For what? A potential marriage? A chance to finally right Dad's wrongs and so give Mum some peace? I have it in me just as he did. It's different, but it's there, lingering.

I couldn't resist.

'*Consequences*,' says Frannie. 'The word inside the box. What do you think that could mean?'

'Means what happens when you do something,' I say. 'The knock-on effects.'

She breaks into a sad smile. 'I know what the word means in a literal sense, Caroline, I'm not a complete idiot. But for us. What's the significance for us?'

'Could be negative, could be positive. Although, to be honest, I'm not sure how our experience on this ship could become much more negative. So I'm choosing not to worry about it.'

She stands up and points off the starboard side of the ship.

'It's just the wake of the ship,' I say. 'The disturbed water from the propellers.'

'But why can we see it off to the side?'

'Because we're turning,' I say, standing up to join her, understanding. 'We're turning back.'

56

We stand by the stern railing and watch the shape of the ship's wake. It casts a long, gentle arc in the water far below us.

In a typical landscape with signposts, trees, landmarks, house numbers, you know where you're turning away from and moving towards. There are clues and markers everywhere. People to guide you, technology to assist. It's even possible to glean from the slope of the land if you're near a river or approaching the coast. But here we have nothing. Discombobulated doesn't start to cover it. I have no notion of direction.

'We've turned before,' says Smith, approaching with a bottle of Japanese whisky under his arm. 'Not this sharply, but I think we've been doing circles in the middle of the ocean. And by the freezing night-time temperatures I'd say we're close to the southern tip of Greenland.'

Frannie shivers. 'I read about ocean routes in a book in the library before Daniel and Caroline found me. The main shipping routes are far south of here if you're right, Smith. They're kind of like motorways: narrow channels that commercial ships stick to. We might be north of all that.'

My head spins from the elevation above sea level. I rest, leaning against the safety railing, an overhang directly below us, and I have the strangest compulsion to fling myself overboard. I won't do it of course but the sensation is there nonetheless, stronger than it has ever been, stronger even than during the summer the café almost went under, or when a blue-haired woman travelled from York to scream at my mother, directly to her face, spitting and swearing at her about how we all ruined her life. Our collective shame faded gradually over the years only to resurface again, resurrected by an outside force.

Frannie, Smith and I walk back along the running track to the centre of the ship.

'Shipping routes are not what concerns me,' says Smith. 'What concerns me is that we've been on here for days and how long will our fuel last? Unless they plan to refuel us at sea we could lose the TV, propulsion, and lights. Not only that, but if we lose power we'll be at the mercy of Atlantic storms. They're not a challenge for a liner cutting through waves head-on, but if we're bobbing around like a sitting duck in November seas we'll be extremely vulnerable.'

A sitting duck. What does that make us? Four starving parasites clinging to its feathers.

'The viewers will insist they give us more fuel,' says Frannie.

'It's a TV show,' says Smith. 'Why would viewers want to help people like us? Most folks at home are streaming this on their smartphones and they'd give a kidney to swap places with any one of us. Guaranteed fame and fortune, at least for a month or two. There's nobody searching for us. No coastguard all the way out here. People watch their LCD screens and they see four regular people out to win five million dollars and then they flick to the next channel. The media company's likely planning season two right now as we sit here warming ourselves by the bonfire. This is transactional. To you and me and Caroline here, it's a disaster vacation, a threat to life. But to the folks pulling the strings this whole operation is a carefully considered business venture.'

He stops talking. Looks startled.

We follow his gaze back to the stern of the ship.

'Nobody say a word,' he says.

A long pause.

Wind whistling around the funnels and towers of the ship.

And then the distant sound of Daniel screaming for help.

57

We hurry down the port side of the *Atlantica*, following the outside lane of the running track.

'We're coming,' yells Francine.

'He's fallen?' I ask, sweating, the arch of my right foot aching. 'Overboard? He's not screaming any more?'

'Consequences,' warns Frannie, speeding up, outrunning me and Smith.

When we arrive at the rear of the ship Daniel's standing there shirtless, his trousers soaking wet, netting gathered all around his feet, holding a small fish above his head like it's a sporting trophy. The fish is the size of a wine bottle.

'We thought you were hurt,' I say, panting.

'You caught that?' asks Frannie.

'*We* caught it,' says Daniel, smiling, freeing himself from the nets around his ankles. 'We caught an empty detergent bottle and a piece of driftwood, and one beautiful fresh fish.'

We help Daniel cast the nets again and then we walk back triumphantly to the fire. I prepare the embers a little way from the flames. After carefully gutting the fish I grill it over a scrap of wire mesh we found in the engine room workshop, head and all. Smith tries to name it Nemo and

Frannie protests. We share the fillets out evenly and they are flaky and delicious. I slice a lemon and squeeze juice on to each portion. Crispy, charred skin and tender white flesh.

'Watch out for the bones,' says Smith.

We sit around the fire, licking our fingers and feeling better about life. If it happens to rain then we'll collect clean water. If we keep catching fish, we'll have a food supply.

There is hope.

You might think you are a sophisticated, twenty-first-century human, but when your body is depleted of the nutrition it needs, no prospect of a meal, you lose that sophistication so fast it takes your breath away. I've had half a serving of fish and the effects are immediate. My mind loosens, my blood plasma feels rich in my veins, my thoughts are ordered again. I boil water in a casserole pan to brew tea.

'Not a bad consequence as it turns out,' says Frannie. 'Catch of the day, and as fresh as can be.'

'I wish that . . .' I say, and then stop myself.

Daniel glances at me. 'Go on.'

'I wish that I'd left when Lips gave us all the chance. Maybe I'd be home by now, sitting next to Pete watching you guys on TV after I finish work, understanding the truth of the show, the endgame, the risks, knowing who is really in control and what the world is making of all this. You're all so much better at being here than I am. I wish I'd said no to the chance to win. It feels tainted, somehow. As if I'm participating in an evil game and I'm playing against you all.'

Frannie nods. 'The worst part for me isn't the competition so much as I can't stand being appraised. I'm happy living a quiet, private life and doing my own thing. My Instagram's locked and I keep myself to myself. I've never told anyone outside my family this but I go and visit the Catholic church near campus, even though I'm an atheist. Don't laugh, but I love how quiet and settled the place is. The stone steps worn smooth over centuries. So now, here, the idea that people are gossiping about me and comparing me to you guys and zooming in to unflattering photos of me and digging into my past relationships fills me with utter dread.'

My chest tightens.

Of course.

I didn't think this through. They'll be digging into my family history. It's not difficult to find. Tabloids will be doorstepping Gemma and the café crew again, photographing them through car windows and dredging their old social media posts. What have I done?

'You might want to keep in mind the five million,' says Smith, licking his fingers. 'I worked my first job at our trailer park aged twelve. Earned a buck a day plus tips, except there were no tips. Then two paper rounds and a car-cleaning job. Two bucks a day. In school vacations I'd work with the janitor fixing equipment and doing maintenance work on the furnace and grounds while other kids went away to the lakes or the mountains.' He looks at Daniel. 'Kids like you, I expect. I was at school throughout the year, never managed to venture far from the place. And for the first ten years of my adult life I never made enough money to scrape by. This isn't a sob story; I had friends much worse off than I ever was. I started moving from state to state. I remember cashing pay cheques at the cheque-cashing place in Fayetteville, paying my rent weekly with those same bills. If I needed a tooth out, that could end up getting me evicted or in trouble with a loan shark. And now we have the chance to pull in five million. If you feel bad when you win, you can give it away, simple. Help out a charity. But don't for one minute feel sorry for yourselves because you might get a windfall. The price may be loss of privacy, on here and back home, but one-in-four odds to win is a once-in-a-lifetime privilege and we should all view it that way.'

Is he saying all this because he believes it, or because he knows the viewers will agree?

'I'd keep some of it for myself,' says Frannie. 'I'm just being honest. But I'd give my dad what's left. He had a new heart valve and a triple bypass. Mum was sure it'd kill him, but he pulled through. He can hardly walk for five minutes without doubling over and spraying nitro-glycerine down his throat. And yet he won't close his machining plant. Says it just needs three or four good years to turn around and be profitable again. Couple of significant orders might be in the pipeline, you never know. He's been saying that since I was a girl. Thirteen men relying on the wages he pays them. He won't stop until it finishes him off. If I'm able to buy him and Mum a few peaceful years then I'll do it.'

I throw my fish bones into the fire.

And then the ship's foghorn blows.

Smith peers over at me. 'Challenge two.'

58

We douse our fire with garbage can water and run inside.

The lights are off.

'Why did they cut the power?' asks Frannie. 'Why do they keep doing these things?'

Nobody answers her. We walk briskly through the murk, deeper and deeper into the cold bowels of the ship. Some corridors and atria are lit from window light but as we descend lower, taking staircases in silence, the walls covered with black-and-white photos of the original Queen Mary ballroom, the gloom intensifies.

'Wait for me, would you?' says Smith.

We slow a little, urging him to hurry.

By the time we enter the Ocean Lobby the whole place is almost completely dark. The casino is unlit and the Nantucket Spa entrance is difficult to make out, and in the distance the arcade of shops, some of them violently trashed by Smith, are too murky to see. The only light source in the lobby is one solitary TV screen attached to a panel.

We walk to it, moths to a flame, prey drawn towards a shadowy watering hole.

The only details I can make out are tennis balls. Dozens of them. Smith and Daniel's old games.

Frannie taps my arm.

The image on the screen is that of a wave. Next to the image is the word WATER.

My challenge.

'It's OK,' I say, more to myself than the others, my throat constricting. 'Smith managed his. I'll do the same. It'll be OK. We might even earn some food out of it.'

Daniel gently squeezes my shoulder. I have an instinct to run away, some animal urge to turn and flee, but you cannot flee an ocean liner. You can try but you will fail.

Lips appears on the screen.

'Good afternoon, passengers. Your next challenge is *Water*. You have agreed among yourselves that Caroline will complete this challenge. I will outline your instructions, and then you will have precisely ten minutes to move into position. Water is a physical challenge with a team element. Caroline, you'll find a hatch located at the front port side of the ship, accessible via Deck Three. The hatch has been opened remotely. Caroline, you will proceed, after two sharp horn blasts, to jump into the sea.'

What? Jump into the sea? Did she actually say that? I start to look around the room, into the shadows. I can't breathe. She keeps calling me by my full name and now I have the lyrics of 'Sweet Caroline' looping in my head. Mum's singing voice.

'Do not attempt to jump from one of the main decks; the fall would be too high. Jump only from the hatch on Deck Three. The hatch is designed for a pilot to access the ship when entering a harbour or canal. Caroline, you are the only passenger permitted to access either the room or the hatch.' I can't keep up. 'It is the responsibility of your fellow passengers to position themselves wher-ever they choose on the ship. The water-level shell doors on Deck Three at the rear and centre of the ship will be accessible to all remaining passengers. These shell doors are used to access tenders at water level. They turn into stable pontoons. You can decide among yourselves who should be positioned at which location. You are permit-ted to assist Caroline in her challenge, but you may decide not to do that. I repeat: you do not need to assist if you do not wish to. It is your choice. Once, after two sharp blasts from the ship's horn, Caroline jumps from the pilot hatch at the front of the ship, you may, as a team, help to pull her back aboard. There will be no assistance available from outside. I repeat, no outside assistance whatsoever. If you fail this challenge, Caroline, you may be left stranded many miles from hope of rescue.'

'Wait,' I say.

The others stare at me, their mouths agape.

'This is nothing like Smith's challenge,' I tell her, trip-ping over my words. 'The bookmarks? The puzzle? This is completely different. It isn't . . . I can't do—'

'If you fail this challenge you will be eliminated from contention for the main prize and you will no longer be entitled to your participation fee.'

'This clearly isn't fair,' says Daniel, standing up straighter. 'Come on. This should be more equal.'

Lips swallows.

'All actions have consequences,' she says, her voice deeper than before. 'You had the option to leave. You had the option to select your own challenge. The box is now open.' She pauses. 'It cannot be closed.'

'Please . . .' I say.

The lips grow in size on screen. Zooming in so we can make out pores and fine hairs. 'Please do remember that you brought this upon yourselves.'

'There will be a lifeboat somewhere,' says Smith. 'She's bluffing. There will be someone close by.'

'Consequences,' says Lips.

I walk closer to the TV. 'I'm not doing—'

'You have ten minutes to reach your locations,' she says. 'I wish you all fair winds and calm seas.'

The screen goes blank.

59

We don't move; we just stare open-mouthed at each other.

'You can do it,' says Daniel, his voice unsteady. 'But, if you don't want to do it, then sit this one out. You always have that option.'

Sit it out.

She wants me to jump in the ocean?

'Let's move to the light,' says Frannie.

When we can see each other clearly again I look at Daniel and say, 'What would you do?'

He rubs his injured eye. 'I might just say no to this one.'

'Sure you would,' says Smith, a little removed from the rest of us. 'One-in-three odds would be preferable.' He looks at me. 'Someone tried to talk me out of doing Mind, remember. Someone would love for all of us to bow out one by one so they can win.'

I lick my dry lips and I can taste salt on my tongue.

'What did—'

I interrupt Daniel. 'I'm doing it. I'm doing the challenge.' I feel giddy. Adrenaline pulsing through my body. 'I've come this far, I'm not quitting now.' I take a deep breath. 'You three go to the shell doors. I'll go to the pilot hatch. Deck Three.'

'Wait, please,' says Frannie. 'Hold on for a second. Are you sure? Who do you want on each pontoon? All of us on one, or spread out?'

'I don't know. The ship's moving so fast. I need you all to reach out for me. Maybe you'll need to hold on to each other as well. So we don't all go overboard. Use ropes, maybe. Do we have ropes?'

I'm gambling again. I hate myself for it but I could not say no. I sense a little of what Dad couldn't resist. The high stakes.

'You need a life vest,' says Daniel.

'And water,' says Frannie. 'Take rainwater in a bottle. Tie it to your life vest.'

'Water?' I say.

Frannie swallows. 'Just in case we can't catch you, Caz. In case we miss. Insurance. Thirty knots, it's something we need to think about. You'll need water if . . .'

She trails off.

'Daniel and Francine on the centre pontoon,' I say, frantically, running out of time. 'That's where I have the best chance. After that I might be too far out from the ship for anyone to reach me. The two of you, wearing life vests, with ropes, and anything else that floats. Tie yourselves to the ship if you can. If you miss me then it's down to you, Smith. You understand?'

He doesn't look confident. 'I'll do my best.'

'I'll swim close to the boat. Just grab at me and pull me in. I'm not a bad surface swimmer.'

As long as I don't go underwater I'll manage.

They all look terrified.

'I'm doing it. Don't look so damned scared. We haven't much time. Go.'

They don't go. They hug me in turn, surprisingly tightly, and then all at once, one messy embrace. They sprint away and I'm left alone. I jog towards the stairwell and descend to Deck Three. Almost complete darkness.

I made my choice. Nobody forced me.

My stomach is churning: sweet lemon tea and bile. I panic and fumble and check the deck plans screwed to the wall. It's crew-only down here. Grey rubber floors and bare steel; no wood veneer or Art Deco mirrors. The cameras are all out in the open, swivelling and focusing on my frown lines and grey roots whenever I move. I approach the front of the ship and take a life vest from a row of hooks.

A chink of daylight ahead of me.

Pale light pouring in from outside of the ship, and it feels dangerous this close to sea level. Normally if you see daylight down here it means the hull has been compromised.

The sound of waves lapping against the steel superstructure of the ship.

I pull on my lifejacket and fasten it and tighten the straps, finger shaking, and then realise I forgot to take any water. The lifejacket will prevent me from going underwater, it'll be OK.

I step towards the open hatch.

60

One thing I didn't expect on an ocean liner of this size and luxury is the sheer number of safety signs and muster protocols. You don't get those in a normal hotel. Each one is a reminder that you chose to take your well-earned holiday on board something inherently dangerous.

This is a red zone.

Do not approach the opening.

Do not work in this zone on your own.

Do not attempt to assist a pilot embarking without being tethered to a harness.

The water level is only a few metres below me. A short hop, really. And yet, as I bend to look out, my body judders.

Brilliant blue skies.

I look up instead and I'm confronted with the dark blue hull of the ship and the towering bridge high above. It looks like a tower block from down here. I turn my head. Tiny figures of Frannie and Daniel perhaps a hundred metres away on their pontoon. I can't see Smith at all. Either he hasn't reached the rear pontoon yet or else he's eclipsed by the others.

Sea spray hits my face and the cold water stings my skin and drenches my neck.

How did I reach this point? Why am I not home with Gem?

I wait for the horn to blow.

Shivering.

The sound of steel cutting through water.

Daniel and Frannie have something with them on their pontoon. A white object. They look busy, as if they have a plan. I'll jump in and then they will pick me up. The media company must have completed comprehensive risk assessments and their insurers will have signed off on all the details. I'm not actually alone. My shipmates will pull me out of the water.

There's padding on the side of the door. Orange safety padding designed so a pilot won't be injured embarking and disembarking in rough weather. I tear off a section and drop it into the water. In a matter of seconds it's past the central pontoon. At this speed I'll need to find my bearings quickly and then reach Frannie and Daniel. I'll only have one shot.

Lips's words fill my head.

Consequences.

Please do remember that you brought this upon yourselves.

The ship's foghorn blows twice.

61

I slip off my shoes and socks and start shivering violently. From the cold but also from the knowledge of what I'm about to do. Why don't I have life insurance? Where did I put my will? Maybe I'd be more responsible if I had a dependant at home.

How dare they ask me to jump into the fucking ocean like this? I can pull out. I can refuse to play this stupid, reckless, empty game.

A wave splashes my legs and I gasp, retreating a step, and the others are shouting words of encouragement from their central pontoon. Unintelligible reassurance. Irrational enthusiasm and support diluted by this incessant maritime wind. Because they want me to fail so their odds will improve? No, I do not believe that.

A ticking clock in my head.

If I don't leap, I can't repair the damage. The harm we endured is one thing, but the families did nothing to deserve being ripped off like that. Dad's colleague was an insider. A book-keeper. He was a short, handsome man with a dimple in his chin. He wasn't a gambler, just an enabler. A pitiful creature who took a small percentage of Dad's withdrawals in exchange for his silence.

I step to the edge of the hatch, my toes overhanging the metal lip of the door. This is not a class of maritime vessel you jump from. My body is begging me to seek safety, find another way. But in my mind's eye I see a Royal Marines sergeant's widow. Her pallid, betrayed face on the front cover of the *Yorkshire Post*. Locals assumed we'd all benefited from Dad's actions. *Fur coats and diamond rings*, one neighbour shrieked at us over the garden wall. But we never benefited in any way. Dad wasted every penny.

It's now. It has to be now. I steel myself and go to jump in the fast-moving water.

This is my only chance to make things right.

I hesitate. Voices yelling in the distance. Memories of what I gave away in that stuffy hospital room all those years ago. I squeeze my fingernails into my palms and bend my knees.

My teeth chatter.

I take a step.

62

Regret, so much regret before I hit the water. But tinged, unexpectedly, with exhilaration.

Then, reality.

The water's so cold it burns.

Tumbling under the surface, round and round.

No air in my lungs. Winded. I burst back up, gagging, coughing up salt water, noise returning. I can't see properly. I wipe my stinging eyes and I'm not next to the ship. I thought I'd drop adjacent to the hull.

Voices yelling instructions but I'm only focused on keeping my head above the water. My breathing is fast and my heart feels as if it might stop pumping any second.

I spit out water.

Another wave hits me square in the face and I rise with a swell that might be as large as an Olympic pool. Larger, even.

My throat hurts.

A mile or more of darkness underneath me. Bobtail squid and jellyfish with names like Bloodybelly Comb, Black Sea Nettle, Atolla. An alien world covering two-thirds of the planet. Unimaginable depths and no chance of retrieval.

'Caroline!' yells a voice. 'You need to . . .'

I don't catch his words. The wind is whistling and the waves are breaking over me, pushing me under. I have never been this cold.

Gemma's voice in my ear. *Go to them.*

I'm not close enough to the ship.

I start paddling, frantically, flailing with my arms. I want to swim, to power myself to the pontoon, but the lifejacket and current make it almost impossible. Short, ineffective strokes.

Seconds like hours.

The *Atlantica* is a cathedral or a futuristic prison wing scrolling past me. I am so infinitesimally small in this moment.

I kick and paddle with all my might.

'Caz, you need to swim harder,' roars Frannie, her face appearing and then disappearing again through the waves. A flash of her red hair. 'Swim harder!'

I kick out and push with my arms but the waves are too high, the surface too choppy. Whatever strength I had is leaving me. I am faint; shivering and exhausted. Freezing cold. Pathetic, alone, starving. Coerced into open ocean.

Something splashes next to me.

'Hold it,' says Daniel. 'Take it now!'

I swim to where I think it is but I cannot find anything. I see him pull the rope back through the water and throw it again.

Gemma is a strong swimmer. Far stronger than me.

'Help,' I say, desperately. 'Help me.'

But they do not dive into the water to save me. They shriek, and the look of desperation on their passing faces is a still frame from a nightmare. Them moving by as I bob up and down, powerless in dark grey sea water. The look in Frannie's eyes as I hit the next wave and go under, resurfacing past them. Past their reach.

Past any realistic chance of rescue.

I'm left to perish from hypothermia in this unforgiving sea.

My only hope is Smith, but my faculties are dimming, my vision fading with every passing second.

I can't see him or hear him.

I kick and paddle to move closer to the ship but with every ineffective motion a wave pushes me further away again, deeper into open seas. I ponder if Lips underestimated the Atlantic.

Or, perhaps, she didn't.

My body is chilled to the bone; heavy and clumsy in the water. After days with no real food I have nothing left to give.

A wave throws me against the side of the ship and I try to cling to the smooth metal, my fingernails digging in around flush rivets, but I fail. There is nothing to grip. Flat steel two inches thick, designed for minimum friction. No barnacles or hand-holds.

I see Gemma now. She is smiling, quietly. She looks anxious. As if she wants me to come home to her.

Another wave hits and I go under, spinning around, resurfacing spluttering and heaving.

The pontoon is there. The rear shell doors open.

But no sight of Smith. He must have failed to locate the room quickly enough. Without thinking, I forgive him.

I must do this on my own.

'Grab hold,' shouts a muffled voice far away.

I'm still twenty metres from the pontoon but it's coming up on me fast. It floats half a metre above sea level except for when waves break underneath it.

I try to keep my eyes on the unmanned pontoon. My breathing is slower. It's as if my body is taking over from my mind, screening out the noise and the pain and the cold.

The pontoon is close.

Water in my throat, stinging my tonsils.

I steady myself and throw up my arms and cling to the pontoon and Daniel and Frannie both cheer behind me. I clench my chattering teeth together and haul myself up, an overwhelming sense of relief flooding my head as I look momentarily inside the ship, and then a heavy wave breaks over me like a brick wall collapsing and my numb, icy hands lose purchase and I slip beneath the black waters.

When I surface my head smashes up into the under-side of the pontoon and I am trapped.

A solid kilometre of water beneath and a solid steel door above.

I begin to lash out, breathing in sea water, coughing and flailing; kicking out into nothingness, and the ship moves and the steel above my head pushes me down deeper and deeper under the water.

I come up coughing a deep guttural bark from a different world, a different species.

The pontoon is out of my reach.

I am past the last point of hope.

Alone.

64

'Help me,' I yell, but a wave crests ahead of me and I may as well be screaming into a cliff, negotiating with a basalt mountain.

Time slows.

I see myself from above: a flailing seabird.

The *Atlantica* is immense from this angle and I despise every bolt and rivet. A whole city block powering away, leaving me here with whatever eyeless creatures lurk below.

I'd swim to chase the ship but if it's travelling at twenty-nine knots, or even just nine knots, there's no way I'll catch up. My heart sinks in my chest.

Be careful, Caroline. The words Mum would mutter before I'd head off to the moors with my one-man tent for a quiet night by myself. Back when she knew who I was.

Something on the rear deck, far above me.

A pair of eyes.

'Help,' I shout. 'Please, you must help me!'

Smith is shouting back but I can't make out his words. He bends down and then he throws out Daniel's fishing net.

I swim as hard as I can, through wall-size waves, gulping down water and spitting it up again, burning salt inside my nostrils, and I lurch for it. Nylon rope. Webbing. I miss. This is too difficult. I reach out again, kicking with my legs, and my fingertips find it. I pull it to me and hold on and wrap it around myself. I twist my arm through the net and wind it around my leg as though I'm a herring he's caught.

'Pull me in,' I shriek, my voice hoarse.

But he does not pull me in. I see him far above, struggling to hold the line, gritting his teeth, losing purchase. He's going to drop me. He's going to fail and leave me tangled in a net.

And that's when I hear something truly terrifying.

I hear him, this man, my only chance at survival, yell, 'Help me.'

65

'Tie it off,' I say, my voice straining. 'To the railings.'

He's trying, I know he is, but the net, plus my weight, is too heavy for him. He's almost sixty. He's struggling; the end of the line is pulled tight around a rail pillar, but the line's not secured. It's extending. I'm being left to trawl further and further behind the ship.

'Help me, goddammit,' he shouts.

'If you drop me then send a raft,' I say, pathetically. 'You must drop a raft.'

I'm hit by another wave, this one pushing me further beneath the surface, but when I recover myself, coughing up water, there are three people on the rear deck. They're heaving the nets.

I let myself go loose and I am so very cold. My hands are wrinkled and blue, my feet completely numb. Daniel, Smith and Frannie lift me closer to the underside of the stern. My peripheral vision is dark.

'Please,' I say, too quietly. 'I can't feel . . .'

They pull but I am too heavy for them. Me, drenched, plus the wet net – it's too much to heave as dead weight. The stern of the ship is an overhang. I remember the muster drill – they called it the Fantail. They manage to pull me clear of the water but then I sit motionless, clinging to the netting, rope burns scarring my forearms, swinging in the cold Atlantic air, sea water dripping back to its source.

I'm shaking. The relief of knowing I might yet see Pete again, my sister, my niece, my nephew. But also I'm crying from this wretched game. Today, and each sorry day that went before. This whole trip growing worse with each passing nautical mile.

I rise past the huge lettering on the rear of the ship, lifting higher in slow jerky movements.

RMS *ATLANTICA.*

'Almost there, Caz,' yells Daniel, from above, his voice straining. 'Hang on a little longer.'

I rise up like a newborn wrapped in a handkerchief carried by a stork in some ancient folkloristic tale, higher and higher. To the lip of the ship's stern.

Six hands reach over.

I'm almost asleep. The chattering of my teeth and my shivering shoulders the only things keeping me conscious.

Hands grab at my life vest.

They pull me back on board the ship I long to leave.

66

I can hear their muffled voices but they seem distant. Blurry. As though I'm unwillingly sinking back into an unreliable dream.

They help me to my feet, supporting me, dragging off my soaking life vest.

I can hardly stand.

Daniel unbuttons his shirt and pulls off mine and embraces me. Frannie does the same at my back, skin-to-skin, while Smith bends down and rubs my calves and feet. I am caught within a tight embrace.

'You're going to be OK,' says Daniel, slow and clear, his breath warm on my ear. 'But we can't warm you up too quickly. That would be dangerous. I've seen hypothermia treated by medics on the beach. We need to increase your core temperature gradually. Can you hear me?'

I nod, my teeth chattering, my peripheral vision still hazy.

Frannie rubs my arms with her hands. 'When you're warmer we'll take you to the fire. We'll make you better, all right?'

I try to speak but I fail. An empty croak. I'm too empty. Too frozen.

'There was no safety boat out there,' says Smith, standing, angling a bottle so I can sip water. 'I thought they'd have a lifeboat on the horizon waiting but there was nothing out there at all. If you two hadn't showed up when you did I'd have . . .'

'You did great, too, Smith,' says Daniel, using his warm hands to gently cup my neck, to heat up my throat. His thumbs flank my mouth and I could kiss them.

I want to thank everyone but I am paralysed. Completely shut down from the inside.

An hour later we're seated by a bar stool fire on the front section of the ship, sheltering from the wind behind the tall steel breakwater. I'm covered in four blankets and I'm sipping warm tea with plenty of sugar. Daniel says I can't have hot tea yet. I need to do this step by step.

'How are you feeling, sweetheart?' asks Smith. 'You worried us back there. Couldn't heave you up on my own, couldn't even hold the net steady. It's the water, the drag; it was too much for me.'

Was that how Dad felt? Was that what he faced when he took that solitary decision?

'You saved me,' I say.

He shakes his head. 'I'm too old. Those two saved you.'

Frannie and Daniel are talking on the far side of the fire, and they both have concerned expressions.

'What's wrong?' I ask, my voice croaky from all the screaming earlier, from all the salt water.

They throw a stack of Nantucket Spa treatment brochures on the fire and walk over to us. The scent of paper burning. I am too tired to move far but I try to sit up straight.

'Are you warming up?' Frannie asks. 'How do you feel?'

Numb from the cold and the adrenaline, but also from the realisation that this experience, this show, is not at all what I thought it was.

'I'll be OK.'

'What's my name?' she says.

'I'm OK, Frannie, thank you. But I never want to jump in water again, never into the sea. I don't even want to step close to a safety rail or a beach promenade. Thank God you all came. I don't know how to thank you.'

'I have a feeling we'll all need to look out for each other from now on,' she says.

'We already were,' says Smith.

'Well,' she says, 'that was then and this is now. The inside of the box said *consequences*. Someone opened it and let them out. Unleashed them. We need to watch each other's backs, because, whatever happens next, I doubt it'll be anything good.'

67

Daniel has cast the fishing net after spending hours detangling it and reinforcing the ropes. We are down to our final two lemons. Frannie uses a knife and a marble-handled grater from the Captain's Lounge bar to squeeze lemon juice into china cups. She follows that up with sugar from sachets, zest, and warm tea.

'Vitamins are important. I don't want to see you all bow-legged,' she says, smiling. 'Drink up. I'm an unqualified pretend nurse and I know what's best for you.'

We drink the lemon tea. I have so little energy since my challenge I can hardly keep my eyelids open. That experience, facing the vastness of the Atlantic Ocean all on my own, so insignificant and impotent next to the mass of the ship – it took something out of me. Changed me forever. I haven't felt that way since sixth form and now I doubt I'll have time in my life to rebuild whatever confidence I managed to accrue.

'We didn't get access to a room with water or food like we did with my Mind challenge,' says Smith. 'They could have at least given us sandwiches and potato chips, cold hamburgers, even, for what they put us all through. BLTs. Cheeseburgers with pickles and relish. I'd take an old slice of pepperoni pizza.' He closes his eyes and his voice trails off. 'Roast beef subs with horseradish and caramel-ised onion, or ham and wholegrain mustard on freshly baked bread.'

'What they put *her* through,' says Daniel.

'That's what I meant.'

The last time I was this out of control was at school. Even during the worst times Gem, Mum and I could pull together, come up with a plan to muddle through another week. At school I was constantly out of my depth. I never had a best friend, was never in a group. Teachers didn't warm to me and I couldn't blame them. I was lost. Everyone else seemed so together, so integrated, so easy. I could tell they weren't taking walks in the street close to traffic, in front of lorries, weaving through speeding cars, not looking both ways, pathetically, laughably. Trying, half-heartedly, to escape.

'Consequences,' says Daniel. 'It's like they changed the rules of the game. We didn't know the rules before and we still don't know them; we just understand that they have changed substantively.'

He throws a card table on to the fire and I watch as the green felt bursts into flame and I am glad to see it go.

'I'm going to ask her at six o'clock,' says Smith. 'I'm demanding answers this time, after what they put Caz through.'

'Lips will answer or she won't,' Daniel says, flatly. 'The screen will be on or it will turn off. You can't demand anything here. You tried that before.'

'So we give up?' says Smith.

The question is left lingering in the air.

I force myself to stay awake a little longer. The fire flares bright as a stack of newspaper catches. Papers dated almost a week ago, each one in a different language from a different country. Out-of-date French and German news burning to keep us alive through the dark hours.

'We have Body left and we have Air,' says Daniel. 'We need to expect those both to come tonight. Body and Air. Me and you, Frannie.'

'Both tonight?' says Frannie.

He nods.

Her cheeks swell as she grits her teeth.

'They completed theirs so we'll do ours,' she says, coughing from the smoke. 'Air. If I need to hold my breath then I'll do it. If I need to crawl through air-conditioning vents, well, I'll have to try my best; do the Stoic philosophers proud then deal with the mental trauma after I'm home. There's no way Air could be worse than what they put Caz through.'

68

'Caz, you need to wake up now.'

My vision is blurry.

Frannie's face comes into focus. Freckles. Hazel eyes. She's gently shaking me.

'Are we . . . OK?'

'You need to get ready. I wanted to let you sleep as long as possible but we're off to the Ocean Lobby soon. It's twenty to six, Caz. How are you feeling?'

I struggle to sit up. 'I'm tired.'

'It's the shock leaving your body.'

I move and my whole body hurts. Bruises and rope burns. 'Sorry?'

'Shock. You're adjusting. The adrenaline's still draining away. That's what happens. When I was nine, just before Christmas, my dad crashed outside Cardiff. It was slippery and he lost control on the ice and mounted a pavement. We ended up careering into a tree.'

'Were you all OK?' I croak.

'We emerged with cuts and bruises but the car was a write-off. Dad had to fight with my door for a long time to pull me free. He was worried the petrol tank might catch. There was no fire in the end but our car had hit a pedestrian before it hit the tree, a lady from our street. She didn't make it through the night.'

I place my hand on hers.

'Adrenaline can push you to do remarkable things. The fire crew were surprised Dad managed to pry my door open that day. They said the way it was crumpled you'd need machinery to do what he did. You've done something similar. I'm glad you slept a little, I've been keeping an eye on you.'

'Do we have any water?'

She hands me a plastic bottle. 'The last of the drinkable water we collected.'

I sip it. That's all there is in the bottle. One sip.

My face is dry from all the salt.

'If my phone worked, or the computers, at least we could check the weather forecast,' she says. 'At least we'd know when we'll next have rain. It's infuriating having no information. We can brace ourselves for the dentist's drill because we know it'll be over in minutes. This unending information vacuum is a new form of torture. Maybe I could ask the Admiral?'

'Don't waste your question.'

'Your lips aren't blue any more,' she says, smiling, blinking. 'They're not blue.'

'They were blue before?' I trail my fingertip over my lip.

'Bright blue. It was awful. They're pink again.'

I stand up but she needs to steady me. I frown because this physical weakness is alien. This lack of kinetic strength and energy. Even when I've been emotionally on the floor, angst-filled, ashamed, unsure, I could always rely on my body to push harder.

I stagger to the bathroom, each mirror and dial draped in newspaper and tape, and I weep when I see my reflection in the unused shower head. A tired-looking person, more similar to Mum than how I hope I usually look, with unwashed, tousled hair and white crystals in her eyelashes and brows. Not a drip to wash with, not a drip to drink.

We join the men and walk together down our corridor.

A funeral march.

'I took the dogs for a runaround while you two were sleeping,' says Smith. 'I like the one with the lazy eye the best. Suzy, is it? She's a real character, a *Sesame Street* dog if I ever saw one. Chased her tail a little up by the lamp post. I've fallen for her.'

It's almost six o'clock.

We keep walking. The lights are off but we're growing accustomed to the layout of the ship, and to the darkness. Four emaciated bats, fluttering, beating their wings, sensing where the hard edges are.

As we descend the stairs, my hand firm on the rail the whole way down, I am nauseous. Not because of the amount of sea water I swallowed, but rather because I step outside of myself and look back and I see a troupe of tragic figures. Powerless bodies unable to escape whatever labyrinth they've found themselves contained within. A game inside a nightmare. Levels of isolation and manipulation I wouldn't inflict upon a mortal enemy.

The lobby is gloomy and silent. Four elevators sit in frozen animation on different floors. The Nantucket Spa is dark and the arcade is smashed to pieces. The casino has murals and paintings of well-dressed people, and, bizarrely, dogs in bow ties, playing cards around a table.

The television screen gradually lights up on the pillar.

We take our seats.

Her mouth appears. You might think I'd be livid at this moment. Angry at the glossy lips and the corporation they likely represent. At the grave danger they seem willing to subject us to. But I don't have enough energy to be angry. I am not becoming resigned to this miserable reality, I will fight it in my own way, but now, so soon after my challenge, I am left with nothing. The hunger and lack of autonomy are wearing me down slowly from the inside. I jumped from a moving ship because they told me to.

'Good evening, passengers.'

69

We sit motionless awaiting the next challenge. Crash-test dummies driving towards a concrete block at breakneck speed, safety symbols painted on our blank faces.

That poor pedestrian Frannie told me about. Her relatives. And I can only imagine the complex feelings of guilt and relief her parents were left with.

'Good evening, passengers. Please do not curse. Congratulations, Caz, on completing Water.'

We don't say anything.

I can hardly keep my eyelids open.

'As a reward the RMS *Atlantica* would like to invite you and your fellow passengers to an exclusive gala dinner reception this evening in the Diamond Grill restaurant. You will have time to dress and make yourselves presentable. Dress code is strictly formal: tuxedos for men and long dresses for ladies. Please ensure you're in the restaurant by seven p.m.'

'Food,' says Smith. 'Does this mean food?'

I shake my head. My blood boils in my veins and I blurt out, 'No, not so easy, you don't get to do this. You're not training dogs or breaking in cadets. You made me jump off the ship to entertain viewers and now you want us all to dress up? So they can watch us devour meat because you chose to practically starve us this whole time? I'm not playing your games.' I stand up. 'Unlock all the food stores. We bought our tickets; now let us live freely on the ship. Enough is enough. Spy on us if you've got nothing better to do, but let us eat and drink, for pity sake. Treat us humanely.'

I am shaking with anger.

Lips says, 'The gala dinner will begin at seven sharp. Now, does anyone have a question?'

'Yeah, I have a question,' says Daniel. 'How are you allowed to do this if we are not consenting to it?'

The lips purse for a moment, skin wrinkling slightly, and then she answers, 'In fact you each consented when you booked your tickets.'

'That's bull . . .' says Smith, before he stops himself. 'You know it is. Would never stand up in a court of law.'

'You consented when you completed RMS *Atlantica* booking forms. Your tickets and itineraries clearly laid out this possibility. Clause seventeen, subsection D, paragraph six. *By purchasing this ticket and boarding the RMS* Atlantica *you hereby consent to participation in whichever events, group activities and performances the crew and entertainment staff deem necessary.* Even though your tickets were booked by others – Daniel by your agent, Frannie by your parents, Caroline by Peter Davenport, Smith by your friend John – you signed the papers and are nonetheless bound by those contractual terms.'

I can't compute what she's telling us. This is not the time for legalese. 'Would you have left me out in the middle of the ocean all on my own?' I say, my teeth gritted. It's not the question I had planned but it escapes from my mouth.

'The aloneness of any terrestrial ocean is merely an illusion,' she says, robotically. 'You are never alone in the Atlantic. You're one of a million or more people on boats, on ships, in the water, on jetties and beaches. You would not have been truly alone, Caroline.'

I push my hands to my eyes and force my knuckles so deep into my eye sockets that I start seeing kaleidoscopic phosphenes: psychedelic swirls and luminous spirals. My instinct on hearing the answer is to sob, but I refuse to give her the satisfaction.

'Which direction are we headed in?' says Frannie. 'Towards New York?'

'Only one question per passenger, per day, please. Francine, the *Atlantica* is currently headed in a south-westerly direction.'

'Ask her if we're headed for New York,' Frannie says to Smith. 'You can ask her that. Are we still going to the USA or not?'

Smith sniffs and looks at the screen.

He scratches his wrist and looks at me, then at Daniel.

Then he asks, 'Out of the four of us, who opened the box?'

70

'Wait,' says Daniel, staring down Smith. 'What did you just do?'

Smith stands up and shrugs.

Lips says, 'The passenger who opened the box . . .'

'None of us,' says Daniel firmly, standing up and scowling at the man by his side. 'Not one of us. We did not open that box.'

'. . . was . . .' says Lips.

'We *all* opened the box,' says Daniel, much louder now, lifting his hands in the air. 'Let's not do this.'

A long pause.

'Francine,' says Lips.

Smith and Daniel both take a step back away from her.

Daniel loses his composure and slams his fist into the back of an armchair.

'Frannie?' And suddenly I have sea water in my mouth again, spluttering, desperate to reach that pontoon, to find safety. 'You?' I say, coughing. 'You opened the box?'

She shakes her head. 'I did not open the box. I wouldn't do that. We agreed we wouldn't touch the box so I didn't touch the box. I swear I didn't.'

'Passengers have forty-five minutes to prepare and

dress for the gala dinner in the Diamond Grill,' says Lips. 'I wish you fair winds and calm seas.'

The screen turns off.

'You opened the box?' shouts Smith. 'These consequences are all because of you? Why did you do it? So you'd be noticed on the show, finally, is that it? So the viewers would remember you for something?'

'I'm serious,' she says, pleadingly, her palms out in front of her. 'I didn't open it! I promise! I was a little drunk that night, we all were, but I'd remember something like that. I didn't open it.'

She looks over towards the box itself, still perched on top of the drip tray under what was once an ice sculpture of the RMS *Atlantica*.

'She said you opened it,' says Daniel, taking a deep breath. 'They have all the cameras they need. They'll have footage. Tomorrow I'll ask if we can view the video evidence. Until then I think we should all take a breath. Innocent until proven guilty.'

I keep coughing.

'Are you OK?' asks Frannie.

I look at her like *Don't you dare. I do not understand whose side you are on so do not pretend you're concerned with my welfare.*

We head back to our rooms. No talking. Changing into a silk dress and high heels is absurd but at this point I'll do anything Lips asks if it means we are fed. Even if it turns out to be a sandwich and a bottle of orange juice, it'll be worth this incremental loss of dignity. I'll play the games to stay alive; ultimate humiliation to entertain the anonymous masses through their touchscreens.

I'll give in to it.

We all will.

'I didn't open the box,' mutters Francine, reaching back to zip up her black dress. 'I can't prove it to you yet but I'm telling the truth. I wouldn't jeopardise our safety. And if I had opened it in a moment of drunkenness I'd have confessed to you, Caroline – Caz. I hate this.'

'I hate it, too,' I say, but there's no warmth to my voice. I've lived through too many betrayals in my life to forgive easily. Gemma moves on faster than I can. She'll offer people second chances. 'That Water challenge will give me nightmares until the day I die. I keep thinking about the depth underneath me. Not imagining my death exactly, but sensing my body sinking slowly into darker and darker water. Fading away. The silent, chilling loneliness of it.'

She comes over to comfort me but I pull back. 'We should go,' I say. 'If I don't eat soon I'm going to pass out.'

She applies a quick brush of lip balm and then we join the others in the hall.

Daniel doesn't say anything, but seeing us both in formal attire for the first time, with everything else degrading around us, he can't help but smile.

'Here,' he says, removing a hair from my shoulder. He smells different. A woody scent probably scavenged from someone's wash bag. It suits him.

'Thank you.'

'We're going to get fed,' he says. 'Because of you. Food, could even be a lot of food, enough to keep some back for whatever comes next.' He glances at Frannie. 'We mustn't fracture as a group.'

'Sometimes a fracture doesn't heal the same way it was before,' says Smith, scowling. 'You were the one I trusted most of all, Francine.' He looks more sad than angry. 'Why did you open it?'

I know these three intimately through our shared trauma, but, at the same time, I realise I don't really know them at all.

'We still have Body and Air to come,' says Daniel. 'From what I saw of Water, the team element, we'll need all of us working together just to make it through. We fall apart now and we'll stand no chance. We split and people could get lost in the ocean.'

I adjust his black bow tie. He's shaved, fine red bumps on his neck. I breathe him in.

We walk past dozens of empty rooms to reach the stairwell. Four people in evening dress scuttling around on Beelzebub's yacht.

The lights dim and then they switch off altogether.

Smith uses his torch to illuminate the steps for us. We can't afford anyone breaking a leg or wrist. I take it slow. We walk tight together through dark restaurants, lounges and passageways, our eyes acclimatising.

The wind is picking up and the ship pitches from side to side, but not to the point where we lose balance. Through the lobby, on towards the Diamond Grill. Cameras hidden behind mirrors and air vents watch our every step. A parade of squinting, overdressed captives marching through a floating penitentiary. Are the cameras infra-red? Or night vision? How must we look? The inmates of some hitherto unimagined concentration camp, starved, dressed up in clothes a size too large, being forced to perform for some unseen guard. A chain gang with no hope of escape.

Music pipes through from speakers. 'Rhapsody in Blue' by Gershwin, but you'd be hard-pressed to identify it. The volume is low and the track is playing at half-speed.

A single light up ahead, guiding us.

We enter the Diamond Grill itself, the restaurant class Pete and I never had tickets for, and the entire room is dark save for one table in the far corner. A round table with four chairs picked out by a theatrical spotlight somewhere high on the ceiling. The table is set with fine china. Plates, bowls, knives, forks, fish knives, teaspoons, wine glasses, water tumblers, bread plates, butter knives, folded napkins, elaborate floral centrepieces. The flowers are drooping, though. Each stem is limp, the tablecloth covered in discarded petals and pollen smudges. Yesterday we discussed drinking from the vases but Daniel informed us that flower food can be toxic to humans. There is so much water on and around this ship and yet we cannot drink any of it.

The soaring trumpet solo of 'Rhapsody in Blue', that epic musical portrait of New York City, is unsettling when slowed down. That rise in pitch, triumphant at its normal tempo, resembles something from an exorcism. Like a final scream for help.

The white spotlight is dazzling. It makes us appear pale, heavy shadows under our eyes and chins. A black and white photo from another era. We each stand behind a chair, boy-girl-boy-girl, the way we've been conditioned to do.

'Where's the food?' asks Francine, desperation in her voice.

'You thought there would be real food?' says Smith, snorting. 'There is no food, Francine. Thanks to your actions there's nothing here to eat. All the food's down in the locked stores on Deck Two. Refrigerated and secure. There is no gala dinner, only *consequences*.'

'Well,' she says, 'I think . . .'

'Treating us like rhesus monkeys,' he goes on, squinting up at the spotlight. 'You want me to dance on a table, Admiral, is that what you want?' He looks around the room, spinning, pointing at different mirrors, jabbing with his finger. 'Anything for another thousand paying viewers. We're hungry. I'm sixty years old and I demand some food.'

Daniel sits down. We all sit down. The light is directly in my eyes so I have to raise my hand in order to see the others. Smith does the same. Francine appears as a silhouette.

'They're evil,' mutters Smith. 'How do they think they're going to get away with this?'

Daniel frowns. Then he smiles and pulls up the edge of the tablecloth and peers under.

71

There are three small plug-in refrigerators under our table.

'This one says *First course, start here*,' says Frannie. She goes on, '*Do not open second course until first course is complete.*'

My mouth starts watering. 'Mains and dessert on this side. Three-course gala dinner, kind of.'

'Let's lay it all out on the table,' says Smith, his eyes wide. 'See what we have.'

I wince as my stomach growls so loudly I'm sure the others can hear it.

Daniel says, 'We should follow the instructions to the letter. Last thing we want is to break their rules and the fridges to lock shut.'

'He has a point,' says Smith, disappearing under the table on his hands and knees. We hear him whistle, then, clutching a chilled bottle of Pol Roger champagne, he reappears. 'French champagne. You won't have had this in Gold class. Who wants some?'

'All champagne is French champagne,' says Frannie, acid in her voice. 'I'll open it.'

She removes the foil and holds the bottle at forty-five degrees, twisting the bottle, extracting the cork expertly, and then she fills our flutes.

'Take it easy,' I say. 'The state we're in, it'll go straight to our heads.'

'I'd like to make a toast to young Francine over here,' says Smith, standing, raising his glass. 'Because if these are the kinds of consequences coming our way after her little box incident then I'd say we all owe her a sincere apology.'

She sets her smile and says, 'I never opened the box. I already explained that.'

'To consequences,' says Smith, sipping his champagne. 'Delicious consequences.'

I drink and it is sublime. Cold and fresh and quenching and it feels wonderful to be sitting at a table doing something relatively normal. The only thing that's jarring, aside from being under constant surveillance, is the bright spotlight illuminating us. The rest of the cavernous Grill Room is pitch-black. The lamp makes us all look terminally ill. Smith unshaven and tired-looking. Daniel gaunt and anxious in his tux. Francine looks as if she has vitamin deficiencies. We're well-dressed tonight but viewers will note that we don't look healthy. Thin, unwashed, shadows under sunken eyes. Like a group of homeless people dressed up for some exploitative magazine photo shoot. And I can only guess how I must look under these harsh lights.

They all appeared healthy enough before we walked down here.

'First course,' says Daniel. 'I'll serve.'

Vapour from his breath. The restaurant is almost as cold as out on deck.

He brings out bowls and sealed boxes from the fridge and places them down on the table. Upon opening the containers we come to understand that our gala dinner first course comprises of mini blinis, sour cream, packs of chopped chives, vacuum-sealed chopped hard-boiled eggs, and sealed tins of beluga caviar.

'I'd have opted for a hamburger or pork tenderloin,' says Smith, ripping open his packages. 'But fish eggs and mini pancakes look pretty good from where I'm sitting.'

We sip champagne and eat delicate mouthfuls of blini covered in sturgeon egg and sour cream. I've never tried caviar before. Pete likes it; he's told me so. On recent dates he said he'd like to take me to Paris and Madrid and Bologna one day. He's obsessed with Bologna. He talks about it being home to the oldest university in the western world, how the pasta is to die for, how it's a centre of culture and radical debate. I'd give anything to be with him tonight. Watching him crouch down in his old jeans to light the fire in his log burner, using his late father's bellows to get it going. The weight of him when he joins me on the sofa. The feel of his chest as I rest against him. Pete's mentioned caviar twice in the past, and, now, as of today, I can say I love it as well. Salty and fresh. I had imagined the eggs popping in my mouth but they seem to melt instead. I'm not ready for oysters, but I could definitely eat caviar again in future.

'My belly was completely empty,' says Daniel. 'Like, on zero. I had to make a new hole on my belt.'

His smile has turned boyish. We're seated here, an unlikely table of four, and this place is more manageable with food. I am positive all of a sudden. My mood has transformed and I have a droplet of hope. We should all have been enjoying a luxurious ocean crossing but right now, for once, it almost feels like we actually are.

'What was that?' asks Frannie, sitting straighter.

I look where she's looking.

'Check the fridge, Danny,' says Smith. 'Are there any more fish eggs left?'

'It's nothing,' says Frannie, relaxing back in her chair. 'I thought I saw something move over there in the far corner. My mind's playing tricks.'

'Go easy on the drink,' says Smith.

Daniel shines his light in the direction Frannie gestured to and there's nothing there.

'What did you see?' he asks.

'Just my imagination,' she says, biting into another blini. 'This ship's driving me half-insane. Doesn't matter. It was just a shadow. I'm sure it was.'

72

I use my last blini to mop up the remaining sour cream and caviar, not wasting a milligram, and Smith refills our glasses.

'This fizz is going straight to my head,' he says. 'I'm not complaining. Wine is fine but liquor is quicker, my old momma used to say, God rest her soul.'

'Main course?' says Daniel. 'I'm still half-starved.'

I open the main course fridge door.

Three shelves with various glass containers and sealed boxes.

Frannie clears away our old plates and because of the strange lighting she almost disappears as she leaves to place them down on the next table.

'What is it?' asks Smith. 'Don't tell me, don't tell me. Let me guess. Beef Rossini, no, no, I take that back. Turbot with buttery mashed potato and string beans. OK, I got it. Rack of lamb with garlic breadcrumb crust and a medley of vegetables?'

He looks excited as I start unpacking boxes and pulling off lids. Daniel helps me arrange the food on the table and Francine pours the last of the champagne into our glasses.

I'm dizzy from the alcohol.

'There any water in that fridge, Caz?' asks Daniel.

'Bottle of white wine,' I say, staring at the bottle. 'Montrachet.'

'Expensive,' says Smith, slurring his words. 'Five-star wines. That's why I'll only travel Diamond class, even though it's a stretch. This is my usual Grill so I feel right at home. That's a Diamond-class burgundy.'

Frannie finds a corkscrew at the sommelier's station and opens the wine.

'Tinned duck rillettes,' I say, reading from the top of the container. 'Sourdough bread. Quince jelly. Roquefort cheese. Watercress salad.'

'Canned duck and cheese?' says Smith. '*Duck and cheese*? That's Gold-class dining. We don't have any hot food?'

'It's been here for days,' I say. 'All this is food suitable for long-term storage, I know about these things. This won't spoil. I guess they planned our special meal in advance.'

Frannie rubs her eyes and says she's feeling tired.

'Me too,' says Smith. 'All that stress from the challenges, the sabotaged sand timer, not knowing when I'll get fed. Listen to me, Frannie. What you did: opening the box and all. It's better to get that kind of thing off your chest. Tell the truth and move on, you know?'

'I didn't open it.'

I take my knife and spread some of the coarse duck rillettes on a slice of sourdough bread. The bread feels chill from the refrigerator, and they probably treated it with some kind of preservative to make it last this long, but still, I'm eager to taste it.

'Maybe dessert will be hot?' says Smith. 'Self-heating packets or something? I could murder a hot waffle with maple syrup and heavy cream.'

I bite into the rillettes and then, as discreetly as I scan, spit it out into a napkin.

'Not what you ordered, *madame*?' says Smith.

'It's ninety per cent salt,' I say, wincing, swilling my mouth with wine and swallowing. 'It's inedible.'

Smith takes a lick and his face contorts. Daniel takes a small bite and then spits it out on to his plate and stands up. He uses his napkin to clean his mouth.

'They got the seasoning wrong?' says Frannie, probing her food with her fork.

'Very wrong,' I say.

Daniel sits down unsteadily and slumps in his chair.

'Are you OK?' Frannie asks him.

A noise from the distance.

'I saw it, Frannie,' says Smith, and then he coughs and collapses against the table, his arms pushing plates into the dead floral centrepiece, knocking over his glass of wine.

My vision starts to blur from the alcohol.

'So many,' says Francine, slurring.

'Frannie,' I say. 'I don't feel right.'

And then everything goes black.

73

'Gemma?' The word emerges from my dry mouth as a wheeze.

Where am I? Everything's dark. I reach out and touch the weave of a carpet or rug.

The room is cool. Vague. As if my eyes are still closed. 'Gem?'

Someone moans next to me and I am brought back to reality. The ship. Lips. My fellow passengers.

'What happened?' I ask, coughing.

But nobody replies. I use my hands to lift myself, use my chair to stand upright, but the room has no light whatsoever. The spotlight has turned off.

Something moves. I can't see it exactly but I can sense it.

'Frannie?'

It scuttles over my foot. I scream at the top of my voice and my heart races. I start panicking, running around, crashing into other tables and chairs, tripping over, one shoe on, one shoe lost.

'They're everywhere,' I whisper.

'What?' says a man's voice, drowsy. 'What happened?'

'Daniel.' I reach out in the darkness, my arms outstretched. More squeaking from the floor. Sounds like dozens of them. 'Daniel, switch on the light. The torch. Flashlight. Switch it on.'

'What happened?' he asks, slurring his words.

I step towards him, reaching out.

'Where are you? You need to switch the light on.'

The sound of a chair falling over and then more of them start screeching. I scream again, a piercing shriek, and run, hitting a table, and then I stand precariously on a chair.

A beam of light points up at the ceiling.

'Caz?'

The light moves around the room, hitting mirrors and polished wood veneers. Daniel gets to his knees, the light from the torch shaking, and then he shines it at our table.

They're running frantically over our plates, grazing on our leftovers, gnawing through paper and cardboard containers, mating, biting each other, drinking from glasses, each one with a tail as long as a carving knife.

74

Frannie wakes up and she is too terrified to scream. She opens her mouth in horror but no noise emerges. She clambers to her feet and stumbles over to me and climbs up on the table and holds me firmly by the shoulders and she says, 'We have to escape here. What is this?'

'I count to three and then we all run,' says Daniel.

I look around. 'Where's Smith?'

Daniel moves, kicking them out of the way, them screeching, him swearing under his breath, his pathetic light flying around the room. 'Smith, wake up. Get up right now.'

The weak beam of light fades as Daniel moves around the table, the noise of scurrying and biting. 'Wake up!' he yells.

The torch light goes off.

'Daniel,' says Frannie.

'He's unresponsive,' answers Daniel. 'We'll have to leave him here. He's not waking up. I don't know what's wrong with him.'

The torch light reappears and Frannie jumps off the table and runs over to them both, shouting on and off, muttering and cursing.

Five minutes later she's managed to rouse Smith. He throws up, and then, when he sees what's happened to our table, he throws up again.

The four of us run, Daniel's light dancing off the Art Deco paintings and murals as we flee for the exits and head up the staircase.

Smith sits down on the third step, holding his chest. 'I can't. I need to rest. What was that?'

'We left a full fridge back there,' says Frannie.

'The desserts,' says Daniel.

The ship has turned wild and now there is no reasoning, no rationalising the pros and cons. This place is our enemy.

'I'll go back,' she says. 'You wait here, give me the torch, and I'll go and take the food. I'll collect it.'

'Are you insane?' I say.

She wipes her mouth on her wrist and says, 'We're not getting the food and water we need. Whoever's in charge doesn't care about our welfare, that's clear now. We don't know what's happening in five minutes' time, never mind five days. I'll go and retrieve the rest of the food.'

Frannie runs away from us. We don't hear her scream this time. One of the rats emerges as she heads in and Daniel throws his shoe at it, causing it to divert down to a lower deck.

She returns holding a piece of paper.

'No food?' I ask.

She shines the torch on the paper.

Dessert is for passengers who finish their main course.

75

With every flight of stairs we climb, visibility gradually returns. Splinters of dirty moonlight from small windows, and then thick shafts through glass doors. We arrive back at our cabins.

'I want a hot shower and a cooked breakfast and a newspaper,' says Daniel. 'That's all I want. Enough of this game-playing. I'm a grown adult. I obey laws and I pay my taxes in full. I just want a coffee and some clean clothes. We're not prisoners.'

'You wanna win the money, you gotta roll the dice,' says Smith in an exaggerated accent as he disappears into their duplex cabin.

Daniel looks up at the unconcealed CCTV camera by the ceiling in the corridor. 'You can't go around drugging people.' His voice is cracking as he speaks. 'That's criminal behaviour, and I don't care what you say about consent and terms and conditions. It's not morally right. We retain autonomy over our own bodies. Do you know how dangerous it is to medicate someone unwillingly? You don't do that . . .'

He's shaking with rage.

Francine smiles a desperate smile.

'What?' I ask.

'I took a module in public international law before I switched to philosophy. Diplomatic immunity, human rights conventions, treaties, proportionality. Admiralty courts and the Law of the Sea,' she says. 'I didn't really pay that much attention to it at the time but I remember the basics because the lecturer was so charismatic. I think he was a QC barrister. He talked about the way sovereign law, the rules governing individual nation states, doesn't apply out here in the middle of the ocean. It's not quite the Wild West, but it's close. Ships hire mercenaries and ex-soldiers to repel pirates; war-fighters armed with automatic weapons. Captains are allowed to marry couples. It's almost akin to being in Outer Space, he explained. Countries, authorities, they might claim they can impose their rules but in practice they can't. Something about the flag of the ship, and customary rules that have come about over the centuries. But, you see, it's not like there are police out here to oversee compliance. So, in a sense, Lips and her people can do pretty much what they like.'

I try to digest what she's said.

'They haven't met my attorney,' says Smith, stepping back out to join us. Was he eavesdropping? 'Drugging our champagne? My head still doesn't feel right. My attorney's settlement will make the prize money of this so-called show look like nothing.' He stares at himself in the mirror, talking to the camera that's surely behind it. 'You cannot do this to law-abiding people.'

Daniel opens the collar of his dress shirt. 'I'm going to build a fire on deck. For all we know we could be headed up into the Arctic. It feels cold enough for it.'

'I'll feed the dogs,' says Frannie, removing her heels. 'Give them a walk.'

I long to be with someone I know and trust. What I wouldn't give for an evening in front of the television with Pete, him answering all the impossible questions on some quiz show, curtains drawn, mug of tea in my hand. I'll never take that security for granted again.

'How long were we out for, do you think?' I ask, looking at the dawn light on the horizon. 'I'm losing all sense of time. One day and two nights? Or just one night?'

Smith looks at his wrist and starts to talk but then his mouth falls open.

'What?' says Frannie. 'How long were we out?'

'I'm not saying it out loud, but I think I just remembered something that could get us off this ship. Follow me.'

76

We head down the corridor in single file, down the stairs, through to the unlit Ocean Lobby.

'What are we looking for?' I ask.

Smith keeps jogging. He has extra vitality.

Past the blank TV, past the open box, past the silent piano, past the threshold of the casino.

Daniel helps us with his torch.

'Shine it over here,' says Smith. 'The watch counters.'

He points to something in the obliterated Breitling counter.

'You brought us back down here for this?' I ask.

'That large one,' he says. 'It's called the Breitling Emergency. Designed for mountaineers and adventurers. You see that little screw on the bottom right? You loosen that and pull out a long piece of cable. That cable forms part of an emergency beacon that transmits on a special wavelength. It's the international distress code. As long as the watch has battery power we'll be able to put out the signal and we'll be able to get help whether Lips likes it or if she doesn't. Food and water. We'll be able to leave this ship.'

Two hours later we're sitting around the fire at the front of the ship, burning walnut coffee tables from the

Cape Cod Lounge. Heavy clouds have moved in with the breeze. We boil the last of the garbage can water in kitchen saucepans and I can't wait for mine to cool before I drink it. It's scorching hot and yet it tastes divine. Lubricating my throat as I swallow, filling my empty stomach.

Pale magenta sparks drift up into the sky, and the paintwork around our fire site continues to blister and blacken and peel away like burnt skin. There were no fish in the net when Daniel checked. Possibly because of where we are in the world. Possibly because the webbing was damaged from my rescue.

I keep imagining Pete arriving on a speedboat with a team of rescuers. I'm so desperate to see him.

The Breitling watch is strapped securely to Smith's wrist.

He keeps looking at it.

We all do.

'I don't know,' he says. 'Maybe I should never have remembered this.'

Frannie frowns. 'We pull the cord and then we get a hot meal. A boat comes to pick us up, possibly later today. We'll get bottles of mineral water; we'll have warm clothes, working toilets. What don't you know?'

'I don't know either, if I'm honest,' says Daniel, moving a table around on the fire, poking the embers with the end of a parasol. 'It's the easy way out but I keep thinking of how my parents moved to the States from Korea. They still talk about those days. They tell us stories of the journey, of how difficult it was to settle and be accepted by neighbours, how hard they had to work and save just to get by.'

'Harder times back then,' says Smith.

'Dad told us they had to jump on opportunities whenever they arose because they didn't come along often for people like them. He talked about rising to the challenge. Seizing every chance. Not backing down when the pain sets in, but rather gritting your teeth and seeing something through to the end.'

'You cannot be serious,' says Frannie. 'This is completely different.'

'Is it, Frannie?' I say. 'We must be halfway through now. Maybe we shouldn't stop just before the end?'

Frannie nudges a half-burnt stack of newspapers with a mop handle. 'Easy for you to say. No offence, but you've already completed your challenge. Now you're drifting through to the finish line. I still have no clue what I'm about to face.'

I watch Daniel shake his head. 'The way I see it, I'll never be able to build anything permanent or useful on what I earn. But if I were to get through this I could make a difference to a lot of children. Maybe I haven't been there enough for my own daughter, but that's going to change, and I can help other families too.'

'I say we pull the cord, Smith,' says Frannie. 'Let's end this farce. Return to our lives. Pull the cord and at least we'll all make it off this ship alive. A lifetime of PTSD, but we'll live.'

'And . . . I hate to say it, we'll be poor,' says Daniel.

After Dad died, Mum was terrified of letting us all down. She started economising harder, skipping meals again, buying discounted food and turning her central heating right down. Poverty is only understood properly by those who have lived it.

'We're all on an ocean liner,' says Frannie. 'I have to break it to you, Daniel. We're not that poor.'

'I live in a van. I think I qualify.'

'Yeah, but you're *alive*,' she says. 'Actually alive. With options. You can sell your story, Daniel; I'm sure magazines will want your face and torso plastered all over their covers. We can all sell stories. *The reality show that pushed the boundaries*. We can each come out of this with a pay cheque.'

I take another sip of hot garbage can water.

'Is it wise for just one person to wear the watch?' says Frannie, pointing at Smith's wrist. 'It's too much responsibility. And no offence, Smith, but you tend to drink more alcohol than we do.'

'No offence taken,' he says. 'You tend to open boxes more than we do.'

'We should take it in shifts to wear it,' says Daniel. 'I keep changing my mind about pulling the cord or not. I'm so hungry I can't think straight.'

Eventually, after much discussion, we agree to leave the watch strapped around the base of a leg of the Ocean Lobby grand piano. We agree to activate it only when two of us agree to do so. And we agree to release half of the dogs to help with the vermin problem.

The question whether or not to pull that cord qualifies as yet another gamble.

A hideous coin-toss.

Fifty-fifty.

77

Frannie volunteers to select which dogs to set free. She says she'll choose the six that most resemble *ratting* dogs: small terriers and Jack Russells. And she'll continue to look after the rest in the kennels. They'll keep each other company that way and we'll limit the amount of defecation and wildness on the ship. Although to me it already seems as if we've descended, in only a matter of days, from a luxury vessel, to an abandoned post-flood arc: a decrepit boat with backed-up toilets and burnt air, overseen by some faceless group of outsiders.

Frannie hands us each a roll of liner bags she found in the housekeeping area. She says it's vital for cleanliness and health that we all pick up and dispose of all dog waste as soon as we find it.

I head down to the Platinum Grill kitchen. I do three trips in all, carrying back up every saucepan and mixing bowl capable of collecting rainwater and putting them into position for next time we have a downpour. We desperately need water. As I pull open stainless steel doors and empty the shelves of bains-marie and stock pots, I realise how short-sighted we've been, laying out such a small variety of buckets each night in the hope of some moisture. Not capitalising on storms, instead retreating to our doorless duplex cabins. We need to stop acting as though a benevolent force will intervene on our behalf, and start acting as if we're shipwrecked.

Three of them in the Gold Grill kitchen, and a dozen more scurrying down the stairwell.

When I surface on the main deck there are dogs wandering around in a pack hunting precisely nothing. Over by the fire there are two more being petted and stroked by Smith as he reclines on a deckchair, heating his sockless feet close to the flames, a magazine and empty martini glass by his side.

The saltwater pool on the top deck, the largest pool on the ship, is still concealed. The hard shell, constructed so people can dance on top of it, covers the water and we cannot remove it.

If Dad were still alive he'd be betting heavily on who the winner will be. He would choose who he thought had the best odds. I doubt he'd put money on his own daughter.

I walk down into the Ocean Lobby. There's something about the screen where Lips appears each evening that's perversely comforting. Maybe it's some twisted form of Stockholm syndrome, but she answers our questions. I am desperate for insights, about home, about Pete, about what comes next, and she is the only source we have.

The piano starts to play and I turn on my heels to face it.

Two keys over and over: F, and F-sharp.

Down on the floor by the piano stool is the watch we left there. It's still strapped securely around the piano leg. But leading away from it is a metre-long metallic cord.

Someone has activated the emergency beacon.

78

I walk to the watch and use my dying torch to illuminate it.

The coiled wire leading from its case is the length of my arm. The dial clearly shows it has been activated.

'What the hell have you done?' asks Smith, suddenly behind me.

'It wasn't me,' I say, startled. 'I found it like this.'

He unfastens it from the piano leg and says, 'How do we deactivate it? There must be an abort switch.'

'It wasn't me.'

'You're the only one down here, Caz.'

An hour later we're on the fire deck, as we now call it, and the seas are choppy. Not so rough where the waves break over the front of the ship and extinguish our heat source but we may be heading that way.

'Who pulled the cord?' says Daniel. 'No repercussions. Let's clear the air.'

'Don't look at me,' says Frannie, cradling a miniature poodle. 'I didn't open the box and I didn't mess with that watch. I wouldn't even know what to do with it.'

'Well,' says Smith, 'I did see you reading the instructions from the box earlier. You unscrew the cap and you pull, it's that simple.' He turns to face me. 'Caz, Daniel, are you sure we can trust her?' He turns back to Frannie. 'You want to win that bad? You're prepared to fight against us for the money?'

'You're a fool,' she says. 'A hungry fool, which is worse still. Take my word for it or don't. I never opened the box and I never touched your watch.'

The day after Dad's funeral I walked, in a complex fog of grief, numbness, regret and relief, down our local high street. It felt as though everyone was staring at me, as though they all knew. Without thinking I crossed the road and walked into a betting shop. Nobody looked at me. They were all too engrossed with their betting slips and the horse-racing on the TV. I felt unseen. I pushed a coin into a machine and pulled the handle. I played on. I lost all the cash I had on me and I told myself it was one final goodbye to my father.

I never told Mum or Gem.

Some secrets must be kept.

Frannie's dog starts writhing so she sets it down. It barks. Daniel says, 'Wait a minute. Is that . . .?'

We look out to sea, at what he's staring at.

'I don't see anything,' says Smith.

Frannie runs to the metal steps leading up to the observation deck where spare propellers are displayed like fine art installations. She reaches for the telescope installed on the guard rail.

'Is it?' I yell.

'Headed right for us,' she says, relief in her voice. 'Looks like a fishing trawler.'

79

The boat grows slowly on the horizon as it approaches, black smoke spluttering from its engine as it pushes hard to reach us, to save us.

'How far away is it?' asks Smith.

'Five miles, maybe,' says Daniel. 'Trawlers aren't quick. They're built to withstand storms, not for speed.'

'They'll have food,' Frannie says, smiling, wiping her eyes. 'Lots of food. Biscuits, eggs, rice. Water. A phone or at least a radio.' She looks at me, tears forming rivulets down her dirty face. 'I'll be able to speak with Mum.'

I put my arm around her.

'I think I might stay right here,' says Smith. 'Try my luck.'

Daniel and I turn to him.

'I mean, I've played this long, managed through my librarian test – why not see it through? I might even take up reading. You guys should go with the fishermen, though. Enjoy the hot food, the snacks, the sodas. I'll be OK here by myself.'

'You wouldn't do that,' says Frannie.

Smith looks out at the boat. The engine noise is intensifying. 'Oh, I'll be fine,' he says. 'Now, Frannie, go get your belongings.'

She detaches from me and jogs away, turning back to say, 'Why are you like this, Smith?'

'I'm going with Frannie,' says Daniel. 'Might not be safe for a young woman on that trawler all the way out here.'

'Good for you, Mr Cho,' says Smith. 'What a gentleman. You should absolutely go with her. If I were your age I'm sure that's what I'd do. Same for you, Caz. Your sister's running the coffee house, right? You'll be wanting to get back to make sure she's managing. Make sure they're all—'

'My sister,' I say, cutting him off, 'will be managing the business perfectly well. She's capable. You really ought to think before you speak.'

'Oh, you won't be bothered by me and my clumsy old mouth any more once you set foot on that cosy fishing boat. They'll have crispy French fries and a heater in every room. Snickers bars and Coca-Cola in glass bottles. Might even have DVDs.'

Frannie returns with her few belongings in a carry-on bag. Seeing her drag it behind her makes our existence on board seem all the more preposterous. This crossing was supposed to be relaxing. Cocktails and ballroom dancing lessons. Fine dining, aromatherapy massages, and watching the ocean pass by on the way to New York. There were supposed to be shows in the theatre each evening and lectures in the daytime. Working through a stack of novels. Foxtrot lessons and afternoon tea. The voyage of a lifetime.

Daniel lifts his arm, pointing out to sea.

He says, enunciating each word, 'That doesn't look right.'

80

We are no longer the only vessel on the sea.

I sprint up to the observation deck and take control of the telescope. A heavy mass inside my stomach. Through the scope the orange flames are visible, and I can make out one man in a wet weather suit. He disappears from view.

I have no words.

'Are they saving us or are we saving them?' says Smith.

'They'll put out that fire,' says Frannie, taking her place at the telescope. 'I already have my bag packed so they'll extinguish their fire; there's no other way. I'll talk to Mum later on the radio. Professional fishermen. They'll all be trained for this kind of eventuality. They have drills and exercises and . . .'

The flames are visible with the naked eye now. No screams or cries for help. Just a burning trawler a few miles away, silent, so small I can eclipse it with the tip of my index finger.

'We need to help them,' I say.

'We can't even help *us*,' says Daniel, resigned, his brow furrowed.

Smoke rises at an angle, joining the heavy clouds above.

We jog around to the lifeboat deck and Daniel removes the steel pin. The mechanism activates. Pulleys and cables swing over the side of the ship and the lifeboat starts to descend towards the water. I should be hopeful but I am not.

'It'll work,' says Daniel. 'This time it'll work, I think. If it hits the water and unlocks I'll shimmy down the cable and set off to help them.'

The lifeboat hits the water and Smith says, 'It's all right. Look, this one is fine.'

And then, as if in slow motion, it pitches slightly to the port side.

Bubbles emerge.

The lifeboat sinks beneath the waves.

81

'This is the devil's work,' says Frannie, wide-eyed. 'They lie over and over again. They don't seem to place any value on human life, only trickery.'

She has a vacant look.

The trawler has gone under. It had a flag at its stern. I saw red and I saw blue. Could have been an Icelandic vessel come to save us.

'They force us to eat lemons and drink rainwater we collect in pans,' mutters Daniel. 'But they cannot tamper with lifesaving equipment. We can't deal with this.' He rips a life ring off its base and flings it out to sea. It lands perhaps twenty metres from the hull of the ship.

I wait for it to sink like the lifeboat.

It stays on the surface.

'Anything that floats,' I say. 'Throw it all overboard. They might be able to swim to it. Quick, before we move out of range.'

We drop over forty life vests and seven rings. Most, if not all, float. And we don't know – they may have their own lifeboat, a proper one, but somehow I doubt it. Not on a trawler that size. They could have an inflatable raft, but the speed with which the fishing boat sank means it's unlikely they had time to deploy it.

We reconvene by the fire and the low-lying clouds are silver-grey. We scanned the horizon with the scope and there was no sign of any survivors in the water. We can still track some of the floating debris.

'It'll have a radio,' says Daniel. 'GPS tracking. The captain will have radioed for help. There will be others who detected our distress signal from the watch signal. You see. Pretty soon there will be other vessels here to help them and to help us.'

'They should go find the trawler crew,' says Smith. 'I don't need help. I'm almost done; I'm not quitting now. You three leave if you can't stand it here but I'm staying where I am.'

I throw the broken fragments of what were once our duplex cabin doors on to the fire and the flames jump out and almost scorch my eyebrows.

The mood is subdued.

Even more subdued than before.

How did the show's producers select the four of us? I feel sick at the thought of middle-aged men sitting around a boardroom table comparing notes on a shortlist of potential passengers. I can picture them assessing our photos and reading bios provided by minions, analysing our chances of success, discussing the private motivations we each might have for playing on despite the obvious risks.

The wind changes direction and I receive a face full of smoke.

'I still don't know if I'll leave,' I say, sitting down cross-legged on the far side of the fire. 'I want to see Pete, talk to my family. I want to eat a normal meal. But we're close.

It's like when you wait for a bus and no bus comes and you keep on waiting and then as soon as you quit and walk away the bus arrives and you miss it.'

'Except,' says Frannie, crouched, her knees up by her chest, 'the bus stop isn't intent on torturing you. And charging onlookers for the privilege of watching.'

We wait for other ships to arrive.

Four broken people pacing, scoping, staring at the horizon.

No one comes.

Perhaps because the trawler told other vessels it would answer our distress call. Or because in this part of the ocean, far away from coastlines and shipping lanes, past the continental shelf, there are no other ships.

'Where are we?' I ask myself out loud.

A dog trots by with something hanging out of its mouth.

'East coast of Canada?'

Smith steps to me. 'I always thought I had a good sense of direction but we could be off Newfoundland or Antarctica by now. Always on the move. Turning, spinning, pivoting. Honestly, I don't have a clue. Feels like I'm going around in circles waiting to sink.'

'Could be close to Russia,' says Daniel.

'We doubled back?' I say.

'West, past Ireland, then north between Iceland and Greenland, or Iceland and the Scottish Hebrides, doubling back, past the Arctic coast of Norway. I don't know. We could be headed for Siberia.'

I imagine us waking up to snow, sheet ice covering the decks and railings, polar bears observing us in silence from the mainland. We're not an ice-breaker. We wouldn't fare well that far north.

'You think people died on the trawler?' asks Frannie. 'Fishermen with families. Young kids back in their homes waiting for a call from Dad. Or were they picked up?'

'I don't think anyone died,' I say.

'How do you know?'

I pause for a moment. 'Instinct. I think they were doing a good thing and they've been rescued. Either by the people attached to the show, or by a passing ship. They're all professionals; they have to be, to work all the way out here. They know what they're doing and they have access to equipment. Not like us.'

Mum's first husband was a trawlerman out of Grimsby docks. She didn't tell us about him until Gemma and I were teenagers. They had two years together before he died from an aneurism. I don't know much about him to this day except for what Mum shared in the years between Dad's suicide and her decline. But I remember he worked on a boat called the *Ross Tiger* and I understood, from the look in her eye, that she loved him with all her heart. She said he had sparkling blue eyes and he didn't talk very much. She said he wrote short poems for her. She said he could ride a horse. She has his photo framed by her bed in the care home.

'Lips stepped over a line,' says Frannie. 'A red line.'

'Yes, you told us before,' says Smith. 'Talk to the camera. Tell them. We already heard it. Does anyone have any secret food hidden away? I'll pay cash.'

Frannie puts her head in her hands. I'm worried about her. She seems more fragile with every passing day.

Then the ship's horn blows.

'I knew it was coming,' says Smith. 'I felt it.'

We walk away from the deck fire. Anxious, half-starved, exhausted.

We don't douse the flames because a heavy mist has set in. The pans will be filling. At least we have that.

Down in the Ocean Lobby the TV screen is glowing as we arrive.

We walk in, dejected.

A pair of Lips.

And one word.

BODY.

83

We stare at Daniel.

'You don't have to go through with it,' says Frannie. 'It's your choice. They cannot take that away from you. If you decide to sit it out, you can.'

'Sure,' says Smith. 'Sit it out. Let the three of us play on. You go take a nap or something.'

I think about uttering something reassuring but Lips starts talking so I stop myself.

'Good afternoon, passengers.'

We look at her, leaning in closer.

'Today is the Body challenge. Daniel, I will brief you on the safety features and goals of your challenge. This is a solo event so the rest of you will be housed temporarily inside an observation room on deck with access to a TV and window overlooking the main event. Daniel, after this conversation ends you will have precisely ten minutes to arrive at the base of the climbing wall located at the rear of the main funnel. Once the foghorn blows twice in succession, you will begin your ascent. You can wear the clothes you're in but you must remove your shoes and socks for health and safety reasons.

'At the uppermost section of the climbing wall the face moves from vertical to an overhang. That is the expert climbing section, designed for experienced climbers, and at the top of that section you'll see numerous artificial crevices and cracks. Secreted inside one of these cracks you will find a zipwire handle. Once you have located the handle you can position it over the steel cable leading from the top of the funnel down to the deck. You will exit the zipwire directly into the saltwater swimming pool. The cover has now been remotely retracted. Dive to the bottom of the deep end and retrieve a room key. The room key is the same colour as the pool lining. Once you exit the pool with the key in your hand you will be deemed successful in this challenge. The key will allow you and your fellow passengers to access a rewards cabin. Is that understood?'

Daniel says, 'I understand.'

'I wish you fair winds and calm seas.'

The screen turns off.

84

You think you'll never be stuck in a situation like this.

Until you are.

We walk briskly up staircase K3 and Daniel is quiet. He's mentally preparing for the climb. I open the door to the main deck and the wind almost blows me back inside: diagonal rain blowing across the ship. The deck is soaking wet and I can't see the far end of the *Atlantica*.

A dog howls faintly in the distance.

Daniel sets out towards the funnel and the rest of us shelter in the observation room, the door locking securely behind us. Glass walls, glass roof. Frannie takes a rolled towel from a recliner and pats her hair dry. Empty wine coolers and a marble bar at the far end.

'He doesn't have ropes,' says Frannie, peering through the glass. 'He should have ropes, surely. A harness. The top of that wall must be twenty metres off the deck. And that overhang, in these slippery conditions. You can't do this without safety gear.'

'It's what the masses want,' says Smith, his voice flat. 'Real jeopardy. Not manufactured reality TV, but genuine danger. God, I'm too hungry to talk. Listen, Caz survived when she jumped off the ship, didn't she? Must have made great TV. This is the same. Feels strange to us, here, now, but other shows have done worse. Daniel's reliant on himself now. He needs to face the wall.'

'Caz had help, though,' says Frannie, under her breath. 'From all of us. It was a team challenge. There's no way this is fair. He's out there all on his own in this weather.'

'Life isn't fair. That's something my generation understands. And, as you know better than the rest of us, Frannie, there are *consequences*. This is one of them.'

The foghorn blows twice and there's a sharp pain in my chest. My fall into the sea. How painful the water was on impact and how the salt burnt my throat and I couldn't tell which way I was facing.

'Look at him go,' says Smith.

Daniel moves elegantly and smoothly. He reaches for hand-holds and then swings his legs where no easy foot-ledge is within reach. It almost looks easy for him.

'He can actually do this,' says Frannie, smiling with relief.

I look away for a moment, to a section of deck I walked with Pete mere days ago. I wish I'd told him about the family history sooner. I guess when you finally meet the person you can imagine growing old with, you'll do anything not to ruin it. I held on too tight, trying to project the idea of a functional family, and now I don't know if I'll ever see him again.

The monitor shows a close-up of what we can see for ourselves through the raindrop patterns on the window. Daniel's face. The focus and determination in his features. He's saying *one hold at a time, one hold at a time* like a mantra. His face is lit and the icy rain is running off the tip of his nose. *One hold at a time.*

'What do you suppose is in the rewards cabin this time?' asks Smith. 'I for one will be eating a few mouthfuls and saving the rest. We have to assume the food is drugged from this point—'

'Son of a . . .' says Daniel, the camera zooming in tighter on his face.

The camera pans to highlight his right hand. He pulls it away from the wall and inspects his fingertips. They're covered in something dark blue. Some kind of viscous fluid. He rubs it between his fingertips and then wipes his hand on his soaked jeans.

'Some kind of grease,' says Smith. 'Engine oil.'

Daniel slows his pace. He takes a few deep breaths and then continues up the wall. His face is drenched with a mixture of rain and sweat, and his hair is plastered across his forehead.

'Those gusts aren't helping him,' says Smith.

Daniel is halfway up the wall. He does not look down. From that height I'm fairly sure a fall would be fatal.

He reaches for a foot-hold, his knee tucked up close to his chest, and then as he pushes himself up he lets out a scream of pain.

'What just happened?' asks Frannie.

The camera zooms in to focus on his foot.

It's dangling in mid-air.

The sole of his foot is red.

85

For a split-second the camera focuses on a short spike protruding from a hold. The upright nail gleams in the spotlights.

'Whoever set this up is sick in the head,' says Frannie. Then she turns to the camera in the corner of the room and says, 'You don't need to do this to him. You can stop, be merciful. You're pushing this too far.'

Daniel climbs on. Up, not down. I'd have quit by now. The thought of reaching up and gripping a shard of glass or an upturned nail is unbearable fifteen metres above a hard deck in a gale with no harness. And yet he keeps on climbing.

I back away from the window, unsteady as the ship pitches one way and then the other. We are alone. So extremely alone, and yet it's possible we are the most watched people on the planet.

'Another spike,' says Smith, cringing. 'His other foot. That one had to hurt.'

A close-up on Daniel's face: his jaw is clamped shut and he is hanging on by his fingertips. He reaches up carefully to probe the holds above the overhang. The muscles in his forearms tense. He lifts and swings but he has no foothold.

'Please,' whispers Frannie. And then she bangs her fist on the glass.

'Don't,' I say. 'He needs his concentration. He's strong. All that water-skiing and surfing. He can do it.'

He has to stretch up in the most unnatural way to make the next hold, using the weight of his body as a pendulum. The sinews and tendons in his hands are protruding like piano strings and his face is rigid with focus.

Smith stands with his nose up against the glass. 'He needs the handle or he'll fail.'

Daniel probes the artificial crevices for a minute or so and then pulls out a V-shaped metal object. He holds it in his teeth, still at the overhang section, and heaves himself up to the cable. The camera angle changes and I see him slip. He scrambles and his other hand catches a hold, his body hanging in dead space.

Frannie turns away, her head in her hands.

'Come on, Danny,' says Smith.

I brace myself against a recliner. This would be too much on a full stomach but, as weak as we are, it is torture.

We haven't known Daniel for long. I'm not religious but I recite the Lord's Prayer, memorised in primary school, inside my head.

Daniel reaches up and hooks the V-shaped bar over the cable. He's unsteady for a moment, turning on his axis, but he manages to begin his descent. The line is shaky. He descends slowly towards the water, shaking in the wind.

I see Smith's face fall.

Daniel drops down into the saltwater pool.

And the hard cover silently, smoothly, starts closing over the top of him.

86

A moment of silent panic.

Paralysis.

And then we bang our hands on the glass, and shout his name.

The cover keeps on moving, silently sealing the pool.

'Daniel!' says Frannie.

I can't speak. Everything slows down, the way it did when I leapt off the ship. The noise melts into an echoing buzz. On screen we watch Daniel as he looks up from the bottom of the pool and sees it now for the first time, the shadow creeping over him. On the TV, as part of the audience, violent in our inaction, I watch his face, underwater, in close-up. The disbelief and then the quiet horror. His mouth wide open, his eyes filled with the panic of a childhood night terror.

He starts to wriggle, pushing up off the bottom, room key in hand, but it's no use.

The pool cover seals shut like the lid of a pharaonic tomb. The scene is shrouded with rain and darkness and the ship is constantly in motion.

'They need to open it now,' says Frannie, shaking. She turns to the camera. 'Is this an accident? Did you mean to shut it over him? You must open the cover.'

We continue to watch Daniel kick and punch at the cover, the room key still in his hand, but the cover is almost flush with the water. There is so little air for him. A thin layer above his head.

'It's no good,' says Smith.

His head is tilted to the side so he can breathe.

I push my shoulder against the door but it will not budge.

I couldn't help Dad. For a long time I could help Gemma. And now I can't help Daniel.

'He won't be able to hold his breath much longer,' says Smith. 'I can't watch any more.'

The ship tilts hard to the port side and Daniel's air pocket disappears.

We fall silent.

He swims around, frantically searching for a way out. The storm intensifies and a deckchair is blown across from starboard to port.

I think of his daughter.

Four years old.

Quietly, with no screaming or hand-waving, he goes limp for a moment.

He kicks out again and we watch on, powerless. Bright lights erupt in our faces, blinding us. I turn to the screen and there is no image. Only a single line of text.

This content is for élite tier subscribers only.

87

There are some moments in life where you realise, deep inside yourself, that nothing will ever be quite the same again.

Frannie and I cry out. Smith rushes the door but it is still locked. We try everything to break through.

I move to comfort Frannie but she pushes me away, wailing, fighting.

'He has no air,' she says, between sobs, 'They trapped him down there.'

I hold up my palms and say, 'We don't know that. He might be OK. It could have been a malfunction. The cover might be off by now. He may have been evacuated from the ship.'

Smith's face is white from the harsh spotlights that shine directly at us. We can't hear what's going on outside and we cannot see a thing.

Frannie folds down into herself, kneeling on the floor. 'I can't.'

'I know,' I say.

'He died. You saw his face, Caz. You saw the look in his eyes.'

'He could have got out,' I whisper.

She stares at me, still crying, but quieter now. 'There's no way he could have survived that. They trapped him right in front of us, with everyone watching. What have we all done?'

The air has changed in this room.

Everything has changed.

'I never thought they'd go through with it,' mutters Smith. And then he turns red in his face and picks up a wooden chair and throws it at the door but the door does not give. The glass does not break.

'Don't,' I say.

'We need to do something.'

'If they don't want us out they won't let us out. They're in complete control.'

Frannie looks up at the camera and then slowly rises to her feet, wiping her face on her sleeve. She stands shaking with her head tilted up to the camera lens. 'You all watched him and now you're gawping at us, aren't you? I don't know how you can live with yourselves.' Tears stream down her face. 'You will bear this like a scar. There are some things you should never watch. You turn away. But you're all still viewing all this, aren't you?'

We try again to see out of the window, shielding our eyes with our hands.

'I can't make out a thing,' says Smith. 'The lights are too bright.'

Frannie beats on the glass with her open palms. 'Let me off this ship.' And then, in a smaller, frailer voice. 'He has a daughter.'

88

Before you lose someone, you cannot predict the shape or depth of the hole their absence will leave in your life.

By three the next morning Frannie has cried herself to sleep. Smith and I are talking in hushed whispers. He's resting with his back against the wall and I'm laid out with Frannie's head heavy on my lap. The bright lights are still pointed right at us in the observation room.

'I never thought they'd take it this far,' he whispers. 'Danny didn't deserve that.'

I stroke Frannie's head lightly, my hand barely running over her red hair. 'They went too far a long time ago.'

'Kind of reminds me of a country in civil war, or a dictatorship collapsing. No accountability.'

Frannie twitches so I soothe her back to sleep.

'Sooner or later someone will put a stop to it,' I say. 'Somebody has to decide enough is enough.'

He chews his lip and shakes his head. 'You think there are people out there helping Danny? Medivac, or something like that. Giving him oxygen, taking him to a hospital?'

I shrug. 'What hospital?'

He rubs his eyes with closed fists.

'Whatever it is they're doing,' I say, 'they don't want us to see.'

'Or they don't want us to know he's still in the pool. They couldn't have showed it all live, could they? There are rules.'

'I don't know. You'd hope so. But every now and then some new format comes along and stretches the boundaries. A groundbreaking idea that shocks and achieves record audiences and changes the ethics of broadcasting for ever more.'

He thinks about that.

'She looks like a child on your lap.'

'She almost is a child.'

'Did you ever, you know – want . . .'

I squeeze my eyes tight together.

'Sorry, I shouldn't have asked. The nonsense that comes out of my big mouth. Forget it.'

Frannie moves on my lap. Swallows.

'It's difficult.'

'I apologise,' he says. 'Honestly, you don't have to—'

'I was very young.' I set my jaw and take a deep breath. 'I didn't know anything.'

'You don't have to tell it if you don't want.'

I stroke Frannie's hair again, and smile. 'Sometimes life happens whether you're ready for it or you're not.'

'That's the truth.'

'When I was seventeen, still in school, I had a daughter. A beautiful seven-pound-two-ounce baby girl with a birthmark behind her ear.' I clear my throat. 'My boyfriend was already out of the picture by the time she was born. He was an apprentice mechanic. Wasn't a bad person – actually, he was a sweetheart. I still see him in town from time to time, outside the chemist or queuing at the post office, and we exchange a sad glance. We thought we knew it all back then, but when we found out I was pregnant we were both so scared. I thought I was grown-up but my first instinct was to run back to Mum. He moved on to a classmate of mine when I was about six months. She fell pregnant too, but he stuck with her. For a while at least.'

'I'm sorry.'

I shake my head. 'I made my peace with him leaving us. Mum helped me a lot; she was there at the birth, passing me the mask, giving me sips of water. I had wise, good-hearted, practical women all around me telling me it was my decision to make: I could choose what happened to the baby. They weren't talking down to me or trying to teach me lessons, they were just doing their best to help. A midwife from Leeds told me about her aunt doing the same thing years before, about the joy that baby boy had brought some other couple, and about how her aunt had made peace with it, eventually.' I close my eyes and let out a long sigh. 'I never really made peace with it, though. Not really. How could I?'

He nods, one side of his face bright white, the other half in shadow like some court jester from a bygone age.

I stroke Frannie's hair, red strands smooth under my fingers.

'Feels strange to say I had a daughter. I *have* a daughter. She's someone else's daughter now. She's been raised. Fed and changed and soothed in the dead of night. Taught and loved. Looked after. My precious little girl is part of another family and I take a walk by the river to wish her a happy birthday every spring. I look into the water and tell her. I talk to her sometimes, you see, even though I haven't seen her since the week of her birth. She'll be thirty-two next April the seventh. A grown woman. She might even have a family of her own.' I look at Smith through tears, smiling. 'I might even be a grandmother. I might be a nanna.'

He nods and smiles.

Frannie murmurs something in her sleep and I stroke her brow. 'I'll never know if I did the right thing when I was seventeen, but I know I'm not ashamed of it. Secrets eat away at you over time. Shame eats away, I know it does.'

He nods.

'Part of me went numb that year and that part never really came alive again. It lies dormant.'

He sniffs and says, 'I'm going to help out Daniel's family in some way. College fees for his daughter or something. If I win, or even if I don't, I'll see them straight.'

I smile at him. 'I'll try to do the same.'

Frannie starts twitching in her sleep so I caress her cheek with the back of my fingers.

'Go to sleep,' I whisper. 'It's all OK. Go to sleep, little one. You're safe.'

I wake at six a.m. Frannie's sitting up, watching me.

'Are you OK?' I ask.

She shakes her head. 'I had strange dreams.'

'I know, sweetheart.'

'The door's still locked and the lights are still on but you can see a little now in the daylight,' says Smith. 'Look.'

I stand and step closer to the window. Frannie tenses up and starts shaking as she looks at the pool, the retractable cover still in place as if nothing happened.

'Did someone come in the night?' she asks, squinting as she stares at the pool. 'A team of medics? Did you hear anything?'

'I was awake the whole time,' says Smith. 'Nobody came.'

The spotlights switch off.

'Oh,' says Frannie, clutching her chest.

There's an audible click and Smith tries the door. It opens. We walk outside but we do not run. It's not as though there could be any good news out here. There never is on this ship. The seas are calm and the air is fresh and cool. Sunshine breaking through thick, unmoving clouds.

We approach the pool cover.

Frannie points at the zipline running down from the funnel.

'It's all here,' she says. 'The climbing wall looks the same.'

She tries to remove the pool cover but it must weigh several tonnes. It's solid enough to be used as a dance floor for outdoor dance classes and club nights.

'Is he . . .?' she says, her lip quivering. 'Could he still be under there?'

'Oh, no, sweetie,' I say, glancing at Smith, then back to her. 'No, Frannie. He'll be in a hospital somewhere by now. He'll be receiving treatment, fluids, specialist care.'

I feel the need to protect her in any way I can, even though she's far stronger than I was at her age.

'His fiancée and kid might be with him already,' says Smith, helping me reinforce this white lie.

She shakes her head. 'He's gone. His body is here in the pool but Daniel is gone.'

The next hour passes slowly.

We are mourning a man we've known only for a few days. Remembering him.

One of his last acts was to place out even more receptacles to catch rain water. Those pans and buckets are now full to the brim. The three of us drink straight from the saucepans he arranged, letting the water flow, cascading from the sides of our mouths.

'That's the most I've drunk in three days,' says Smith, wiping his face with his hands.

'Thanks to Daniel,' says Frannie. 'We can't carry on. But how do we quit?'

I look at them both in turn, and then I stare out to sea. There are so many things I miss this morning. Daniel, mainly. Having him here with us. But also Pete, the smell of him, the feel of his hand in mine. Simple things like going out for a drink together in the village pub and being completely at ease. Sitting by the fire reading our books and not worrying about what the other is thinking about. I miss the warmth and safety of my café. Gemma, my colleagues and regulars. Nature: the infinite shades of green. I miss hearing birds, and crossing through traffic. Noisy children out playing football in the street, coats and bags for goalposts. Everything here is hard and manufactured. Cameras, microphones, hidden recording equipment. The pervading sense that whatever has happened is inconsequential relative to what's waiting for us around the next corner.

'We can't give up,' says Smith. 'Daniel fought hard for his challenge. We should do the same to honour his memory. Support those he left behind.'

'But she still has her challenge,' I say. 'Sweetie, listen, if you skip it nobody will judge you, not a single person.'

'Don't call me that, please.'

I nod. 'Of course. Sorry. If you skip it, Frannie, then whoever wins will share their winnings with you. God, I can't believe we have to talk about money on a day like this. But we agreed last night. We're a team, a family of sorts; we're not competing with each other any more. Right, Smith?'

'I'll help out, that's what I said, but I didn't agree anything about an equal split. I promise to help out his family and do what I can for the rest of you. I'll stick to my word.'

'I want to walk off the miserable ship,' Frannie says, and the look in her eyes worries me. There's something about her gaze that reminds me of Gemma the time she almost lost hope. 'I want the ship to pull up and dock against some barren rock and then I'll walk away to be on my own. I can't spend another day here.' Her expression is vacant. 'It's not a sick game any more. This is a burial ground.'

She tells us she needs to feed the dogs and give them water. I haven't seen the six we released. I guess they're downstairs hunting on the lower decks. No animals up here. Just shiny wet decks and the sound of the engines. I offer to accompany her but she smiles flatly and tells me she needs some time alone.

Later, the mood around the fire is solemn. Frannie found a half-full power-bank in the dog kennel lockers. She's charging her phone with it. Smith suggests, out of the blue, that we sing, and he starts off with a passable solo rendition of 'Walk the Line'. Frannie and I don't continue. Instead, we gaze into the spitting flames. Silent and reflective. Our thirsts are quenched but our souls are permanently bruised.

There are four stacks of cushions and mats arranged around the fire.

Four.

Before it becomes too dark, Frannie builds a kind of makeshift shrine to Daniel close to the library. She drags over a heavy table. There is an ornate crystal vase with dead flowers and no water. There are items from Daniel's jacket. Personal belongings we'll pass on to his family. I add a single battery-powered flickering candle and the copy of *The Hitchhiker's Guide to the Galaxy* that Smith found. Smith places down a magazine about water sports. We take a moment with our thoughts and then we return to our cabins ready for six p.m.

Frannie has an energy I haven't seen before. A cold, galvanising fierceness.

There's a knock on our cracked doorframe. Smith's standing there with one foot in and one foot out in the hall.

'It's a shallow thing to say but it's strange in that duplex without Danny,' he says. 'It feels empty without him.'

I pat his shoulder and we make our way silently to the Ocean Lobby.

No dogs out hunting.

No prey for them to stalk.

One minute before six. We assemble in our three chairs facing the TV on the pillar. The other chair is obscene: a pathetic memorial to our fallen friend.

The alarm on one of Smith's expensive watches goes off.

We wait.

One minute past six.

'She's late,' says Frannie.

This is out of kilter. The one thing we have relied upon, the one constant, our metronome, has let us down.

Two minutes past six.

My stomach is queasy.

Chalkiness inside my mouth.

The sound of a door opening behind us.

'Good evening, passengers.'

90

We turn to face the Admiral.

She's poised but her hands are shaking.

'No,' says Frannie. 'Is it *you*?'

She walks down the stairs elegantly, holding the hand-rail firmly the whole time. Heels. Asymmetrical scarlet dress.

'I don't get it,' says Smith. 'You've been on the ship with us all this time? Where have you been hiding?'

She's trying to smile, adjusting her posture for the multiple cameras she knows are focused on her face, but her eyes betray her. She looks terrified. Maybe she thinks we'll attack.

When she reaches the base of the stairs we stand a metre from her.

'From now on you can call me Michelle,' she says, holding out her hand for us to shake. 'Caroline, Francine, Mr Smith. It's good to finally meet you all.'

This is not us all.

Frannie tries to embrace her, arms open wide, and Michelle laughs awkwardly as Frannie holds her. I hug her tentatively. Smith shakes her hand.

'It's finished?' he asks. 'Who won? It's over now, right? We can eat?'

Michelle takes a deep breath and straightens her off-the-shoulder dress. She looks so pretty next to us. She's clean. Her face isn't gaunt. She has laundered clothes and floral perfume. Her hair has been styled.

'Did they bring you on board today?' I ask. 'The bright lights were covering that up? Is Daniel OK?'

'Caroline, let me explain something. I've been here with you the whole time. I had a cabin and an exercise area and a small studio down on Deck Zero. You won't find it on any of the deck plans.' She takes a deep breath. 'It's so good to see you three. It's nice to finally meet you all in person.'

'You too, Admiral,' says Smith, frowning and smiling at the same time. 'Are we reaching land today, then? Can we eat dinner now?'

'Call me Michelle.'

'New York City?' he continues. 'You can tell us. Do you have a canteen on Deck Zero? A stocked fridge, even? I'll pay you good money.'

Her smile fractures.

'What?' asks Frannie. 'Something's wrong. What is it? Too many questions? Is Daniel alive?'

'I don't know.' She looks flustered before walking closer to the open box at the centre of the lobby to compose herself. 'I don't have any more answers for you. In truth – and I know you might not believe me, and I can't blame you for that – but really, regarding Daniel, I'm just as much in the dark as you are.'

91

It's a cold, clear night and the sky is awash with stars. Frannie and I helped make up a seat for Michelle by the fire. She's in between us and she looks awkward. We didn't re-use Daniel's cushions.

She's so pristine compared to us, it's as if she's been dropped from another world.

'Just relax, Michelle. Take your time and tell us every-thing,' says Smith. 'Drink your water; we have plenty, for once. But share the information now. We've had so little. What happens now?'

'Is Daniel OK?' asks Frannie, again, but her voice betrays her. She already knows the answer. 'I have more than one question, right? That part's over? Is he in hospital?'

'You have to believe me,' Michelle says. 'I have no idea what happened to Daniel. I hope he's all right. I prayed for him.'

Frannie shakes her head.

'I never knew the challenges would turn the way they did.' She looks at us all in turn, then back towards the climbing wall. She swallows hard. 'I wouldn't have accepted this gig if I'd known the full facts.'

'Who hired you?' I ask. 'What did they tell you?'

She pulls a blanket tightly around herself and says, 'I was recruited for a presenting role on a new reality show. Board and lodging included, all expenses covered.' She sighs. 'Came in via my agent, first exciting job opportunity in a while to be honest, and she warned me it might be intense. After signing NDA documents I was told the basic premise. Removing everyone from the ship, leaving a few bewildered passengers, etcetera. Originally we'd planned to keep six of you on board, all pre-screened – that's why there were six boxes in the rewards room after the Mind challenge – but the other two woke up when everyone evacuated.' A shooting star streaks behind her. 'Everything here is operated remotely. Navigation, engine controls, camera operation, mics, production, editing. Five of us on the ship, you four in the dark.'

'What went wrong?' I say. 'After the box was opened? The consequences. Something went very wrong.'

'I expect that was a pivot-point so they could maintain audience attention. Grow numbers. It's not like a typical show. I mean, it is, in a lot of ways – like, on a typical show you'd have people texting and calling in to vote, live audiences interacting, that kind of thing, but this is more than that. It's significantly *more* interactive than anything before. People comment in real time because the shows are streamed in real time. Teams of editors and producers, along with computer algorithms, scan the comments and analyse data.' She backs away as the smoke blows in her direction. 'Sometimes the teams will make a viewer's suggestion come true, simultaneously displaying that viewer's reaction as their wish plays out in the real world. The whole ship is set up for it. Every remote-activated lock. The food and water situation. Heat and light. It's not just the production company controlling you passengers. This is far more unpredictable. The viewers at home are in charge.'

92

'But where is Daniel?' Frannie asks Michelle, again, as Smith places another bar stool on the deck fire. 'You know more than we do; you *must* have something you can share with us.'

She sniffs and says, 'My feed was cut at the same moment yours was.'

I've always had good instincts with people. Usually I know who I can trust. That list is small because once you've been betrayed by a loved one you never quite recover from it. I sense I can believe what Michelle says. But, then again, after so many days without food, perhaps it's my own instincts I shouldn't trust.

'Did he have enough air left to breathe?' I ask. 'Was he taken away?'

She takes a deep breath. 'Some viewers zoomed in, scanned the pool walls, tried to decipher if there was an escape hatch of some kind. I hope he had help but I'm not optimistic.'

She is not optimistic.

I take a moment for that to sink in.

'Who is running this,' asks Smith. 'Who's in charge?'

'You need to understand that I don't want to be here. Like you, I wasn't told all the facts.'

I nod. 'Go on.'

'It's a new production company. Most people watch the show through their phones. Virtual reality is popular: being able to virtually stroll around the ship, virtually walk past you guys, sit next to you at the deck fire. Some watch at work in their coffee breaks. A whole side industry has popped up: reaction videos and spin-off cable shows. The thing that got it all started was the pilot episode being shared for free on YouTube with links for how to watch the rest. It's already the most watched video in the history of the internet.'

Smith turns his head to her. 'Not that it's important after what we've been through, losing our friend and all, but the prize is real, right?'

'As far as I know. I've been paid half my fee in advance to host the show, with the rest later on. The payment cleared and checked out.'

'OK,' says Smith, nodding to himself. 'OK, that's good.'

'Is Daniel off the ship now, or is he lying dead at the bottom of the pool?' asks Frannie, glaring at Smith, her eyes wild.

'I don't *know*. You need to stop asking me this.'

She is starting to lose her composure.

'I'm sorry, Michelle,' I say. 'But he was our friend.'

'Really, I honestly don't know,' she says, backing away again from the flames. Her forehead is creased. 'I'd tell you if I knew anything, I swear. They kept me on Deck Zero the whole time. They told me what to say to you all at six p.m. each evening. I had to keep to the script. They only let me know the details of each challenge immediately before I explained it to you. I had no say in what

347

happened. You have to believe me. The way I see it, we just need to keep our heads down and finish this thing safely.'

'Safely?' says Frannie, nodding in disbelief. 'We're being gaslit, all of us. You included. They can't toy with us in this way. We're not pieces on a board game; they can't manipulate us. We have rights, even out here in the middle of the ocean. Human rights. The UN ratified a universal declaration, for God's sake. Entitlement to dignity and liberty. The right to life, prohibition of torture and slavery. Freedom of thought and expression, the individual's right to healthcare and a basic standard of living. They can't do this. I won't go on.' She stands up. 'I refuse. You can keep playing this game if you want. But I'm done.'

93

How can you be *done* on a show like this? Who gets to decide?

When we walk back to our duplex, Michelle probes the wall fittings and doors and ceiling vents with her eyes.

'You know where all the cameras are, don't you?' I ask.

She shakes her head. 'It's not like I ever had access to full schematics. I just saw what the viewers at home saw. But I know there are cameras everywhere. All angles covered. They're in the rails and the decks and stairs, not just the obvious places. Tiny cameras implanted in library books and bottles of bourbon, in piano keys and floral centrepieces and gym treadmills. They were in the climbing wall on the funnel, recessed, flush with the vertical surface. We could see you all clearly in the dark. We could even see you, Caroline, when you jumped in the sea. Thermal imaging. Cameras below the water level. We could hear you pretty much wherever you were talking, and we had lip-readers as back-up.'

She looks up. Places her hand over her mouth.

'What is it?' Frannie asks.

Michelle scratches her ear. 'You know what, go and fetch a duvet, Frannie, would you? I'm cold.'

When she returns, Michelle looks up to the ceiling again and then says, 'You all need to take a little walk with me. Mr Smith as well.'

'Where are you taking us?' I ask.

'Yes,' says Frannie, suspiciously, passing Michelle the duvet. 'We need more answers before we—'

Michelle nods and then interrupts, 'Come with me if you want to. I can't make you.'

We follow her through myriad corridors and stairwells. Deeper into the ship. Passing by the Grill restaurants and the locked doors of the ballroom. Past the signs to the fine art gallery and the backgammon room. Exiting the passenger areas and passing through narrow crew-only corridors with snakes of exposed cabling up by the ceiling.

We keep on walking, through the control room, through the workshop, until we reach the diesel engines themselves. Metal walkways. Pipes and pistons and dials and warning signs.

Michelle pulls the duvet up over her head and gestures for us all to join her underneath it.

I crouch and move under. Smith and Frannie do the same.

'What are we doing?' says Smith.

'They can't hear us under here,' says Michelle, in a nervous voice. 'Come near. Faces almost touching.'

We move closer. It's hot under the blanket. Hot and damp from our collective breath.

'This all started off as a new reality show to reignite the genre, to disrupt the media status quo. You were each selected because you were deemed to be essentially good.

But you all have something complicated or unresolved in your pasts.' Her voice starts faltering. 'What's happening now, what happened to Daniel in that pool, and now to me, isn't just reigniting the genre. This is different.'

94

The colossal Rolls-Royce engines throb all around us: a constant drone. The smell of engine oil and grease, even under the duvet.

'This premise isn't like the others,' she says.

Smith says, 'You don't have to—'

'Not so loud,' she cuts him off. 'Their microphones are sensitive. We need to whisper; our faces need to be this close, however uncomfortable it is. We cannot let them hear us.'

I am on the edge of a fresh panic attack under this duvet. Complete darkness. The drone of pistons pumping. Nervous, rancid breath mixing with my own. I've never felt so far away from home.

'The show is only available on the dark web,' she says.

We stay quiet for a few seconds. Taking that in.

'Not . . . television?' I say.

'Full uncensored shows only on the dark web. It's available there to stream. Pay-per-view, with all payments via cryptocurrencies. All anonymous and encrypted. People access links through social media, through the pilot on YouTube. Every time the pilot episode, or a new, shorter clip is removed from YouTube, someone else posts it again with a slightly different title, different keywords.

They can't remove them fast enough. A whole subculture has emerged, proficient at disguising the clips. Different theme music, pixelated faces, new metadata, digital camouflage. *Atlantica* has revolutionised reality shows.'

'But it is a real show?' asks Smith. 'With an end?'

'It's real,' she says. 'All too real. But it is far from the opportunity I signed up for. The show is run by people focused on viewing statistics and interaction metrics. They always demand more. Those in charge break a record and they want to go further to break the one they just set. If one show has lower viewing figures than the last they'll activate some new sub-game or rule. Escalate. The episode where Daniel died had over three hundred million views in two hours. That's more than the Olympics.'

'He's . . . dead?' asks Frannie.

'I'm sorry,' she says. 'That was clumsy of me. I really don't know for sure.'

'He is dead, isn't he,' Frannie says, her hair touching my cheek. 'He's still in the pool, under that hard cover. There's nobody around to help us.'

She has the same look in her eyes as Gem had when the police told us they'd recovered a body in the Humber estuary. Acceptance and deep sorrow.

'I don't know, Frannie. That's the truth. Whoever funded this, whoever masterminded every detail, is an expert in reality media. Specifically, in seizing and holding attention. I was told during my interview process that live births out in nature had already been done on mainstream TV. Plastic surgery makeover shows have shown it all. People are growing increasingly immune to click-bait and, as we all know, attention spans are shorter than ever. There have been survival programmes where people almost drown. There have even been several well-documented fatalities on prime-time reality challenge shows. So whoever is behind this knew they needed to go a step further. They wanted you all to not even know you were playing, that's the first hook. And then they planned to push you as far as possible, aided by viewers' suggestions. Slowly increasing the stakes.'

I lift the duvet a little to get some air.

'When will it end?' whispers Smith, desperately. 'The prize is genuine? There will be a series finale?'

'As I said, I was paid properly. The winner will receive their prize. Same with the participation awards. That part is legitimate.'

'But?' I say.

'But this is the dark side of the internet, Caz. That's what I'm trying to explain to you all. There is no broadcasting authority or regulator ready to step in. We're talking about the shady underbelly of the web which hosts illegal images and narcotics markets. Photos of JFK's assassination. Marilyn Monroe's autopsy footage. This is the place people try to buy and sell illegal biological agents. Uranium, even. It's the murkiest place you can imagine. And now *Atlantica* has brought hundreds of millions of new users to its hidden world. Doctors and teachers and high-school kids downloading Tor for the first time and logging on. There is speculation that whoever masterminded this isn't doing it for the show itself, they're doing it to accelerate adoption of the dark web and increase mainstream crypto acceptance. To increase the popularity of onion-like software. They're changing the online world, pushing it forward a decade in a single week. And they're doing it by sacrificing us.'

95

I am entangled in something much larger than myself. Something dangerous and out of my control. It's happening again.

Smith starts coughing and choking. Frannie pats him on the back, all while still under the duvet.

None of this has anything to do with Pete and me. We did nothing wrong. Years ago I used to attribute any bad luck to family karma. The idea that Dad's theft caused so much harm that the family must pay somehow. He left it all behind and Gem pays with her recovery, Mum with her dementia, and now, I pay with this.

We are still paying.

'The ship will run out of fuel eventually,' I say. 'So if we focus on staying safe and working together, the ship will eventually drift to some country's territorial waters. And then we can be rescued. This can't go on forever.'

'That's what I'm worried about,' says Michelle. 'Up until Daniel's challenge this was much like a regular format. Spectacular in scale and ambition, sure, original in format, but not so out-of-the-ordinary that it scared me. The Body challenge broke the rulebook. I honestly don't think the show's owners have *time* for the ship to run out of fuel. My guess is that assistance is already on its way. I don't know for sure because I never had access to the media from my studio, I was given curated snippets and I wasn't allowed to bring my phone on board, but, once that pool scene broadcast, some branch of law enforcement must have been mobilised. Even though we are in international waters, Daniel's challenge would have triggered some kind of rescue. I think it's our location that will determine how long we have. If we're in the middle of the Atlantic it may take them a while, but I'm convinced they're already on their way.'

Trapped beneath a duvet, inside an engine room, on a runaway ocean liner. I try to calm my breathing. It is immature for me to feel so aggrieved, furious even, at being placed in this situation. Others have it worse, I know that. But I can't help feeling incensed.

'If we get rescued, taken off, nobody wins, right?' says Smith. 'We entertain viewers, risk our safety, lose thirty pounds, the owners reap all the benefits and we never even have a chance. I don't think that'd be fair. If people come here to rescue us I think I'll tell them I'll stay put instead. I paid for a valid ticket. They can't force me to leave.'

'Mr Smith,' says Michelle, 'I think it's more serious than you imagine. We're in the escalation stage of the show. Do you think they care any more if you complete a challenge or not? It's not about that. It's not about you playing the game. It's about the game playing you.'

Frannie's eye twitches. 'What do you mean?'

If Pete could burst in now I'd give anything. I'd sacrifice all comforts and luxuries for the rest of my life. I'll live on water and gruel.

Michelle adjusts her position under the duvet. 'Have you ever heard of a red room?'

We don't answer.

Hot breath and damp, stale air. My knee touching Smith's.

'No,' I say, finally. 'I haven't.'

'A red room is something that exists on the dark web. It's where anonymous individuals pay significant sums to watch someone die in real time.'

'What?' I say.

'It's essentially a live execution. People have been watching executions for millennia. Road sweepers, actuaries and carpenters all queued up to watch. They hold some morbid fascination. But this is entertainment for money. Unpoliced.'

Cold sweat on the back of my neck. 'This actually happens?'

'Nobody really knows the true extent of red rooms,' says Michelle. 'Because the dark web is the shadiest part of the internet. No law enforcement there. Nobody to help.'

'Sounds familiar,' says Smith.

'Daniel's challenge,' says Frannie. 'The premium subscription message on screen. Was that a red room?'

Michelle pauses for a moment and then whispers, 'I think this whole ship is one.'

96

I'm an optimistic person. Even now, desperately sad and hungry, a part of me hopes our situation can improve. And yet, after hearing Michelle's words about red rooms, and how public executions were normalised through history, about how people watch longer when the content is extreme, I am losing my optimism. The facts are stark. People *are* drawn to violence and jeopardy. They do, repeatedly, watch their peers in distress. The veneer of civilisation and human decency is more fragile than I feared.

'So what do we do now?' I ask, hot under this duvet.

'I don't have answers for you,' says Michelle. 'Perhaps we should hang tight until help arrives. That will happen, you know. Help will come.'

Frannie coughs under the duvet and I pull my head back, an automatic response. 'But we have no food,' she says. 'We have no idea where we are. And now you say people are paying to watch us all perish? I say we abandon ship. We launch a lifeboat and abandon this place.'

Michelle moves her head. She speaks slowly. 'None of the lifeboats are operational. I'm not even sure all the life vests are. The boats are all the same as the ones you launched. Some will sink; others will burst into flames as soon as a pressure gauge activates. They are literally the opposite of lifeboats, Francine.'

My breathing quickens.

No air under here.

'It's like we're trapped in a board game,' says Smith. 'But you still think the game itself is on?'

'Why are you so obsessed?' asks Frannie.

'I think they'll pay out to the last survivor.'

We all go quiet at that.

The last survivor.

'What if we all survive? Then they'll pay the winner?' he asks.

'I can't predict what they will do. I don't speak for them in any capacity. The way they changed my role, my job, with no notice, no discussion . . . I have no way to predict what they'll do next.'

'You never planned to join us today,' I say. 'They tricked you, too?'

'Of course I didn't plan this. I was simply asked to move room for twenty minutes. Leave my studio, my cabin, and enter the next room while they conducted a remote soundproof check. I was ready for the six p.m. screening. Then they locked me out. They opened the far door, an airlock of sorts, and they told me I was to join the other passengers now. They thanked me for my diligent work. I laughed. I actually laughed. Thought someone back at editorial was playing games with me. I suppose they were in a way. And then, pretty soon after, I fell to my knees and I pleaded with them. I threatened them. I begged to speak with my agent. Nothing. No phone, no food, none of my clothes or personal items, no purse, nothing.'

Perversely, I miss having her on screen. Back then she had authority. Now she's just one of us.

I lift one corner of the duvet again to let in some air. 'What do we do now? There's nobody here to plead with, right? Is that true, Michelle? Are we really the only people on board this ship?'

'You've been tracked with thermal imaging on every deck. The five of us are the only ones here. You three, or four if Daniel's still trapped in the pool, and me. I saw heat registers from the dogs in the kennels, half of them now loose. From the pool. From the vermin, even. But there are no other passengers on board.'

'We can't just passively continue to let this happen to us,' I say. 'We deny them their red room. This is a ship. We're passengers. That's all. We reject the game and stay put until rescue.'

'Sounds simple when you put it like that,' says Smith.

'It might be that simple,' Michelle says. 'The only real dangers you've faced so far have all been self-inflicted. You consented to participating in the show. You stayed because of the game and the participation awards. You played dangerous challenges so you'd have a chance at winning significant sums. So, yes, we could resist all that temptation. If you want to stop, we stop. Only I'm not sure how they'd react if we stay in the duplex cabins and wait.'

She's right. In a way this has all been self-inflicted. We failed to resist temptation. The curse of my family. The curse of many families.

We remove the duvet, now damp and hot. Everyone looks flushed. Red cheeks and dishevelled hair. There was a before and an after. We were largely innocent of the truth before disappearing underneath the blanket and now we're contemplative.

But at least we know.

My ears are ringing and I do not feel hungry any more. Despite my proactive words I'm becoming resigned to my fate. There's only so long a person can fight on for.

We walk slowly through the corridors. Frannie drags her feet. In the Diamond Grill restaurant a troupe of rodents gnaw away at a partition wall, ripping out polystyrene and particle board.

'Except,' says Smith, 'how do we know for sure that you're not still part of it? How do we know you are who you say you are, Michelle? Nothing personal, but I'm not sure I should trust what comes out of your mouth. I've not seen you placed in any kind of danger. No jumping in the ocean or climbing up a funnel. You're not even hungry yet. How do we know you're with us now, and not them?'

'I guess you don't,' she says. 'But I know who really opened the box.'

'Sorry? You mean it wasn't Frannie?' I say.

'I told you,' says Frannie. 'I never opened that damn box. I wouldn't. It never even crossed my mind. All of this, the consequences – it was never me.'

97

It's as if I'm back at school again. Out of the loop. Excluded from conversations, from birthday parties, from jokes. They all know more than I do. The hunger is exhausting, the challenges are draining, but the game-playing, setting us off against each other, is perhaps the most unexpectedly awful aspect of this.

Michelle avoids answering my question. 'It doesn't matter now who opened the box,' she says. 'I should never have brought it up. What matters is that you all understand how this game has multiple levels, challenges within challenges. The rules update daily and nobody knows who is pulling the strings. So, I suggest, firmly, that we go back to the cabins and erect some kind of barrier, something to stop the pests at least. We take stock of our water and food and we hunker down.'

Gem and I used to hunker down in our bedroom when Mum and Dad were arguing. It was always about money. Bills unpaid, bailiffs visiting, cash taken. We'd sit close together and we knew we could muddle through if we had each other.

'We can't stay in there,' says Smith. 'Not the whole time. You don't understand it like we do. We need to check the nets, to boil water, to warm ourselves by the fire. You don't have any concept of how cold it can get at night. You had heating down in your presenter cabin, did you?'

She nods. 'It wasn't luxurious, not even a porthole. Nothing like the duplexes. I was below water level. But I was comfortable.'

'Oh, you were comfortable, were you?' says Smith. 'Heating, a/c, running water, cooking facilities, hot showers, plenty of food, drinking water. You had all that?'

She looks down at the floor.

'You don't have the first idea of what we've lived through. After a day and a night without the basics you go through evolution in reverse. After seventy-two hours you live like stray dogs. So, you sit and do nothing inside the cabin if you want. But we know it doesn't work like that.'

We decide to share one duplex from this point on. The four of us, one on sentry duty each night, two-hour shifts. We start work erecting a new barrier, so we can at least sleep more soundly. Frannie places fire extinguishers and our fire axe and a range of Japanese chef knives by the door to our cabin. It's not easy waiting for a foe when you have no idea what form it will take or when it might board the ship. But on a morale level we're slightly more prepared with Michelle here. With our barricade made from beds and side tables and chained-together wheelchairs and broken vodka bottles, we're more ready than before.

More ready?

What have we become?

There is a noticeable shift when a group adopts a siege mentality. Like rural townsfolk digging anti-tank ditches or a family taking to their hurricane shelter, the level of paranoia intensifies. Before Michelle joined us we were afraid when we had challenges to complete. Now we are afraid, and vigilant, all the time.

In the morning, after a restless night, Michelle and Frannie leave to feed the dogs. It's unnerving to witness our new passenger grow more dishevelled and tired-looking by the hour. Michelle doesn't look as unkempt as the rest of us yet but her descent from TV anchor perfection has been abrupt. Smith leaves to collect saucepans of rainwater to store in our cabin. I set off to find life vests.

I'm holding three when I hear it.

A noise so alien to me after these long days at sea that it stops me in my tracks and I drop the life vests gently in a heap by my feet.

The dialling tone of an old-fashioned telephone.

98

Memories of payphones at the bus station. Putting in coins so I could tell Mum I was running late.

Years later, the call at Gem's old place to say I had secured the lease on my café. The landlady, Mrs Newton, explaining that she shouldn't even contemplate me with no guarantor, but she wanted to give me a shot.

The police ringing. The look on Mum's face when they told her they'd found him floating in the brown waters of the estuary.

I kick the lifejackets out of my way and run down the hall towards the dialling tone. It's barely dawn but there's some weak illumination from the windows. It sounds like an old phone box. It grows louder as I run. *Ring, ring.* I meet up with Francine and she has a broad smile on her face.

'You think this is it?' she asks. 'It's the end, isn't it?'

Ring, ring.

We run together.

Close to the library plaques we join up with Smith and Michelle.

'You knew about this?' I ask.

'No,' she says. 'I swear. The phones weren't connected before.'

'It's coming from over there.' Smith points to the internet room. A dozen computers and a line of phones, each one in an ornate Art Deco booth.

'All four are ringing,' says Frannie, giddy, moving her hand closer. 'This one has my name on the screen.' She picks up the receiver, 'Hello?'

I find the phone displaying my name and pick it up. The others do the same.

The ringing stops.

'Caz, it's Gemma.'

My chest fills with happiness. With relief. 'Gem, oh, my God, how are you? Listen . . .' I start to cry. 'Oh, Gemma. Are you OK? Is Pete OK? I need you to—'

'I hope you're feeling good. We're all managing here. Nothing to worry about. Mum's fine, eating a little better, infection cleared up with the pills just like Dr Sanderson said it would. She's doing her own thing, you know how she is.'

'Gemma, I—'

'They've explained it all to us, Caz. The show and everything. The prize, oh, my God, I never understood why you went in for it, especially not telling us, warning us, but now it all makes sense. You're doing all this to pay it back, aren't you? Well, you go and win that show, sis. I know you can do it. You win that money.'

'Gemma, I . . .' And then I stop, because what's the point in trying to talk to a recorded voicemail message?

'I'll take care of the business; you don't have to worry yourself. I know it all, anyway. It'll be good for me. Extra responsibility and all that. I'll make sure invoices get paid on time. I'll put the orders in and keep on top of the takeaway team, especially Johnny; I'm keeping my eye on him after last week. You can relax, OK? Enjoy the break; you deserve it. And we're all going to watch you, even Maureen and Fred from over the road. The people at Amp Media said we'll get free links so we can watch and even leave comments for you. You're going to fix what he did, and you're going to be known all over, Caz. Don't forget us normal folk, will you?'

'I miss you so much, Gem. I miss you all.'

I close my eyes and sense Frannie slump to the ground, her phone still clamped tight to her ear. She's sobbing.

'They told me Pete's on his way back up here,' says Gemma. 'Mum reckons he should help me out in the café, step into your shoes, but I can't see him rolling up his sleeves making sandwiches and heating up lasagne, can you? I think her new morning carer, Jenny, keeps her up to date when I'm busy. Even on good days Mum can't remember Pete's name, bless her; she calls him *Caroline's friend*. I told her he'd be no use to me at work. Marigolds, loading the dishwasher, spreading butter. I can't see it.'

She laughs. And I start to cry again. I picture Mum and I wonder who will cut her hair if I don't make it off this ship. I do it each and every month. I use kitchen scissors even though they're not really up to the task. She wears my white robe and we put on Glenn Miller, Dad's favourite, and it relaxes her. Who'll do that now?

'Anyway, I won't rabbit on longer, this call might be expensive. Just to say you should have told us you were going on a reality show, you cheeky cow, and we wish you all the luck in the world. Whatever it is, you'll be ace. Hope you don't have to eat a caterpillar or anything awful like that. But if you do you just pinch your nose and swallow it down. You're the best big sister, Caz, you always have been. We'll all be watching you tonight.' I hear Martin and Alice yell something unintelligible in the background. 'Quiet, you two. Good luck, Caz. We all miss you.'

I am shaking, crying hard, gripping the phone as though it's her.

'I miss you, Gem,' I whisper, sniffing. 'I miss you so much.'

99

Without saying anything, we come together in a messy embrace after listening to our messages. And yet it is not awkward. We are each surrogates for loved ones. An outpouring of emotion with nowhere else to go.

You can't measure our time away from home in days.

That linear, universal scale is an insufficient yardstick to quantify what we continue to endure.

'My room-mates from university all spoke over each other,' says Frannie, grinning, her eyes wet. 'I could hardly hear their words but it was so good to listen to their voices. Their normal lives with the communal kitchen and the shower that doesn't drain properly and the bike Amit hangs on the wall because there isn't enough space on the floor. It was great to hear their relaxed voices. Noise. Normal, everyday noise. Who called you, Caz?'

'My sister,' I say, nodding, breaking into a smile. 'My little sister.'

'Gemma?'

I nod. 'She sounded really well. Said I should have told her I'd signed up for the show. She didn't know this was all a surprise to us too.'

'Calls were recorded before the pilot aired,' says Michelle.

'Who called you, Michelle?' I ask. 'Your family?'

'I wish,' she says. 'I could do with hearing my dad's voice right now. He was always wary of anything that seemed too good to be true. He can always soothe my nerves, you know?'

'I'm sorry,' I say.

'That was Daniel's ex-fiancée, calling him.' Michelle looks down at her shoes. 'I even heard their little daughter's voice.'

A lump in my throat.

We all stop talking.

'Those poor people,' says Frannie, shaking her head. 'I hope his ex didn't watch the challenge. I hope the girl never sees it online when she's older.'

I squeeze Frannie's arm and then I turn and say, 'Who called you, Smith?'

'That was my good old neighbour, Marlon.' He looks surprised that he received a call at all. 'Said he expects me to be thrown off the show within the first twenty-four hours, my tail between my legs. Said I'll annoy the other contestants and anyone else who might be watching. But in case I do stay on, he promised to feed my cat and check my mail.'

'I didn't even know you had a cat,' says Frannie.

'Scraggly old one-eyed tom cat. I left food for a week but now Marlon's looking after him. I was half-expecting it to be . . .'

We wait for him to continue.

He looks over at the phone. 'Well, anyway, it wasn't. It was Marlon.'

We wait some more.

He takes a deep breath and rubs the grey stubble on his cheeks. 'It was ninety-three; Clinton had just been sworn into office.' He pauses and nibbles the nail on his index finger, glancing at it. 'I was a kid myself back then, scrawny little bastard with no money and no plan. Anyway, long story short, we had a little boy, Ruth and me. A little son. His mom and I never really got on, not past that first month or so. She had her own issues and I surely had mine, a whole catalogue of them. I think about him every so often, the boy, when I'm sat on my back stoop with a beer or a smoke listening to traffic after work. What he's doing and what he looks like now, if he looks anything like his sorry old man. He'll be all grown up now, you believe that? Hope he's doing well, I really do. A start like that, he deserves a break, and I hope his mum's doing OK, too, if she's still with us.' He pauses for a minute and frowns, glancing at his hangnail again. 'I've been thinking about finding him, setting him up with a car or something.' He looks back up. 'Maybe a Toyota, something reliable that he can afford to run himself without racking up bills. Maybe a deposit on a condo one day. College money for any kids he might choose to have. Was pondering it well before I boarded the ship, and with the prize I could make a difference to his life. But it wasn't even him who called so I don't know why I'm wasting all your time blabbering. Was just my pal Marlon from next door. Runs a computer repair store, pretty sweet operation. Good of him to call, I'd say. Good of him to look after Draken, too.'

I pat him on the arm and then I turn to Michelle and say. 'Is this them being kind? The producers finally showing us some mercy?'

'I'm not sure about that,' she says, narrowing her eyes. 'I think they're working for audience reaction. For viral clips. Views, comments and think-pieces. They released these calls so people will feel more invested in the three of you, that's my best guess. And if they want viewers to be invested, then that has me worried about what they're about to do.'

100

We sit huddled around the fire at the very front of the ship. The heat is our only comfort. After the phone calls we gravitated back here because for some reason you can't tackle existential questions or discuss loved ones inside a soulless duplex. With a flame you have hope and with the horizon you have perspective. When I camp on the moors, my mind drifting to happier memories with Dad, us all together in blissful ignorance, I'd light a candle before I zipped up for the night. I'd turn off my phone and the dancing flame would afford me some peace. It'd quieten my mind for a time.

The ocean is one of the most unforgiving places on the planet, and the light from our fire, besides being a beacon, a plea for help, sustains us a little longer.

'Hearing their voices on the phone,' says Frannie, wrapped up in her coat, a blanket covering the top of her head, a lifejacket by her side. 'They sounded close by but also a thousand miles and a hundred days away. Like they exist in the past. A predictable, secure world with laws and rules and people to protect you. Phones numbers to call in an emergency. Courts to decide who was right and who was wrong. They're probably watching us now, glued to their laptops.' She sighs. 'I don't want them to see us.'

'Frannie,' I say. 'Would you come with me, please?'

We head all the way back to the stern. Frannie's talking softly as we walk, contradicting herself, shaking her head. She sounds as though she's drunk, or under the influence of strong painkillers. Her eyes are wild, and I hope this is hunger and grief and not the start of something worse.

'We'll leave this place,' I tell her. 'You and me. All of us. We'll leave this ship.'

'It's the waiting,' she says, still shaking her head. 'Always waiting for the next thing. This, then that, then this other thing. I don't have any say, do I? Even though I studied this stuff – personal autonomy, concepts of individual liberty – I never understood until now. Kant said something about how moral autonomy is the capacity to give yourself moral law, rather than obeying the rules of others. Personal autonomy is the capacity to decide things for yourself and pursue a course of action regardless of moral factors. Personal versus moral authority, you see? These bastards will do whatever they have planned and we are expected to take it. I've had as much as I can take. Any other show you just walk off the set and call a minicab. This is a prison camp, not a TV programme.'

Her eyes look blank. Out of focus. As if the phone call made everything worse not better.

I feed the half-dozen captive dogs with her and the Caucasian Shepherd watches our every move. He is quiet, but his teeth are exposed, his gums twitching.

We let the other five out to relieve themselves in their designated area. The half-dozen that are free to roam are already making the rest of the ship foul. But there are fewer vermin. Significantly fewer. So it's a price worth paying.

I pick up four cans of dog food.

She frowns. 'You're feeding the other six?'

'No, they're feeding themselves.'

I borrow two large skillets from the Diamond Grill galley kitchen, together with oil I forage from the base of a deep-fat fryer. I take salt and pepper and chilli flakes. The rest of the herbs and spices are locked away down in the stores but at least I have these.

The others are sceptical when I return.

'You have to be kidding,' says Michelle, grimacing. 'I don't think I can.'

'Well,' says Smith, 'you're not as hungry as us three are. I'll try them. Go on, Caz, cook them up.'

Bile rises within me. I'm not comfortable with how he expects *me* to serve *him* food. It's different in the café; that's a transactional relationship. Mutually beneficial.

'If I cook for you, then you clean up the dog mess tomorrow. Deal?'

He nods.

I open the cans of dog food and empty them with a spoon into a large mixing bowl. I nestle the skillet on the embers. The dog food is wetter than the meat I'm used to, it has more jelly in it, but I do my best to form meatballs, rolling each one in salt and pepper and chilli to disguise what they are.

'Fry them for a long time,' says Smith, his mouth watering. 'Deep-fry them, if you can.'

The meatballs spit and sizzle as I move them around gently in the pan. A copy of *Vogue* magazine burns brightly in my peripheral vision. My stomach rumbles and my head is conflicted because although this is food, it is not food intended for us. We're taking from the dogs. I've judged that to be fair because so far they haven't missed a single meal.

We sit around the fire eating six meatballs each.

'They're not bad,' says Smith pushing his second meatball into his mouth.

Frannie doesn't talk, she just eats.

Michelle says she can't stomach them so offers hers to us.

They are revolting, to be fair, but they're edible. I force them down, mindful that I need energy for whatever struggles lie ahead. I heard my sister's voice today and that spurs me on. It reinforces my resolve. I must see her and Mum and Pete again.

Michelle tells us stories of her dad bringing her and her brother up all on his own. How he sacrificed his comforts, his personal relationships, to make sure they were provided for. She tells us how he walked them to school each and every morning on his way to work, telling them about faraway countries he'd visited in the Army.

My mind wanders to the walks Pete and I take around his village. Conversations, guarded, tentative, about moving in together and adopting a dog one day, a retired greyhound or a bull terrier from the rescue home. He brought it up on the way back from the pub after a Sunday roast. I've always been awkward around these decisions, these big life changes. But I started imagining what might happen after we adopt the dog. I started to think about this very trip, and if we might talk openly about making longer-term plans together.

'You think we could season these up with something spicy next time?' says Smith.

'Sorry, I was miles away. What?'

'Season them. With—'

But he's cut off by the deep bellow of the ship's foghorn.

Two blasts.

Frannie stands up.

She's next.

101

The bitter taste of over-fried meat on my tongue.

Our final challenge.

We leave the deck fire burning, drizzle holding it at bay, and we enter the ship. We walk without speaking. All of my thoughts are for Frannie's welfare right now. Before Daniel's challenge she'd already told me she'd had vivid nightmares of having to hold her breath in a vat of engine oil or being zipped up inside a hard-shell suitcase, so I can't imagine her anguish at this moment. She told me this morning she woke up in a cold sweat, convinced she was already dead. I didn't need her to tell me what she dreamt. I was right there next to her.

Still no vermin in the corridors. Strangely, unnervingly, no evidence of the dogs, either.

Down the stairs, into the murky, quiet depths of the RMS *Atlantica*. Will this vessel be scrapped after what's happening to us? Sunk in some maritime trench complete with fire damage and feral dogs and a looted arcade of shops? Who'd ever set foot on this ship again after this?

The Ocean Lobby is lit only by the TV screen.

'This should be interesting,' says Michelle. 'I wonder who they've cast to replace me. If it's Miranda Wallace I'll . . .'

No face on screen. No mouth. Just the word AIR.

Frannie looks pale. She's muttering something under her breath and she's rubbing her palms up and down her arms.

A pair of lips on screen. Red. Pixellated.

We sit down.

Four chairs.

Don't you dare, I think. *Do not hurt this precious girl.*

'Good evening, passengers,' says the new set of lips. She sounds almost human but it's clear her voice originates from a computer rather than an organic larynx.

We don't say anything. This is far from a good evening.

The lips have an androgynous tone: calm and composed. 'Your final challenge is Air. Francine, this is your personal challenge.'

Frannie, once again, mutters something indecipherable under her breath. She's whispering a mantra. I place my hand on her shoulder and she flinches.

'Francine, after I finish speaking you will proceed to the top deck. This is a solo challenge. The other passengers will enter the observation room at the front of the ship, immediately behind the main mast. Francine, you will proceed to the base of the main mast, one-hundred-and-twenty-two feet above sea level. Please note this is not the funnel or observation room used in the previous challenge. You will climb the external ladder to the halfway point. At that point you will need to cross the mast to the ladder a quarter-turn around. Clockwise. You will then climb past the radar and wind gauges to the top of the tower. One-hundred-and-ninety-one feet above sea level. Collect the room key attached to the top of the ladder. Make your way down to the base and open the observation room door and then, with your fellow passengers, proceed to enjoy your rewards.'

'*Atlantica*,' says Frannie, her hands balled into tight fists.

The lips do not reply.

'I nominate Caz.'

102

My stomach tightens.

'No,' I say, but the word is almost silent. A gasp. 'You can't . . . we don't do that, Frannie. I've already done my challenge.'

'Nomination accepted,' says the pixellated lips. 'Good luck, Caroline. Passengers . . .'

I stand up. 'No.'

'I wish you fair winds and calm seas.'

The screen goes blank.

'What . . . what the hell did you do?'

Frannie shakes her head. She looks haunted, dark circles under her eyes. 'I couldn't go through with it, Caz. You should hate me, that's OK. Hate me forever. But I can't climb that ladder, there's no way. I'm sorry; you're much stronger than me.' Her voice has reduced to not much more than a whisper. 'I wouldn't make it.'

My whole world has turned upside down.

Again.

'You can do this, Caz,' says Smith.

I shake my head. 'I can't do it and I won't.' At the top of my voice I say, 'I demand you take us off this ship now.'

'Then congratulations, Mr Smith,' says Michelle, shrugging. 'I guess you just won.'

I frown at her, at this shift in tone.

'I'm sorry,' says Michelle. 'But Frannie nominated. She won't be disqualified but there's no way she'll win after that move, even with her enormous legion of loyal fans. Frannie was by far the most popular, you see; at least that was true before I was thrown in with you. If you quit, Caz, Smith will win by default. Maybe we'll dock later tonight and he'll be presented with the prize and a bottle of champagne and you'll go home having *almost* won. You'll get a few decent paid-for interviews in magazines, I guess. You might—'

'You think we're that close to the end?' I ask. 'You know it, or you think?'

'I don't *know* anything,' she says. 'But I can sense it, can't you? The show's almost finished.'

Smith is walking around in circles trying to make sense of all this. 'Frannie's the most popular?' he says.

'I'm sorry,' says Frannie. 'I know it was wrong. But my nightmares. What happened to Daniel. I just couldn't.'

They all stare at me.

'I don't hate you, Frannie. I don't like you much right now but I don't hate you.'

More than any moment before, I crave distance from them all, from this place. I crave a long walk on my own to clear my head.

Smith looks at Michelle. 'Are you saying all this to grow the viewing figures, to make sure somebody, anybody, completes this challenge? Michelle, tell us the truth, are you still on the payroll?'

'Ah, you're saying that because you want her to abstain from the Air challenge,' says Michelle, her threaded

383

eyebrows raised. 'I understand. Play chess when others are playing chequers, right, Smith?'

I rub my temples.

And then I walk out of the lobby.

103

Alice, my niece, says that when she was twelve she felt so much pressure at school, with ongoing assessments and homework, that her anxiety negatively affected her grades. She cared so much it was counterproductive. She eventually learnt ways to maintain perspective. She told me how she worked out that if she takes breaks, and sometimes gives herself permission to fail, she performs far better. I'm proud of her. Next year she will be the first Ripley ever to attend university.

My knees are weak as I exit the lobby to climb the stairs. Mirrors recording me. Light fittings observing. My own friends following and watching my every move.

All I can do is my best.

Alice is right.

The others enclose themselves in the safety of the observation room, and Frannie has the audacity to wish me luck.

Blustery showers spraying across the ship from the starboard side. Wind whistling, and the smoke from the extinguished fire hanging heavy in the air.

It's not that I started to think of Frannie as an adopted daughter or anything, but I did regard her as a friend. A younger version of Gemma, perhaps. Bright, honest and decent. Why would she do this to me? She could have just refused and bowed out gracefully. This action is the most painful slap in the face I've had since the morning I picked up our local newspaper from the front step and realised the true extent of my father's deception.

I've walked past the mast a dozen times but I've never looked at it closely before. Why would I? The mast is immense. White-painted steel with a horizontal arm at the one-third level and another at two-thirds. It looks as tall and as steadfast as a lighthouse from down here. Flashing lights at the apex like an aircraft passing overhead.

I glance back over my shoulder. I can't see their faces inside the observation room; just raindrops and my gaunt reflection in the glass. Turning to face the mast head-on, I take my first step up the ladder, gripping the verticals so hard my knuckles turn white. I climb a few rungs. It's slippery from the rain and it is cold to the touch. No safety harness. No chance of rescue or medical assistance if I mis-step.

I tell myself that this is what sailors have been doing for centuries. Climbing the rigging, reaching the crow's nest, repairing and maintaining the mainsail. But not like this. Not filmed from all angles, starving, viewed across the world, streamed for light entertainment.

The wind gusts and I have to flatten myself against the ladder, my arms looping through and around to keep myself from being blown off. I must only be five or six metres above the deck but well over thirty metres from the water, perhaps three thousand metres from the sea bed. The ship is moving in the swells and bucking against the waves and if I fall I can't predict whether I'll crash down into solid wooden deck or into the sea itself.

I'm not sure which would be worse.

I climb up another six rungs, my hands soaked, past a slowly rotating radar beam.

In small orange text, too small to read from deck level, is written *Proceed higher* and then, when the radar beam completes its rotation, the other side says *at your own risk*.

104

Dad never talked about his gambling. It was something he did on his own, in secret, late at night or hiding on his lunch breaks. When I was in my early twenties I lived through a difficult winter, sharing my then flat with my then boyfriend. As soon as he moved in, he became jealous. He demanded to know my routes to work at the kindergarten, and which dads came by to pick up their children, and what they said to me. He wanted me to remember their exact words. It became so intolerable in that one-bedroom flat that I began to gorge myself on snacks. That may seem like an innocent vice compared to Gemma's problems, and in many ways it was, but it took over my life. Dad would hide his betting slips and winnings. Gem hid her stash. I hid chocolate and sweets all over the apartment. I had to know I'd have access when I needed comfort. There's an incurable canker disease running through every root and branch of our family tree.

I flatten my body against the ladder. This storm is growing louder. It is intent on ripping me off and throwing me into the ocean. The ship rolls from side to side and there is nobody here to encourage me or yell my name. I am being watched by millions and yet I have never felt more alone.

I climb one rung at a time, slowly, carefully, gripping the horizontal rung above with all my force, holding myself against the ladder, against the mast. The scattered deckchairs below look like splinters of driftwood and the freshwater pool spills on to the deck with each swell. I think of Daniel still trapped inside the other pool. The wind gusts. Far above me a gauge spins so fast it's a whirring blur. My face is wet, my hair drenched. I'm shivering, my teeth knocking together as I step up another rung. Look ahead. Look up. Resist the temptation to look down.

Three more rungs left.

The sun has already set and what little light remains is leaching away into the horizon.

I step up and the ship lurches to the port side so I stop climbing and just hang on for dear life. Salt in my mouth. Water down my back and in my socks. A ragdoll in a spin cycle.

My fingers are numb. They are less reliable than I need them to be. I climb up to the top of this section of the mast and look over. I need to step out and stretch to reach around this monolith. The mast has the circumference of an industrial chimney at this level. I must straddle it, shuffle around, find my rung, and then join the next ladder higher. I reach out my leg and feel for the rung but it is too far away. Ice water is streaming down my face. I lean further out into the growing darkness and find the edge of a foothold. I'll have to commit to this. I must make it to the next ladder. I squeeze my eyes tight shut and in my head are Mum and Gemma and her kids, all looking back at me, all horrified. Mum shakes her head, frightened, frail, confused, agitated. I reach out with my shoe and let that rung take my weight and then I swing my body around and cling to the next ladder.

Spluttering, panting, I hold on. White ladder, white mast, white radar beams, white wind gauges. But then I look around and everything else is black. If I look up or down I find only darkness.

I flex my fingers to get the blood circulating and then I move up a rung. Two more. I have a steady rhythm. I climb up one more and that's when the ship's whistle blows right above my head.

105

My feet are dangling in mid-air. I'm hanging on, wretched, screaming into the void. I hold it together for long enough to regain my composure on the ladder. Clinging to it the way a baby monkey might hold on to its mother.

I climb.

The distance below me is too great to comprehend, and the ship's lurching like a drunkard, each movement exacerbated by my height above sea level. One moment I'm over the deck and the next we've moved so much that there's nothing between me and the cold ocean below.

I'm being filmed every second. Cameras watching my technique, people analysing, judging, commenting with their opinions. But this is our final challenge, and that thought gives me energy.

I climb towards the top of the mast, Dad's face in my head for a moment, past another radar device, and there are lights above me, bright lights to show other vessels and planes where we are. One of the lights is red and it reminds me of the lamp outside Gemma's ex-husband's building. He thought he was being smart, replacing the bulb with a red one. Thought that was hilarious. But I wasn't laughing the day I found her on the floor of his living room, slumped down between the wall and the arm of the sofa. She'd missed picking up Alice and Martin from school. Gemma overdosed that day. He claimed she didn't, claimed she was just high, but I could see for myself. Her lips were blue, just as mine are now. Her skin was losing its colour. My little sister, who at school was better than me at pretty much everything – academics, sport, friendships – was jammed between a wall and a filthy sofa.

I'm operating on some kind of primitive survival mode, some animal instinct or autopilot I never knew I had. One foot after the other.

Some of the rungs are greased with oil or some other lubricant. It doesn't shock me or disgust me; I just accept it. I wipe my palms and take my time, and continue. There are moments I almost lose purchase but I hold tight. Aching wrists and knees, shivering so violently I fear I might bite through my tongue, but I'm moving higher.

Will I even be able to climb down again?

I peer around at the velveteen blackness of the sea, of the skies, and then I look up.

The wind lashes rain into my eyes, my ears, and I struggle to maintain grip, my hands imprecise and numb from the incessant sleet. Is this how a firefighter feels climbing the rig from the roof of a fire truck? But they have a basket. Training. A reliable team. This is not the same.

Writing in italics. Bright green paint on the mast.

Higher or lower?

I climb another rung.

Stick or twist?

My heart sinks. Who wrote this? When? Is it intended for me? Of course it is.

I'm making the choices he would have made.

History repeating.

Heads or tails.

I swallow hard and go on.

I'm swinging back and forth, left and right, and at times I'm climbing an overhang just as Daniel did. The ship looks like a bath toy far below me. Barely connected. Pitching and rocking on the surface of miles-deep water.

Two more rungs and then I have to pause for breath, my arms aching, my shoulders on fire, my hands wrinkled from the endless tempest. My fingers looked like this on the day we buried him. It wasn't raining this hard, just Yorkshire drizzle, but I shunned the umbrella that Uncle William, the scaffolder, offered. I wanted that rain on my face. I wanted to feel something straightforward and clear and honest, something that wasn't shame mixed with loss. He was buried next to his parents and hardly anybody turned up for the service. His old colleagues shunned us. His friends made their excuses. I don't know why we wanted a good turnout but we did. Mum did, especially; she was desperate for it. But it was as if the shame was contagious. People didn't want to be tarnished. Shame for what he had done, lying to us and to the charity, hurting so many people for no good reason. He never even enjoyed his gambling. Never enjoyed the money or the buzz of a win. It was something he had to do. A form of gradual, mindless self-harm that, in the end, harmed families all over the region.

One more rung. I can see the grey clouds moving in the wind and it's as though I'm up inside them. Turbulence brewing in a part of the ocean so remote, so devoid of light, that God himself would struggle to find us.

We couldn't have a proper reception in a hotel or a café, Mum couldn't afford one, so we hosted it quietly at home, before they took the house from us. I made ham sandwiches, his favourite, and sausage rolls, and Mum cleaned every surface and every floor until the house sparkled. It was her last desperate attempt at respectability. She never deserved that. She didn't profit from Dad's behaviour in any way.

It cost her dearly.

It still does to this day.

Rainwater in my ears, and soaking through my underwear. My back is stiffening from the cold and the exertion. I heave myself up higher and higher and the top still seems a hundred metres away. It's as if the ladder extends each time I step up. A Sisyphean trial I'm too exhausted to fully comprehend. All I can do is cling on, shaking, not progressing. Static. No hope of assistance. I loop my arms through the rungs and I cry out like a wounded creature. For Mum, for Gemma, but mainly for my father. I cry out at the heartache, his pain, and the legacy of his choices, and my own. We try, and fail, to rectify mistakes.

Our shame is indelible.

History repeating.

If I don't continue I know what will happen. Hypothermia will set in. I'll turn dozy. Lose clarity. Maybe I'll even drift off to sleep, and in that slumber I will fall. A few seconds of anguish followed by a sharp crack. A head hitting the shuffleboard deck or a thirty-metre dive into the water below. Sinking, not rising. Blessed relief. Falling through the midnight zone. A thousand metres deep, two thousand. My body collapsing in on itself, crushing, compacting. Capillaries bursting one after the other. Three thousand metres. And then, gently, like an invisible hand placing me gently on a mattress in an unlit room, I'll settle on the sea bed.

106

It's the ship's whistle that shakes me back to lucidity. I can reach the top. I've come this far. There's no way I'm going to fall asleep and fall. I can still win, repair damage, allow the families some comfort, a little security well-earnt through sacrifice and service.

It's Gemma's voice in my ear as I move higher. *One at a time. Just keep at it. It's just a ladder; climb up it, then, go on. Don't fret it now; once it's done there will be plenty of time for all that overthinking you're so good at.*

The end is in sight. Seven more rungs. I climb, my trembling hands like thawing ham hocks. My teeth chattering in their sockets.

I spot the room card at the top of the mast. The final key attached to the top of the ladder by carabiner. And then the wind blows so hard it roars like thunder. The ship lurches and I lose my footing and I'm left hanging by my hands high above the deck and the ladder feels as if it could snap.

I'll die here, in this twisted place, with nobody to see me but everyone to bear witness.

The ship lurches again and through no skill or strength of my own I'm sent crashing back into the ladder and I grab on to it with all my might, looping a foot around, bringing the structure close to my chest as though it's a lover or a lost child.

When I reach the top the sleet is threatening to turn to snow. I've seen the camera lenses implanted into the structure, dead eyes flush with the rungs, but it's as if I'm waking from a fever dream, my back drenched, my pulse racing, my breathing shallow.

I am the highest point on the *Atlantica*.

Placing the key card between my teeth, biting down into the plastic, I begin my descent. Part of me, the part that's tempted to jump off a cliff or crash a car, that tiny fragment of insanity buried deep within all our brains, is ready to loosen my grip and slide all the way down. I grin manically at the thought of it.

I pass the radar and the wind gauges and the lights and make the transition to the final ladder stretch and maybe, I'm not sure but maybe, if I fell from here I might survive. A broken pelvis, perhaps, a shattered femur, but I could live to see the end of this hideous charade.

When I make the final step down to the deck, suddenly feeling like the most solid thing in the world, like basaltic bedrock rather than teak on steel over water, I collapse into a ball and weep. Voices through the rain, through the darkness. Hands on me. Blankets. A coat placed over my head. Words. Kisses. Voices urging me out of the sleet.

Was this how you felt, Dad, each time you won? Each time you lost?

Inside the observation room the others are jubilant but I start to shut down. My vision is cloudy, as though I'm seeing them all through an antique scope, and I can't hear properly any more. I can't speak. They rub me. They strip my wet clothes and wrap me in blankets and Michelle moves her hands up and down my back and I start to make out their voices clearly again. The room comes into focus.

'Where is she?' I ask.

'What do you mean?' asks Michelle. 'Who?'

I look around. 'Where's Frannie?'

107

There are times in life when you have a sense that something terrible is about to happen and yet you are unable to do a thing to stop it.

Frannie's not inside.

She's nowhere to be found.

I run through the storm on deck, my knees still unsteady from the climb, and I yell, 'Where are you?' but the wind takes my words as soon as they leave my mouth.

Squally gusts from the starboard side.

Smith's torch beam picking out overturned deckchairs and doors jarred open with bar stools.

'Francine?' he yells. 'Frannie?'

She will be OK. Gemma was OK. We'll find Frannie taking a moment for herself, sheltering inside a corridor or crew room.

Michelle points.

I dash across the deck to the port side, slipping on the sleet, stumbling. 'Frannie. Get down, please. This is almost over. Frannie, please, sweetheart.'

But she stays up on the safety railings, one leg over the side of the ship.

The storm subsides for a moment.

A few seconds of peace.

Frannie stares back to us. Her red hair is plastered over her face in curls. Her expression is blank.

'You did the right thing, nominating me,' I say, stepping closer. 'You were right all along, Frannie. I made it, didn't I? I'm fine. Come back now, come on. Let's warm up together and talk about it.'

Slowly, she turns her head.

She looks away from me.

Frannie does not fall or slip. She steps off.

My voice fails. We dash, all three of us, to the rail. I can't see her all the way down there. And then she surfaces, spluttering, very small, and almost instantly she disappears under a wave.

The ship powers on, leaving her behind.

'Life vests and buoyancy aids,' says Michelle. 'Throw over as many life vests as you can.'

Smith is crouched on the deck, seemingly in shock. His chest is convulsing and he's mumbling.

'He's praying,' says Michelle. 'We need to get vests in the sea for her. She'll find one because she's young and strong. But you have to help.'

I snap out of it and collect vests and throw them all into the sea. I throw dozens overboard.

'The rescuers will find the vests,' says Michelle. 'And then they will find her.'

108

The kind of sadness where you forget how to speak or move.

You forget how to be.

We search for her with torches but they are weak. We try to shout encouraging words but our voices are drowned out by the raging winds. We attempt to spot her in the sea but it's too dark and the ship has sped away from her location.

Powerless, again.

I scream so fiercely my voice fails me.

Held hostage on a maleficent ship. And now another soul lost. An innocent. Some might say she took her own life but I will tell you it was stolen from her. This ship, the men who installed the cameras, the faceless executives who profit – they killed Francine, and I swear on my life some day I will make them pay.

The three of us look like survivors from a natural disaster we wish we'd perished in.

We don't talk about it because what is there to say?

Lightning on the horizon. It forks before it meets the water.

Silence. An absence of everything. Then thunder.

We move to the bow of the ship but we can't light a fire in this weather so Michelle, Smith and I retreat to the duplex cabin and there, in silence, without discussion or planning, we construct a kind of fort from blankets and duvets. With no external source of heat, and the ship's metal structure ice-cold to the touch, with all residual heat long-ago sapped or wicked back into this antagonist of an ocean, we're reliant on whatever body heat we have left. The layers of blankets over our heads will trap some of our malodorous warmth. And if we suffocate in our sleep, well, perhaps that will be a peaceful release. We huddle close together as we did back in the engine room, except then we had Francine with us.

Smith coughs. He sounds as though he has pneumonia. How many ways can this ship end us?

We recovered four bottles of water from a crew cabin using the key card I collected from the top of the ladder. Four bottles of water and sixteen packs of instant noodles. Rations for four people, not three.

What was going through her mind as she approached the rails? As she stepped over? What pain must she have been going through? Was it nominating me or just the relentless ordeal of these past days? Dad hadn't seemed especially sad the day before he took his last walk. He appeared at peace, if anything. Mum and I spent hours discussing how we should have seen the signs and talked him out of it.

I honestly don't think there were any signs.

Michelle sleeps, her arms tucked into herself, and I can't stop seeing my young friend every time I close my eyes. Every blink a grainy snapshot of Francine, lost at sea. Being dragged further and further away. No source of light. A pinprick of a person in an incomprehensible body of water. Have you been picked up, I think, or are you out there, waiting? Have you frozen to the point where your heart slows, then stops, still wearing your life vest, or are you sinking, eyes open, staring back at the hull of the ship?

Smith falls quiet and I think he sleeps a little.

Was it filmed? They wouldn't show her jump. They couldn't screen something like that.

Of course they could. They wanted this to happen. They probably designed all this for one of us to step over into oblivion.

We each ate, in silence, a pack of noodles mixed with cold bottled water, raw, uncooked, before we buried ourselves in these stinking blankets. I can still taste the powdery bouillon and the onion on my tongue.

Michelle wakes, panics, calls out for her father, jerks her legs, and I soothe her back to sleep.

I sit here in a Diamond-class duplex cabin on the finest mid-size ocean liner in the world, clutching the note Frannie left safe inside a plastic Evian bottle.

I read her note one last time before huddling under the blankets.

I love you, Mum, Dad. And I'm sorry I didn't tell you. I couldn't do this any more.

109

The next morning the wind has dropped but the air is still bitter and the waves are silver-white at their tips.

My heart aches.

The haphazard saucepans and mixing bowls are full of rainwater and we have more food than we've had for days thanks to the rewards cabin. And yet our collective mood is defeat. We completed all four challenges successfully but we are beaten. None of us starved or froze to death, but we all lost and we all *are* lost.

Daniel and Frannie are gone.

Both sacrificed to this ship.

I finish the makeshift shrine to Frannie as Michelle and Smith build up the fire, sheltered from the breeze by the breakwater. We have a week or more of bar stools and deck-chairs left to burn. If we were to tear out wood panels and doors, and the stage from the theatre, we'd be able to heat ourselves for years. Unseen and yet seen, cannibalising this decaying vessel from the inside out. We know it won't come to that because we sense the end approaching. There's no way human rights organisations will let this continue.

In my bones I know it ends today.

Her shrine is next to his. Flickering battery-powered candles. Passenger voyage passes complete with photos and barcodes. Frannie wanted to free her father from the burden of employing friends and neighbours in a failing business, and enable him to retire, to spend some time with his wife and their friends. She knew he was ill, his body weakened, and she wanted to buy him a few easier years. I battled with myself whether or not to place her message here with the photos and her yellow-rimmed sunglasses and lip-gloss but I couldn't bring myself to do it. The note is too private. I'll keep it in the duplex and if we ever reach shore I'll make sure her parents receive it.

Lost at sea. I keep thinking of newsreaders using that phrase to describe Frannie's fate. Some form of maritime purgatory. This is not a river or a lake. There will be no bloated body washing up on a pebble beach in a week's time. This is the mighty Atlantic Ocean and it will take her for itself.

She is lost.

We all are.

We don't discuss it directly, how our situation will end soon, but we all eat more instant noodles than we ordinarily would. I watch their faces and they watch mine. We eat at least half of what could be rationed out to a five-day supply. We don't explain to each other why we do this because we don't need to.

The sun breaks through the clouds and the tip of our fire flares higher as if to meet the rays. A union of flame in a cold, unholy place.

'The ship was empty before,' says Michelle. 'But it feels emptier now.'

Smith stands up with his saucepan of noodles and he walks slowly over to the closest all-weather CCTV camera and he says, 'I don't have the right words. I don't know how to do this. But I want to leave a message for Frannie's mom and dad. I never was a public speaker but we owe it to you and her to say a few words. I'm sorry – we all are. Never should have turned out this way. Never needed to. Someone was greedy and it went too far. Anyway, that's not for you. I wanted to say that you raised a really great kid.' His voice breaks. 'A great woman, I mean. Frannie helped out and she kept a cool head. If it weren't for her the dogs might not have made it. I think she'd have gone on to become an important person, someone who could make a difference. She made a difference to my life and I knew her less than a week. You should both be proud. She was an asset to you.'

His chin falls to his chest and he walks back to us and slumps on his lounger.

'That was nice,' I say.

He brushes that away with his hand and probes his saucepan half-heartedly with a fork.

'I mean it,' I say. 'Not nice. It was decent. Gracious – is that the word? You gave them some comfort.'

'I have none for myself; I may as well offer some to others.'

'You guys,' says Michelle, a piece of grey ash lodged in her hair. 'Do you ever think about the anchor?'

'What do you mean?'

'The ship's anchor. It has two, I think.'

'That's a no-go,' says Smith. 'Didn't you ever watch the old diving films back in the day? Jacques Cousteau?'

We both shake our heads.

'He switched me on to diving and the underwater world. I was fascinated by minke whales and porpoises and hydrothermal undersea vents when I was younger. Anyhow, I subscribed to a magazine when I lived outside Gastonia. Heavy anchors are useful in a cove, in a channel, close to a landmass. They might even be of some use further out; all depends on the depth of the sea bed. But way out here, assuming we still *are* out here, in the middle, I mean, past the continental shelf, there isn't an anchor in the world that'll go that deep, nor a motor powerful enough to lift all that chain back up again. It's an impossibility.'

'I don't know,' says Michelle. 'I think a six-hundred-million-dollar ship like this must have some trick up its sleeve. Some tech we're overlooking. I'm going to search the bridge again. Shall I go on my own or do you want to come with me?'

We follow her.

No rodents in the corridors but no dogs either. Perhaps the dogs killed the vermin and now they're resting. Or the other way round.

We pass a restroom area and the air is foul.

On the bridge the screens are all off and the GPS is blank. The joysticks are inoperable.

'Who's steering the ship?' I ask.

'I don't know. Way over my pay grade, Caroline. Someone in an office somewhere.'

'You must know something more,' I say. 'You have to know more than we do.'

'Remote control,' she says.

Something crackles. Michelle flinches. 'What was that?'

We run our hands over the instruments and screens but they all look blank.

Another crackle.

And then, faintly, with a backdrop of static, we hear the words, '*Atlantica*, *Atlantica*, this is the *Belgoness*, please come in, are you in need of assistance?'

110

We stare at the receiver.

'Pick it up,' I say.

Smith reaches down by the seat and removes the handset.

'*Atlantica*, we detected your signal. Are you in need of assistance? Over.'

Smith presses the button and replies, 'Yes. Jesus Christ, yes, we need your assistance. Urgently – get over here. Where are you?' He scans the horizon. 'I can't see you. Please. Come and help us right now.'

He releases his finger.

Static.

Crackles.

No answer.

Michelle takes it from him and says, 'This is Michelle Jones on the *Atlantica*. I'm contracted by Amp Media and we need urgent support. We have no food or water or navigation. No control of our ship. We have injured people on board. This is an emergency, over.'

Static.

We all look at the hand receiver.

Crackling.

We wait for what seems like minutes but there is no answer.

I take it gently from Michelle and press the button and say, 'Mayday, mayday. This is the *Atlantica*. We're sinking. Taking on water. We need your assistance immediately. Over.'

Some white noise and then they reply, 'Hello, *Atlantica*. This is the *Belgoness*. We heard your distress signal. Are you still in need of assistance? Over.'

'They can't hear us,' says Michelle, panic in her eyes. 'It's not working.'

I go to press the button again but a new voice emerges, crisp and authoritative. 'Good morning, *Belgoness*, this is Commodore Harrison from the RMS *Atlantica*. Happy to report no need for support, all under control. We were running a scheduled exercise which we've now successfully completed. Apologies for any confusion, I've spoken to the engineer involved. Won't happen again.'

The response is almost immediate. A relieved voice. 'Thank you, Commodore. One more time, just to be cautious. Are you in need of any support at this time? Over.'

'No, no,' says the man's voice. 'We're serving breakfast to the passengers and all systems are green this end. Thanks again for checking though, we're grateful. Wishing you fair winds and calm seas. Over.'

111

We each try to activate the hand receiver, to press the button in a different way, adjusting pressure, but it's no use. The *Belgoness* has gone quiet. They're satisfied. They followed up on the distress signal and to them everything seems fine.

'They need to stop,' whispers Michelle.

Smith is over by the telescope.

'I thought that was our exit,' I say, breathing fast. 'I was starting to feel hopeful. He had a reassuring voice, like a pilot or a priest.'

Smith scans the horizon. 'Nothing out there I can see. Who knows if they were even real? How can we know what's real and what's designed to make us lose our minds?' He walks over, scratching his cheek, frowning. 'Could be they were both in some studio, two voice artists in separate booths. Could be that the *Belgoness* doesn't even exist. Michelle, where's the main studio?'

'Me? I have no idea. I received instructions through my agent and was paid half up front. The money was above market rate and now I understand why. I swear to you, I don't know how this ends. I don't think they do either.'

'I'm starting to think they do know,' says Smith, a little crazed. 'I think they're pulling our strings every single minute of every single day. You ever read the pulp books back in the eighties and nineties? *Choose your own adventure.* You'd reach the end of a chapter and you'd have to decide to do this thing or that. Choose a sword and jump to chapter sixty-two or choose the medical kit and jump to chapter ninety-seven, that kind of thing. It's like we're in one of those books right now.'

'I liked those books,' says Michelle. 'My brother and I would borrow them from the library.'

'How did you know to come up to the bridge right now?' he says, one eyebrow raised. 'We were warm by the fire and you start your ridiculous anchor monologues and then you want us all to come up here with you. Why did you get an urge that just so happened to coincide with the *Belgoness* talking to us over the radio?'

I look at him, then her.

'Well?' he says.

'They're getting to you now,' she says, tapping her head, retreating a step. 'I was with you both the whole time, remember. You think I'm talking to them? How would I do that? I'm always with you. They can see us, remember that. Maybe they timed the distress call for when we arrived here. Anyway, if you hadn't opened that box Daniel and Frannie would still be alive and I'd still be working down on Deck Zero with a stocked fridge.'

'What did you just say to me?'

'OK, cool down,' I say. 'This is exactly what they want. This is the in-fighting they're looking for.'

'She's still working for them.' He points at Michelle, wagging his finger. 'We didn't see any rats outside but there's one in here right now. Are you lying to our faces? Wearing a wire?'

She pulls up her shirt and turns around. 'Why would they even need me to wear a wire?' she says. 'Everything we do, everything we say, it's all picked up and broadcast. Some viewers pay for live streaming. Others pay for premium all-access with commentary. They can hear me already.'

'Did you open the box, though?' I ask Smith.

He looks at me and says, 'I'm not explaining myself.'

I try to focus on the practicalities of our day, to let these two calm down. We decide eventually that Smith and I will feed and walk the dogs, and Michelle will keep watch over the fire.

One minute I find myself thinking about Frannie's words, the next I'm craving food, the next I'm wondering what Pete is doing. I can't hold on to one cohesive thought for more than a minute.

'I didn't do it,' he says, as we walk under the lifeboats toward the rear of the ship. 'I do not trust her.'

'How can we trust anything?' I say. 'The lifeboats sink, the ladders are greased, our radio is answered by some-one pretending to be on the bridge. I don't think you need to trust Michelle. But I do think you need to work with her.'

'I get a bad vibe.'

I hit him on the shoulder and say, 'Yeah, well, I get a bad vibe from you sometimes, but I still slept with your head on my lap most of last night.'

We feed all six dogs and walk the five that don't look like they'll tear us limb from limb.

A heavy scent lingers in the air as we lock up the kennel. Something acrid.

We walk around the side of the kennel block and the whole of the front of the *Atlantica* is ablaze.

112

Black smoke rising vertically.

We run to the stern. Michelle is crying out for help, staggering around, her clothes blackened from the fire, coughing, calling out our names.

'Go inside.' I say to Smith. 'Bring out all the extinguishers you can carry.'

I can hardly breathe as I reach Michelle. The smoke is thick and noxious. Burning wood, but also white maritime paint and synthetic cushions.

'Are you all right?'

'I tried to contain it,' she says between coughs, her eyes watering. 'The wind gusted and it all went up.'

I point to the freshwater pool. 'Take buckets. Go back and forth. Bring as much water as you can.'

'It's too hot,' she says. 'You can't step close enough.'

'Buckets of water,' I say again.

She runs off and I duck under the smoke and crawl over to the saucepans we've accumulated. Mixing bowls and food processor tubs and industrial-size baking trays, all filled with rainwater.

I start throwing the water as best I can, but Michelle was right, it's impossible to get close. The white steel under my feet is hot to the touch and the rubber soles of my shoes are starting to melt.

The water evaporates on impact but at least it cools an area enough for me to access the roaring heart of the fire. I retch from the fumes and Michelle returns with two buckets, her face drenched with sweat, her boots soaking wet, and together we swing the buckets and throw water at the fire. It doesn't land where we want it to but it helps.

This is what hell looks like.

Smith runs to us with one red extinguisher and pulls out the hose. He looks at the instructions for a second and then coughs and activates it.

Nothing happens.

'You can't trust it,' shrieks Michelle, shielding her eyes from the flames. 'You cannot trust anything you see.'

I kick cushions out of the way, depriving this fire of its fuel.

The three of us rely on the saucepans and garbage cans of water, and Michelle leaves again to fill up her buckets from the freshwater pool.

'It's calming down, I think,' says Smith, the soles of his shoes misshapen. 'Running out of fuel to burn.'

The whole centre of the front of the ship has turned from marine white to black. A smudge of soot runs all the way up to the bridge high above us.

My shirt is drenched.

A rush of wind forces the flames to leap higher into the sky, almost knocking us over.

'We need more pool water.'

I am faint from lack of calories. I turn on my axis, trying to make sense of this, trying to see a way out of it.

He raises his hand to his eyes. 'Where's Michelle gone?'

We stagger back from the heat towards the stern of the ship. After twenty metres we both stop in our tracks.

At the far end of the *Atlantica*, close to where we cast our fishing net, there's a grey helicopter hovering over the rear deck.

Our rescuers are finally here.

113

My heart lifts.

It's over.

Smith laughs with delight and runs faster than I've ever seen him move before. I keep up and the sound of the fire is slowly replaced with the comforting, whirring noise of the helicopter's rotor blades. There's a cable dangling from the body of the aircraft.

'They're winching us off the ship,' he says.

We jog side by side, past the lifeboats and windows, along the dark green running track. By the time we're halfway there we see the cable go tense and then a basket starts to lift into the air.

We gaze skyward.

The basket rises up to the open door of the helicopter and a man in black uniform helps pull Michelle inside. Then they start lowering the basket down again for us, all the time hovering in place like a hummingbird, matching the speed of the ship perfectly.

They came.

The basket is ten metres above us.

It moves lower.

Eight metres.

Five.

And then the helicopter starts to turn.

I swore on top of that funnel ladder I wouldn't put myself in that situation again but here, now, I know I won't hesitate.

The helicopter returns to its hovering position, the basket only three metres above us.

'Ready,' says Smith. 'Are you ready?'

It flies a little way from the port side and then comes back.

We are in its shadow.

'I'll go next,' says Smith. 'I have a heart condition.'

The basket lowers again but, just as Smith reaches up to touch it, the helicopter lurches and flies off the port side.

'Steady,' yells Smith, his hands cupped to his mouth.

The helicopter rises up a little.

Tremendous noise from its engine and rotor blades.

Smith gives the pilot a thumbs-up signal and then gestures for him to lower the basket again.

Instead, it flies thirty metres out to sea.

A hundred metres.

It climbs.

'Where are they going?' says Smith, waving his arms around to get the pilot's attention. 'She needs to tell them to pick us up. We need to leave now.'

My heart sinks.

Smith jumps up and down, waving his arms.

The noise of the helicopter fades, quietens.

We both watch, our bodies pressed up against the safety rail, as the helicopter shrinks into the distance.

Leaving us behind.

114

We both yell and wave manically at the helicopter but it's already flying away, shrinking into the clouds.

'Would that have been recorded?' he says. 'Taking her away like that?'

'Maybe this was off-camera. They have full control over what narrative is presented to the world.'

I rub the bridge of my nose. Being that close to the end, to escape, and having it yanked away at the last moment is too much to process. I allowed myself to imagine my homecoming. Pete and Gemma picking me up from the airport, the café team, hugging Mum awkwardly as she tries to remember who I am.

We turn back to face the fire at the front deck past the breakwater, and the whole area is soaking wet. The fire's been extinguished and the steel floor is covered in thick grey sludge: ash and water and melted paint.

'How?' I ask.

'Sprinkler system, I guess,' he says, in disbelief. 'They wouldn't have let their ship burn up completely. I think it was a decoy. Something to hold our attention while they approached from the rear, hidden by the bridge and the bulk of the ship. I never saw it coming. Whoever is orchestrating this is some kind of sick genius.'

'I think they're probably just sick,' I say, flatly. 'And Michelle was never on our side. We've lost two friends now. That's not genius. That's psychopathic.'

Before this I took my privacy for granted. My right to say no. I never realised how my quality of life, those I hold dear, my ability to schedule and plan, could be snatched away. My father couldn't make plans. He and Mum would argue if she ever raised the idea of saving up for a family holiday to Blackpool or the Peak District. Because he needed the money to feed his habit and, more importantly, he needed private time. He became antsy if we were with him for a long stretch. He'd leave in the night to search out an opportunity to place a bet. I think he loathed the transparency; the way we could see him all day long, see what he was really like.

We all grow accustomed to being in control of the image we present to the world.

Smith and I reinforce the door barricades and huddle together on the sofa bed on the ground floor of our duplex. Discarded Twinkie bar wrappers and buckets in the corners. A café owner and a vending machine businessman hunkering down and trying to make sense where there's none to be found.

And then there were two.

It's horribly empty without the others.

He sighs. 'Even though they're safe in a remote studio someplace, to me they killed Frannie and Daniel with their bare hands.'

I stir instant noodles with the last of our water. From a luxury cabin to a grimy bedsit in a matter of days.

'You think one person's orchestrating this?' he asks. 'Directing the show, I mean. Or is it a team?'

'Some faceless man with an ego as swollen as his bank account. I imagine him with two screens; I was thinking about it last night. One screen has a live link to the *Atlantica*. He has a safe button. When a challenge goes wrong or the fire starts burning out of control, maybe his manicured fingertip hovers over that button. If he presses it, a rescue team will swoop in from the helicopter we saw and rescue us. But, of course, he never quite presses it. Because of the second screen. He watches the escalating drama, the fresh danger, and part of him thinks *press the button, they've been through enough.* Dr Jekyll and Mr Hyde. Just as he reaches that point, he notices that viewing figures have hit a new record. So he hesitates. Something even more dire takes place on board. Maybe Daniel starts his descent and the viewers know what we don't: they've been told the pool cover is on a timer. The interaction numbers spike. The countdown runs. Comments and likes start to jump higher. The algorithmic data is more mesmerising than the format driving it. The humane part of him may consider pressing the button. But the other part, the base part, knows the show must go on. Because those numbers have to go up a little more each day. The good and evil we all have within ourselves. Now we know what we're dealing with but we're afraid to call it by its name.'

He slurps his cold noodles. 'In the old days I always had a back-up plan. Skip to another state, set up a new hustle.' He shakes his head. 'Right now I have nothing. I have no idea how to get away.'

'You can't leave if there's no safe place to run to.'

He rubs his eyes.

'We had TV shows in the past,' I say. 'Prime-time shows in the UK where people were filmed going to the toilet, taking showers, having sex, cooking breakfast, all inside a fake house.'

'I remember it,' he says. 'We had our own reality-show president, don't forget that. And another show where people displayed their embarrassing body parts on live TV: haemorrhoids and infected piercings. All out for us to gawp at from the comfort of our sofas and recliners. The business model is corrupt. It leads to a hunt for the most extreme.'

A hunt for the most extreme.

That's exactly what this is.

'So, then, we should give them the opposite,' I say. 'We sit tight in this room and sleep. We give them absolutely nothing. The viewers will start to watch something else; go back to streaming nineties sitcoms.'

'They won't let it happen. You know they won't.'

'I am staying inside this cabin whether they summon us to the lobby again or not, water or no water, food or no food.'

'You'll resist if they offer food?'

'What can they do to me if I stay in here, Smith? I will wreck this show by making it pedestrian. There is nothing they fear more.' I look at the mirror on the wall. 'You might as well watch football, people. This is over. We're done.'

115

We rest, and the light outside our duplex fades to dusk.

There are no more fires by the breakwater. There is no more scurrying around for food, arranging saucepans on deck, sending out pointless mayday calls.

We are steadfast.

Smith and I have agreed not to leave the duplex. We don't want to give them anything to watch. We decide to use the balcony as a makeshift bathroom, utilising what buckets we have, screening it with sheets for privacy. They have pushed us to this new low.

I was planning to wash my clothes in the bathtub with hand soap and rainwater. But what's the point?

I sit and read through all the brochures and spa leaflets while Smith sleeps. Body wraps and energising organic scrubs. Pedicures. Deep-cleanse vitamin C facials and aroma-therapy massages. Caviar algae detox. Eyebrow-tidying.

I don't think Michelle is a bad person. Quite the contrary. She was a pawn in this game just as we are, and I worry about where she is and what she's going through now. The guilt and regret.

I know all about guilt and regret.

After Smith wakes, the atmosphere in the room is subdued. He pads up to the top floor of the duplex to be alone for a while. To think, I suppose. To process what we're dealing with. An hour later he walks back down the stairs with a puzzled expression on his face.

He shakes his head, half-smiling, half-confused.

'Tell me.'

He drags a blanket over and gestures we should both huddle underneath it. I'm suspicious of his motives, some autonomic reflex, but I climb under. He puts his lips to my ear. I feel the warmth of his breath. He says, 'I found something, Caz. In the bathroom upstairs.'

I turn my face to him and move my lips close to his ear and whisper, as quietly as I can, 'What is it?'

He places an object in my hand.

'I can't see,' I whisper. 'What is it?'

He moves his lips to my ear again. 'Michelle left a key.'

I shrug but I can't tell if he understands in the dark under here so I say, 'So?'

He whispers something too quietly for me to make out.

'I can't hear you.'

'The ballroom,' he says. 'At the back of the ship. The key tab says *The ballroom*.'

'Closed for renovation. They told us before we boarded in Southampton. Laying a new parquet wood dance floor. It's . . . locked.'

116

The air under the blanket is sour and hot: stale breath and smoky, unwashed hair.

'Do you think there's food in there?' I ask, my spirits rising. 'You think it's some kind of special rewards room? Like, a feast? A grand finale?'

'I have no idea.'

'Quieter,' I whisper. 'They'll hear us.'

'Let them.'

'Probably just tools and timber and gear. Still, that could come in useful.'

'I thought we weren't going to leave this cabin.'

'I don't want to. But who knows how far north we're headed? We may need fresh material for fires.'

'I didn't think of it that way,' he whispers, then pauses. 'Who's to say the ballroom isn't some kind of editing suite? Part of me suspects there might be a small team of people in there directing us. Some kind of hub or control room. Maybe they navigate the ship from there, or sneak around making arrangements when we're all asleep.'

'Seriously?'

He moves his lips closer to my ear, reduces his volume. 'Caz, there might be other people on board our ship.'

Our ship.

'Michelle said there weren't,' I whisper. 'She said they have thermal imaging cameras.'

'We can't trust a single word she said. Are we going to rot in this cabin, or are we going to see where this key leads us?'

I take a moment to think. 'They're playing us again, you do realise that.'

'Maybe,' he says. 'But we have no food and no heat. Little water. No idea what's coming next. We can't stay holed up in here forever.'

'I say we wait a while longer,' I whisper. 'At least for tonight. We don't rush into a decision this time. We play them, not the other way around.'

We emerge, flushed, from the blanket.

Two hours later we're both asleep, me upstairs, him downstairs on the sofa bed.

A strange, shallow dream. Pete and me at a party in an old hotel. Some kind of waltz in the background. Tuxedos and a full orchestra. A bar backed by a long mirror. My father siting at the bar shuffling a pack of cards, drinking a glass of milk. Mum a few bar stools down with her trawler man, both of them beautiful, laughing. The barman pours my father another glass of milk. A line of them. a little girl in a long dress with a bow walks around crying, looking for something. Everyone ignores her. My father drinks his milk and the tempo of the music intensifies.

I am awoken by a drip of ice-cold water falling on my forehead.

One more.

I sit up in the darkness and there is water streaming down the walls, soaking the floors, cascading down the stairs like a waterfall.

My throat starts to constrict. We're going down. They didn't let us sabotage their ballroom or their show. I'll be in the ocean again. Water flooding all around me. No lifeboats. The cabin is filling up.

'Smith,' I say.

No reply.

The emergency lights come on for the first time in days and I see the state of our room.

'Are we sinking?' asks Smith from the stairs, his grey stubble picked out by the low lights.

I run down to join him and we look out of the window.

The beginnings of a moon.

Calm seas.

'We're still far above sea level. The water's coming from above?'

The water stops abruptly.

The ankle-height lights stay on as the last drips fall from the ceiling.

From somewhere inside the cabin music starts to play. Some orchestral piece piped through at low volume. It's a Viennese waltz, I think. Was it playing before? The emergency lights at ankle level flash and dance around the walls.

'They're telling us where to go,' says Smith.

We cross through the barricade and head into the corridor. I don't want to leave but I feel compelled. My clothes are soaking and my shoes squelch as I walk. The pale lights pulse in one direction. Towards the stairwell. The music plays on. Violins and cellos.

'Do we go *there*?'

'Maybe we shouldn't.'

The fire alarms all burst into life at once.

We cover our ears with our hands.

Flickering emergency lights low on the walls. The lights move, pulsing, changing colour, urging us to keep moving.

'Is this it?' I say, trying to be heard through the pulsing alarms. 'A live broadcast and one of us wins?'

Smith walks ahead of me and says nothing. Wet footprints for me to follow. The ballroom key is held tight in his hand.

Down the stairs, I'm careful not to trip but the constantly changing light levels make that difficult. My feet are sodden and freezing cold. The alarm quietens. It morphs into the noise of people talking. Conversations and laughing. Stock recordings of café small talk.

'This *is* the end,' I say, to myself as much as to Smith. I jog to join him at his side. 'We did it. We're going to leave now.'

He doesn't look convinced. And I feel guilty and shameful for that expression of hope. Daniel and Frannie never had a chance. So, even if this is the end, it never will be. I know that from my family's legacy. There are some things that never really end, some situations that live with you until the moment you take your last breath.

Through the Ocean Lobby, past the drip tray and the piano, through the Gold Grill restaurant with its chandeliers and double-height ceiling and then the even more elegant Platinum Grill and Diamond Grill.

Will I see Pete tonight?

'Why are they playing that noise through the speakers?' asks Smith, scowling. 'All the talking. Why do you suppose they play that?'

'Why do they do any of these things?'

'Maybe the film crews are here and they're covering their noise? Setting up lights and mics. Bringing on presenters?'

We pass the entrance to the library, leaving more wet footprints in our wake. We pass the impromptu and wholly inadequate shrines erected to honour our friends.

We arrive outside the ballroom.

There are signs.

This area is closed for refurbishment until further notice.

Three sets of double doors lead to the ballroom atrium.

The captain and crew apologise for any inconvenience caused.

Two sets are boarded over. The central doors are chained together, fastened by a large padlock.

For private ballroom dancing lessons please contact the purser.

'What's inside?' I say. 'We should go back.'

His face is exhausted, his eyes bloodshot. 'I don't know. There might be food in there. Sandwiches and hot soup. There might be a way off this ship. Or someone holding a cheque.'

'Are we doing this?' I say.

He looks up at the ceiling. A prayer or a silent plea. And then he hands me the key.

'You decide.'

117

I move towards the padlocked door, key in hand. Smith raises his palm in the air and says, 'Wait.'

We pause.

We listen.

I cup my hand to the crack in the door but on closer inspection I find that there is no crack. The whole thing is hermetically sealed. There is tape or some kind of membrane sealing the gap between the doors.

'I hear something in there,' he says. 'Whispers?'

There is hope.

'I don't hear anything,' I say. 'Just my heart beating like a bass drum.'

'I'm not sure we should. The dice are always loaded against us.'

My stomach groans. The dice. The cards you are dealt in life. The coin toss. The odds of survival. Red or black. Heads or tails.

The house always wins.

It just does.

'You go back if you want to,' I say. 'Choose a new cabin for us. I'm going inside.'

He doesn't leave.

He braces himself as I insert Michelle's key into the lock.

Before I have a chance to turn the key, the light levels soften around us. The LEDs integrated into the walls bathe the atrium and the warning signs in an imitation candlelit glow.

I begin to turn the key.

It clicks.

I look at Smith, sweat beading on his brow.

Together, we push the door open and eventually, with one hard shove, we break the seal. Then, after a second or two, we slam the doors shut again and retreat, coughing and gagging, our hands over our mouths.

Smith throws up clear liquid into a planter.

'What was that?' he says, wiping his chin.

I shake my head. 'Some kind of chemical leak?' I lock the door back up. 'Sewage?'

'I heard something in there.' He rubs his lips on his sleeve. 'Caz, there's something inside.'

'Yes.' It was dark but I sensed it too.

We stop talking.

My stomach is twisted, knotted.

I approach the door again and the air around me is still heavy and sour. I place my sleeved arm over my face and Smith does the same.

We unlock the door and push it open.

Gagging, coughing, we move back inside. Two steps. Staggering forward. The room is as large as a nightclub and almost pitch black. The smell is unimaginable: the worst thing I have ever encountered in my life. The carpet feels sticky underfoot. The lights are low and the sound of people chatting still flows through the audio system. Conversation and laughter and that delicate background waltz.

Smith grunts. He won't move his sleeve from his mouth and neither will I. Feels as though I might pass out from the fumes as it is.

He points awkwardly.

I take another step and the floors are tacky, like walking over freshly chewed and discarded gum.

Something scurries across my foot and I stifle a scream.

The lights flash on full for a fraction of a second.

A strobe.

Smith wails.

A glimpse into a hellscape.

In the centre of the ballroom, on the free-sprung parquet dancefloor, sits a stack of people. A mound of bloated passengers, their arms and legs positioned at ungodly angles. An unimaginable vision from some faraway genocide. My arm drops from my mouth and I fall to my knees, gasping for air. The rodents are here. They are frenzied.

I stumble backwards. My breathing stops and my brains fogs. This cannot be. I can't be seeing this.

They've been here all week?

Hundreds of people. Liquid seeps from the pile. The vermin squeal in the darkness and the dogs are already here. The animals found a way; they always do. I take a step back, and then the emergency lights switch off and we are left in complete darkness.

118

We stumble back into the atrium.

My hands are shaking. I manage to hold the padlock and secure the door and then I run to the far wall, gasping for breath.

Smith lifts his shoe and looks at whatever is stuck to the sole. He says, 'They weren't in there, there was nobody in there, that didn't happen, I didn't see anything, nothing changed, that ballroom was empty. I didn't see anything.'

He slips off his other shoe and then he pulls off his shirt, buttons falling to the floor.

I catch my breath but I am faint.

'Wait.'

He just keeps repeating the same mantra. 'I didn't go in there. There was nothing to see. It wasn't anything. Nothing in the ballroom.' He spits on to the floor. 'There were no people in there. Nobody.'

'Smith, please.'

He pulls down his trousers and pulls off his socks and stands there in his underwear, shaking, mumbling.

'We need to get out of here,' I say.

His eyes lift slowly to meet mine and, silently, he mouths, 'There is no place to go.'

I approach him and he steps back.

'It's me. It's only me.'

He stares at me the way a timid dog might look at the tyrant who beats him.

'How many people?' I ask him. 'Listen to me. How many do you think are in there?'

He shakes his head.

I cannot form cohesive thoughts. I'm losing my balance.

'I'm serious. How many?'

He goes to speak but then he starts to break down instead. He gurgles. Sobs.

'It's everyone.'

119

Sepia-tone flashbacks, each one a splinter of time, a millisecond. They merge together and overlap. The moment they took my daughter. I never gave her a name because they told me that would make things harder. As if it could ever be harder than it was. The emptiness of the room after. The look on Mum's face when the police arrived in our front room that day. The empty church pews at the funeral three weeks later. The time we found Gemma unresponsive.

'That can't have been everyone,' I mutter.

'There's a thousand in there,' he says, wiping his face on his bare arm, his voice growing louder. 'It's everyone.'

I stare at the mirror on the wall and say, 'Did you all see? You have to help us. You have to come.'

'They've been watching all along. Maybe they know what'll happen next, maybe they don't. We're not leaving this ship, Caz. Why would they let us go now? They sacrificed crew and passengers alike.'

No.

I need to talk to Mum one last time. Have her recognise me.

'Most elaborate red room in history,' he says. 'They forewarned us. Michelle told us exactly what this is. She explained it to us clearly, to our faces, and we chose not to look into that darkness.'

I drag him away from the doors, urging him out towards the stern deck for air.

'I can't get the smell out of my nose, out of my throat,' he says, spitting. 'I can't get away from it.'

I gag once we're outside. It's as though my nostrils are coated with a film, as though my mouth is infected.

'I saw the concierge,' I say between dry-retches. 'Still in his uniform. Very tall man. More bald than you. Birthmark under his eye. He was lying under somebody else, a woman, and his face was turned towards me and I saw his swollen face. I recognised him from a week ago.'

Smith throws back his head and releases a cry that makes me jump. He stands there, skinny and bare-chested, shaking in the harsh Atlantic air.

'My friend,' he says, shivering. 'My friend was there in the room.'

'You saw him?'

'I felt his presence. I know he was there. How can they leave them? You wouldn't do that to an animal. They deserve some kind of burial at sea or cremation. You bury your enemy in a war. You can't just leave people in a room like that.'

I sink to the deck and rock backwards and forwards on my heels. 'Pete's in that room.'

He doesn't say anything.

'My Pete.' I want to cry but I can't.

'Breathe slow,' he says.

'I can't,' I say, rocking, and it's true, I can't take in a full breath. I'm wheezing and my body is shutting down.

Rocking and fighting for air. Pulling my arms tight around myself and gasping as if I'm choking on a chicken bone.

Smith sits beside me and says, 'Breathe, Caroline. Breathe. Just slow down.'

'I saw handbags,' I say. 'I saw a phone on the floor and the case had a photo of a little boy. I saw a man's tie loose around his neck.'

'This is the end.'

Gemma in my mind. She's not pleading with me to survive any more. She's not telling me Mum needs me or she loves me. I see her back in her ex-husband's place. Down close to the wall, the room bathed in gentle red light, her shoulders crumpled, a belt tight around her arm, veins bulging, blue lips, her eyes rolled back in their sockets.

I take Smith and we stagger through to the Gold Grill restaurant.

'We're closer to land,' I say.

'You saw it?'

'No, but the helicopter that came for Michelle . . . they can't fly all the way to the mid-Atlantic. It launched from dry land.'

He looks at me for more answers.

'In the middle of the ocean maybe we wouldn't choose to jump for it. But here, with people on their way to rescue us, I say we flee while we have the option.'

He drags his fingertips down his face. 'How do we even know they *are* coming?'

'The authorities can't let this continue. As a show, making us hungry and thirsty, shocking us, that's one thing. But this . . .'

'When I saw them,' he says, his lower lip trembling either from cold or shock, 'all piled up like that . . . it looked like a mass grave.'

'We have to jump, Smith, you realise that, don't you? We'll do it as safely as we can.'

He doesn't reply. Part of me wants to give up and crawl under a blanket, lock myself in the duplex and clamp my hands over my ears. But I keep seeing Gemma's face. She looked after me at school despite being younger. She watched my back and stood up for me when I was hounded. I can't leave her now the way Dad left me.

In the cabin I tell Smith to rest for a while because he looks as if he's on the verge of a heart attack.

I lash two life vests together. Then I do it again. I pour the last of our water into bottles and use curtain ties to attach them to our vest rigs.

'How can you be like this?' Smith says, his eyes red, watching me tie the knots. 'How can you do this? Your partner's in there.'

I stop dead.

Turning my back on him, the grief begins to rise up like a wave, but I summon every ounce of strength I have left to force it back down.

'I know how you're feeling,' I say, squeezing my eyes tight shut for a moment, turning to face him. 'But we need to leave. Collect anything you want to take with you and wrap it in a plastic bag and make sure it's watertight.'

He pulls on a shirt. 'What if we say one, two, three, and I jump, but then you stay here on the ship?'

'What? Why would I choose to stay?'

'Oh, I don't know. Because you get scared at the last minute. It'll be a much higher jump than the one you did last time, you know. It'll be like falling off a ten-storey building.'

'We jump together.'

He narrows his eyes. 'It's a gamble.'

I throw him his two vests. 'You come or you stay.'

He checks the watches strapped to his wrists: 'All diving pieces,' he says, touching them one by one as if they boost his confidence. And then he puts four gold watches into a plastic bag and inflates it like a balloon and ties it off on the vest.

'They won't help you,' I say. 'Water. Food.'

'Let's say we wash up in Senegal or Honduras. Who'll get us home then? I will, with these. Gold is hard currency everywhere in the world.'

The light outside the window saps away and I still smell that hellish ballroom as though I never left it. The wooden parquet floor warping and bending.

What were their last thoughts? Did they get any warning? I often think about Mum and how much she understands, these days. In the early days after her diagnosis I'd look for signs of it slowing down, signs that she was still there – we'd do crosswords together – but I knew. I used to lie awake at night thinking about Dad's last thoughts before he jumped. I hope to God he balanced the bad with the good, and knew that Gem, Mum and I, despite everything, still loved him.

'Are you ready?' asks Smith.

I nod. But I am not ready.

We approach the barricade. There's a familiar noise on the far side.

Through the interlocking beds and wardrobes and desks I can make out a pair of eyes at shoulder level.

121

I hold out my hands instinctively and the Caucasian Shepherd dog growls, rearing up on his hind legs to test the barricade. His teeth and his eyes are bright. The dog barks and I try to soothe him with my voice but his tail is stiff in the air and I can sense the power of him from here.

'It's OK,' I say, my palms out. 'We're not going to hurt you. We've been feeding you all this time, haven't we?'

He barks and jabs his head through a gap in between the upturned beds and desks and he tries to bite me.

'Behave yourself,' I say, frowning. 'We're coming through whether you like it or not.'

Smith joins me.

'Where did you go?' I ask.

'Trying to find something it might want. If I had a steak or something . . .'

He picks up a carving knife.

I don't want this dog to get hurt. An irrational reflex after witnessing the ballroom, but I can't help it.

I pull a section of bed away and the dog snarls and barks, its fur sticking straight up, its ears pricked.

'I'm coming out,' I tell him, trying to sound authoritative. Like a trainer. 'Calm down, boy.'

I push a desk to the wall and the dog leaps at me. Before I know what's happening I'm down on the ground, my head ringing, and I can sense the sourness of his breath and then the pressure of him biting down.

122

The dog's teeth sink deeper and deeper into my life vest, his immense neck writhing, thrashing one way then the other. His claws dig into my chest.

'Smith!'

And then my eyes are stinging. My face wet. Some kind of gasoline. Smith stands back at the cabin doorframe with a fire extinguisher in hand. The pressure of the jet forces the dog to disengage, so I run for the barricade. Smith puts himself between me and the beast, walking backwards, keeping him at bay, spraying him in short, sharp bursts. Once he's through the barricade I push the desk back and trap the dog behind it. His growling turns to barking and then howling and whimpering as he comes to terms with his fate.

We stand, dripping wet, panting.

'Are you hurt?' he asks.

I have to check myself. Gasoline from the phoney extinguisher, saliva, chunks of material missing. 'He bit my lifejacket but I'm OK. How did he get out of his cage?'

'They let him out. They are in charge of all the locks and they wanted him to hunt.'

When we arrive on deck it's still dark. The clouds move

gracefully across the speckled sky and the ship has slowed.
It may have even stopped.

'Are we at anchor?' says Smith. 'Maybe this *is* the end?'

'Don't trust anything you see or touch.'

I walk slowly to the covered saltwater pool and crouch
down on my knees. The petrol stench is overpowering.
As I kneel I detect a whisper-thin chink of light inside
myself for taking the positive decision to leave this
grotesque spectacle. I pause to say goodbye to Daniel. I
apologise for it all and tell him I am complicit because, in
past years, I watched many of these shows; I binged them.
I even called up to vote, years ago. I contributed to this
arms race for attention and clicks. The drama, the hurt,
the raw emotion was addictive. I tell him if I have the
chance to meet his family I'll tell them how resilient he
was.

The dog's still audible from our duplex corridor. A
faint howl in the distance on this cold, clear night.

Looking out at the horizon, there is no reassuring glow
from a distant city or harbour. There is only blackness. It
is all there has ever been on this voyage.

We make our way to the front deck, down past the
stowed propeller blades and below to the angled breakwater. *No passengers beyond this point.* The white steel
plate is the colour of the sky and in places it is still
smouldering.

Smith says, 'We can't go anywhere near the fire, not
like this.'

I check Smith's life vest rig and he checks mine.

Our breath vapours mingle and hang heavy in the still
night air.

I have two water bottles and Frannie's phone and Pete's watch in a bag. Smith has his watches except for one Omega that he's strapped to my wrist. He has his own water bottles, and Frannie's suicide note securely sealed inside an Evian bottle.

We step to the edge. Only the steel railing between us and the water below.

Ten storeys down.

I climb and swing one leg over the edge. I'm not afraid any more.

Smith does the same thing.

'How will it feel?' he asks, meekly, already shivering in the night breeze.

'It's going to be good,' I say, trying not to laugh at the absurdity of my words. I am light. Relieved. And I should not be feeling this way. 'Hold your breath and jump on three. The life vest will bring you back up almost immediately.'

'Wait. We should jump from the back of the ship. It's closer to the water.'

'It's not closer,' I say, placing my hand on his. 'It's the same. I'm terrified of going underwater and look, I'm not scared.'

He glances over the edge. 'I want to see John again. I have to see him.'

'Are you ready?' I ask.

He closes his eyes tight.

'Deep breath. One, two . . . three.'

I step over.

He does not follow me.

123

'What are you doing?' I say.

I cling to the side of the railings, my toes barely fitting on the lip.

'I'm sorry,' he says. 'I can't jump that far, Caz. I can't do it.'

I pull him closer to me, my fingers grasping at his life vest straps. 'You can do it. If you stay here, you'll perish like everyone else.'

He shakes his head, his vest butting up against mine, trying to back away from me. 'Or maybe I'll be picked up in a day or two. Did you ever think about that?' He peers over the side.

'What's your name, Smith?'

'What?'

'Your *real* name.'

'People call me . . .'

'I know what people call you, but what is your name, the name your mother gave you? I want to know it.'

The breeze blows my hair across my face.

He looks over the rail again and I adjust my grip.

'My name is Walter.'

124

A week ago we were strangers.

Now we're clinging to each other across a railing on a deserted ocean liner.

'Let's do this together, Walter. Let's end the show on our terms. I'll hold your hand. It'll be OK if we jump together. They have plans for us on board this ship. You know they do.'

'It's dark,' he says.

'It's dark, and it'll be cold as ice down there. But we'll be doing it together. Nobody interfering with us, pulling strings behind the scenes, controlling our destinies. Just you and me. No cameras.'

'I don't know.'

I take a deep breath. 'We'll sue them together, how's that? For more than the prize winnings. We'll do that together and we'll go after the show's owners.'

'I can't swim so good.'

'Walter, you won't need to. You saw me in the water before. The life vest will do all the work, I swear it will. We jump and paddle away from this ship and then someone will rescue us. We're not far from shore. Do you trust me?'

He looks out. Scanning the horizon. The petrol smell is fading away.

'I can't see any shore.'

'Do you trust me, Walter?'

He nods.

'The shore is out there,' I say. 'Look into my eyes. We'll make it together.'

'Promise?'

I smile. 'I give you my word.'

He holds the rail, his knuckles white, and swings his leg over. His foot's shaking. We stand together on the wrong side of the safety barrier.

What are we doing?

We have no alternative.

'Don't look down,' I say. 'Walter, you keep hold of my hand when we jump, OK. Squeeze it tight.'

He doesn't say a word.

'Are you ready, Walter?'

He nods.

125

We are both silent as we fall.

We have screamed enough already. At Daniel's fate. At Frannie's solitary decision. At our fellow passengers in that unspeakable locked room. The air is cold on my tear-slicked cheeks and we drop like two children stepping into a pool.

The impact with the water is immense, like hitting asphalt. Freezing water rushes up my nose as I'm pushed beneath the waves. I lose Smith's hand. Spinning, my leg is bent backwards. Sinuses burning. I surface, gasping for breath, and the sea is calm but the sky is on fire. Dazzling stars around a ship the size of a city block.

I splutter and cough up salt water and look around, paddling furiously with my hands.

'Smith!' I shout out, catching my breath. 'Walter, where are you?'

I cough and try to push myself higher in the water to see. I swim around, the tethered water bottles knocking my arms and getting tangled, my leg throbbing, but he is not here.

I watch as the tips of his fingers poke up out of the water.

'Smith,' I gasp.

His fingertips disappear under the waves.

I start to tug off my life vest. Gemma's voice in my head. *What are you doing?* I unclip the straps and wriggle out and suddenly I'm free in the water. I dive. I buck and lift my feet above my head and slip under the black waves.

Nothing.

I cannot see him.

I cannot see anything.

A mile or more of blackness below me. Not a single sign of Walter Smith. No life vest or bottles. Nothing.

'Smith,' I yell as I surface, spitting up water.

Silence.

I dive again, my eyes bulging, stinging, as I try to find him.

Acres of dark, empty space.

I surface coughing up water, my heart racing in my chest.

No talking or birdsong. No noise at all. The ship's engines are off.

'Smith?' I say, desperately, my voice failing me, swimming around in circles, never losing sight of my life vest. 'Walter. I need you. Walter, where are you? Please.'

The sea is flat.

The air is still, and it is laced with something metallic.

My friend is gone.

126

I have felt alone many times in my life.

But never, ever like this.

The life vest keeps my head clear of the water. I let my head rest against it, my feet up close to the surface, my eyes tracking the vast, drifting ship and the stars beyond. I am as isolated as anyone on the planet.

Plastic bags float around my face like translucent bladderwrack seaweed. Bottles of water. The phone in its own bubble. Frannie's note that must have broken free from poor Smith and surfaced. I'll pass it on to her parents if I ever have the chance.

I failed Walter.

I told him to trust me and he did.

It's odd how your perception of life and death, fear and hope, risk and reward, changes when you live through something like this. It's unlikely they'll find Frannie or Smith. But I expect they'll find me. Alive, perhaps. Or maybe not. If they're too late, my family will at least be able to bury me properly, next to Dad, and, in a way, they'll have been with me, virtually, through these unfathomable days.

Gentle waves slap at my life vest and every time the current moves me around to face nothingness I manoeuvre myself back to see the *Atlantica*. I know it's a bleak memorial of sorts, an open grave, but I can't float facing the other way. It's too lonely and blank.

I suspect Smith had a dysfunctional vest. Michelle said something about not relying on the lifeboats or the safety gear. I think at least one of the vests on his rig dragged him deeper. He jumped and fought and then he sank and I cannot imagine how awful those final moments of consciousness must have been. He saw me on the surface, his arm outstretched, and I failed him.

No birds.

No fish or debris.

Beneath me is an ocean so vast it may as well be bottomless. Millions of cubic kilometres of water. Countless whales patrolling the depths, feeding on krill, sleeping vertically like strands of kelp. There are barracuda beneath me. Giant moray eels and blacktip sharks.

I try to think of something else.

Pete deserves a funeral in the church he visits each Sunday. He's one of perhaps a dozen regular parishioners and he's even stepped in to read on occasion. He should be surrounded by his community, dressed in one of his fine wool suits, and the small nave should be filled with the hymns he sang at school as a boy. He deserves peace and dignity.

Something touches my leg and I flinch, desperately paddling away from that spot. A fish, perhaps, or a piece of debris from Smith's life vest rig. It was nothing else. Nothing sleek, manoeuvring quietly beneath the surface.

Dad was always wary of the sea. He'd swim out a little way when we were kids visiting the beach but one time he panicked. The water turned from aquamarine to dark blue. He'd gone too far. Gemma and I were building sandcastles and he was only fifty metres out. He was a strong swimmer, it wasn't that, and the North Sea is hardly Great White territory. It was just the change in colour that shocked him. That was all it took. The depth of that cool water. The pressure below.

Will they arrive by helicopter?

I'm moving away from the ship. Slow, but steady. Some maritime current my niece would know the name of. At what point will my blood temperature fall too low? I'm becoming resigned to it. If hypothermia takes me it'll be gradual: the inverse of dropping a frog in a pan of warm water and gradually increasing the temperature until the water's boiling.

At least I have my watch. *Walter's* watch. I thought he was ridiculous but he was right all along. Out here, with no control over my direction of travel, or anything at all, with no idea what lurks beneath, no clue what country I'm nearing, at least I can check the time. There is that one abstract universal constant to rely upon. I have Pete's old watch in a bag and Walter's on my wrist. Each minute feels more like an hour. The miles-deep ocean and the sparkling cosmos. Me trapped somewhere in between.

My lips are dry as if the skin is starting to peel away. My throat is sore. My leg doesn't hurt any more because it is too cold to hurt.

Gemma would say, *You figure it out, sis. You came this far. They bullied you at school, those Watkins sisters. They bullied you for three years, day in, day out, hiding your things, sticking gum in your hair, calling you names. They teased you for your hand-me-down clothes and your second-hand shoes.*

For your hairstyle and how your coat was four sizes too big.
The whole school gossiped about Dad. The teachers knew.
They gave you looks. They whispered about him behind your
back. The kids called him a loser. But you found your own
path in the end. You scraped through.

My teeth are chattering.

She's right. Gemma's usually right. Not about her own
life, but about mine. She'll manage looking after Mum as
well as her kids and the café. I think she'll stay away from
her ex-husband. She's older and wiser. With me lost out
here she'll step up, and I know she'll cope with it all. I
should have given her much more responsibility earlier
on. Trusted her. Maybe I held her back.

I'm sorry for that, Gem.

God, I wish I could talk to her one last time.

A single cloud moves slowly across the sky, eclipsing
the stars behind, those galaxies and unseen worlds, and I
think about Frannie's words. She called it *old light*. I
should have listened more intently but she talked about
the wonder of us looking back in time when we stargaze.
I squint at a shooting star but it's moving too slowly to be
that. My heart lifts for a split-second, thinking it's a plane
at high altitude, but what help would that be to me down
here? It's not a plane. It's a satellite. It might even be the
space station in orbit. Them looking down, surrounded
by survival gear and state-of-the-art communication
equipment. Me looking back up.

Frannie's with me in this ocean.

We are together once again.

I take a generous sip from my bottle of water. My body
is giving up, slipping slowly into some other realm.

Between you and me, I'm not fighting it any more. Not, really. I am allowing myself to quench my thirst in full.

I can no longer feel the lower half of my body.

Gemma will do her best to repay what she can. If she continues my instalments she'll never get there, not even close, but she'll do some good with what the café brings in. Perhaps her children will take over the responsibility but somehow I doubt they will. Alice and Martin won't feel the burden in the same way we do. They won't squirm inside with the ignominy of what their grandfather did, the scale of his deceit and the ripples still radiating from his lies. When he hurt us, his immediate family, we could deal with that behind closed doors. We could absorb the impact the way sand or water might absorb a blast. But then he went so much further. Neighbours shunned us. The corner shop stopped serving Mum after knowing her for twenty-seven years; they wouldn't even deliver papers to our address. The community turned their backs and I never for one moment blamed them for it.

I open my eyes wide to take in the starlight.

I'll not forget what he did. Using my saved-up birthday money to back a horse. Ruining the plans of local families. But now I, too, have had a taste of being completely and utterly out of control. Dad didn't have true autonomy over his actions. He told me once he was in a kind of sad trance, as if something else had taken him over. If he was up one afternoon he'd keep on gambling until he lost it all. He couldn't break free. Wasn't strong enough. And on board the *Atlantica* I felt that, too. We were both being played. Him by flashing lights and the odds of winning, me by some insidious media company.

Maybe we're not as different as I thought.

I'm sorry we both had to jump, Dad.

Pushing my head back, tears rolling down my face into the sea, focusing on what I think is the pole star, my hands numb from cold, I whisper, 'I understand now. I forgive you.' And yet, I wonder if I'm worthy of that same forgiveness.

I've discovered that keeping air pockets in my sleeves helps with buoyancy and guarding against the chill. I must look like the Michelin man. Air pockets and two life vests. I'm aware I must do everything in my power to keep myself conscious. I have a duty to my family and to myself, but the responsibility feels lighter and more abstract with every passing hour. Now, at 5.14 a.m., I could close my eyes and fall into a deep slumber. I am lighter having let go of my anguish about Dad. Anguish doesn't cover it. Resentment, fury, sadness, longing. A hundred other things. Guilt. Erosive guilt for doing what I thought was right. Gemma's ex tipped me off one summer evening as I was closing up the café. He told me Dad was placing huge bets with local bookkeepers in a desperate attempt to cover his losses. When I confronted Dad he denied it, but I'd heard his lies before. I saw through them. I told him he needed to talk to the police and put together a payment plan or something. I said if he wouldn't talk to them then I would. I thought I was helping but I made things ten times worse.

I know if I give in to my weariness it will be my final sleep, but my body is willing me, tricking me, to consider that option. Not to give up but rather to stop fighting. To let the tension release from my muscles and, perhaps for the first time since I was a child, since Mum and Dad were good together, be at peace.

If this has taught me anything it's that life can change in an instant. I can continue to dwell on my mistakes and push away every chance of happiness. Or I can move forward.

A plastic bag, bleached by the salt and the sun, drifts past me out of reach.

I'm moving away from the ship but I'm still facing it. I cannot look at the area containing the ballroom. I will not.

Pete and I deserved more time together. Time for me to tell him secrets and for him to share his. I never told him about my daughter. We deserved more than thirteen proper dates.

We deserved years.

There is no light except for the twinkling above and there is no noise. If there were birds or outboard engines or people talking in the distance I'd have something to anchor my consciousness to, something to swim towards. But here, in open water – dark, metallic, uniform – I am untethered. No, that's a lie. Rather absurdly, I'm tethered to the ship. It looms like an uninhabited island in front of me. I drifted from it and then I drifted back closer. Like we're connected under the water by some kind of umbilical.

By 6.57 a.m. I've finished one of my two water bottles. In just a few hours. I spend twenty minutes deciding whether to keep it as a flotation aid or release it. This is what my life has become. I untie the bottle and it leaves me behind.

If I could look at my face it would be blue. My lips and skin would be wrinkled. Wet and dry at the same time. Edging closer to my fellow passengers on that sprung parquet floor. Closer to Pete.

I splash and turn from the ship for a moment. If you've ever lain in a deep bathtub at night during a power cut you may understand how this feels. You may *think* you do. The alien sensation of floating freely in dark water. The sudden change from security to unease.

The horizon begins to brighten.

Why haven't I watched more sunrises in my life? Why did I not prioritise this miracle?

I sit up higher in the water.

My mother's voice deep inside my head. *You made it through the night, Sweet Caroline. I knew you would. Now, don't do anything rash and it'll all turn out all right. Don't I always say it'll turn out all right if you leave it long enough? Don't I always say that?*

She always did say that. Back when she recognised my face. Even when she was unsure whether we'd be evicted that week, she maintained poise. When she learnt the food budget was suddenly gone, or there were bailiffs at the door, us squatting nervously behind the sofa, she kept positive, at least in front of us. Perhaps all that resilience took its toll over time. She spared us and now she pays the price. There were a few times when she broke down but she hid it as best she could. Mum could always understand, or at least forgive, the small lies. If Dad took the gas money, or the time he sold our oven in the council car park without telling her, she knew we'd get by. That was why the truth hurt so much. When he stopped robbing from us, when we thought he'd changed his ways, he was just hurting her more, only it was building up quietly like a pressure cooker. And when it blew, when the news broke, it broke her.

My eyelids grow heavy and I shudder, shaking myself awake again. Coughing and clearing my throat. *Stay awake, Caz. Stay lucid.*

I start to sing.

The song my parents shared, 'Love Me Tender', the song they danced to at their social club wedding the year before I was born.

Shivering, I sing the lyrics.

And then I sense something in the water.

I splash with my arms to sit back upright.

The bag attached to my life vest.

It's ringing.

128

I wrestle with the thin plastic bag, desperate not to drop the phone, for it to sink and be crushed in the midnight zone. I half-untie the knot, but my fingers are so cold they're not working as they should. I don't want the phone to ring off. When it's free, I hold it high out of the water, as high as I can, firm grip, six per cent battery, teeth chattering, and I answer the call.

'Help me. Please. I'm in the sea. I'm so cold.'

A pause.

'Good evening, passenger.'

Who is this?

'I'm near the ship. Help. Send help. You have to get me.'

Another pause.

'Caz Ripley.'

'Mayday. Please, I'm not, I can't . . . Mayday. SOS.' I lose any composure I had. 'Help me!'

'It is my pleasure and honour to inform you that you are the winner of *Atlantica*.'

'Send someone now. The coastguard. A lifeboat. Walter's missing and I have very little water left. You need to help me.'

I start to weep.

'Look behind you, Caroline.'

I try to turn my head but the life vest won't allow it so I kick with my legs. *Don't drop the phone. Whatever you do. Do not drop it.*

'You need to come and help me right now. I'm so cold. I don't know how much longer I can . . .'

There are lights on the horizon, clear in the dawn haze. Red lights. Green. Boats: at least a dozen of them.

'Oh, thank God. Thank you so much. Oh, thank goodness.'

'The people on the boats will take good care of you now, Caroline.'

'My family. Are they OK? My sister?'

'You'll be able to speak to them soon.'

One of the boats approaches at a tremendous speed, its engines roaring. It's a small RIB boat.

'Who are these people?' I say to the voice on the phone. 'Who are they? How can I trust them? Who are *you*?'

'We are Amp Media, the makers of *Atlantica*,' says the voice. 'The boat will help you back.'

The boat comes alongside me, four men on board wearing dark wetsuits and balaclavas.

'Caroline?' the voice says.

'Yes?'

'Go with them. I wish you fair winds and calm seas.'

129

'Give me your hand,' says a man with a midwest American accent.

'Who are you? Where are you taking me?'

'Your hand. We'll pull you in.'

I look around frantically, at the ship, at the phone, at the inflatable. 'I don't know. I can't . . .'

Two of the men use a hook on a stick to pull me closer to their boat and then they drag me over.

They take the phone from me.

By the time I know what's happening the boat is speeding away towards the *Atlantica*.

'No,' I croak, pointing at the monolithic hull. 'I'm not going back there. I left the ship. I will not go back. Turn the boat.'

But they do not turn.

'Help! Help me!' I yell, wriggling, but there is nobody to listen to my pleas. Two men hold me in place and wrap me tightly in a Mylar foil blanket. I can't move my arms. The other boats are motoring with us towards the *Atlantica*. It looks like a solid mountain in the morning sun. It is immense.

I grapple to loosen the blanket and reach the side of the boat, the edge, but a man pulls me back and offers me a bottle of water.

I shake my head and shriek, 'I won't drink it.'

The boat slows.

The man, covered head-to-toe in black neoprene, points to the *Atlantica*, to the bow deck where our deck-chair fires used to burn.

Operatic music plays from the deck speakers.

A figure appears.

130

The masked man beside me passes me his binoculars.

I hold them up to my eyes but my hands are shaking too much. The volume of music increases and I struggle to keep them steady. A figure on the deck. Waving.

It's Michelle. She's back, and she's waving at me.

Fireworks rise up out of the main funnel of the ship.

One of the other people in my small boat removes their wetsuit head covering.

I stop breathing.

'Caz Ripley,' she says, smiling. 'Congratulations. You're a worthy winner.'

She moves closer to me.

'Frannie?' I rub my eyes. Her red hair has been cut since she jumped. 'It's not possible. You . . .'

She hugs me gently and I step back, nauseous.

'I'm not seeing this.'

'I'm OK,' she says. 'It was a big jump, but I'm completely fine. Now, look.'

She points to the ship.

There's a screen on deck, close to the breakwater, showing what's happening. People walk to join Michelle, all waving and smiling as if this is a prom or a normal cruise ship.

I put my hands up to my face.

'All these people? You?'

I watch as Daniel and Walter join Michelle. Daniel has the Caucasian Shepherd dog on a leash and now he looks as gentle as a puppy. The ship sends up more fireworks from the funnels, filling the ocean air with sulphur.

I lose whatever strength I had left in my legs and stumble.

Frannie helps me up.

She gestures for me to look at the screen on deck again. I see a parade of ten or more people in grotesque costumes, with scars and wounds and bloated faces. One of them wears a concierge uniform. Another has an imitation gash in his abdomen. They smile. They wave enthusiastically.

Frannie puts her arm around me. 'It's all fine.'

131

I wake up, dazed.

Yesterday morning I reboarded the ship. I had no choice. Taken in via the same pilot's hatch I was persuaded to jump out of. I could not compute what I was seeing. They had no comprehension of what that level of shock can do to a person.

I check my watch, Walter's watch, and I have slept for fourteen hours straight. That's what having a lockable door on dry land and a room with no hidden cameras does for you.

I'm told I was hysterical when the presenters tried to interview me on camera. I hid and I wouldn't believe a word they told me. Then, I collapsed.

I stretch and sip from the water on my bedside table. I will never take clean, reliable, flowing tap water for granted ever again.

Last night, after Daniel had calmed me down, their medics gave me a thorough examination and transferred me by boat to the shore. Seeing *terra firma* was almost a religious experience. After over a week at sea the relief was overwhelming. Rocks and trees. Birds. Traffic. A vast continent.

The drapes in my Hilton suite are pulled. Blackout curtains. The door is triple-locked and I've pushed all my cases behind it for extra protection.

Once I reached shore I was transferred by helicopter to the city. I could hardly stay awake. Walking to the hotel entrance was surreal. Thousands of screaming people, all holding their phones, all chanting, 'Caz Ripley, Caz Ripley.' Some of them sang the lyrics to 'Sweet Caroline'. I'd had enough of cameras. Lenses. I wanted the opposite. Frannie helped me, along with a dozen security officers, and they gave me small bites of food. But later, when I reached my room, I could still hear the people outside chanting my name.

Frannie debriefed me along with an executive from the show. From his demeanour I suspect he was a lawyer. She explained how six TV networks were lined up to interview me tomorrow along with Walter, the show's runner-up. I told her I refused. They said it was a stipulation in the contract and that I should really use the chance to tell my side of the story. I refused again.

They tried to give me a psychological examination. I screamed when they suggested that. I demanded to be left alone.

Frannie and Daniel are professional actors. When Jen, who played Frannie, told me the truth, I felt like such a fool. I was duped by my father over and over again and now I've been duped by them. She told me their job was to add an extra level of authenticity. She told me the game was elaborate but that I was never in any genuine danger. I didn't respond to that. I didn't tell her that I grieved for her after her jump. How it had brought back memories of Dad taking his life. I didn't explain how that kind of psychological pain is a form of genuine danger. Perception is in the eye of the beholder. I was pained; I still am.

I sit up in bed. Fresh sheets and soft pillows and new cotton pyjamas supplied by the hotel. Heat, light, food, privacy.

Frannie, sorry, Jen, also explained how she and Daniel were given rigorous training. First aid, resuscitation, life-guarding. They were our first line of assistance.

Last night I ordered room service. I was so tired, so hungry. The woman arrived with the trolley and I asked her, through the peephole, to leave it outside and go. She told me I had to sign. I started to cry. In the end she left me the food and she walked away. I could hardly eat any of it. A club sandwich with string fries and mineral water and apple pie. I tasted the water and then spat it out, convinced it was spiked. Then I tried it again and ate a sliver of sandwich and a few salty fries and a taste of the apple pie. I wanted to feast but I didn't trust any of it. Perhaps my stomach had shrunk. Then, an hour later, after a hot bath, I ate most of the rest. The flavours were more intense than anything I'd ever experienced. The chargrilled chicken in the sandwich, the sweetness of the diced apple, the smokiness of the bacon. I ate in stunned silence, relieved the ordeal was over but broken inside by the gaslighting and trickery, by the treachery and lies.

I check my phone. Forty-three new messages. I can't face them yet. I turn it off.

Last night they explained on camera how I'd won five million dollars. I told them I didn't want any of it. That was a fit of juvenile fury. I saw Walter's face when I said those words. His eyes. I thought about giving it all to him. Shunning it. But then I told them, 'Walter won with me. Give half to him.' My expression was flat. They were filming us both, live-streaming, and they expected appreciation of some kind. Excitement, maybe, I don't know. An emotional post-show interview. We did not give them that. Walter and I gave them one-word answers and haunted expressions.

I walk over to the armchair and sit down heavily in it, rubbing my eyes.

Last night I panicked in the bathroom and started covering the mirrors and light fittings with towels and bed sheets and anything at hand, collapsing in the corner, bringing my knees up to my chest, shaking.

I consider switching on the TV but I don't want to see it. I don't want to face, over and over again, the reality of what I have lived through.

Before midnight, I FaceTimed Gemma and Mum. Through the crying and the smiles we managed to talk a little. Mum was confused, bless her, but I think, for a split-second at least, she recognised me. Gem asked how I'd coped, whether I'd suspected, how I'd managed the Air challenge. I couldn't answer. None of that mattered. I wanted to know how my mum's arthritic thumbs were, if the new pills were working. I wanted to know how Alice and Martin were doing at school, how the café was managing. They tried to tell me about journalists and interviews but I couldn't hear any of it. I craved normality. My old life. I told them how next week we'd pay off the debts once and for all. We'd do it together, with Mum, make restitution to the charity so the families would finally have what they deserved. I told them I'd be flying home soon. I told them I missed them.

132

At noon there's a knock on my hotel door and I check the peephole.

I hold the handle for a moment. Steadying myself. And then I open.

Pete's standing right there, smiling, relieved. No flowers or empty gestures. His arms are open.

I step towards him and he holds me and without wanting to I start beating his chest with my fists and weeping.

'You left me. You left me there.'

Tears in his eyes. He takes my knocks and whispers his apology over and over.

We step inside the room and lock the door and then I apologise. I kiss him and we stay that like for a long time, entwined. I look at him properly. I smell him in, his after-shave, his hair. He holds me and rests his face in my neck and I can breathe properly for the first time in a week.

'You were strong,' he says.

I shake my head.

'I missed you so much,' he says. 'I was worried.'

I can't articulate all my feelings and thoughts so I smile and nod and kiss him again. I kiss his lips and his cheek and the back of his hand.

'Are you OK?' I ask.

He nods. 'I am now. They say you want to go back home right away.'

'Yes.'

'I've booked us tickets tomorrow. We fly back together. Straight back home. Is that OK?'

'I love you.'

'And I love you.'

'Where did you go that night?'

'How did you manage it all that time?' he says, not answering my question. 'With those awful challenges? No water, no food? I'll never set foot on a ship again in my whole life.' He gestures towards the window. 'It's like something from The Beatles out there. People have banners and T-shirts. They worship you, Caz.'

'They don't know me.'

'They think they do.'

I shake my head. 'I want my life back. My friends, my neighbours, my walks, our takeaway and movie on a Monday night. Going out for a roast at the weekend. I just want it all back to normal.'

'You'll have all that,' he says. 'This will die down after a few days. The news moves on fast.'

He pours us each a Diet Coke from the minibar.

'What happened that night?' I ask. 'You left me in the cabin. I understand why everyone else left. Some kind of alarm. I heard. Some kind of made-up emergency. But why didn't you wake me, Peter?'

133

He looks down at his hands and then says in a quiet voice, 'I tried as hard as I could. There was a pulsing alarm and I stepped out of bed to check what was happening. I was gone for seconds, that's all. I called out for you and then as soon as I opened the door of our cabin I was swept away by the crowd. Hundreds of panicked people surging down the corridor and I couldn't fight my way back against the flow. I thought you'd wake up, Caz. I was trying to force my way back to you but there was no way to get through. It was a stampede.'

'What happened?'

He wipes his cheek with the back of his hand. 'It was one of the worst moments of my life. I was told five minutes later that you'd evacuated the cabin, that you had been accounted for. I thought I'd meet you at the terminal. But when I disembarked in Cork you were nowhere to be found. I demanded to see you but by then the *Atlantica* had already disembarked and I was assured you were in a sports hall assembly point in the city centre.'

I shake my head. 'But your luggage was gone. It doesn't make any sense.'

'They removed my things before you woke up. The sedatives were that powerful. By the time Walter's friend

John and I had been briefed on the true story, the reality format, it was too late to do anything about it. You were already steaming out into the Atlantic Ocean and I was being told, shown evidence, that you had consented to being part of the show.'

I stroke his arm. His wrist. I unfasten the watch on my wrist and place it on his.

'What was it like, watching me go through all that? Did you try to get help to me?'

He shakes his head, his eyes sad and heavy. 'Up until Daniel's death, *supposed* death, we thought it was all rather exciting. Like an illusion or something. We were concerned, of course, glued to our screens, but we weren't overly worried. Proud, mainly. Everything changed that night. The show received even more attention and I was pulling every string and every business and old school contact I had to get you taken off that ship. I talked to my MP, to a maritime lawyer in Washington DC, to a private security group to see if we could extract you by force. I offered them my *house* in exchange for help. They wouldn't do it. I set up a meeting with a senior civil servant at the Ministry of Defence in the end. I went to school with his husband. Travelled down to London and pleaded with him. We went to his club and I got down on my hands and knees to beg him for help.'

'Last night I couldn't tell what was real and what wasn't. I kept checking the bathroom mirrors for cameras.'

He kisses the top of my head. 'They went way too far. I couldn't sleep, I was so furious. They pushed you all to the brink.'

Over the next three hours Pete tells me more about Deck Zero. How the deck plans and diagrams had all been altered to conceal its existence, and how it was much more extensive than Michelle had divulged. The sub-deck, as they called it on the show, housed a small editing team, two producers, eight ex-navy divers, three medics and one attorney. The team had spacious accommodation. Food, drink, hot water. There was a hidden population below us. They had to wear padded socks, never shoes. The rooms were soundproofed and carpeted. Nothing over a whisper was permitted. The divers could enter and leave through a moon pool, and, in addition, there were sufficient functional lifeboats and life rafts in case of a fire or serious incident.

'But they let us set fire to their ship. They let us damage it?'

'The *Atlantica* was due for a refit,' he says. 'The damage you inflicted was fairly superficial, I'm told. The actor playing Frannie knew to set the fire on the bow, on the steel plate. They wouldn't have allowed you to sink the ship – not that you'd have managed that, as the people on Deck Zero were always in control. The fires could have been damped by remote-activated hoses and sprinklers if necessary. The latest episode showed some of the *How We Made Atlantica* details for an additional fee. One of the presenters explained it like this: the illusion is the big show, but what everyone *really* wants to know is exactly how the illusionist pulled it off.'

I shake my head. Exhausted.

'They even had underwater footage from Smith's rescue. Three professional divers with extra breathing apparatus collected him and brought him back into the ship.'

'There should never be another show like this one,' I say, fiercely. 'You don't know what we went through. Nobody knows.'

'I don't think there *can* be another show like this one,' he says. 'Everyone will be half-expecting it now. *Atlantica* is a true one-off.'

I shake my head. 'My Air challenge. That climb. I was in genuine danger.'

He smiles.

'Don't look at me like that.'

'I'm sorry. You think you were in danger but in fact there were huge airbags and nets ready to deploy if you fell. It was all explained on the show. There was no significant danger. Same with the other challenges. Only Daniel suffered a genuine, unscripted injury, to his eye, and that's been taken care of. On the whole there was only *perceived* danger.'

But there was danger, significant danger: to our minds, to our wellbeing. I don't know how I'll process any of it.

Pete goes on to tell me how beneath the saltwater pool cover Daniel was fine. He had the diving gear he needed as soon as our screens went blank and the spotlights came on in our faces. He says *Atlantica* is the most popular show in history, more popular than the moon landings or the last Olympic finals. How it alone drove up the price of certain cryptocurrencies used to pay for access.

'Walter's going to sue,' I say.

'They'll settle long before it reaches the courts,' says Pete. 'They probably even factored that into their calculations. They'll still make their return.'

'What did the other passengers think? Being removed from the ship?'

'Oh, we were all offered the same voyage on a sister ship, with cabin and dining upgrades, plus free premium viewing access to the show, plus cash compensation. Most of the others were very happy. Those who were not happy were given additional benefits. I think a lot of them were pleased to have been part of history.'

'History?' I say.

He nods and pours two glasses of water.

'The ballroom,' I say, wincing at the memory. 'Seeing all those people. That was one of the worst things I have ever experienced. They made up that smell?'

'It's not so difficult, apparently,' he says. 'They had teams of make-up designers and props engineers working for weeks behind the scenes while the technical crews connected the cameras and microphones. The ballroom had to be closed to you until the end; they explained it on the *How We Made Atlantica* show. That set-piece was too elaborate to put in place when you were all asleep in your Diamond duplex cabins. Dummies and synthetic aroma and imitation carcases with real food sewn into the imitation body cavities.'

'Food?'

'To entice the rats. Genuine rats, but harmless. Bred for the job. Clean. Certified.'

'I feel ill just thinking about them.'

'Caz, they mentioned they'd like for me to ask you again.'

I don't say anything.

'Entirely your decision, but there are TV studios desperate to interview you. They'll pay significant sums.

Newspapers want exclusives. There are even politicians who'd like to shake your hand.'

'I won't do it.'

'Are you completely sure?'

'I want to go back to my old life, Pete.'

'You think that will be possible?'

'I'll make it possible,' I say, setting my jaw. 'They're not controlling things any more. I will go back to Yorkshire and I will go back to my café. They can't touch me ever again.'

134

Pete smuggles me to the airport after booking tickets from another city as a decoy. He bought me a grey hoodie and he keeps me shielded the whole way through check-in. I'm back in the shadows where I belong.

I've been thinking about contestants on other reality shows, shows I've watched obsessively in the past. Social media stars and people made famous for fifteen minutes. Who takes care of them afterwards? Who is there to steward, counsel and guide them when their lives change overnight? I'm old enough and supported enough to make it through. But what about the others?

I've never even flown economy before on a large plane like this, let alone first class. We board first, separately to most other passengers, and we're taken to our seats near the cockpit. Pete removes the newspapers and suggests I should avoid the TV headsets and rest. When the hostess checks my ticket she looks up and recognises me and after a silent gasp she switches back to professional mode. She's attended to Oscar winners and senators so this is something she will be able to handle.

I keep my hood up the whole time.

As we're flying over Greenland the tension in my shoulders begins to ease. Pete's reading an Iain Banks novel with a glass of red wine and I'm curled up in a ball under a cashmere blanket. I'm about ten hours from home, from Mum, from Gemma, my niece and nephew with their chemistry experiments and their weekly swimming lessons. I know where I stand with them. They've seen me at my lowest and at my most desperate. They understand me.

I take Pete's advice and avoid all screens and news sources. I don't want to see myself. I don't want to hear or see anything relating to that awful ship. I need distance from it so I can heal.

The plane is quiet.

No significant turbulence.

I touch my hand to Pete's cheek and he smiles and I go to the restroom to brush my teeth. It's small but lavish. A real, living plant. I touch its foliage and smile. Marble sink. Expensive-looking lemon blossom handwash and cream. I brush my teeth facing the mirror and I seem to have aged a decade in the last days. Sunken eyes, grey roots and gaunt cheeks. Wrinkles I don't recognise. I have seen too much.

My phone vibrates so I unlock the screen as I brush.

I didn't expect any connection on board.

A text message from Gemma.

We want you home, sis. I'll be at the airport with Alice and Mart. Mum and Dad would be so proud of you.

I slump down and sit on the toilet, smiling, holding back tears.

There's a photo attached to the message. The four of us in our back yard when Gemma and I were in primary school. Dad with his arm around Mum. Gem and me laughing, stroking Buster the dog. I can just make out the neighbour over the fence. Mum looks happy; she looks as though she has everything she ever wanted.

I finish brushing my teeth and then I unlock the restroom door, fumbling with the awkward handle, and step out into the fuselage.

The cockpit door is open, swinging slightly on its hinges.

I peer out into the first-class cabin.

Empty.

I check the first few rows but there is nobody in the seats.

I dash back and check the cockpit, knocking on the wall as I enter.

Unoccupied.

Silent.

There is no one else on this plane.

Acknowledgements

As a child I used to reread the introduction of Danny, The Champion of the World so I could experience the quiet safety of Danny's world, the world he shared with his father in their caravan. Now, in my mid-forties, I'm lucky to live in a boggy clearing at the centre of a wild Swedish forest. Together with my wife, we built a wooden house here. We have to put up with a tremendous amount of darkness in the winter (we're as far north as Alaska) and the moose devour everything we grow, but we love it here. My son, now eight, will be able to spend his entire childhood playing in these woods. I am very happy for that.

My grandad died in 2011, a few months after my wife and I married. He had a tough childhood and yet he somehow maintained a childlike sense of wonder and fun even into his eighties. Grandad never flew on a plane, bit he did have lifelong interest in trains and ships (especially steam engines). I like to think he'd have enjoyed reading about the RMS *Atlantica*.

It takes a village to make a book. I'm lucky that in my little village live the most passionate, smart, talented, and fun professionals you could ever wish to meet. Heartfelt thanks to my visionary editor, Jo Dickinson, and her supremely capable Hodder team: Alice, Jenny, Sorcha, Alianna et al. When I first met with my agent, Kate Burke, for lunch, back in 2016, we talked about our favourite Stephen King novels for a full hour. I knew right then that she was the right agent for me. Huge, ongoing thanks to her and the rest of the Blake Friedmann team: Isobel, Conrad, Lizzy, Sian, James et al.

And I need to thank my incredible US team: Emily Bestler at Emily Bestler Books (Atria, S&S) and her brilliant team: Lara, Maudee, Megan, David et al.

A special thank you to all the booksellers, librarians, bloggers, festival organisers and reviewers. And thanks to the people at the printers who turn pallets of paper into books. I appreciate you all.

My wife says being a writer, from her perspective, looks a lot like being an eternal student and always being slightly behind with your homework. Writing sometimes (often) means having to work evenings and weekends (and sometimes holidays and Christmas day). I owe a huge debt to my wife and son for allowing this ridiculous behaviour. I love you both. Thank you.

R.M.S. Atlantica

Ship's Manifest
Crew

* * *

Caron Yeaman
Chief Officer

Jan Tomalin
First Officer

Emma Alvey
Quarter Master

Suzanne Finn
Safety Officer

Suzy Grant
Security Officer

Roxanne Butcher
Staff Captain

Steve Walsh
Engineering

Emma Kilner
Assistant Engineer

Karen Royle-Cross
Chief Engineer

Wil Carpenter
Chief Electrician

Christine Taylor
Chief Radio Officer

Neil Tabor
First Assistant Engineer

Lucy Hilton
Motorman

Oliver Nokes
Motorman

Shamiela Ahmed
Motorman

Melanie Naylor
Plumber

Sally Milton
Plumber

Thanhmai Bui-Van
Oiler

Antonella Gramola Sands
Oiler

Caroline Chapman
Oiler

Lee Matthew
Chief Purser

Chris Stamford
Purser Staff

Lindsey Cross
Purser Staff

Lisa Fuller
Purser Staff

Rebecca Donaldson
Chief Cabin Steward

Donna Gallagher
Chief Steward/Housekeeper

Kathryn Sandison
Senior Watchkeeper

Caroline Rhodes
Senior Watchkeeper

Steve Hillman
Cabin Steward

Penny Carter-Francis
Deckhand

Hannah Lawson
Deckhand

Tracey Harriman
Deckhand

Marion McDonald
Able Seaman

Leighton Cairns
Able Seaman

Roland Fairlamb
Able Seaman

Brian Fairlamb
Bosun

Sarah Oliver
Bosun

Breda Guy
Carpenter

* * *

The Captain appreciates their
dedication and loyalty.

ORDER THE NEXT BOOK FROM WILL DEAN

ICE TOWN

The explosive new thriller
featuring Tuva Moodyson . . .

Deaf teenager goes missing in Esseberg.

Mountain rescue are launching a search party but
conditions hinder their efforts.

The tunnel is being kept open all night as an exception.

When journalist Tuva Moodyson reads this news alert
she knows she must join the search. If this teenager is
found, she will be able to communicate with him in a
way no one else can.

Esseberg lies on the other side of the mountain tunnel:
there is only one way in and one way out. When the
tunnel closes at night, the residents are left to fend for
themselves. And as more people go missing, it becomes
clear that there is a killer hiding among them . . .

HODDER &
STOUGHTON